Death Across the Pond

By
Karin Ficke Cook

PublishAmerica
Baltimore

First printing

At the specific preference of the author, PublishAmerica allowed this work to remain exactly as the author intended, verbatim, without editorial input.

ISBN: 1-4241-5114-7
PUBLISHED BY PUBLISHAMERICA, LLLP
www.publishamerica.com
Baltimore

Printed in the United States of America

ACKNOWLEDGMENTS

I am especially grateful to the village of Bolton-by-Bowland in Lancashire, England, for allowing me to use their lovely village, set among the beautiful hills and valleys of Ribble Valley in Northern England. The parish is introduced at the end of this book, expanded upon in the third volume, "The 'Ghost' in Bolton Hall" and in the fourth, "Tuscan Flowers of Love." You can actually see more of the area on their web site at: *http://www.bolton-by-bowland.com/village/virtualtour/index.htm* and take a virtual tour of the village. The stores and businesses written into the story line are actual places in the village and worth visiting if you holiday in BBB.

And great thanks to Roger Wood, (one of the real people in this book!) Bolton-by-Bowland, who is the Web Master and photographer for the village archives. He has captured the vitality and warmth of the people—the charm of the area and incredible beauty throughout this corner of Lancashire.

To Wikipedia—the on-line encyclopaedia for the information on churches and locations in Rome. And to the Ford Motor Company for allowing us to use their vehicles in these books.

Prayer book used for reference and quotations: The New Saint Joseph "People's Prayer Book", published by Catholic Book Publishing Company. Excerpts from the English translation of the *Rite of Funerals* © 1970, International Committee on English in the Liturgy, Inc. All rights reserved.

And to my dear friend, Nives Jelich, owner of Queen of Peace Travel, for her invaluable help in conveying the beautiful pilgrimage to Medjugorje. The host family, the taxi driver, Cano, Father Jozo Zovko, Nancy Latta and visionary Ivan Dragisevic and more are real people. Information on a pilgrimage to Medjugorje, Catholic Shrines, Rome or Greece can be found on the web site at *http://www.queenofpeacetravel.com* or by writing to: Mrs. Nives Jelich, Queen of Peace Travel, 9806 Westlawn, Wichita, KS 67212. Telephone: (316) 722-0514.

DEDICATIONS

To my husband, Lancashire-lad, L.M. Cook, for his resolve to get these novels published. It takes time, energy and dedication to get a book noticed by our readers and he has spent countless hours in this effort. He has my thanks and an extra custard tart with his cuppa!

To my Muse, Tyler Jalen—my cinnamon and white Turkish Angora cat, who sat for hours on the computer terminal watching me type. He is the inspiration for the cat, "Tyler—TT" in this series of books and is featured in my children's series as himself. His photo is on the back cover of this volume.

And last, but certainly not least, to my sister, Debra K. Osmun, for her continuing support. As a writer herself, she understands the time it takes to produce an entertaining and informative book people will enjoy reading.

DISCLAIMER

Because the phenomenon of the "alleged" apparitions at Medjugorje, in the Hercegovina Province of Bosnia-Hercegovina, it is appropriate to explain this has been ongoing since June 25, 1981, when six children of a neighbouring hamlet were supposedly experiencing a visitation by the Blessed Virgin Mary.

This year, 2006, marks the 25th Anniversary of the first vision and because the visions have not ended, the Roman Catholic Church cannot make a determination if anything is truly happening of a spiritual nature. This is the most investigated and thoroughly tested series of events in modern times, but until the "alleged" apparitions cease, no determination can be made.

The Church does cover personal pilgrimages to Medjugorje. However, there cannot be approved or sanctioned pilgrimages until a determination has been officially made. The Declaration of Zadar covers personal pilgrimages and there are clergy assigned to care for the pilgrims' needs.

The Parish of St. James and the Village of Medjugorje are beautiful places to visit in Hercegovina. This is an area of peace, pastoral beauty and friendly, hard-working people. The local wines are International prize winners and the food is exceptional. I highly recommend this part of Hercegovina for a quiet retreat to shake off the dust of our hectic lives—kick back and relax. If a religious pilgrimage is something you wish to explore or simply for a peaceful vacation, the Village of Medjugorje, the nearby Adriatic Coast and its resorts or the offshore islands make perfect getaways for individuals or families.

This book is fiction, set in 2004, with this particular segment being based on the author's personal experience with the events taking place in Medjugorje and I do not refute nor endorse them in this book due to their ongoing nature.

Chapter One

The silence was deafening. The friends were paralyzed with a gripping fear deep in their souls. The room was so silent you could hear the residue falling from the candle smoke. Shauna sat motionless on the sofa as Jim and Katie simply stared out the front window toward the lake. There was no way Roan could have died in the crash—impossible.

Charles filled a carafe of coffee and brought it over with a tray of cups. The friends sat with cell phones in hand, waiting for some news of the plane crash. Roan's last words were of love and Shauna simply couldn't believe her husband didn't survive. Maybe if she re-dialed his cell phone, someone would answer.

Shauna picked up her phone and hit redial. All she could hear was static and intermittent beeping. It sounded as if Roan's phone was still on.

"Jim," Shauna motioned. "Can you call someone to home in on Roan's phone signal? Maybe they can triangulate the exact position of the signal to locate the plane?"

Jim said, "You know, Shauna, that's a great idea. I can make a couple of calls to some ham radio operators and the cell phone company here. I wish I'd thought of that earlier. Guess my mind isn't focused very well."

Charles poured some of the coffee for Shauna and Katie. Marie put on a brave face and went downstairs to check on all the children, who were watching videos in the game room. Conor was unaware his new Dad was missing. No one would tell him until they had something definite to say.

The ice and wind continued to batter the house. Everyone was glad to be inside and Charles, along with his wife, were especially grateful to Shauna and Roan for their hospitality. With their home destroyed, they had nowhere else to go and the Sanderson home was always welcoming to guests. Even as grateful as everyone was at that moment, the uncertainty of Roan's status was the biggest concern.

After Jim had made a few calls, he strolled over into the living room to read the information from his notepad.

"The Civil Air Patrol has the plane's transponder beacon clear and strong," he explained. "It's just this wind and the heavy ice, which are making it bounce, making it difficult to get the exact location. A local farmer saw the plane spiraling into one of his fields, then slam into the woods. The lake is right next to a stand of trees and that's where the plane is resting. It's half in the trees and half on or in the ice. But no one can actually get to the site until this storm subsides."

Marie came back upstairs with an idea.

She said, "I have a cousin with a 4x4 who belongs to an off road club. I'll try him and see if they can get through. He lives down in Walker and I'll also call Mark Foster, their Chief of Police who is also a friend of ours. I'll try to get some answers."

Shauna felt a little more hopeful. Her friends would eventually come through for her. Time didn't move and the tension began to build. Without anything conclusive, the waiting became almost painful. Charles kept the coffee hot and busied himself with baking. He had a feeling there would be more people at the house soon and he wanted to be prepared to feed them. And busy work kept his mind off his troubles and his missing friend.

"Honestly," said Shauna. "I don't know why we haven't heard anything from the authorities. Someone had to have seen the plane close enough to see its condition. Is there smoke or fire? Is the plane crushed, what?"

Shauna's frustration was becoming rage.

Katie had to intervene and calmly say, "Listen, Shauna. We don't have a way to rush this. We have no information to answer our questions. It's imperative to stay focused, keep our thoughts positive and pray for a miracle.

And you can't tell me miracles don't happen because you are living proof they do."

Shauna stared at Katie and said, "Yes, I know you're right, Katie. I'm just so frustrated."

Before Shauna could say anything else, the phone rang. It was the police chief in Walker. His news wasn't great, but at least it was something. Jim put the call on the speaker phone in the living room.

"Marie, you there?" he asked. "This is Mark and I have some news—not much, but it looks like the plane's fuselage is intact, sitting half way in the woods and half on the lake surface. The trees are holding it back from falling through the ice. The right wing is almost completely torn off, but there doesn't seem to be any fuel leaking. There is a thick, black smoke coming from the cockpit, so it looks like electrical and petroleum-based items burning. But the rest of the plane looks okay. It's highly possible there are survivors, but from the way the cockpit was smashed, the pilots didn't make it."

Marie said with relief, "Thanks Mark. You have no idea how much this means to all of us, especially Shauna. Can this person see any movement?"

"Not yet," Mark explained. "But we have a rescue team in place to get in there as quickly as possible, but the ice and wind are still too strong to get the team mobile. Keep tuned to the CB radio and CAP. I'll call as soon as there is more news."

Jim disconnected the call and sat down in the chair across from the couch.

You could see the emotion sweep over him as he said, "This has to be good news. There is a chance Roan survived the crash. We just have to continue being positive here and get as much information as we can, when we can. I have a few more ideas—people to call."

Shauna could sense things might be more hopeful. She got up and walked into the kitchen just as a knock could be heard through the garage door. Her heart felt like it could leap right through her chest.

Who could be knocking at the garage door and not the front?, she thought to herself. As Shauna opened the door, she saw Stephen, their lawyer.

She immediately said, "Come on in here. You must be frozen. I assume you have heard."

Mr. Brennan said, "Yes, I heard about the crash on the radio, then I contacted friends who live near the crash site. Their cabin is right on the lake and they had a bunch of friends over for a football weekend. They heard the plane go down and have taken in the survivors. Roan is with them, but he's in bad shape."

Shauna turned ashen, started shaking and gasped, "Roan's alive? How bad is bad?"

Stephen explained, "From what they said, he has broken ribs, a deep head wound, a broken left arm and his upper left leg is severely gashed. He was trapped between seats when a tree smashed through a window and pinned him in. Luckily my friends are paramedics with their own ambulance service at their home. Fortunately for everyone involved, they had just come back from restocking their ambulances with emergency supplies, so they have been able to treat Roan and four other passengers. The roads are impassable because of the ice and downed power lines, so they will transport the survivors to the hospital when the weather clears. But Roan is unconscious right now and there is no way to speak to him. He was fortunate my friends were so close and could treat them at the scene, with all this ice everywhere. Just as soon as I can, I will take you down there."

Shauna dissolved into tears again, but this time in relief.

She slumped against the kitchen counter and Charles grabbed her just in time to support her, saying, "Shauna, you can see your prayers are being answered. Now we need to pray for the others on the plane. Mr. Brennan, what about the pilots?"

After pouring himself a cup of coffee, Stephen continued, "The pilots didn't survive. When the plane hit, the trees impacted the cockpit first. Everything shattered and some of it burned. But the fuselage could be structurally sound, even with the trees coming through. Most of the passengers were pinned like Roan. Two of the people sitting in the back weren't even hurt, except for a few bumps and bruises. There were only two deaths and in my estimation, those pilots are heroes."

Katie walked over and put her arm around Shauna's shoulder giving her a hug.

"It looks like this might turn out okay, Shauna," Katie explained. "It's just like Conor. That was an awful experience, but he's going to be fine. Roan will, too. You must stay positive."

Charles announced lunch was ready, called the kids on the intercom to come up. The adults would have to tell them something because they all looked so distressed, it would be hard to hide it. Mr. Brennan said he would handle it.

Antoine, who is eight, came up first, followed by Chloe, five and Renee, who is just three. Their shiny faces were a joy to behold and immediately cheered up the gloomy cadre of friends. Conor came up last with Janet pushing his chair, with Jimmy lost in a gameboy.

But Conor twigged the mood and asked, "Okay, would someone say something. I'm not liking what I am seeing with you folks. Mom, what gives?"

Stephen asked the children to gather in the living room so he could explain what had happened. As Jimmy walked past, Jim grabbed the game from his hands, giving Jimmy no excuses not to hear what Mr. Brennan had to say.

"Kids," said Jim. "There has been an airplane accident and it involves your Dad, Conor. We don't have much information yet, but what I can tell you is your Dad is alive and getting medical care. No one can get to the airplane because of the ice and wind, but they are all safe and warm. As soon as I know more, I will tell you, okay?"

Antoine piped up and asked, "Mr. Brennan, did the plane crash?"

"Yes Antoine. The plane did crash because of the storm," replied the attorney. "What we need to do now is have some lunch to keep us strong, then say some prayers to give Conor's Dad and the others strength, too. Shall we do that?"

The children nodded their heads and slowly walked to the kitchen table.

Shauna made her way over to her son and calmly told him, "Your Dad will be fine. God will grant us a miracle with him as He did with you. Now I don't want you to worry, just eat your lunch and you can hear all the news as we do."

This time Jimmy pushed the chair over to the table. Everyone stood behind their chairs and Jim led the prayers for their friends:

"Dear Heavenly Father. Please keep Roan and the others safe in your care. Help them to be healed and enable their rescuers to get to them quickly and safely. Strengthen us for the many difficult days ahead as we struggle with recovery. We ask for Your miracles in our lives. We ask this through your Son, Jesus Christ, who is our salvation and our life. Amen."

Everyone said a collective, 'Amen', then sat down for lunch. About half way through, the phone rang again. This time it was Franco, who by now was frantic. He almost shouted through the receiver when Shauna answered.

Franco's plaintive voice yelled, "Mrs. Eets me, Franco. What happened to de boss? We are scared heeeer and we know nothing. The tv says plane crash, but where? Who is living? Eees Mr. Roan okay, Mrs. Shauna?"

Shauna loves Franco's goofy accent and it makes her smile each time she hears him. It did again this time, too. She quietly explained to Franco about the plane crash.

"Franco," Shauna said quietly. "You need you sit down for a minute and listen to what I have to say. Are you in the chair, Franco?"

"Yes Mrs. I am sitting," he replied.

Shauna continued, "The storm was much worse than anyone thought and the plane crashed into a grove of trees and partially onto a lake. Five people were injured, one of them Roan, two not injured much, but the pilots were killed. Then everyone was taken to a nearby home and they are being treated by the owners, who are trained paramedics. When the storm clears enough, they all will be taken to the hospital in Brainerd. This is all we know right now, but I will keep you informed as we get more information."

Franco was silent. Can you imagine Franco silent?

After a few moments passed, he spoke up again, "Mrs. Shauna. Eet will be okay. Franco can tell. Should I tell everyone here yet? Everybody anxious about the Boss, you know. They love him."

Shauna tried to reassure Franco by telling him, "Now Franco. You get all the employees and your family together and explain to them what I have just said. And tell them I will call you the moment I get news. Do you understand?"

Franco acknowledged by whispering through his tears, "I do, Mrs. Shauna. I can do that now. Theese is so haard to tell dem. Okay, I go now. Bye bye."

The receiver clicked and within another moment, it rang again. This time it was Stephen's friend, Bob Thomsen. He had some additional news about the crash victims.

"Mrs. Sanderson? This is Bob Thomsen on the lake here in Walker. I'm Brennan's friend taking care of the wounded from the crash. I have someone here who wants to talk to you—just a second."

A moment later, Shauna heard a very weak, but familiar voice.

"Shauna, Honey?, mumbled Roan. "Are you there?"

She nearly fell over, but Jim held onto her, then reached over and put the phone on speaker.

"Roan, Roan? Yes, Dear, I'm here. Are you okay? We are all here trying to get news. Honey, I love you," Shauna sobbed.

"Shauna, my head really hurts. It hurts so bad, my hair hurts," he muttered, as he tried to make light of his injuries. "I'm not sure what all is broken, but I feel like Conor must have after his accident. I think we need more insurance."

That broke everyone up in laughter. Roan knew, even as severely injured as he was, that Shauna would be frustrated and scared for him, so he tried to make her feel a little more at ease.

Roan added, "I can hear everybody laughing. Jim, you there? Charles, Marie, Katie, Conor, kids—everybody?"

Mr. Brennan also spoke up, "I'm here, too Roan. I'm the one who got you to the Thomsens. Don't worry about a thing—already working on the insurance angle. I'll get Shauna down there as soon as this storm clears. You have my word, Buddy."

Roan replied, "Thanks Stephen. Take care of my family up there for me until I can do it for myself. Hey Conor, can I borrow your chair?"

Conor started to grin and yelled into the phone, "Sure Dad. I'll see you soon. I love you, Dad."

Bob Thomsen asked if he could speak with Brennan off speaker for a moment. He wanted to prepare him for an additional complication with Roan.

When everyone had continued with their luncheon chatter, Mr. Thomsen said quietly, "I didn't want to say anything to Roan's wife or have everyone overhear, but Roan's head injury is severe, really bad and it has put excessive pressure on the optic nerves. For all intents and purposes, Roan is totally blind. I explained to him it was the injury, but until we can get an MRI done, we have no way to tell if it's permanent. Please, not a word, okay?"

Stephen Brennan had to agree, then Thomsen put Roan back on the phone for a brief moment to conclude his call to Shauna.

"Honey, are you there?" gasped Roan. "I'm not feeling too well. Call Franco and tell him I'm okay. You know how upset he gets. I love you, Sweetheart."

Shauna choked back her tears and said softly, "I adore you, Roan. I know you will be just fine. I have spoken with Franco and will call him again now. Please don't worry about a thing. I'll see you soon. Remember how much I love you."

The phone disconnected and Shauna had to sit down to catch her breath.

She turned around at the group, staring at her with gaping mouths and said, "You see? He's going to be alright. You heard him. He's just fine—a little sore, couple of broken bones, but hey, we can all deal with those, can't we Conor?"

Conor grinned and said, "Guess I better get this chair shined up for Dad when he gets home. I won't need it after next week. Might as well get as much use out of it as we can."

Chapter Two

The afternoon went past quickly and about 4:00 PM, Antoine looked out the front picture window and exclaimed, "Look. People outside. Some people are coming to the front door."

Sure enough, neighbors were coming up to pay their respects to Shauna and her family. Some of them carried food. Some had bottles of wine and bags of coffee. It was amazing. Roan's next-door neighbors came, too. Everyone wanted the latest news.

Shauna quickly ran over to the door and opened it to see fifteen or so friends shivering in the icy wind.

She exclaimed, "Please, friends. Come in. There is plenty of room and we have news."

As the neighbors came inside, they gave Shauna their precious gifts and the goodies replenished what they had eaten during the day. At least Charles wouldn't have to bake anything else! Jim and Charles pulled several chairs up around the fireplace in the living room, asked for coffee orders, then got everyone settled. Stephen Brennan basically took over and began to enlighten the friends as to the situation.

Jim took phone duty, while Stephen spoke, "Friends, as you know, Roan and six other passengers on the daily commuter flight from the Cities to Bemidji crashed near Walker in the ice storm. The plane's fuselage remained together, but the impact killed the pilots and there are five who are seriously injured. The other two were very, very lucky. Roan has a broken arm, some broken ribs, a head injury and a badly gashed leg. Those are the injuries we know about. He is conscious now, understands where he is and that he is being treated by skilled trauma paramedics. He and the others will be transported as soon as the storm allows their ambulances to get trough to Brainerd. If anyone has questions, please feel free to ask and I will answer the best I can."

Julie Cavanaugh raised her hand and spoke first, "Steve, what can we do for Roan and the others? I think we all feel really helpless right now and we need to do something."

Mr. Brennan replied, "If you want to say some prayers, I think that's needed right now. And you might get on the phones to call your friends in town and explain what has happened so no one gets the wrong idea or misinformation. We need to keep the lines of communication open. Harrold, you contact your people at the newspaper and run the story on the front page. Call me if you need anything else but above all, please, people, stay with the facts and don't make anything up. Everyone on board?"

The group acknowledged, finished their coffees and said 'goodbye' to Shauna and Conor. Katie had finished cleaning the kitchen and Marie had the kids back downstairs playing games. Jimmy was a good 'camp counselor' for the younger ones and they were having a blast, except that Jimmy totally understood the gravity of the adult situation upstairs. Conor's accident was very fresh in Jimmy's mind and there was no forgetting about it.

By now the phones were ringing off the hook—land line, cell phones, even the Internet Ims were going nuts. Sharon Landin, the neighbor to the north, stayed behind to watch over the Internet inquiries. The media had tagged the story and were beginning to descend on the house—again. It was like reliving Miss Lulabelle's death all over, as well as the fire. There was no mercy from these people.

"'Vultures' is too polite a word for these freakin' idiots," shrieked Shauna. "Why can't they just leave us alone to get on with life?"

Jim, Charles and Stephen made their presence known to the media and they backed off—a little. Shauna immediately went into the studio, locked the door and pulled down the shades. A little too much 'deja vue' for her.

Even little Flash couldn't stand all the big people and ran inside the house for protection.

Shauna realised she hadn't called Franco yet, so she walked into her bedroom, cell phone in hand. When she got there, paparazzi were peering in the French doors. She calmly locked the doors, pulled the drapes and called the police. But you could literally see the rage in Shauna's face. The veins in her delicate neck were beginning to bulge and she was becoming flushed. However, she held onto every scream for later, when she was alone. She sat on the bed and hit speed dial, 2 for the restaurant.

Franco answered, "Mrs. Shauna. How ees Mr. Boss? We heer things on thee radio and tellevizun. Ees bad, huh?"

Without missing a beat, Shauna replied, "It's okay Franco. Mr. Boss will be fine. He is badly hurt, but I spoke to him a little while ago and he told me to call you because he knew you would be worried. Now, I want you to tell everyone Mr. S will be going to the hospital soon and I will call you again when I know more. But your Boss doesn't want you to worry. That's exactly what he said. No worries, Franco."

"Okay Mrs.," Franco gasped. "I am sorry because I cry for so long today, Mrs. I am so upset. But I tell the staff and friends he will be okay. Momma and Gramma Giovanna have gone to Mass and will light a candle for him. We will do our best to keep happy because that is what he wants us to do, right?"

"Right, Franco," replied Shauna. "Now go and take care of the business. I will call you in the morning at the house and give you all an update. Talk to you then."

Shauna closed her phone and sat on the edge of the bed. Roan's side of the bed was still covered, since he hadn't slept in it for a few nights. She picked up their wedding photo on the nightstand by her side of the bed and stared at the happy memory. *It was such a glorious day for us*, she muttered. Shauna stroked Roan's face trough the glass, then smiled. She placed the picture back on the stand and went out into the living room to find the police had arrived. Stephen was dealing with them, instructing them to wait until the private security firm could get there.

Several of the officers had part-time security jobs on their time off and were familiar with the house. They volunteered to stay until reinforcements could get there. One of the officers was Jim's brother, Alan. It was comforting to Shauna to have more family there.

The media circled the homestead with lights, cameras and reporters ready to pounce on anyone who came out of the house. Stephen and Jim went outside to deal with them, while Katie and Marie kept the household running. Shauna checked the messages, stacked them by priority and returned the call from the White House. But she left the rest until morning. It was now 11:00 PM. The children were tucked into bed, with instructions to keep all the doors locked and shades drawn downstairs. Flash, TT, Mickey and Cookie were fast asleep in their respective beds and Shauna said goodnight to her friends. Jim, Katie and Stephen stayed, while Sharon put the computer on standby and went home. The security people stationed themselves on the perimeter of the property and kept the madding crowd back, allowing the family some much needed respite from the insanity of the day's events.

The morning broke with sub-zero temperatures and a clear, starry sky. At 5:00 AM, not much was scurrying around, except Flash. But even he wasn't moving very fast. Shauna got up, put on her bathrobe and fuzzy slippers, padding into the kitchen to make coffee. Charles had already done that the night before by putting the coffee makers on timers. The coffee was in middle-brew, so Shauna thought she would wait until it finished. She wandered into the living room, made up the fire, turned on a few lights and checked out the baked goods the neighbors brought. A large serving tray was lying on the table and Shauna filled it up with the tasty treats, got out six coffee cups and made up the tray for the security guards. Then she got the idea, perhaps the media personnel might be half frozen outside in their RVs. Maybe this battle could be won with cinnamon buns instead of venom?

Katie heard noises and came in from the studio with one eye open. Yesterday had been too wild, but no matter how tired she was, there was work to be done.

She yawned her greeting to Shauna saying, "I think it's morning, isn't it, Shauna? This is no dream, right?"

Shauna responded with her own yawn.

All she could muster was, "Not a dream, Katie. I wish it were, but this is that nightmare you were always hoping would never happen and is. I just hope my brain works halfway this morning. I must have left the other half in the bedroom!"

Once they had some coffee and toast in them, Katie and Shauna came up with a game plan for the day. Shauna made a quick inspection of the media trucks, while Katie gave out the coffee and breakfast rolls to the security guards. They came in one by one to get warm and fed. Talk about icicles with a badge! These men were frozen to the bone.

There were about ten of the big RVs and trucks, so Shauna asked a security guard to knock on the RV doors and invite the media people into the house for some breakfast. She went in to take a quick shower and get dressed so she could present her best face to the world.

Katie went downstairs to tell Charles and Marie about the plan, then woke up Jim and Stephen to tell them. Janet got Conor and Jimmy up to put everyone on schedule for the day. Yes, it was very early, but this would be a very long, tense day and the game plan needed to be in place.

Charles came up first and checked out the larder. He pulled out all the bacon in the freezer, plus eggs, bread and whatever else he could find to feed these folks. He knew camera people were always hungry and news crews nibbled on celery! But today, January 2nd, was way too cold for anyone to be on a diet. Within minutes, people dribbled in looking for coffee and a warm, welcoming fire to sit around. Because the living room was huge, everyone could fit, steady cams and all. It was a better way to get information passed around, interviews to be done without much fuss or resentment.

Stephen Brennan came into the living room wearing a bright red sweater, dark brown cord jeans and boat shoes—with no socks. Quite honestly, he looked like a preppie professor rather than an attorney, especially without his buckskins. Once he got his coffee, he sat among the media, chatting affably about Bemidji and what had transpired in the past few weeks. Shauna's idea was working better than expected.

Jim had been on the phone and by now it was 7:00 AM. There was news about the crash victims. Jim brought his coffee cup and a donut along, sitting down at the island at the end of the kitchen, so he could face everyone.

He spoke succinctly, but quietly and said, "Listen up people. The latest news from Walker is this. The weather has cleared enough to get the ambulances to the hospital in Brainerd. I have the status of each patient."

All cameras turned on Jim as he spoke. The results of his investigation were these: Alice and Harriet Foster of Bemidji (sisters in their late 60's) were in serious but stable condition with multiple broken bones, contusions and lacerations. Stan and Tanner Miller, father and son from the Cities were also in stable condition with the same injuries. Roan was the most critically injured, but he spent a decent night. The other couple, Marjorie and Bob Lassiter, were beaten up, but could be released. Jim advised news crews were on the scene at the hospital and if the Lake crews wanted a more precise update, they can check in with their networks.

Shauna came in and sat down in the middle of the white couch. Tyler was following but when he saw all the people, he turned around and ran into the kitchen. Unfortunately for everyone in the room, Mickey showed up and did what Mickey does best.

"You can clear a room faster than a bomb scare with that dog," Jim chortled. "That dog has more gas than a utility company!"

Everyone had a good laugh at the comic relief, but once again the mood turned more somber. Several reporters started raising hands and asking questions, but were basically polite and waited for Shauna to speak. Since Jim had given an update, Shauna explained it was time to talk with the hospital directly, then begin answering the plethora of calls, emails and notes. If she had new insights, she would have the media come back for a short interview. The news crews thanked Shauna and Jim, departed quietly and left the family alone for a while.

Shauna took the phone number of the hospital from Jim and called their direct line to the nurses' station to get an update.

The doctor on call, Dale Shauver, was at the desk and told Shauna, "Mrs. Sanderson, I have a little good news about Roan. He spent the night as comfortable as he could. He is alert some of the time, but drifts in and out. The head injury is quite severe, but we are monitoring it closely. There is a nurse in with him at all times. His broken arm has been set and his broken ribs and leg are extremely uncomfortable, so we have him sedated. It's the best way for him to let the body rest. My concern is what I saw on the CT scan and MRI, but I want you to be here so I can show you what I mean. Can you get through to Brainerd?"

Shauna was concerned but said she would try to get down there as quickly as possible.

"Yes, Dr. Shauver," Shauna responded. "I will take a helicopter down later this morning. Our attorney has arranged for one and we should be there sometime around 11:00 AM. And you had better start calling me Shauna because I think we will be spending some time together over the next couple of days."

"Agreed Shauna," replied the doctor. "This is going to be a long recovery for you and Roan, so it's best to get it off to the right start."

Katie needed to get to the shop to open for the deliveries coming in. The holidays had literally wiped out most of their stock and although the shop would be closed for a few days while they replenished the merchandise, Katie still needed to be there to sign for each delivery. Jim would unload and Marie would be in charge at the house. Charles had to get his restaurants open and meet with contractors. It would be a busy week for everyone in Bemidji.

Shauna quickly packed a bag, intending to stay in Brainerd for a while. Stephen arranged for the helicopter pickup and a vehicle for Shauna while she was there. Once Roan is stable, he can be moved to the hospital in Bemidji, so the apartment will work for Shauna to stay in, but if necessary, there was one on stand-by in Brainerd for her, too.

Stephen told the security company to continue monitoring the situation for a couple of days, then maintain their regular patrol of the area. He could see the RVs packing up to go to another destination and a normal routine could be re-established at the Sanderson home.

Shauna quickly called Franco at home and relayed the latest news. He seemed relieved, but still very upset. She would call him again at the hospital after she had seen the doctor and Roan. She said goodbye to Conor and the rest of the family, then left with Mr. Brennan. Now it was 10:00 AM and as she was leaving, the florists were delivering arrangements to the house.

I guess these folks have recovered from Christmas, Shauna mused. *I won't be able to enjoy these flowers, but everyone else will.*

They got into Mr. Brennan's SUV and drove out to the airport. The copter was waiting and took them directly to the heliport at the hospital. They landed in no time and found the critical care floor immediately.

Shauna walked up to the desk and said, "I'm Mrs. Sanderson. Can I see my husband?"

A nurse responded, "Hello, Mrs. Sanderson. I'm Jenny, one of the nurses taking care of your husband. The doctor wants to chat with you first and he is waiting for you in his office. I'll let him know you are here."

"Thank you, Jenny," replied Shauna. "I'll just wait over here on the bench."

Stephen and Shauna waited in a cheerful waiting area, then saw the doctor heading toward them.

"Shauna? I'm Dale Shauver. Nice to meet you but it would be nicer under different circumstances. I know your work and I'm a fan! But I want to show you something before we go in to see Roan. Steve, it's good to see you again."

They walked into the radiology lab and began looking at Roan's test results.

Dale began softly, "Shauna, I don't want you to be alarmed, but these tests show the head injury has left Roan blind in both eyes. There is severe pressure on both optic nerves. Now, it could be simple swelling from the brain injury and will go away at some point, but it could also be irreversible. I don't want to be an alarmist, but I wanted to you see for yourself."

Shauna looked at the x-rays, turned to Stephen and slumped against his shoulder.

"Oh hell," she cried. "This can't be. He's an artist and his sight is everything to him. Does he know he's blind—you said he has been sedated?"

"Yes he has been sedated," replied Dr. Shauver. "But there were a few flash burns on his eyes and they are covered, so he really doesn't know. We will take the bandages off this morning and with you there, the results will be a lot easier for him to accept. Let's just see what happens."

Shauna nervously walked out of the radiology lab, cautiously observing her surroundings. Stephen supported her arm and when she stood at Roan's hospital door.

She took a couple of deep breaths, then said, "Okay, I'm ready. Steve, keep holding my arm. I'm so overwhelmed right now, I'm almost sick."

Dr. Shauver opened the door and they could see Roan sleeping peacefully. Shauna walked over to the side rail to look at her battered husband. There was a huge bandage over his left temple, bandages on his eyes and his arm was in a cast. She couldn't see the stitches in his leg, but she knew they were there. He was hooked up to oxygen helping him breathe due to the broken ribs. All in all, he seemed in better shape than she expected. Shauna said nothing, but took Roan's other hand in hers and sat down on the stool next to the bed. It didn't take long for Roan to wake up.

"Ah, Shauna is here," he said groggily. "I'd know your Chanel No. 5 anywhere, Honey."

Shauna stroked his hand and said lovingly, "Hey handsome. I hate it when you miss a party. I guess we will just have to do it all over again when you get home. Good idea?"

Roan smiled wryly then said, "Ah, I see Stephen is also here. I know that Jade East after shave, too. Dang it man, get into the 21st Century!"

"Oh yeah, hi yourself, Roan," barked Stephen. "No brain injury there. What's wrong with my after shave? The ladies love it. Besides, I got a great price on six cases of the stuff."

Roan replied with a grin, "Ladies? You mean those moose you hang out with at your cabin in the woods? Ah, I don't think so. I may be injured, but I'm not blind. Or am I, Dr. Shauver?"

SNAP. No one expected that response.

But Dr. Shauver explained to Roan, "I don't know yet, Roan. I want to take the bandages off and see what's under here—other than your eyes. Jenny, hand me those scissors, please. I'll take the pads off and we can see how your eyes are healing. Now, if you can't see right away, don't worry. It's probably temporary due to the injury. Okay, here we go."

Dr. Shauver carefully cut away the gauze holding the cotton pads on Roan's eyes. He took off the pads and lifted the last layer of cotton, wiping away some of the antibiotic, careful not to tear any burned skin. Roan's eyes were red, black and blue, swollen and almost unrecognisable.

"Okay, Roan," said Dr. Shauver. "Open your eyes slowly. Let's find out how you are doing."

Roan cautiously opened his left eye, then the right. You could see him trying to focus on something but the results were frustrating.

When asked again, all Roan could say was, "No. Nothing. I can't see a thing, not even light. Shauna, where are you?"

"I'm right here, Roan," she replied. "I am just at your side, holding your hand."

You could see the despair in Roan's face. He couldn't see anything.

"Damn it, Shauna," Roan cried. "I can't see you. I can't even tell how many people are here."

Dr. Shauver reassured Roan this could be temporary and they would know more in a few days. He put new patches over Roan's eyes, then left the room with Stephen in tow.

The doctor said to Mr. Brennan, "It will take a couple of days for the swelling to go down. We are talking some major head trauma here. Thank goodness for the Thomsens. They did everything exactly right and Roan is alive today because of them. Just don't let Roan give up hope if his sight hasn't come back in a few days. It might be then, a month from now or never. We simply don't know at this point."

Stephen nodded and went back in to talk with Shauna and Roan.

He felt it was best to leave them alone and he had his law practice to get back to, so he said to Roan, "I hate to watch you lolligagging around here, so I'm going home and leaving Shauna to deal with you. Just call if you need anything, except a bottle of Scotch. You need two good hands to drink my firewater!"

Brennan kissed Shauna on the cheek and said farewell. Now Shauna was left to cope with the aftermath of the accident. You could feel the tension building up in the room, now that Roan discovered he couldn't see. Shauna was going through this all over again. It seemed she had just gotten her strength back after Conor's accident.

But with Rosary and Prayer Book in hand, Shauna drew in a huge breath and said, "Roan, I'm here. You will get your sight back and you will be fine. We're just side tracked for a little while, but not to worry. Everything is running smoothly and all you have to do it get better."

Shauna stroked Roan's hair and beard. His medication had him drifting off to sleep often, so Shauna took this opportunity to call Franco and the store. Then she would sit in the recliner in the corner of the room and take a rest.

Time seemed to fly by and when Shauna awoke from her nap, it was 5:00 PM. I guess you never really know how tired you are until you drop off and wake up hours later. Roan was still sleeping peacefully, so Shauna went out to the nurses' station to see where the cafeteria is located. She went down for a sandwich and coffee, plus she wanted to check in on her messages and Katie's day. Everything seemed so mundane—ordinary. She seemed to be the only one out of synch.

Once Shauna sat down, she noticed a woman roughly her age sitting alone. She got up and went over to introduce herself.

"Excuse me, but I couldn't help but see you eating alone and I thought I would introduce myself. I'm Shauna Sanderson."

"Oh, Sanderson?" the woman replied. "Was your husband in a plane crash? My husband and son were on that plane. It's a miracle anyone survived. Please, join me. I'm Betty Miller, by the way."

"Yes, I guessed you might be," Shauna replied. "My husband Roan is upstairs in ICU, but I should be able to take him home to Bemidji in a few days. It's going to be a long recovery, but he is strong and will be fine. How are your men?"

"They should be released in a couple of days, too," explained Mrs. Miller . "Their injuries weren't as severe as your husband's, but I would assume there are hurting just as bad. My son is thirteen now and he wants to take care of his Dad. I'm going to have to get in some help just to keep sanity around my house!"

"My son Conor is recovering from a bad fall," Shauna explained. "Just when he gets out of his wheelchair, his Dad needs it. I'm so lucky to have a great support team working for me at home."

The women ate lunch, then went back up to the ICU. Roan was awake— kind of groggy, but still aware.

He heard Shauna talking with Jenny in the hallway and began to call out, "Shauna? Shauna? Where are you?"

"Oh oh, I'd better get in there, Jenny," Shauna exclaimed. "No need to make him anxious."

Shauna returned to the room and grabbed Roan's hand. She reassured him she was right there and wasn't going anywhere.

"Some honeymoon, huh?" sighed Roan. "Here we had all these plans and starting our lives together. How much more do we have to endure?"

"Well Roan," Shauna replied. "This is only a setback. We have handled a lot in the past six months and we can continue handling it with prayer, faith and the love we have for each other. I'm not giving up and you aren't going to either. Got it, Mister?"

"Guess I deserved that one," Roan grimaced. "We really have accomplished a lot and there is so much more to do. I need to get out of here."

"Oh yes, there you are in there. I knew my husband was inside that mass of bandages," Shauna laughed. "Okay, okay, one day at a time. I've got permission to take you home to the Bemidji hospital in a couple of days, but then you will be starting rehab once they give you the go-ahead. Just don't try to be Conor too quickly. You're no Spring chicken, you know!"

"Very funny, Shauna," moaned Roan. "But at least there is a plan in place. Leave it to you to put it in place early. Glad Janet is still with us. These drugs are making me sleepy again. You go home and get some sleep. I'm not going anywhere, so get some rest. See you in the morning, Honey."

Roan was off in lalaland again and Shauna knew it was time for some real rest. The hospital had the keys to an SUV for her, plus keys to a self-catering motel suite close to the hospital. Everything had been taken care of and Shauna needed to get changed and eat a little supper. She gladly took the keys and grabbed her bag. All would be peaceful until tomorrow.

Chapter Three

Mariachi Band. There is a mariachi band playing near the room. This is too bizarre, mumbled Shauna. *Where on earth is this coming from?*

Within seconds, Shauna opened the curtains to see a parade marching past the motel. There were all kinds of bands and marching units. A sign said something about a winter carnival. *Here it is, 7:00 AM, the middle of January and there is a parade screaming past her doorway. Guess that's one way to get a wake-up call!*

Now that Shauna was awake and motivated, she grabbed her coat and went off to the hospital to see her husband. The florist had struck again. The room was filled with arrangements, plants, small trees—you name it, someone sent it. However, there were no balloons. Roan awoke to smell the overpowering aroma of flowers. He was pleased at first, then got angry.

"Jenny, Jenny, what is this a funeral home?" Roan yelled. "Get these things out of here!"

Shauna arrived just in time. She walked in the room, took some photos with her digital camera, took the cards off each arrangement and told Jenny to take the flowers to patients who had none. The green plants would be nice for the chapel or nurses' station and the trees would be great for the cafeteria. That was easy enough to do.

"Well, I see you are almost back to normal," Shauna cracked. "I admit, those were a lot of arrangements and probably overpowering, but let me tell you this, lots and lots of people care about you and are concerned for your recovery. I dealt with it, took some pictures for you and will send the thank you cards. We seem to have a few thousand left from Lulabelle's thank you's. Oh and by the way, there were no balloons in the arrangements. You satisfied now?"

"Feeling sorry for myself, aren't I?" Roan asked. "I'm sorry. I should know better. I'm just so frustrated I can't see anything or do anything. It's a control issue, yes, I admit it. Am I hopeless or what?"

"Ah no, Roan, you aren't hopeless," replied Shauna. "You are just a typical man who isn't used to being confined to a bed. So let's see what the doctor says about you getting out of here, back to Bemidji and into rehab. I don't want you here any longer than you have to be. I'm sure the NTSB will want to talk with you as well. How do you feel this morning, by the way?"

Roan thought for a moment and said, "I know I feel better, but there is still so much pain. Dr. Shauver told me what got broken, bruised, gashed and dented, but he didn't tell me how I got this way. He told me the plane had crashed and for the life of me, I can't remember a thing about it. Maybe that memory will come back, but for now, I don't remember a thing."

"You don't need to worry about that," explained Shauna. "When you called on your cell phone, I recorded your messages on the home phone, so that gives the NTSB something to go on. I met Mrs. Miller downstairs and her husband does remember. So it's okay, Roan—got it covered."

Dr. Shauver came in to give his daily report on the tests and give Roan a quick once-over. Roan was a fast healer and the doctor determined Roan could go home—not to the hospital, in two days. He would arrange for a life flight to take Roan back to Bemidji. Fortunately, since they had just gone through the process with Conor, all the support people, physicians and therapists were in place.

Dale Shauver explained how Roan was doing, "I'm pleased with the progress you are making Roan and don't hesitate in sending you home. Let me take the bandages off your eyes and see how they are healing. I know you probably can't see yet, but the new MRI shows promise, so I don't think this is permanent."

But Roan still couldn't see. He couldn't even make out shapes or colours. It was unbelievably aggravating, but Roan accepted that reason for the time being and readied himself to go home. Shauna got out her planner and began writing out the rest of the plans for the thank-yous, the trip home, therapy, etc. Then she began making calls to set everything up. Shauna was excellent at planning and taking charge of difficult situations. In an hour, her task was complete and she spent the rest of the day chatting with Roan.

The next two days went by quickly. Then it was time to thank everyone and go home to Bemidji. The ride home was excruciating. Roan's broken ribs pressed in against his chest and the gash in his leg was giving him phantom pain where the nerves had been severed. Every move, every jerk brought tears to his eyes, but Roan was determined to get home to Conor and his friends. Roan's sense of smell took over for his eyes and he could smell the diesel fuel in the helicopter engines. The blades made a deafening sound as they took off and the pressure on his head injury was immense. The ride home was only 20 minutes long and when they landed, Roan finally felt relief.

"Remind me not to get in any more accidents, Shauna," Roan exclaimed. "I don't think I can take the pain!"

The ambulance whisked the Sandersons home to the lake house. It was a quiet ride (without the siren) but not so quiet homecoming when they got to the house. All the neighbors, friends, business acquaintances and reporters lined the driveway cheering for Roan as the ambulance pulled into the driveway. Roan managed a little wave with his good arm but that was about it. Glad to be home, Roan was tucked into his own bed and Janet gave him some sedation to calm him down from the trip.

Katie and Jim came out to the house that evening to fill Shauna in on the progress at the store. Charles also had a report on the rebuilding of their home, plus there were calls from Franco and others. Shauna called the florists and asked the gifted items be given to a nursing home, so the smell of flowers wouldn't overpower Roan. She would thank each person via personal note, but this way, others would benefit from the lovely floral arrangements. Fortunately, after Miss Lulabelle's wake and funeral, the florists knew to write a description on the back of the enclosure cards, even if the flowers were delivered somewhere else.

Once Roan healed from his injuries, he had to deal with the blindness. That might prove to be the most difficult injury to heal. Dr. Shauver called a colleague who dealt with trauma induced blindness and when the time came, he would call on Roan. But now, the physical damage had to heal.

The first month, Roan progressed as one would expect, but the second month, February, brought on a mild depression. Of course, that isn't unusual in trauma cases, but with the blindness, this added more strain. Roan was restless. He couldn't sit still for very long and although his arm was still cast and he was confined to the wheelchair, Roan's distress was obvious.

Determined to get out of the wheelchair and fend for himself, Roan felt around for the brake, shoved it down and attempted to climb out. Janet was outside with Conor, so they didn't see him. But they heard him when he crashed against the kitchen island onto the wood floor. Roan screamed in pain and frustration. His cast was split from hitting the sharp edge of the cabinet and he was tangled in the spokes of the chair. When she heard the cries, Janet ran back inside to find Roan in distress.

"Conor," she called outside. "Conor, get in here, call the doctor and the hospital. Your Dad's had an accident."

Roan began pounding his fist on the floor, more out of anger than anything else.

He immediately addressed the situation to Janet and between sobs cried, "Janet, I can't get up. Help me, please."

However, Roan didn't know about the split in his cast and the fact it was twisted up in the spokes of the chair's right wheel. Emotions were running high and Roan kept pounding his good fist on the floor.

"Janet," said Conor. "The doctor is on the phone and he needs to speak with you."

Janet picked up the phone as Conor rushed over to his Dad to comfort him. Janet spoke quietly with the doctor and said, "Hello, Dr. Drummond. Roan took a spill in his chair and split his cast. I don't know if anything else is damaged, but I had Conor call for the ambulance to bring him in, just in case, but right now, we can't get him untangled or off the floor. We'll just let the paramedics do that. But Doctor, my real concern is for the depression he is exhibiting. It's getting worse and he's really frustrated with not being able to see. I thought you should know."

"Thanks Janet," he replied. "I'll reassess his progress when he gets here to the hospital. Have you called Shauna yet?"

"No, not yet," she answered. "But I'll do that now and have her meet you at the hospital. I can hear the siren now, so I will see you in about fifteen minutes."

Shauna was advised of the accident and agreed to meet everyone at the hospital. The paramedics were able to cut Roan out of the chair, but the wheel needed to be replaced, as did his cast. Guess if you are going to mess up, get it all done at once!

Conor and Janet followed the ambulance into Bemidji. An anxious Shauna was at the emergency entrance, pacing around the lounge area. Once she saw Roan, she calmed down a little, but the concern was still evident on her face.

As they brought him into the bay, Shauna grabbed Roan's hand and said, "I'm here Honey. Don't worry."

She could tell all Roan wanted to do is jump up and scream in frustration, but Shauna calmed him down by saying, "You will be fine, Roan. It doesn't look like you have really hurt yourself again, you just tore the cast. They will look you over and give you a new cast for your arm. I'll wait outside while they help you, then sit with you until I can take you home."

Dr. Drummond whisked in to check on Roan and came out in a few minutes.

He didn't seem that concerned, but told Shauna, "Roan seems fine. I have ordered new x-rays just to be on the safe side. It's the depression over his sight that has me concerned. Knowing Roan as I do, he wouldn't want medication for it, so I am bringing in a psychologist who works with trauma patients. Maybe he can come up with a treatment plan to help lift this. I can have him consult with you first, then have him come out to the house."

"Thank you, Doctor," replied Shauna. "This will be a relief when he's back to being himself again."

Roan was patched up and released within an hour. A new chair could be delivered that afternoon, so Shauna took the family back to the lake house.

The next few weeks drove Roan into silence. The psychologist came by to talk with Roan and felt he could be helped by therapy a few times per week. Maybe it would help, but maybe not.

The next months went by too fast. His vision hadn't changed, but Roan's injuries repaired themselves. His memory of that fateful day began to return and he was able to record more details of the crash itself. He could remember the plane on its belly as it skidded toward the grove of lodge pole pines. The visions in his mind were as clear as they day they happened. Roan remembered hearing the pilots as they angled the plane the safest way possible, but the ice made any control impossible. The wings had iced over and strong cross winds forced the plane down as if it were made of lead. In an instant, the fuselage slammed into the ground as the trees impaled the cabin, breaking the windows and forcing their way into the steel skin, ripping huge holes like shrapnel from a hand grenade. The smell of burning insulation and rubber choked the passengers and stung their lungs. There were flashes of flame coming from the cockpit, which is how Roan's eyes were burned.

As Roan talked into his hand recorder, his memories became more intense and he shouted, "Crash. We crashed. I can't move, I'm pinned in here. Oh God in Heaven, there's blood everywhere. Shauna. I have to get to Shauna. There's no way out…I can't get out. No. No. No."

Roan dropped the recorder and Shauna came running into the room. She found her husband sobbing uncontrollably. She tried to keep her composure, but the tears overwhelmed her.

Trying to choke them back she held her hand to her mouth, then cried, "Roan, you did make it out. You're here with me. You're home. It's over."

Shauna embraced her husband and they held each other for a long time. Conor came through the room, saw his parents in such emotional distress, turned right around and went back up to his room. This was not the time to say 'hi' and Conor was old enough now to realise it. But there had been a breakthrough. Now Roan's memory of the crash had resurfaced and he could give it closure.

Although Roan still couldn't see, he turned to Shauna and asked, "What day is it? How long have I been like this, Shauna?"

"It's April 12th, Roan," Shauna replied. "You have been home for a little over three months. Your cast is off, your leg is almost healed and your ribs aren't cracked any more. I'd say you are doing very well, Roan. I'm really proud of the way you are working for a full recovery."

"But Shauna," he gasped. "I still can't see. Why can't I see?"

"I don't know, Roan," she said. "All the tests say you should have your sight back. Dr. Shauver has a specialist lined up if you want to see him, but I have another idea if you trust me."

"Of course I trust you Shauna," Roan exclaimed. "You of all people know how much I count on you and trust you with my life. What have you got in mind?"

Shauna had been thinking about a trip to the place she had seen in the photo book on the coffee table. It was a spiritual place—a place of healing. It would be an arduous journey, but it had been part of Miss Lulabelle's wedding gift to them. Shauna decided to tell Roan and get his opinion.

"Alright Roan," said Shauna with a steadfast voice. "Do you remember Miss Lulabelle gave us those tickets for our honeymoon? Well, they are out of date now, but I think we can trade them in given the circumstances and take the trip whenever we want. But maybe we should do only one of the destinations this trip. What do you think?"

"Okay, you have me in suspense, Shauna," declared Roan. "Just tell me and we can decide."

"Okay, I'll tell you," exclaimed Shauna. "This is perfect. Do you remember I told you about the photos in the book, how the people were climbing up the mountain, praying and saying the Rosary? There was a little monk or brother in the pictures and it was he I saw in the chapel at the hospital when Conor was there? I want to go to this place. It's a village called Medjugorje, in Hercegovina. Our Lady has been allegedly appearing there for almost twenty-three years. I truly believe she is and I think we should take a pilgrimage together. There is one leaving next week for ten days, with a stop-over in Rome on the way back for three days. I know there is a miracle for us in there somewhere. What do you think?"

Roan was a bit stunned, but angrily declared, "Why can't Our Lady appear to me here and heal me here? I don't understand why I would have to go half way around the world to do something that can be done at home. It's nonsense, Shauna. I can't even find my way around outside of the house. No, I don't want to go."

Shauna was taken aback, but persevered and replied, "Fine. I'll go. You don't want to try? Fine, I will try. I need a break—I'm tired. I'm sick of you grumping around here all day. Lulabelle's understanding of spiritual matters was not ours, but she understood more than we ever gave her credit for. There was a reason for her to give us those tickets for our honeymoon to these specific places. I won't force you, Roan. But I want you to think about it again before you make a final decision."

Roan got up and made his way to the bedroom, closing the door. He didn't slam it, but Shauna knew from experience he was contemplating something. She decided to bring in the voice of reason—their friend, Maggie McManus. Maggie had been in Medjugorje many times and had seen the little monk in the chapel, along with Shauna. If there was one person Roan would listen to, it was Maggie.

Shauna looked up the number and dialed her. When Maggie answered her phone, she knew instinctively what the call was about.

After listening for a moment, she responded, "Oh, I agree with you, Shauna. Roan needs to go to Medjugorje. And he needs to go now. He has lost his spiritual center and depression has set in. If there is anything I can do, I will be more than happy to do so. How about it if I come over in the morning for coffee—we can go from there. This is such a perfect time to go over. It's less crowded now and the weather is usually brisk, not cold or hot. See you about tenish then?"

"You are a life saver, Maggie," responded Shauna. "I can't thank you enough."

Maggie said, "Oh sure you can. You can take me with you! I am chomping at the bit to get back over and I can help with Roan. I'm the perfect tour guide. This would do more good for Roan than a psychologist. You think about it and I will see you in the morning. Nite, Shauna."

Shauna turned off the lights and went to bed. Roan was out on the deck looking up at the stars, but experiencing nothing, except the cool April breeze on his face. Roan closed the French door and used his cane to tap along the wall toward the bed, then slowly got in. He said nothing, not even good night to Shauna. And she left it that way. He wasn't angry, just 'thinking.'

As the morning doves cooed on the deck, Shauna awoke to their lovely sound. She went into the kitchen to find Charles had left some of his famous cinnamon buns on the stove warmer and the coffee had just begun. Roan followed soon after and continued to say nothing. Shauna poured fresh coffee and placed a bun on each plate on the table, then sat down. Roan sat with her, still saying nothing.

Well, two can play at this game, Shauna thought. When she was finished, she got up and took her morning shower. She put on jeans and a light-weight, bright yellow sweater, her sneakers and watch. Soon Maggie was knocking on the front door and Roan continued to sit at the table, lost in thought.

"Hey Maggie," grinned Shauna. "Out paying a house call?"

Shauna nodded her head and Maggie followed her lead by saying, "I sure am. Hi Roan, you look much, much better than the last time I saw you. Feeling more chipper?"

Roan looked up at Maggie, forced a smile and said, "Guess so, Maggie. Nice to see you again. Well, you know."

Maggie replied, "Sure I know, but this is only temporary. Anyway, although it's always wonderful to see you, Roan, I came for another reason. I am going out of town and need a digital camera. Mine got dropped last time and I have a bunch of memory sticks which fit Conor's camera, but now I have no camera to use them in. Would it be alright to borrow it?"

Shauna loved the way this ruse was going and retorted, "I will go up and ask Conor now if you want. He hasn't used his for a while and it may need batteries. Just a second and I will ask him. Oh, and help yourself to coffee and a cinnamon bun, too."

Shauna waved her hand around in a circle to get Roan talking about where she was going. She also motioned to s t r e t c h it out—so it didn't look like a put-up job.

"Don't mind if I do, Shauna," she said. "It must have been heaven to have a professional chef at the house for three months, Roan. I expect they will be moving into their new home soon. Oh, this bun is divine."

Roan was curious about Maggie's trip and asked, "Where are you going this year, Maggie? Backpacking in the Himalayas? Trekking in the Sahara? There must be some souls who need saving in a third world country."

Maggie tried not to blurt out where she was going, so she merely explained, "Nothing quite that exotic this time, Roan. You probably wouldn't know where it is or why it is, but I have been eight times already."

"You still haven't told me, Maggie," inquired Roan. "Is this the magic kingdom or something like that?"

"I guess you could say something like that," she replied. "I'm going on a retreat and it's so beautiful there, I need the camera. I can walk through the fields, watching the chickens in the people's yards or play with a goat tied to a house (he likes hard candy). There are mountains to climb and places to simply sit and pray. I think it's the most fantastic place on earth and for me, the only place I can strip off the grime of my life and cleanse my spirit. Oh sure, Lourdes and Fatima are always wonderful, but they are so crowded and this village is tranquil. I can join in with the other pilgrims or just be left alone to my own prayers. I've gone with this group every time and now I kind of just 'do my own thing', to coin a phrase."

"And this place is called?" Roan begged. "Come on, Maggie, tell me."

Now for the sales close.

Maggie replied, "It's a place called Medjugorje, in Bosnia-Hercegovina. It's a little village not bombed during the war. I know you probably never heard of it before, but I love it there and I can't wait to get back. Your mom and dad went there, you know. And that's where the rosary came from that Shauna has in her pocket—you know, your Mom's crystal rosary—she was never without it. It was blessed there and it never left her side. It was really your Mother who influenced me to go on retreat there. Oh, I see Shauna with the camera. I'm glad I was able to see how you are doing, Roan. I'll see you when I get back. Thank Conor for the camera, Shauna."

"Yeah, see ya, Maggie," said Roan.

Maggie gave Shauna the high sign and Shauna said nothing about the retreat, only that it was nice to see their friend again.

Roan looked directly at Shauna and said, "Yes it was good to talk with Maggie. She's a lovely woman. Funny though she should mention this Medjugorje place, too."

"Oh did she?" asked Shauna. "I guess I didn't hear her, because I was checking the batteries on the camera. I put some fresh ones in for her. I hope she has a good time there. She mentioned it at the hospital last year, because she saw the little monk in the chapel, too. It's Padre Pio, you know."

"I figured it might have been Padre Pio, but there was such chaos that week, I lost the thought," replied Roan. "By the way, I have always liked your yellow sweater. It suits you."

"My yellow sweater, Roan," asked Shauna. Why do you mention that one?"

"Because it's the one you are wearing, isn't it?" he replied. "Yellow sweater—yellow. Shauna, please tell me you have the sweater on."

"Yes, Roan," she said. "I am wearing the yellow sweater! Can you see yellow?"

"Oh man, I can see yellow, Shauna," Roan shouted. "I can see something yellow. Praise God, Shauna. Call Maggie and get her back here. We need to go to Medjugorje. Now!"

Chapter Four

Excitement swept through the house, as Roan continued to shout. Shauna immediately called Maggie's cell phone to bring her back. She was in the driveway, just stepping into her car and she dashed back in.

Maggie ripped open the entry-door to the garage and yelled, "What's going on? Okay, you two, tell me before someone bursts a gut!"

"I can see yellow," replied Roan. "I can actually see the colour yellow because I can see the sweater Shauna is wearing and that has to be a sign we need to go to Medjugorje. Maggie, are we too late to join the pilgrimage?"

Maggie beamed with glee and grinned, "Nope. You aren't too late because I booked two extra places yesterday! Somehow I just knew you would be coming with us."

Conor came into the living room with a quizzical look on his face.

"Hey, what's all the shouting about?" he asked. "I never hear shouting around here."

"Your Dad has something to tell you, Conor," replied Shauna. "Go ahead, Roan, tell him because this is YOUR news."

"Son," responded Roan. "I can see your Mom's yellow sweater—well, the colour of it, anyway. Isn't that great news?"

"SNAP," laughed Conor. "Dad, that's totally awesome!"

Shauna was already on the phone to Marie and Charles at the restaurant, Franco in the Cities and Katie at the Gallery. This was the most hopeful news they'd had since the accident. There was cause for celebration in the Sanderson home tonight!

Shauna then called Roan's doctor to clear the trip with him. This would be an arduous journey of over 24 hours on planes and in airports, plus a long drive from the Split airport in Croatia down to Medjugorje in Hercegoniva. And this would be the first time Roan had been on an airplane since the crash.

Can he handle this trip?, mused Shauna.

After the conversation with the physician, Shauna explained her discussion with Roan's doctor and explained Roan has clearance to go on the pilgrimage, provided he be supervised and have access to medical care in a crisis. Shauna checked the brochure Maggie had with her, which explained the amenities, accommodation and activities. There is an aid station with paramedics in the village, plus access to the clinic a few miles away in Chitluk. Whatever Roan needed would be available in an emergency.

Shauna thought she should show Maggie the book she had seen with the Hill of Apparitions and the figure of the little monk. She brought the book over to the dining room table, opened the book to the center section and there it was—the photo of Medjugorje.

"Sure," agreed Maggie. "This is it. That's Podbrdo, also called the Hill of Apparitions. It's where the pilgrims say the Rosary, the Stations of the Cross and make their sacrifices to God through prayer as they climb to the top and back down again. So many don't wear shoes up the hill. This place is amazing."

"These have got to be signs we are supposed to be there now," said Shauna. "Maggie, tell me more about this place."

Maggie brought everyone in the living room and began to tell about Medjugorje. As she was starting, Katie and Jim came in the door and joined in.

Maggie continued, "Almost twenty-three years ago, six children were alleged to have seen the Virgin Mary in this tiny hamlet of Bijakovici, next to the village of Medjugorje in the Hercegovina province of Bosnia. Our Lady gave them messages and ten secrets, while speaking to them on an on-gong basis. She has been with the pilgrims during their visits. Some people have actually seen Our Lady and she has spoken to some of them in their hearts.

Others have seen miracles like the sun spinning, the stairway to Heaven or have had experienced a multitude of blessings while there. Some have been healed spiritually, physically and emotionally. Most have taken these 'living stones of faith' as they are called, home with them and these blessings continue there. Blessed Mother asks nothing for herself, only that our hearts be open to the messages of her Son, Jesus Christ and that we pray with our hearts. This is an amazing place to be. The Church hasn't approved of the Apparitions because they are still on-going and until they stop, there can't be a full ruling, but personal pilgrimages are allowed, with priests and religious able to partake under the Declaration of Zadar."

Katie asked, "So, anyone can go to Medjugorje? What's the place like?"

"Oh Katie," responded Maggie. "I am so glad you asked. This tiny village is set in the valley between the hills (which is its literal translation) between Mt. Krizevac and Podbrdo. The homes are made from breeze block and stucco, sometimes rock and marble. We must remember, timber is very scarce and the natural hard-scape materials are used due to that shortage. Each plot of land is small, so most folks build upward. Many people take in pilgrims. Most of the visionaries, who are now adults with their own families, have built on to their family homes and take in groups of pilgrims. Many of their relatives do as well. Yes, there are some hotels in the village, but for the most part, people stay with families. The people work very, very hard to recover from the war."

"What's the church like, Maggie?" asked Jim.

Maggie continued, "St. James Church, named for St. James the Worker, is a beautiful twin-towered building. You can see it for miles out in the country and from the top of Mt. Krizevac and Podbrdo. Most of the time for Mass, you must come early because the place is packed and sometimes people must stand outside. There can literally be thousands of people packed like sardines for Mass or Adoration. Inside there is a large altar and often twenty or more priests concelebrate the Holy Mass. They come from all over the world. And sometimes, the visiting priests are invited to give the homily. It's very, very moving. This is a regular parish church and the people of the parish are very hospitable. During the war, the towers suffered only a little concussion damage, but the towers were strengthened and some remodeling was done inside the main sanctuary to change behind the altar and add the stained-glass windows along the sides. The statue of Our Lady of Lourdes is inside and just magnificent. There are hundreds of flowers surrounding the statue."

Maggie got up to pour herself a cup of coffee, sat down and continued.

"Outside, in the plaza, there is a beautiful statue of Our Lady, carved from white marble," she said. "There is a wrought iron fence around it, with several benches placed around her and there are roses everywhere. People come to pray, to have their photographs taken in front of her and most use the spot as a meeting place. The buses often take off from in front of the plaza. Across the street and along the main thoroughfare, are the shops with rosaries, jewellery, medals, gifts, statues and all sorts of things to bring home. Some say it's kind of touristy, but if you go to certain places, you don't get ripped off and sometimes even get a discount if you mention the group you are with. I'll show you some of my favourites, along with the best places for coffee and pizza, when we get there. The first time you go to Medjugorje, is an experience you will never forget. And Our Lady keeps calling you back, which you will experience after you return home. There is always a reason you are called to Medjugorje. It isn't just a place you want to go—you are called."

Shauna asked Maggie, "The rosary I have with me is Roan's mother's. Did this come from Medjugorje?"

Maggie replied, "Yes. Take a look at the center medal and you'll see it is the statue of Our Lady on the front and the church on the other side. I was with her when she bought it."

Shauna pulled the rosary out of her pocket and examined it carefully, looking at the center in particular.

She showed it to Katie and said, "And here I thought it was a Miraculous Medal! I guess I didn't look close enough at it to really tell. But it's beautiful."

Katie agreed, "Yes it is. This is so pretty. No wonder this is such a treasure. You are so fortunate, Shauna."

"Oh look at the time, " gasped Maggie. "Gotta fly. I have another appointment in town and then I have to firm up the details of the pilgrimage. I'll get them out to you ASAP, so don't go anywhere. I should be back tomorrow morning."

Maggie got up and waved goodbye to everyone. Katie and Jim were almost dumbfounded as they sat with Roan.

Katie was the first to speak up about Roan's news.

"So you can see Shauna's sweater?" she asked. "Can you see the colour of what I am wearing?"

"No, Katie," Roan replied. "I can't see yours, but it must have something to do with the light spectrum of yellow. I am just so thankful I can see a spot of colour. It's wonderful, isn't it?"

"Yes, wonderful, Roan," she said hesitantly.

Katie didn't have the heart to tell Roan she was also wearing a deeper colour yellow sweater, the one Shauna had given to her for Christmas. Maybe it was only wishful thinking on Roan's part or perhaps he had touched the fabric of the sweater, recognising it. In any case, she said nothing. It wouldn't be right to dash Roan's hopes now.

Katie had brought some invoices for Shauna to look over, checks to sign and a few catalogues to look at. They went over to the kitchen table while Roan and Jim continued talking. As Katie laid everything out, Shauna picked over the catalogues, signed the checks and looked at the invoices.

She responded favourably by saying, "Nice, Katie. Very nice. I think we should order several of the lamps from this catalogue and some pillows from this one (pointing out another page from a different mailer). I'd like to make a display of the pillows, with some fabric, pottery, lamps and a few of the framed photographs we found in the basement—all for the front display window. What do you think?"

"Oh fabulous, Shauna," replied Katie. "I have the feeling we are going into the interior decorating business now!"

But that wasn't too far off.

Shauna had been thinking about it for a while and told Katie, "We have the talent and the resources. I think we should do it. We certainly have the contacts and people keep admiring the visual merchandising we do in the store. What about it?"

"Hey," said Katie. "I'm game if you are. Hey guys, we are going into the interior decorating business at the Gallery."

Roan and Jim let out great sighs. They had unleashed an unstoppable force in Bemidji, but at least it was a positive one.

Roan was more upbeat than Jim and said, "Well, at least the girls know what they are doing and it seems to be a natural progression into this kind of business. The Gallery is almost an interiors shop now, if you don't count the books. There are all kinds of decorating items in the shop and all they would need are fabrics, carpeting, wallpaper, blind and tile samples. And if they need additional expertise, there is a decorating class at the university this Fall. I say the girls deserve a shot at it, don't you, Jim?"

"Sure, why not," agreed Jim. "After all, they have the talent, the drive and desire, so they should succeed. I don't think I have ever seen either of them stopped from doing what they do best. Their first clients can be Charles and Marie!"

"Hey girls, did you hear that?" shouted Jim. "Your first clients can be Charles and Marie. They will need a decorator!"

Katie and Shauna just grinned at each other, while they each scribbled down notes for filling up the store with merchandise.

Shauna spoke first, "Let's meet in a couple of days with our ideas, then we can decide and you can order what we need. I also think we need to make some room vignettes with chairs, tables, lamps, etc., to make it look like a decorating shop. There is more than enough room in the shop to display everything and plenty of storage space in the basement for the things we want to rotate. We can get these ideas implemented before Roan and I leave. We will only be gone two weeks and that will give you and Jim the time to see where you want these things placed."

"Super," said Katie. "I'll go back to the shop now and get started. Do you have your passport and Roan's? Will you need any special vaccinations or visas to get there?"

"Maggie will tell me all about it tomorrow morning," replied Shauna. We are meeting at 10:30 to go over the brochure and details. My head's almost spinning with these developments. I need to take a breather."

Jim and Katie left to return to the store, so Shauna sat down with Roan on the couch. Tyler climbed up between them and purred contentedly.

Shauna nestled her head on her husband's shoulder and said softly, "I'm almost stunned right now. All of a sudden, you can see a colour, I am expanding my business and we are going on a pilgrimage in a foreign country.

45

Whew, I am so glad I am sitting down with you, because my knees are buckling!"

Roan was just as baffled.

He tried to explain his feelings by saying, "I agree. This has been one of the most exciting days of my life, except for marrying you, of course. Now we can go on the first leg of our honeymoon and maybe, just maybe, there will be some kind of healing for me. I know I shouldn't go with any expectations, but I am hopeful. I really am."

The lovers sat on the sofa holding hands for a while until they heard Conor racing in with Jimmy demanding supper. Time had flown by and it was 4:30 already. It was time to get back to reality!

"Oooo, bummer Indian," grunted Shauna. "Our food is almost gone! Tell you what. I'll call for pizza and salads and maybe they will deliver in a hurry. Is it unanimous?"

Of course it is always unanimous when it came to pizza and within fifteen minutes, the delivery was on the counter. Janet needed to talk after supper. She told Roan and Shauna she had been offered a position with a rehabilitation hospital in the Cities and she needed to start in three weeks.

"I hate to leave you like this," Janet blurted out. "But this opportunity came up and it's exactly what I want. Are you okay with this decision?"

Janet had gone way beyond her duties with Conor and Roan.

All Roan could do was say, "Of course Janet. You have given us so much and if you would like a reference, please let us know what we can do for you. You are like family to us and if you want to come back for a visit, you know you are always welcome. This is your home."

Janet walked away in tears but it was the right decision for her. Her mission had been completed and the family was well enough to be on its own. So many changes were headed the Sanderson family's way—good changes. Maybe the bad days might be over, except you never know.

Shauna sat with Roan a while, then went in to clean the kitchen. Before she knew it, bedtime approached and the boys went up to bed. Roan could walk to his bedroom without the aid of a cane, so he went ahead. Shauna locked the doors, turned off the lights and followed. This would be a sound sleep for both Sandersons.

Morning came in with rain, lightning and thunder. The smell of ozone lay heavily along the ground and it seeped into the bedroom window.

As Roan woke, his heightened sense of smell kicked in and he groaned, "Rats. This isn't the way I wanted to start out my day. Hey Shauna, how are you doing on breakfast?"

Shauna poked her head around the corner, spatula in hand and grinned, "Denver omelette, bacon, home fries and freshly squeezed orange juice. How does that sound Mr. Sanderson?"

"It smells sensational, Mrs. Sanderson," he replied. "I'll be in there in a couple of minutes."

You could physically see the depression lifting from Roan's face. The lines were gone and the dark circles under his eyes appeared much lighter. Finally, there was something to celebrate. Conor and Jimmy came down for breakfast, along with Janet. Shauna felt now would be a good time to explain the pilgrimage and as they ate, she told them about the village, the country and what they would experience there. Janet had to interrupt, because it was time for the school bus and the boys couldn't be late. But you could tell Conor was excited for his folks.

Katie and Janet were in charge for the next two weeks and in no time, the Sandersons were ready to go. Maggie brought over the final details and they were ready to take their flight to the Cities.

Flying would be difficult for Roan. But the morning of their journey, he had taken something for motion sickness and it made him somewhat groggy. Maggie had arranged for a wheelchair for Roan, plus he had his white cane. This trip is tiring for uninjured people, but for someone who had been through such physical trauma, it might be too rough.

Roan heard the sound of the jet engines and backed away a little.

Shauna gripped his hand tightly and gently whispered in his ear, "I'm right here, Honey. This horse isn't going to buck you off."

Roan smiled, took a deep breath and reached for Maggie.

"Yepper, Roan, right next to you. Watch the first step," she exclaimed.

Roan knew his way around the commuter flight. He made his way to the seat just fine. The plane took off and he sat comfortably for the first leg of the trip. They would take the flight from Minneapolis/St. Paul to Chicago, then go from there to Frankfurt. They have to wait several hours for the next flight out to Zagreb, Croatia and by the time they make the connection to Split, Croatia, it will be almost midnight. Then the bus will take them down along the rugged Dalmatian Coast to Medjugorje and they should arrive around 3:30 AM. Like Maggie said, a very long journey.

The wait at the Frankfurt airport took the longest. There are plenty of beautiful shops there and Maggie knew where all the good ones were. She decided to go on the hunt for something special. Shauna wasn't that interested, so she bought a couple of espressos to share with Roan. They would meet up with their pilgrimage leader at the departure gate. Maggie knew her well, so she knew who to look out for.

Soon it was time to get the wheelchair for Roan, as the departure gate was a long distance and to conserve his strength, this was a better option. Once there, Maggie spotted her friend, Nives Jelich, a native Croatian and leader of the pilgrimage. Nives warmly welcomed Maggie and the Sandersons, then introduced them to other members of the pilgrimage group. There were twenty-two people altogether this time, which was an excellent size group for Nives to handle. Eighteen were traveling with them from Frankfurt, while the others had already made their way to Medjugorje a day earlier.

"I am so pleased to meet you, Roan and Shauna," exclaimed Nives. "It's wonderful you could come with us on such short notice. I feel you will get much from this pilgrimage. Medjugorje is very special and you will sense it the moment you round the corner into the village."

Shauna was impressed with this lovely woman. Nives might be in her early fifties, petite with dark hair, perfectly coifed. She was dressed in a burgundy knit dress with a brocade jacket, gold necklace with a medallion and simple gold earrings. Cell phone in hand, she chatted in Croatian with our host family, cousins of one of the visionaries. All was set for our arrival and Nives explained Roan's room is on the main floor, so he didn't have to negotiate the stairs.

Several of the pilgrims came up to Shauna and introduced themselves. An Irish priest from Cork, Father Eamon Patrick Shaunessey, or Father Pat as he wanted to be called, was the priest going along. There were several religious sisters with the group, along with two families with teenage children, several couples, some older ladies and a few single folk. It was a nice mix of ages and backgrounds.

Nives herded the group together and Father Pat prayed over them to begin their pilgrimage. They made their way onto the Croatia Air plane, a new airbus. It's a far cry from what they originally flew—old Russian Aeroflot planes, which had screws in the windows you could tighten with a nail file! The seats were quite comfortable and Roan had an isle seat right up front, so he could stretch his leg out. The short trip would take around an hour, with less time on the last flight. Everyone was anxious to get a little sleep before starting out in the morning.

Chapter Five

Zagreb was an interesting airport. It was small, but had a lovely little café where you could sit inside or out on the concourse. During the war, the airport was teeming with military security, men with automatic weapons and canines. Now there was only one security officer in sight with his dog, a German Shepherd named Max and Maggie said hello.

"Hello Ivan. Hello Max," she smiled. "And how is my big strong puppy then?"

Ivan replied, "Hello to you again Miss McGuire. I see you more often than my mother. I see Max is happy you are here."

Max was wagging his entire rear end in anticipation of what was in Maggie's sweater pocket. She pulled out a plastic bag with three large dog cookies in it, opened the bag and handed Max a bone-shaped treat.

"Here Ivan. Take the rest of these," she said. "You can give Max the other two later. I see he really does love dog biscuits."

Max continued to chomp on the cookie, came over to lick Maggie's face in thanks, then resumed patrol. Ivan smiled as they walked back along the corridor.

Their flight to Split was on time and Maggie got everyone through to the security checkpoint. Now the guards smiled instead of frowned and of course, Maggie knew most of them by name, all about their families and friends. Maggie McManus never met anyone she couldn't befriend.

She spied one guard, Nico and said gleefully in perfect Croatian, "Mir Gospodnji bio vazda s vama. It's good to see you, my friend. How is your wife? Is your mother-in-law still living with you?"

"Maggie, Maggie, my friend," Nico replied. "Wife and children fine. Mother-in-law not so good. She is driving me crazy. I think go home in a few days!"

Maggie opened her carry-on for inspection and handed Nico a small clear zip bag with American cosmetics inside. Stravka's name was clearly written on it.

"These are for your wife, Stravka. I hope they are the right colour and products she wanted. My card is inside and you let me know if these are okay or if she needs something else," Maggie said with delight.

"You are wonderful person, Maggie," responded Nico. "I cannot thank you enough."

Once they had cleared that inspection point, they went down the escalator to the departure terminal on the lower level. Roan held onto Maggie and Shauna, following their lead.

On the lower level, there are duty-free shops with perfume and liquor, some gift items and candies. Some people opted for cold bottles of juice, water or sandwiches to take on the bus, but most were so tired from the trip, they simply sat on the orange bucket chairs and waited patiently for the flight.

You could see Roan was exhausted, but still excited about the pilgrimage. Not much longer now. After half an hour, it was time to board the 30-minute flight to Split. Then the bus ride would be another three hours, with a short "potty break" stop half way along. Unfortunately, because of the darkness, you couldn't see the coastline, but some of the towns were lighted and enchantingly beautiful. The way back up would be during the daylight and offer sensational views of the Adriatic.

However, before they could board, Ivan came over to Maggie and pointed out something he felt was suspicious.

"There is a man by the staircase with long white hair, dressed in black, who has been watching your group," explained Ivan. "I don't like his look. Is he a member of your pilgrimage?"

Maggie carefully looked around the terminal, spied the man and looked at him for a moment.

She responded to Ivan by remarking, "I don't think so Ivan. But I will mention it to Nives and keep my eyes open during our trip. Thank you Ivan. You are very observant."

"It's my job, Maggie," he replied. "And if something happened to you, Max would lose his American dog treats!"

Maggie grinned, hugged Ivan, careful not to touch his automatic weapon and thanked him. As they boarded the plane, Maggie did so with a more watchful eye.

The flight to Split was very fast. Customs went swiftly, too. When you have millions of pilgrims each year flowing through the gates, the security agents become accustomed to helping thousands a day. Shauna grabbed a luggage cart, located the bags on the carousel and loaded them for the short distance to the bus. Many of the pilgrims were old friends, having been on one of Nives' groups before. They all watched out for one another. It didn't take long to meet up at the bus, find a place to sit and ease into a long bus ride.

When everyone was on board, Nives took the microphone and made an announcement.

"Please rest on your way to Medjugorje," she said clearly. We will make a stop for the bathroom halfway through and you can get soft drinks there, too. We will turn the lights back on as we get closer to the stop. If you have questions, please ask. Our driver for this trip is Vaslav. Some of you know him. He is an excellent driver."

The lights went out, meditation music played quietly over the sound system and the bus drove away from the parking lot. The strange man Ivan warned about was not on the bus. He was waiting for a taxi. Maggie put it out of her mind.

A few people chatted on the way down, but most fell asleep, including Roan and Shauna. Only a handful got off at the halfway point. In ten minutes, they were on the road again. The landscape changed as the bus turned inland, away from the coastline. The hills became higher, almost mountainous. There weren't many lights in this region, so it was difficult to see where they were. The stars were out like a blanket of silvery glitter against a midnight blue sky. A few shooting stars danced across the expanse. It was an unexpected welcome for the pilgrims.

The bus rounded the corner by the post office onto the main street in Medjugorje. Ahead on the right is the church. The bus slowed a little to let the new pilgrims see it lit at night. The lights came on inside the bus when it stopped and Nives tapped the microphone with her finger.

Nives said quietly, "Ladies and gentlemen. Time to wake up. The church of St. James is on the right. We will be driving up the main road, going past Mt. Krizevac and onto Bijakovici to our host family. You will have to carry your bags down to the house, because the bus is too large to get through much of the lane. It will go down as far as it can. Your rooms will be assigned when you get inside. Breakfast is at 8:00 AM, with Mass at 10:00 AM. We will be walking to the church, unless you need a taxi. I will tell you about that in the morning."

Soon Roan and Shauna walked off the bus into the chilled night air. It was quite a change from their warm seats! The bags were quickly unloaded and since the Sanderson's luggage was on wheels, it was easier to move to the house. Maggie grabbed her two bags, also on wheels and the three followed the group to a beautiful house made from stone.

There was an arbor with vines beginning to flower, large porches surrounding the house and a huge dining room off to the left. There were two bedrooms on the first floor for pilgrims, one of which Nives had as her private quarters, while Roan and Shauna shared the second. Each room had a small bathroom with shower. The other rooms were upstairs and could be shared by up to four people. Most had verandas with views to Podbrdo. This trip, the house was full.

Maggie was sharing a room with the two religious sisters, Sr. Monica Thomas and Sr. Scolastica Thomas. Both were Sisters of Providence from Chicago. They had been teachers and were now retired. And, they were actual sibling sisters. This would be a discussion-filled pilgrimage for certain.

Nives chatted with the host family, Jelka, her second husband and her parents. Jelka is the cousin of one of the visionaries. Her first husband was killed during the war and she has used her home to welcome pilgrims since then to earn a living. Her daughter has been growing up with pilgrims since she was a toddler and the pilgrims who know the family, always bring toys, clothes and candy for her.

But now, Nives had to show Roan and Shauna to their room. There was a small step up and one turn to the left. Not too bad. The room was sparsely furnished with two twin beds, a night table with a small lamp, two electrical plugs and small bathroom. There was a window, with a small heater beneath it. It got down into the 40's at night, which is why they were advised to have warm clothes with them, just in case it did. There was a small armoire to hang clothes and put bags away. And a small portrait of Our Lady hung on the pale green wall. It was definitely basic. However, this was not a vacation, but a pilgrimage, as they would soon find out in the morning.

They had only four hours until breakfast, which meant only about three hours' sleep. Roan kissed Shauna goodnight and they literally hit the beds, clothes on, asleep in moments. The alarm shook them awake at 7:00 AM on the dot.

Shauna helped Roan with the shower, then took a fast one herself. She wanted to get the diesel fuel out of her hair. Within ten minutes, her shower was over and she was dressed. She plugged her hair dryer into the converter she brought along and in a few more moments, she was ready for food. No make-up, only jeans, sweater, light jacket, fanny pack and a baseball cap. No one makes a fashion statement in Medjugorje. Prayer, fasting, the Holy Mass, discussion and visits to local places of interest were the fare of the pilgrimage.

Nives was bright and alert at the dining room table with the schedule, information, directions, etc. and once everyone was around the table, she led the prayer and introduced herself again.

Then the pilgrims went around the table, introducing themselves, where they were from and what they did for a living. Most had been on at least one other pilgrimage, while some were newbies. Those who had arrived early were there as well. Nives handed out the schedule and explained nothing was mandatory and if you had your own schedule, that was fine, too. But to get the full experience, it was always wise to follow the entire schedule with the others.

Today would be a quiet day to get acclimated to the regimen, the topography and the time difference. Maggie had it arranged with Nives to take Roan and Shauna around, plus get them to the venues on time. This morning would be Mass, with free time until 3:00 PM, when dinner is served family style. The International Mass is in the evening, with the Rosary starting at 5:00 PM, Apparition at 5:45 PM and the Holy Mass with blessing of articles and prayers at 5:50 PM. Naps were encouraged before dinner is served. Then Ivan Dragisevic, one of the visionaries, would come over to give his talk in Croatian, with Nives as his interpreter. After Ivan spoke, there would be time for questions and additional prayer time. Many of the pilgrims liked to walk a couple of blocks to a local eatery for a libation, perhaps a sandwich or pizza.

The second day would begin with breakfast again at 8:00 AM, then Mass at 10:00 AM. Afterward, the bus would take them over to Siroki Brijeg to meet Father Jozo Zovko, former pastor at St. James during the beginning of the visions. His talks about Our Lady's messages of love and focus on prayer are always riveting. Each person will receive a photograph of Our Lady taken at Tijalina, plus a Rosary, which has been blessed. This is an especially moving talk by Father Jozo, made more memorable if it is held in the auditorium, rather than the church.

Roan didn't seem terribly inconvenienced with his blindness, other than he wanted to see everything around him. People were kind. They were gentle and most of all, understanding. Later in the pilgrimage, there would be a healing service, which Roan and group would attend. What happened in the interim, however, would change Roan's life forever.

Shauna and Maggie dug into the sliced white bread on the table. One slice and you couldn't stop. It was the most delicious bread they had ever tasted. The bread was made in Chitluk and brought over fresh each day. And it was available all over the valley. Wednesdays and Fridays would be fast days of bread and water—not as easy as one would think. But that bread made fasting more palatable.

Nives gave Shauna the business card of a taxi driver named Cano, who would help them to the various locations, should Roan decide not to try the pathways leading into the village. He was at the front door waiting to be introduced and take them into Medjugorje for Mass. This would be a good match, as Cano could take them all over the valley, to spots most pilgrims never see. Shauna knew she should take lots of pictures to show folks back home and to Roan when he regained his sight.

Nives stepped up and introduced everyone, "Cano, this is Roan and Shauna Sanderson. You already know Maggie."

Maggie was delighted to see Cano again.

She exclaimed, "Cano, it's always great to see you. How is the family? How many living with you now? Does your brother-in-law have his hearing back yet?"

Cano was grinning through his stubbly mouth. Although he was handsome, he wasn't one for shaving often.

He replied, "You are still the same, Maggie McManus. Yes, everyone is fine. We only have thirteen living at the house now, instead of nineteen. I am a grandfather now, too. I have lots of pictures!"

They piled into his older Mercedes taxi and went into Medjugorje for Mass. The ride cost $4 for everyone and took about seven minutes. That's quite a bargain in today's market. Maggie gave Cano a $5 bill and called it even. Roan advised he might like to walk back, but asked Cano to watch out for them after Mass, just in case.

Because late April and early May are less crowded, the church wasn't packed. They were there early enough to find a good pew, close to the front. It was still chilly inside and everyone kept their jackets on. The statue of Our Lady of Lourdes sat directly to their right, with the outside doors remaining open for air flow. The altar was draped in white and gold, with white pillar candles bearing the Croatian National flag to the left side. Several priests scurried around readying the chalices for Mass and making a quick count of those who had arrived for the service. Maggie waved at people she knew from other pilgrimage groups. Mass would begin in about ten minutes, as Shauna described everything for Roan.

Roan's first impression was that of total peace. There was something so remarkable about the feeling in the village and definitely in the church. You didn't need sight to pick up on these feelings. From the moment they arrived, there was something mystical in the air. As Roan sat, his mind cleared of the clutter grinding away at his soul. The feeling of warmth swept over him with a wave of uncontrollable emotion and he broke down in tears.

The English Mass hadn't even started and the release of deep, wrenching spiritual and emotional pain was surging through Roan.

Shauna asked if he needed to go out into the plaza for a few minutes, but Roan said, "No, I don't need to. I want to stay right here. There is so much I have been suppressing for the past twenty or more years and it needs to get out. There is abundantly more to it than even Confession can bring. I feel like a broken clay vessel, whose shards lie sprawled out on the sidewalk of life. I'll be fine when Mass begins."

Maggie and Shauna sat there with their mouths gaping again, just like in the hospital chapel.

Maggie turned and whispered to Shauna, "Guess this was the right decision. And it's only the beginning. Think what will come next!"

The distribution of Communion was swift. The priests came down the aisles, plus clustered in the back to be certain everyone received who wanted to. The confessionals outside would be busy today, since there were several new pilgrimages beginning. Priests heard Confession in many languages and each was written on the door to the confessional. In the early days, there were lines outside on the grass, where a small bench or chair was set up for each priest. St. James has come a very long way in twenty-three years!

The German Mass followed, so everyone quickly left their pews and walked into the sunshine. It felt warm and invigorating. The block of new rest rooms was directly before them as they came out of the church. Maggie asked if anyone needed to 'go', but no one did.

Roan remarked, "Maybe it's time to go back home to Jelka's and take a nap. I am really drained."

Shauna agreed and spotted Cano on the street. He waved back and the Sandersons took the taxi. Maggie wanted to visit some friends for coffee, but didn't stay too long. She made it back in time for dinner. Naps would prove a very useful tool during a pilgrimage. This was the time to get in touch with spiritual and emotional needs, sometimes becoming a drain on one's physical resources. Plus, today, it made the jetlag easier to deal with.

Before they knew it, 3:00 PM rolled around and you could smell dinner cooking in the huge kitchen. Today it would be pork chops, country friend potatoes and onions, bread, a spinach salad, plus home-made wine. There was nothing skimpy about the food at Jelka's. Her mother, Katica, made certain of that. Pilgrims brought American-style coffee, creamer, artificial sweetener, tea bags, etc. for the table. The Turkish coffee normally served in their home is way too heavy for the American palate, so you are asked to bring whatever you want to drink with you and leave it for the hosts. They will provide Fanta orange drink. Candy, crackers, cookies, etc., are always welcome goodies, too!

Just about everyone was back for the meal and eagerly awaited Ivan's talk. Roan brought his tape recorder to enable him to play it back later. After dinner, the group stayed together for evening prayers, but this evening there was a twist. Nives asked Roan to sit on a chair and for the pilgrims to gather around to lay hands on Roan. He had never experienced this before. Ivan had arrived and joined in. Roan's emotions became razor sharp and the more the prayers and singing progressed, the more pain and sadness was released. He was totally spent when they finished and had to retire to his room. Nives agreed to run the recorder for him. One of the attendees was Bogdan Caric, a local banker, who stayed to talk with Roan after Ivan left. They had more in common than a pilgrimage.

Chapter Six

After talking with Bogdan for a few moments, Roan went back to the room and fell asleep, while Shauna walked out onto the veranda with Bogdan. She thanked him for taking an interest in her husband. Bogdan had heard of the plane crash on National news, as he was in the States with his family during New Years.

He spoke with a quiet confidence in perfect English and told Shauna, "When we have some time, I want to speak with you and Roan about funding some programs for the children of our country. I know about Miss Lulabelle and her causes. Several of our orphanages are her project, so yes, I knew her well. Maybe when the pilgrimage is over, I can come to Bemidji—put it on my schedule and we can have a few days to go over her plans."

Shauna was shocked. Lulabelle's generosity extended across the world to help orphaned children in Bosnia. *So that's why she gave us these tickets. It all begins to make sense*, Shauna mused. She extended her hand in friendship to Bogdan as he left for home.

It was still early in the evening, so Shauna stayed on the veranda for a while. She could hear Roan if he needed her. The sounds of the birds at night surprised her. This was a rural area and the sounds reminded Shauna of home. Just then, Maggie came tooling around the corner with some of her friends.

She stopped, sat down with Shauna and grinned, "So, you think this will be worth it? I do already!"

Shauna explained about the orphanages and what Miss Lulabelle was involved in. Maggie already knew about them.

She explained, "I know more than you think I do about our beloved Lulabelle Lavinia LaFontaine. Suffice it to say I know most of the pies her little fingers were in. When my husband Paul died in Kuwait, it was Lulabelle who came to my home to comfort me. And it was she who has made these pilgrimages possible. She continues to do so. Oh, this was years ago, when she had her full faculties, but her trust has provided for me very, very well. Does that shock you, Shauna?"

Shauna looked sleepily at her friend and yawned, "Nothing but nothing surprises me anymore, Maggie. I just wait to see what's next! Oh, by the way, is it always this noisy at night?"

"Yes," replied Maggie. "These are part of the sounds of Medjugorje. And every once in a while, when you return home, you will hear them again. I told you how amazing this place is."

"You did, Maggie," replied Shauna. "Just look at Roan. He has been transported somewhere else, almost another dimension, spiritually and emotionally. We have seen some miracles already today!"

Shauna stood up, looked around the hamlet and took a deep breath. She could hear Roan moving around, so she said goodnight to Maggie and went inside. Once in her room, she could see Roan was shivering. She grabbed another blanket from the closet and spread the blanket without waking him.

It might be difficult to sleep because of the birds, but when Shauna's head hit her pillow, the birds made a soothing Lullabye. A knock on her door woke Shauna. They had over slept and it was now 9:00 AM.

Nives brought in a tray of coffee and toast. She wanted to let them know the bus would be taking off at 11:15 AM sharp for Father Jozo's. They could take their time getting into town, maybe do a little rosary shopping for the family back home. There was even a store or two which shipped express to the States and with money no object, Shauna kicked into shopping mode. Even the church would get a statue or three, rosaries for the RCIA candidates, post cards, medals, gifts, etc. And she would pick out a good rosary for Roan, who had somehow lost his.

Shauna found the shop, "Souvenirs Charly"—Maggie's favourite. There were actually three shops, owned by three brothers. This one, however, was usually managed by Josip and Maggie was always trying to fix him up with one of her single girlfriends. Josip was terribly shy, but always took a photo of his new friends to put on his shop wall. Shauna spotted the picture of Roan's parents and Maggie.

She pointed to it just as Josip called out, "You must be Mrs. Sanderson. I'm Josip and I remember them very well. Is this your husband?"

Shauna smiled and said, "Yes and I am amazed at all these photos. Oh Roan, I see your parents on the board. They look so happy."

Josip spoke up again.

"Miss Lillian loved her rosary," he explained. "She bought it here. I helped her select it."

Shauna pulled hers out of her pocket and exclaimed, "You mean this one, Josip?"

His eyes grew wide and he remarked, "Yes, yes, that's it. And now it's yours. I hope you will pass it down to one of your children."

Shauna looked at the rosary for a moment, then asked, "Do you have a nice one for Roan? His has disappeared."

Roan was quick on the uptake and laughed, "Yes, mine has disappeared and I could use a heavy duty one to replace it. I keep breaking them! You'll have to describe it to me."

Josip was stunned he had to describe the beautiful Autumn jasper rosary to Roan. He had no idea Roan was blind. The only clue was Roan's white cane.

But he carefully described it and said, "This is a rosary like your father's. I made it for him. It might be nice to have one just like it."

Roan remembered his father's rosary. It was sitting in the dish at the apartment. He smiled as he remembered his Dad using it. When he put the new one in his hand, he fingered the beads, feeling the smoothness of the jasper nuggets.

He smiled again and said, "This is just great, Josip. I'll take it. You don't even have to wrap it, because I will take it to church and get it blessed."

Shauna paid for the rosary, but before they could leave, Josip asked a favor, "A picture for the wall next to your parents please?"

Roan replied, "Sure, why not. I won't have to see the spots before my eyes because of the flash!"

Josip took the photo, thanked them and put the instant picture up on the wall, next to Lillian and Robert. Once again, life is coming full circle.

They got over to the church in time for the articles being blessed. Now Roan's rosary was "official" and he could use it that night during group prayers. And they were just in time to catch the bus with their new friends.

On the ride over to Siroki Brijeg, Roan kept shaking his head. He asked Shauna if she saw anything funny, like squiggles in front of her.

"Shauna, I keep 'seeing' something like little dots or scenes in the blackness of my eyes," sighed Roan "It seems really odd. And it's almost as if I can see faces flashing in front of me, kind of like neon colours jumping all around in a tv commercial."

Shauna responded quietly, "No, can't say as I have seen anything like that—you mean like what happens when you get your picture taken and you see floating dots?"

"That's right," he responded. "I haven't seen that before. Maybe something is happening with my eyes?"

"Maybe," added Shauna. "But let's take time to evaluate this. Right now, we are on our way to meet someone very important, plus learn about the Martyrs and the International Godparenthood program. This will pass, I'm sure of it."

Shauna kissed Roan on the cheek and settled in for the bus ride, holding his hand. It's just too bad Roan couldn't see the majestic beauty of the hills and valleys on the way over to Siroki Brijeg. Even in early Spring, the fields were lush and deep green. On the other hand, while winding down the mountain, you couldn't help but look into the underbrush to see wrecked and burned out cars, old washing machines and furniture. There was trash from the war, just dumped.

Around another corner was a cemetery. The rows of graves were terraced and immaculate, with a huge white marble crucifix in the top centre. Marble slabs covered the surface of each grave and photographs of the departed were placed securely in the headstones. Sheltered candles flickered dimly mixed in with fresh, but wilting flowers. Soggy teddy bears and half deflated balloons dotted several grave sites in tribute to the little children who had recently died. The graves were well tended, but looked cold—as cold as the senseless war which created many of them. Shauna felt a deep sadness for the families of the Bosnian war.

But as they approached another turn, the Romanesque church of Siorki Brijeg rose from the hilltop like a beacon of hope for the children left behind by the madness of war. There is great love here. And there is also crushing sadness. The group would learn not only about the orphans, but of the Thirty Franciscan Martyrs who died in 1945 at the hands of Communist soldiers.

The bus engineered its way into the parking lot. There were several buses already there about fifteen minutes before the talk was scheduled to begin. It allowed everyone to walk through the plaza outside the church to see the contemporary sculpture of St. Francis and the metal sculpture of a segment of roof from the cathedral in Mostar which had been melted, as if frozen in an eternity of torture. It was a stark reminder of the viciousness of war. As the pilgrims walk to the end of the plaza, many gasp at how beautiful the view was. The mountains and valleys glistened in the afternoon sun. How peaceful it is here.

Father Jozo Zovko, former pastor at St. James in Medjugorje, is always extremely well received by the pilgrims who visit the area and those he speaks to throughout the world. The pilgrims crowded into the large, cold church to hear the soft-spoken priest who had gone through torture at the hands of the Communists. His interpreter, Canadian Nancy Latta, was by his side as he began to speak softly in Croatian. His hearing had been damaged by repeated beatings by his Communist jailers. The insanity of his confinement and political "trial" is depicted in a movie, staring Martin Sheen, called "Gospa" and it shows in detail, the horror and injustice he endured for his faith and the country he loves.

Father Jozo began with prayer, then lifted the crucifix to the pilgrims explaining his devotion to Christ and our Blessed Mother. He spoke of love and hope. He spoke of the Passion of Christ and how we are called to share in that Passion. During the talk, photographs of Our Lady were passed out to the pilgrims. Then small, plastic rosaries were distributed. People are able to come up to be prayed over and Shauna led Roan up to Father Jozo personally.

They stood in line in front of the altar steps as Father came to each person and laid hands on everyone. When he came to Roan, he stopped, looked directly into Roan's eyes and put his hands on Roan's head, then on his eyes. He stayed there much longer than with the others and within a few minutes, Roan fainted. There were "catchers" behind the line of pilgrims and as Roan fell, one of the men caught him, laying him down on the marble floor. Roan was dazed, but could hear everything around him and it didn't matter. The feeling of healing was overwhelming. But Roan still couldn't see. As he got up from the floor, Roan grabbed Shauna's hand and they walked to the back of the church where the rest of the group was waiting to tour the area where the Thirty Martyrs were killed. Roan couldn't stop sobbing.

The group walked to the side of the hill past the offices of the church and down a small incline to a cave of sorts. The guide began to tell of the atrocities done to thirty of the Franciscans from the Monastery at Siroki Brijeg. They were teachers at the school, many were published authors and highly educated, even some who were famous professors. On February 7th, 1945, the Communist soldiers arrived and told them, "God is dead, there is no God, there is no Pope, there is no church, there is no need of you, you also go out into the world and work." The Communists told them to take off their habits and they refused. One angry soldier took a crucifix, threw it on the floor and told them, 'you can now choose either life or death.' Each of the thirty Franciscans knelt down, embraced the crucifix and said, "You are my God and my All." All were taken out, shot and their bodies thrown into a small, dank cave, where gasoline was poured on them, some men still alive. They were burned and guarded to be sure no one got out alive. Their remains stayed in that cave for many years and are now interred in the church. These men were perfect examples of declaring themselves in the presence of others for Jesus Christ. They lived their faith and died in it.

The cave remains closed for most of the year, as rain has seeped in making the cave dangerous to go inside. However, some of the members were brave enough to go in and when they came out, the look on their faces revealed the pain and torture the martyrs must have felt. Even today, their emotions and great faith remain for others to experience.

Roan confessed he needed to sit down. He felt as if something had come down to him and literally cored out his insides like an apple. It left him hollow and walking like a rag doll. Shauna took him inside the bus and gave him a bottled water to drink. There were sandwiches and fruit on the bus and several of the pilgrims were eating when the Sandersons arrived. They had also experienced some of the feelings as Roan, each in their own way. It would make for interesting discussions tonight!

The ride back to Medjugorje was silent. So many had incredible feelings when they were prayed over and most were exhausted. It's difficult to translate one's feelings into words, because words simply fail. Roan said his eyes hurt and kept his dark glasses on, even though the ride back was in shade. Shauna sat motionless as she prayed the Rosary. However, she glanced up to look out at the cemetery as they passed and standing under the large crucifix was the mysterious man in all black. A cold, steel-like feeling crept up her spine and she trembled so hard, her rosary knocked together.

Maggie was out cold and Roan was lost in his spiritual experience, but Shauna couldn't shake the feeling this man was stalking them. She might have felt it was silly, but at this moment, Shauna was taking this man seriously.

The bus eased into Medjugorje, dropping the pilgrims off in front of the church to have lunch at Coco's Restaurant. The reservations were for 3:00 PM and they were a little early, but that was fine. A cold beer tasted good any time of day and Shauna was anxious to talk with Roan and Maggie about the man. Shauna stopped Nives as she was passing and told her she had seen this man here in Medjugorje.

Nives said, "You should go to the police and explain about him. Maybe they have information on who he is or what he wants. Just let me know."

Shauna agreed, then went into the restaurant with the rest of the group. They ordered, ate and conversed, but Shauna excused herself for a moment when she saw an American police office at another table. He was wearing his duty blues and she recognized his patch. It identified him as an Edina, Minnesota police captain.

She walked up to him and tapped him on the shoulder and said, "Excuse me captain, but I need some advice. I think someone is stalking us over here."

The man was shocked, but graciously turned and asked Shauna about the problem.

He began by asking, "Can you identify this man? Is he a local, an American? What does he look like?"

Shauna replied, "He's really easy to spot. The man is tall, well over six feet and very thin. He wears all black—turtleneck, pants, shoes, gloves, but the biggest identifier—his hair. It's pure white tied up in a ponytail. We first saw him at the airport in Zagreb, when a security guard warned us. The minute I turned away to tell someone, he was gone. He's like a ghost."

The officer sat staring at Shauna, trying to figure out why she looked so familiar.

He squinted at her and said, "Say, I know you. You are the artist who did the artwork for the architects in Minneapolis. I was on duty there when you unveiled it. I must say, it's fabulous. Thought I recognized you. Is your husband with you? The name is Tim Sullivan, by the way."

"Yes," replied Shauna. "But although he knows about the man, he doesn't know I have just seen him again. My husband is temporarily blind from a plane crash at New Years."

"Sure, I remember," said the captain. "He's one lucky man. I'm on duty here for six months giving the local police sensitivity training with human rights and interrogation techniques. It's part of the rebuilding of Bosnia. I'll give this matter my attention and get in touch if I find out who this fellow is. Where are you staying?"

Shauna took a business card from her fanny pack, wrote on the back and gave it to Officer Sullivan and said, "Thanks so much. This is unnerving and right now, we need as much peace and quiet as possible. My husband's health is foremost and this guy scares the stuffing out of me."

Tim Sullivan smiled and replied, "Don't worry. This is one of the safest places in the world."

Shauna walked back into the restaurant and Roan was surprised she had left.

He asked her why and she replied, "Oh, just saw someone I knew from home, that's all. It's such a small world."

Maggie looked up from her Coco's Special Pizza, spotted Officer Sullivan and practically shouted, "Oh my goodness, is that who I think it is? That has to be Tim Sullivan!"

Shauna was surprised and asked, "Do you know him Maggie?"

"Know him?" Maggie responded. "He was the best man at our wedding thirty years ago!"

Maggie jumped up, ran over to the table and gave Tim Sullivan a huge hug. The poor man had been in Medjugorje less than a week and already he was home! Once again, that small town feeling abounded in a tiny village halfway around the world.

Roan was concerned about Shauna's absence and asked again, "Where did you go, Honey? I got a little worried."

Shauna replied, "Oh, it's a friend of Maggie's and one of the police officers who was at the architectural firm when I unveiled the artwork. It's nice to see him again. He really likes my work and that makes me feel good. He is also going to check out this man in the black clothes we saw at the airport in Zagreb."

Roan continued to question Shauna, "Well, if he's in Zagreb, why would this officer check him out here? Is there something you want to tell me, Shauna?"

Shauna took a deep breath and decided it was best to explain her concerns to Roan.

"I didn't want to concern you with this, Roan," she explained. "But I saw the man here in Medjugorje. No one seems to know who he is and only a handful of people have actually seen him. But I feel confident Captain Sullivan will get whatever information is available on him. He will alert the local police, too."

Roan reached over and touched Shauna's hand.

He didn't seem too upset but added, "As long as we have this under control, we can go on with our pilgrimage. I have such a feeling of calm here, Shauna. It's just amazing."

Maggie came bounding over to the restaurant, gleefully grinning from ear to ear.

She blurted out, "I'm going on a date tonight. An honest to goodness date. Do you believe it?"

Poor Maggie could hardly contain herself and Shauna picked up on the joyful spirit Maggie brought to the table.

She immediately exclaimed, "There is more than spiritual love in Medjugorje tonight! I have a good feeling about those two—old friends—both single…hhhmmm. Does that sound like a familiar scenario?"

Roan was pleased for Maggie. Paul's death had been traumatic for her. She never got to say goodbye—just like Shauna. A death during war is too swift—too cold. A government car pulls up to your house, you look out the window and see two military men walk slowly up to the door with their heads hanging down. You know immediately it isn't good news. In fact, you feel it in the pit of your stomach because you know the first words out of the captain's mouth will be, 'Mrs. McManus? I'm Captain Jones and this is Chaplain Wilson. May we come in? We have some bad news for you.'

Maggie had been on her own for too long and the chance meeting with her old friend Tim could be her shot at happiness, too. Her work at the hospital was certainly rewarding, but it wasn't enough to round out her life. A romantic relationship with a man she knew and trusted could be built on. Roan and Shauna certainly believed in second chances.

The day had been exhilarating and tiring. Roan wanted to go back to take a nap and Shauna agreed. They decided to walk, rather than take a cab. Maggie needed to shop for parish gifts and opted to come back later for her date. The path back was dry and the fields were just beginning to green up. There was a dewy smell to the ground. Things were fresh and clean. New leaves on the vines peeked around the corners of the twisted branches which were tied up with tiny pieces of blue cloth. Shauna explained what she saw to Roan and he smiled as he imagined what things looked like. They stopped to feel the leaves and vines, so Roan could sense the design in each leaf.

"Maybe I can reproduce the leaf design on pottery when we get back home," Roan exclaimed. "Now I know what people mean when they say when you lose one sense, the others pick up the slack. I'm not saying I don't want to see again because I do, but being able to feel the leaf and see in my mind's eye, it gives me something to remember."

Shauna was excited to see such a beautiful display of leaves and buds. She took out her camera and snapped off a dozen shots. She could paint from the photographs and put her paintings in the Gallery for sale. She could also make up a few for gifts.

Shauna linked arms with Roan and as they continued to walk home, they encountered a group of pilgrims walking in for Adoration. They were praying the Rosary in what sounded like Russian. Everyone politely smiled, then walked along. An elderly woman sat on the side of the road, crocheting doilies. She must have been well into her eighties and she was remarkable because she had several fingers missing on each hand. She blessed Roan and Shauna as they passed and as they walked forward, Shauna told Roan about her.

"I want to know more about the woman we just passed," Shauna explained. "She is missing several fingers on each hand and still she creates the most beautiful lacy doilies. Maybe Jelka will know who she is."

Roan commented, "I imagine this is how she makes a living. Maybe her husband or son was killed during the war and she is alone. I'd like to help her if I can. Let's see what Jelka has to say first. She'll know who the woman is."

Ten minutes later they arrived at the house. Jelka had set out a platter of cheeses and fruit for those coming back to the house. She had a light supper planned for 8:30 PM and this would hold people over until then. There was coffee, soft drinks in a cooler and tea. Shauna made up two small plates and took them back to the room to share. Then she went back to get the coffees when she ran into Nives. Shauna decided to ask her about the woman on the path.

"Nives, can you tell me anything about the elderly woman with the missing fingers," queried Shauna. "She makes such beautiful doilies."

"Oh yes, sure I can," responded Nives. "She is a widow, long time now. She lost her fingers in a farming accident. Her son was killed in the war and now all she has to live on is a small pension. She sells what she makes to keep a roof over her head, but that's all I know."

"Thank you, Nives," replied Shauna. "Roan and I would like to help her and any of the others who might need a little assistance. This would be totally anonymous, you understand. Can you help us set it up?"

Nives was overwhelmed, but replied enthusiastically, "Let me talk with a couple of people in the village an see how we can accomplish this quietly. I think Father Svet will also know what we can do."

Shauna took the coffees back to her room and told Roan about her encounter with Nives. This had been such a momentous pilgrimage so far and they were only half way through. But there was still no healing for Roan's eyes. Shauna could see he was still a little disheartened, but this time away from the familiar things of life, helped Roan to understand there are many ways of seeing than through eyesight. They ate quietly, then took a nap. All the fresh air and excitement of the day had made the Sandersons very tired.

The alarm went off at 7:00 AM. Guess who had slept through dinner? Roan and Shauna were still dressed when a knock came at their door. It was Maggie.

"Hey you two? Late night?" she giggled. "Oh no, you slept through dinner and the night. Guess you were more tired than you realised."

Shauna opened one eye and looked directly at her friend and said, "And?"

"Oh—and," Maggie giggled. "Breakfast is soon and we are going on a drive with Cano. He wants to show you some of the countryside. Tim has a day off today and the four of us can go together, if that's okay with you."

Roan nodded and Shauna indicated it was good for her, too. By the time they were showered and dressed, it was time for a good hearty breakfast. Tim was at the front door at 9:00 AM sharp. He brought Maggie roses and tulips in a lovely bouquet. Maggie was a bit stunned, but she kissed Tim on the cheek and took the flowers to her room.

Shauna told him, "What a lovely thing to do, Tim. I am so glad to see a smile on Maggie's face. She does so much for others and now it's good to see it coming back to her."

"Maggie is a good woman, Shauna," he replied. "We have been dear friends for many years, even before she met Paul. But when he was deployed to Kuwait, we really lost touch. My wife died in a traffic accident a few years ago and I have been alone. I've often thought about Maggie but wasn't sure where she was. Now that I know, I don't think I can let her go. That is, if she wants me in her life. I have to confess, I have always been smitten with her—her spirit, her enthusiasm for life and her uncompromising dedication to helping her hospital patients."

Roan responded to that remark. "Oh, I don't think that will be a problem, Tim," he said. "Shauna and I are proof that second chances can and do work. Ours isn't an identical situation, but close enough and I can sincerely say, I'd go for it if I were you. The friendship is still there. Although I can't see, I can feel the sincerity in your voice and that means the world to me. I look forward to getting to know you, Tim."

"Same here, Roan," Tim replied. "You are also a very fortunate man with Shauna. She's amazing. She's not only beautiful, but she is wise, caring and very loving. And is she ever talented! Now that I have met you both and Maggie is back in my life, I hope we can all be good friends."

Cano honked the horn. Maggie trotted down the stairs and Tim extended his hand to her. Once in the car, Cano turned on the stereo. Maggie had brought country western music for him last time and that's all he blasted through the villages. And he could sing, too! Off they charged into the countryside!

Shauna described the outstanding valleys and rivers. There was a tiny hamlet around most turns and once the travelers got to a small river by a grist mill, they all got out of the car to look at a magnificent site. There was a dam overflow spill that looked like a ski run with water plunging in eight straight lines down into the river. The deep turquoise waters foamed with white froth and swirled with churning undertows. The flowers were just opening along the sides of the river and were brilliant yellow and orange against a bright blue sky. The sunshine gleamed on the babbling waters, just like they did in Bemidji.

Roan could hear this and exclaimed, "This sounds like home. It's beautiful!"

"I don't show his little stream to every tourist," remarked Cano. "But only for special people. This is a favourite spot I come to when I want to get away from everyone. I can fish or just sit and watch the water. Sometimes the cows come down to drink. It is special to me and now to you."

Shauna took photos of the river, the overflow and the grist mill, with a dilapidated house next to it. And she was able to sneak several shots of Maggie and Tim enjoying the pastoral site.

Then Cano took the couples to an outdoor café he liked. It was owned by his brother-in-law. There were several tables with white cloths and an ashtray on each. There was a plastic flower in a glass vase on their table. But overhead was an arbor with hundreds of vines intertwined. These weren't grapes but Kiwi fruit. By the end of the summer, in late August to September, the fruit would be ready to pick. Because this is a more Mediterranean climate, it becomes too hot to eat inside and the arbors provided not only fruit in season, but shelter from the hot summer sun. Almost every house had some kind of arbor either on the ground floor or on the first floor on top of a garage. Rarely did you see air conditioning in family homes, so this was a great way to enjoy the out of doors and keep cool when you eat!

Cano suggested he choose some of the house specials for them to try. If they didn't like them, it didn't matter, but he chose well and it was simply good to eat, converse and soak up the local colour. Tim and Maggie were off in their own little corner of the world, so Cano got to know Shauna and Roan better. Shauna took the opportunity to ask Cano if he had seen this strange man in black.

"No, I don't remember seeing him, but that's not to say I haven't," he replied. "Let me keep my eyes open and I will tell Mr. Sullivan if I see anything."

Cano stopped along the way to show everyone ruins of ancient castles and fortresses. Views from the mountaintops were spectacular.

Roan seemed lost in thought but did say, "Next time we are here, I will be able to see this. Will you bring us back here next time, Cano?"

"I will pray for that day," Cano said. "It will happen. Miracles are here in Medjugorje."

Cano pulled the car into the driveway at Jelka's and Shauna paid him for the journey. His charge was only $35.00 for the entire day, but she gave him $75.00. Petrol was still expensive and Cano had family to support. He was amazed at her generosity, but accepted it graciously.

It was time for lunch, but they had just eaten. Still Tim wanted to talk and he joined the group around the table. He needed to speak with Nives on a matter of the utmost urgency. Once they had lunch, he took her aside and walked out into the flower garden at the side of the house.

"Mrs. Jelich," he said. "I need a HUGE favor. I need to be introduced to a quality jeweller here in Medjugorje because I want to buy Maggie an engagement ring. I don't know many people here yet, but I assume you know someone who will give me a good price. After all, I am still only a policeman!"

Nives beamed, patted him on the arm and told him, "I have just the person to speak to. Come with me now and I will introduce you."

Tim asked Maggie to wait at the house, because he had some 'police business' to do in the village.

"I'll be back in about an hour, Maggie," he explained. "Don't go anywhere until I get back."

Maggie looked at Tim a little puzzled but agreed, "I can take a little nap until you get back, Tim. And I can enjoy my flowers. Or I can just be with Shauna and Roan for a while. I'll see you in an hour then."

Tim kissed Maggie on the cheek, then had Cano take him and Nives into town. Cano had been talking with friends outside, so it was good he was still waiting there. Nives told him where she wanted to go and his eyes lit up.

"Oh oh, Mr. Sullivan," he smiled. "I know what you are planning. And I approve!"

Maggie, Roan and Shauna went outside on the veranda to enjoy the sunset. It was getting a little chilly, but it felt good. The birds were still chirping and a slight fog was creeping along the ground. This was a mystical country. The pace was so far removed from the United States and its hectic life style. Things got done on their schedule. The faith of the people was strong. And it was this strength which enabled the people to survive the war and rebuild their country.

Shauna checked the schedule and tomorrow would be a trip just a couple of blocks away, to the Campo della Vita (the Cenecolo of Life) and to the Oasis of Peace. Both places were just around the corner from the grocery store and the main thoroughfare, within a few minutes walking distance.

The Cenecolo is a community of young men who are recovering from additions of one kind or another. Some are drugs. Some alcohol problems and some of the young men are from dysfunctional families who had gotten into trouble. The center was started by Sister Elvira in Italy and now there are Cenacles all over the world, including those for young woman. These young men built the premises, complete with chapels, by themselves. They get up early in the morning and work hard, physical work all day. There is no television, no newspapers or radio. And they all live by the Providence. That is, by prayer and what comes to them through donation. They speak to various pilgrim groups about their experiences at home and at the community and once they have finished their term at the Cenecolo, they go back into society. And these are the young men who sing during Mass in the village, help disabled pilgrims up the mountains and do other charitable works.

At the Oasis of Peace, the chapel is open to pilgrims for Adoration on a twenty-four hour basis. It is also a hand-built chapel of native stone, with several stained glass windows and a white communion rail. It is part of a community of extremely soft-spoken third order professed religious sisters from a French order. Rarely is a pilgrimage Mass allowed, but Father Pat was able to say Mass in the morning and it would prove to be an extremely special one to Roan.

In the meantime, Nives and Tim entered the jewellers. She introduced Tim to the owner, George and explained he wanted an engagement ring for Maggie.

George looked up and asked, "Is this for Maggie McManus from America? I know her well, as she is a very good client. And I know her taste in jewellery. Just a moment, because I have some pieces you can choose from I think she will like."

George went into the back room and came out with a small tray of rings. George had seen Tim around town in his uniform and knew who he was, so he also knew Tim must have a budget. Two rings caught Tim's eye. He asked Nives what she thought. He first picked up an oval emerald with tiny diamonds surrounding it. It was a rich, clear emerald of medium-dark colour. That would be perfect for the Irish Maggie. He set that one aside. Then he looked at a garnet set with seed pearls and diamonds. That was pretty, but they all agreed the emerald was the best. It had a small wedding band with it, too. Now for the price. Tim closed his eyes as he picked up the tag. He turned it over and couldn't understand the price, as it was in Kunas.

"Oh, oh, sorry," exclaimed George. "Here it is in US dollars."

George printed out a piece of paper with the price. Nives looked at it and gave George a dirty look.

He scratched it out and said, "You get a police discount. Your price is $350.00 US dollars."

"Sold," replied a relieved Tim, as he rummaged through his wallet for the cash. "If I need to, may I bring Maggie back to have it sized tomorrow?"

"Certainly," said George. "I will do that at no charge. Now remember, this is eighteen karat gold."

Tim smiled as George handed him a tiny blue velvet ring box. As they walked out of the shop, Nives asked to go back in. She had more business to conduct. As Tim waited for her, Nives bought a necklace for Shauna, one of hand-painted porcelain with Our Lady on it. Roan had asked Nives to pick out something special. Within moments, they were on the way back to Jelka's. Now Tim had to get up his courage to ask Maggie to marry him. There was no time to waste.

Night was just about upon them. Everyone had gone back inside to change into warmer clothes, then go out to the barbecue area to the fire pit. There was a blazing fire and people were sharing stories of the day's activities. Some had seen miracles, others not. The sisters were making rosaries and teaching others how to make them. Roan and Shauna sat in chairs close to the fire, drinking coffee. Maggie was getting a little nervous because Tim hadn't come back yet.

Once Cano brought them home, Nives walked over to Roan and gave him a little package, telling him what it was and what it looked like. Tim asked everyone to gather around the fire because he had something to say.

He picked up Maggie's hand, then got down on one knee and quivered, "Maggie, you and I have been good friends for over thirty years. Life intervened and we lost each other but now we found our way back to one another. I don't think I can lose you again and I am asking you to be my wife. Will you, Mary Margaret Conroy McManus, be my wife?"

Maggie was stunned. Actually, she was speechless and for Maggie, that was astonishing.

She looked around at everyone and cried, "Yes, oh yes, I'll marry you, Tim. Oh my goodness. I can't believe this."

Tim opened the little box and showed her the rings.

Maggie gasped, then jumped up and down, shouting, "It's beautiful. Oh wow, it's absolutely gorgeous."

Tim put the emerald on her finger and she looked at it with her hand toward the sky. Just at that moment, several shooting stars crossed in mid-air, as everyone pointed to the heavens, ooing and ahhing.

"Magic," exclaimed Shauna. "Pure magic."

Jelka brought out sparkling wine and the pilgrims toasted the happy couple.

Roan took Shauna aside and gave her the envelope saying, "I had Nives get this for you because you and I are always together. I had no way to get for you otherwise!"

Shauna opened the envelope with a small box inside. She pulled the top off to reveal a lovely white enamel oval with Our Lady of Medjugorje on one side and "Kralica mira Medugorje" on the back. The entire necklace was surrounded in gold scrollwork and it had a 20" gold chain with it.

Shauna said quietly, "Oh Roan, it's beautiful. I had admired Maggie's and this is so perfect. Thank you, my love."

Roan put his arms around his wife and looked up into the sky.

He said to himself, *Oh Blessed Mother, if only I can see again. I feel like a broken toy a child can never play with again. I'm not productive as a man or as a husband. I know I'm not supposed to ask for anything for myself, but I long to see my wife's joy in life. I need to see the Blessed Sacrament. Please Mother, help me.*

Roan and Shauna walked back inside, as Tim and Maggie sat with the rest of the pilgrims. It was such a perfect ending to the perfect day. But nothing could prepare Roan for what would happen tomorrow.

Chapter Seven

Mass was at 7:30 AM, so they got up at 5:30 AM for a small breakfast. They would eat lunch at 11:00 AM today, after their trip over to the Cenecolo. Roan seemed to fidget this morning. Nothing seemed to be right. His clothes didn't fit. He wasn't happy with his hair. He couldn't even tie his shoes right. Shauna noticed but said nothing, simply helped Roan get himself together.

They walked over to the Oasis of Peace as a group. Roan and Shauna were hand-in-hand, with Maggie pulling up the rest of the group. She couldn't keep her eyes off her engagement ring!

Nives explained they all must remain silent when they arrived in the chapel. Those were the rules of the order—silence. As they entered, they were met with a life-sized statue of Christ in His passion. It was quite unnerving because it looked so real. Everyone sat on the wooden pews. There was no heat in the building, but that didn't seem to matter. Father Pat was ready to start the Holy Mass.

As Father began Mass, Roan felt discomfort in his eyes. It was so painful, in fact, he began to cry. But he sat there in silent pain until the Elevation of the Eucharist. The moment Father Pat said, "This is the Body of Christ," Roan passed out and fell onto the stone floor. There was a hushed gasp from the group as Father Pat proceeded with Communion. One of the men helped pick Roan up off the floor and set him on the pew. When the Mass was finished, Shauna and several pilgrims helped get Roan outside and onto a bench.

Finally, Roan came around and asked, "What happened to me, Shauna? The pain in my eyes is awful."

Shauna quickly called Cano, who was only a few blocks away.

She explained to Roan, "I've called Cano and we'll go into the aid station. We might have to go into Chitluk to the clinic to see why your eyes are giving you such a problem. You passed out in there."

"I did?" asked Roan. "I feel like I have glass in my eyes, Shauna. I don't understand."

Cano came running into the Oasis and met them near the gate. He helped Roan into the taxi, then sped away to the aid station. The medics couldn't tell why Roan's eyes were so painful, so they called the clinic and made an appointment. Cano drove them over and stayed with them to be sure they got the proper treatment. This was the only clinic within 100 miles with an MRI machine.

A doctor came out to speak with the Sandersons and as he spoke, Roan knew he wasn't Croatian. There was something very familiar about that voice.

"Harris, is that you?" queried Roan. "I can never forget that raspy Texas drawl."

"Damn Roan, I had no idea you were out here," replied Dr. Charles Harris. "It's been a long time since college, huh?"

Roan asked why he was in a little clinic in Bosnia and not back in Texas.

Dr. Harris answered, "I brought the MRI over here a few weeks ago and am instructing the medical staff how to use it. I'm glad I'm here, what gives?"

Roan explained what had happened to his sight and almost as an afterthought, introduced his wife, "Charlie, this is my wife, Shauna."

Charlie stopped in his tracks and almost shouted, "Brewster, you old hag! How the hell are ya?"

Shauna stood there wide-eyed, with her mouth open and exclaimed, "I don't believe it. I really DO NOT believe it's really you, you old dawg."

Roan got a little excited and asked, "Ah, what's going on here? Do you two know each other—oh DUH, obviously you do."

"Roan, don't you remember—at Carleton?" Shauna grinned. "Squidgie here was the college mascot and he was also head over heels in love with that professor what's her name, Bertha—Bertha Billings. That's it. Think back."

Roan tried to laugh, but it hurt too much. He asked Charlie if they could get on with the examination.

"We can get together later, but right now my eyes need attention," sighed Roan.

Dr. Harris shined a light into Roan's eyes and there was normal pupillary response. There was no change, but he thought it best to do the MRI just to be sure. After an hour, Roan was able to sit with Shauna in the waiting room.

Charlie came back shaking his head and said, "Roan, I honestly can't see any change. Your eyes look fine to me. There is nothing prohibiting you from seeing. I'd say hysterical blindness, but I know you better than that. I'll give you some drops, which will help anesthetize your eyes, but honestly my friend, I am at a loss. I'm sorry, Roan."

They all walked out to the car and Shauna gave Dr. Harris her business card with their local address and phone number on it.

"Call us when you get some time, Squidgie," Shauna laughed. "You are such a rascal, I'm glad you are here. We will be here for another three days, but get in touch when you get back to the States, too."

Dr. Harris waved goodbye and Cano drove them back to Jelka's. You could tell Roan was terribly disappointed. But he was glad his friend was around.

They went back to rest until lunch. Roan wanted to go into Adoration tonight and Cano arranged to pick them up.

Roan sat on the edge of his bed with his face in his hands and cried, "I won't ever see again, Shauna. I was so hoping. I have prayed. I prayed on top of prayer. I just don't know what else to do."

Shauna tried to reassure Roan and gently said, "I don't have answers for you, Roan. What I do know is trust and faith are the key. Trust in God and Our Lady. Have faith you will be healed. It's as easy as letting go, my love. Just let it go."

Shauna put her arms around her husband and sang softly to him. After lunch, the day was beautiful, warm and inviting, so they decided instead to walk into town to finish shopping for their friends, plus have a coffee at a delightful café close to the church. They could get their purchases blessed before Adoration. Roan and Shauna took their time and walked another route. They saw several new homes being built, along with two new shops.

Shauna stopped at "Souvenirs Charly" to pick up her order for the church. It was nice to have things taken care of, so she could pack accordingly. The statues of Our Lady of Medjugorje were to be shipped to the States and those were on their way. There was about an hour before Adoration and they walked over to the café for a coffee. Roan sat down under the umbrella facing the road, while Shauna faced the church. Shauna was glad to sit, have a coffee and let the sun shine on her face.

She sighed, "I love it here, Roan. Can you feel the warmth of the sun on your face?"

"Yes, I can Shauna," he responded. "And the sun is spinning, too."

"What?" exclaimed Shauna. "Can you see that Roan? Can you really see?"

Roan cried, "I can see the sun spinning around and rods of light shooting out around it. It's the most beautiful colours of coral, pink and white. I can see yellow rays, too. Oh Shauna. I can see again."

Roan was visibly shaken and began crying. His joy was overwhelming. He was so excited to see the sun spinning he wanted to follow it wherever it went. This evening it went directly over the church and Roan sped across the plaza, up the stairs and into the church. Shauna paid for their coffees, grabbed the packages and dashed off to find Roan. When she got inside, she could see Roan kneeling before the statue of Our Lady of Lourdes—the first statue Shauna told him about. Roan saw her approach, then got up to sit on a pew in front of the statue with Shauna.

"I am so thankful, Shauna," explained Roan. "You told me to just let this go and let the healing begin and I did. I let my faith in God heal my sight. I have seen so many miracles happen to others but not to me and I will never doubt again—ever. Blessed Mother has been watching over me, because I asked for her help and she answered me."

Before Adoration, Shauna took the items up to be blessed, then sat back down with Roan in a front pew.

He was elated and said, "I want to be right in front to see the Blessed Sacrament. I've made a decision about serving Christ in my daily life and I would like to become a Permanent Deacon, but this has to be a joint decision because it involves you. You would need to come to some of the classes—that is, if you want to. Is this something you might consider?"

Shauna told Roan simply, "Hey, slow down a little, it's something extremely important. Let's see how it would fit into our already super busy schedules before we make a final decision. We need to know where classes would be, how long they are and what the time commitment is. Then we can make a judgement. But I like the way you think!"

The priests came in vested in white with gold stoles. The altar was set with a huge gold monstrance, which holds the Blessed Sacrament host. During the service, the blessed host is placed into the monstrance, then it's held up for the faithful to see. The monstrance is incensed and the service allows for prayer and devotion to the Body of Christ. Roan needed to see the Body of Christ and be physically close to Him. The priest holding the Blessed Sacrament brought the monstrance close to Roan and stopped in front of him. Roan literally shook in the Presence of Christ and it seemed as if the host pulsated inside the monstrance—almost like a beating heart.

Even the Protestant pilgrims were impressed with this service. The boys from the Cenecolo came over to sing and there were songs from all over the world, sung in English, French, German, Croatian and one in Russian. The church was packed to overflowing and it didn't matter where you were from in the world, language was not a barrier. You are all one in the Lord.

Once the service was concluded, Roan and Shauna went over to Coco's to have a late supper. No one else knew Roan had his sight back, because he still had his white cane with him. Josip was on his way home after the service and he noticed the Sandersons having supper outside.

He strolled over and said, "I see you are having a meal. It's very good to see you having such a good pilgrimage."

Roan looked directly at Josip and spoke directly to him, "Thank you, Josip. It's very good to SEE you. The rosary you sold me is absolutely beautiful. I've had it blessed and I know my father would be pleased to know mine is just like his. Thank you."

Josip looked quizzically at Roan again and asked, "Can you see me?"

Roan smiled broadly and said, "Yes, Josip. It's a miracle and it just happened."

Josip wasn't shocked. He explained that when we focus on our faith and giving our problems to God, miracles do happen. The food arrived and Josip excused himself to return home for his own supper.

Now Roan could actually see the food he was eating. It made each bite even more delicious. He asked Shauna about the day tomorrow.

"What's on tap for tomorrow? I want to see the river and the mountains. Do you think we can go out there again? Can you call Cano tonight?"

"Whoa, wait a second. Hold on, Roan," Shauna exclaimed. "You just got your sight back. Are you sure you want to do all these activities? What if it's raining?"

"I don't care," replied Roan. "I need to see these things. If Cano is available, I want to see them as soon as possible."

Shauna took out her cell phone and dialed his number. Shauna got the voice mail, but left a message. Cano would scheduled on the last morning at 9:00 to take the Sandersons not only to the places they had just been, but also to Tijalina, the church where Father Jozo had been pastor and where the famous statue of Our Lady of Grace is located. This is the statue often seen in photographs and on post cards. She looks numerous ages when she is photographed from different angles. But unfortunately, Roan eventually had to cancel because their schedule was too crowded for a day away. This journey would have to wait.

Since Cano was off for the night, they took another taxi back to Jelka's. They saw Maggie and Tim saying goodnight and walked up to them in the courtyard.

"Hi you two," remarked Roan. "Nice to see you."

Maggie looked closely at Roan and exploded, "You can see. Oh my word, Roan, you can see!"

Several of the pilgrims came rushing over to see for themselves. What a miracle this is. You could hear everyone clapping for joy!

Roan looked around at all the people clustered around him and told them, "I am so happy for this miracle. Thank you all for your prayers and good wishes. I'm living proof of miracles. I didn't have enough confidence it could happen, but I knew deep down my faith would carry me through. Thank you all, so much."

Roan grabbed hold of Shauna and hugged her. He pulled away from her slightly and looked directly into her eyes.

You could see the love in his gaze, as he smiled and said, "You never stopped believing, did you? I must be the most fortunate man on the planet right now. Thank you, Honey."

Shauna kissed him and picked up his hand saying, "It's a just a matter of faith, Roan. It was always there, but as I have said so often, when the crunch time comes, we must leave our egos and control at the door, then abandon our will to God. He will do the rest and now you see that for yourself. It happened with my moving to Bemidji. It happened when I took the chance on love again and it was there during our crisis with Conor. I have something to believe in and hold onto. That's faith. The healing will come when it's supposed to in God's time, not ours."

Morning came in drizzly and cold, but it didn't dampen Roan's spirits. He arranged to take his visual tour on the last day of the pilgrimage instead, if it wasn't raining. Today would be a day of thanksgiving at Mass and talking with Bogdan in his home about the plans Miss Lulabelle left in place before she died. Things would be preliminary, but Roan took the checkbook along to give them a float for buying supplies, building materials and other needs of the orphans, who were mostly now teenagers. But one of the projects was for babies of drug addicted parents. That was slightly different, as their needs were for diapers, formula, toys, clothing and medications for the effects of the drugs. And it also meant finding godparents for these children. While the children couldn't be adopted from Bosnia, they could be sponsored by someone in another country who could keep tabs on their growth, offering love and support as these children grew to adulthood.

Roan was surprised to see architect's plans to add bedrooms and a dining room onto one of the group homes and a laundry facility to one of the newer facilities for young women. Lulabelle wanted each child to have a good chance in life and the devastation of the war put a halt to that. Each addition offers more hope to the surviving children of war. Once Roan had a chance to look over the plans, he could make changes or additions, then get them back to Bogdan or the builders.

Roan and Shauna decided to walk into town for lunch. The rain had stopped and the sunshine allowed the paths to dry enough to pass. The air smelled sweet, refreshed and the farm animals seemed happy to get a wash-down. The shops along the paved road were re-opening their stalls, putting out displays of post cards, rosaries and ball caps. Although Roan still wore his dark glasses, he removed them often to see the colours of the Spring sky, the green of the fields and the red-tiled roofs of the houses.

As they walked around the remains of the original church, a dark figure caught Roan by surprise. Roan stopped abruptly, staring directly at this mysterious man. He tried to see into the man's features and all he saw was a blank stare from black, lifeless eyes. It was the man dressed in all black and Roan was determined to see him up close. It was the only way to ask what he wanted of them.

Just as Roan began crossing the street to confront the stranger, a car backfired within twenty feet of the men. People ducked for cover, scattered into shops and behind bushes. The war was still fresh enough to frighten people with loud noises and even a car backfire was cause for concern. A few minutes later, people came out of hiding to see a taxi in the middle of the road, its tailpipe surrounded in fumes. And of course, the man was gone.

"Damn it," shouted Roan.

The 'Ghost' had gotten away again. But now he knew Roan had regained his sight and he couldn't just pop up again at will. Maybe he would be easier to catch the next time. Roan and Shauna continued walking to the restaurant along the main street. Mass had gotten out and friends were filtering over to Coco's, but this time Roan opted for something a little more romantic. They went inside to a lovely Continental restaurant Bogdan had suggested. Their specialties were seafood dishes from around the Adriatic, always freshly prepared to order by a renowned chef. Since they would be going to Mass in the evening, Roan could take life a little more leisurely, soaking up the ambience of the village. And after a brilliant lunch, the honeymooners did just that. They strolled!

Time remained submissive to the lovers. It would bend and give without intruding into a blissful afternoon. Shauna pointed out items in shop windows to Roan, said hello to other pilgrims and then took Roan back to meet Josip again. They walked into the shop and Josip looked up from behind the counter where he was repairing a rosary.

His smiled beamed like a lighthouse beacon as he said, "I am so pleased to see you both today. Now you can see your photograph next to your parents."

Roan walked over to the photo wall and looked through the thousands of smiling faces, quickly picked out his parents and said, "You are so right, Josip. My parents look so happy, don't they? Just look at those smiles!"

Josip was a romantic and he wasn't afraid to express it.

He looked over to Shauna and explained, "You and Roan have the same look as his parents. That's the look of true love and eternal happiness. Only God can create that. Your faith and love shine like Our Lady's smile."

"Thank you, Josip," replied Shauna. "I can't think of a better compliment. As much as we would like to stay, it's time for the International Mass and need to go. See you again before we leave tomorrow."

"Tomorrow," asked Roan. "You mean tomorrow is our last day? Time has gone by so quickly I guess I didn't notice."

Josip explained he needed to close up for Mass and they could go together. They walked over to the church, then parted company to enable Josip to sit with his brothers and their families. Roan and Shauna nestled in next to Tim and Maggie.

Tim was pleased to see them and said, "If it's alright with you, Maggie is going to stay and not go to Rome for the rest of the pilgrimage. We need some time to get reacquainted and try to figure out the logistics of planning a wedding with me here in Medjugorje and Maggie in Minnesota."

"Sure, that's fine with us," replied Roan. "We will just see you when we get back home."

Shauna and Maggie sat together, so they could chat quietly before the service. Roan and Tim discussed the progress (or lack thereof) finding the identity of the man in black. After Mass, Cano took them back to the house for a late snack and final directions from Nives.

Morning would be the normal schedule, but the bus would leave from the house at 1:30 PM to drive into Spilt and take the 6:00 PM flight to Rome. Shauna had already packed the day before, but left last minute details for morning. She poured over her planner to see if she had forgotten anything, then packed it. Roan was outside on the veranda looking up at the stars. They were shooting through the sky toward Cross Mountain.

He couldn't contain his excitement and called into Shauna, "Shauna, get out here. You must see these stars. They are amazing."

Shauna walked out to the veranda and could see why Roan was so impressed. All of a sudden, lights shot out across the tops of the hills, almost like the beacon from an airport tower. But there was no airport even close. Lights shot like electric transformers. There was no noise—only the purest white light. The white cross on top of Mr. Krizevec was swathed in bright light, but there were no lights or electricity to power them. The Sandersons stood transfixed as they watched. The rest of the pilgrims joined them, equally mesmerized. This was a sight no one could forget.

Someone noticed it was time for Ivan's prayer group at the Blue Cross. Anyone could join the group in prayer and several pilgrims, including Roan, wanted to attend. Shauna agreed, but with a condition. They needed warmer clothing and she went inside for their jackets and flashlights. Roan made sure he had his new rosary as well.

It was a short walk from the house to the Blue Cross. This was the location the visionaries could go without being seen by the Communist patrols or police. Now it was a place of prayer—a gathering of sorts. Not all pilgrims knew how to locate the Blue Cross, but Roan and Shauna followed Ivan up the cragged, slippery rocks to the most tranquil place they had been. Sounds of pilgrims praying on Mt. Podbrdo formed a backdrop, while people took their places. They would begin with prayers and a Rosary until Our Lady came.

You could sense Our Lady was close. The most incredible feeling swept over the participants as their voices fell silent. Our Lady came in joy, pleased to see so many. Her fervent wish was for everyone to pray for peace in the world, to live out the fruits of Medjugorje in their lives and to keep the unbelievers in their hearts. She indicated to Ivan she had recommended each one there to her Son, especially those who had received gifts while on pilgrimage. There were no names used, only a motherly blessing over all. She had private words for Ivan, then left joyously on a cloud of light.

Roan was stunned to tears. The night air was cold and damp, but all he could feel was his Mother's arms surrounding him.

He reached for Shauna's hand and said, "I am so thankful you brought me here. It isn't the restoration of my sight alone. It's this feeling of fulfilment—of total peace in my heart. I know I need to do more in my life and I'll keep searching for that direction."

By now it was very late and everyone filtered back to their respective homes. Roan helped Shauna back down over the rocks to the road below and they walked arm in arm to the house. When they got inside, there was a message from Tim Sullivan. He might have found the identity of the man who has been stalking them. There was a mug shot coming through the fax from Rome and he would meet us at the main police station in the morning at 8:00 AM. He'd send Cano.

Cano came into the complex to pick up the Sandersons at 7:45 AM. Tension was evident as they drove to the main police station downtown near the post office. Tim said the fax had come through from Rome, so it was possible this man could be some sort of terrorist, maybe even a spy. But why on earth would he want to bother a complete stranger, especially a professor of art from Minnesota?

Tim saw them come in and waved them back into the office. He shuffled some papers and asked them to sit down.

In a matter of moments he said, "I hesitated in telling you about this man, but it's probably wise to just give you the facts and let you sort this out yourselves."

Roan was stunned but asked, "What is it, Tim? Is this man a terrorist or what?"

Tim pulled out the photograph from Interpol and showed it to Roan, Shauna and Cano. The description is as follows:

Name: Michael DuMonde, a/k/a "The Ghost"
Age: 60 Height: 6'4" Weight: 140 lbs. Hair: long white—tied
Nationality: French Eyes: Black Skin colour: pale
Profession: Assassin

Although the photograph was grainy, you could see the lifeless eyes, the blank stare and the chilling personae beneath the pure white hair, which was not in a pony tail, but styled loosely. It was almost as if he was looking through the photograph and right into your soul. The photograph sent that horrible feeling up Shauna's spine.

Tim continued with his description, "It seems this Michael DuMonde has been credited with six recent assassinations of high ranking bank officials in several European countries. And he has been seen in Belgium, Rome and Paris within the last month, during which these murders occurred. But every time the police are close to nabbing him, he disappears. That's how he got his nickname, "The Ghost"—he simply vanishes. And he kills with sniper-like accuracy, usually a head shot between the eyes. Looks like he is a real piece of work."

"But why would someone like this be after us?" Roan asked.

"No clue," responded Tim. "When you get to Rome, I am having a colleague from Interpol meet your plane and I want you both to explain what's happened with your sightings of this man. It won't take long and he will take you to your hotel. Don't worry, I have already cleared it with Nives."

You could see the colour drain from Shauna's face again. That sinking feeling was sweeping over her, but this time, it was more concern for both of them than just one. They thanked Tim and Cano took them over to Coco's for breakfast. Roan asked Cano to join them and he agreed.

They ordered fresh pastries and strong black coffee. There wasn't much conversation. At the end of breakfast, Cano thanked them for their generosity and said he would be available the next time they were in Medjugorje.

Shauna had everything packed and took the luggage out to the veranda to wait for the bus. However, she and Maggie had an errand to do in town and that was their last stop before leaving. Roan wasn't excited about Shauna being out there with this assassin running around, but he agreed.

"Just an hour, you two," exclaimed Roan. "The pair of you are just as bad as Shauna and Katie."

Maggie replied, "I take that as a compliment, Roan."

Maggie and Shauna went to several places for final gifts for the family. Shauna found a lovely necklace and rosary for Katie, some ball caps and t-shirts for the boys, a new rosary for Jim and a pretty bracelet for Janet. All could easily be packed in their suitcase pockets. Rome was next on the list and the shopping would be marvelous, but actually, Shauna's heart wasn't in it. Until this mystery was solved, she wouldn't feel at ease.

The girls came back and grabbed a quick coffee in the dining room. Most of the other pilgrims were waiting outside for the bus. Roan was talking with Tim, who had come out to say goodbye.

"Guess the next time I see you will be at the wedding," Roan mused.

"Yes," said Tim. "That would be about it. I'll keep you in my prayers and hope this mess is resolved quickly. I'm actually quite curious as to why someone like DuMonde would be following you."

"Yeah, me too," replied Roan. "I'll get in touch after we talk with the Interpol agent in Rome. Maybe he has something new to tell us."

Roan and Tim shook hands and hugged. Maggie hugged Roan and Tim hugged Shauna. A huggy bunch, aren't they? Everyone was loaded onto the bus, ready to ride up to Spilt. The day was sunny and the driver went slowly enough to showcase the Adriatic coastline, with the fisheries, tiny islands dotting the shoreline and gleaming white villages clinging to the rock face.

The bus stopped halfway along the route for a potty break and to get a quick snack. Roan followed Shauna across the road to look out over the stone wall toward the Adriatic. The water was the deepest turquoise she had seen and the boats slipped easily through the water on their way to pick up their catch. It was beautiful and very different from home. Shauna took a few photographs and they walked back to the bus.

The flight to Rome was on time and the group quickly boarded for the twenty-minute flight. The Interpol agent, Christopher Cresswell met the flight and took the Sandersons to his station to take their statement. It didn't take long, but he asked them to call him immediately if they spotted DuMonde. Roan programmed the number into his phone. He also gave Roan two minute GPS tracking devices.

Cresswell explained, "Keep these in a pocket or inside your cell phones. Just in case you are taken or get into trouble, we will be able to track you. I think it will be safer to give you an extra tool just in case."

"Thank you, Inspector Cresswell," replied Roan. "We feel better knowing you are watching out for us."

The men shook hands and two Caribenieri took them in a squad car to the hotel. The desk had their keys, plus the bags had been taken up to their room. Dinner was being served in the main dining room in about twenty minutes, so they had to hurry to change and get down stairs. However, Roan took a little time and put his transmitter in the lining of his jacket. Shauna opted for the lining of her fanny pack. Just in case their cell phones were taken, this would be safer.

After dinner, some of the pilgrims wanted to go out to a few bistros, but given their day, the Sandersons turned in. The next afternoon after lunch, there was a general audience with the Holy Father at the Vatican. It would be the last opportunity to see Pope John Paul II in person, as his health was failing and the large audiences were proving too taxing on his fragile body. Shauna respected the Holy Father and his fight for the sacredness of the human being. And she had been looking forward to meeting him if possible.

Roan set a security device on the door. He'd had it for years and never used it when he traveled, but this time, he applied it to the doorknob. Shauna set the alarm and they snuggled in for a good sleep. Even knowing they were secure in their room, Shauna couldn't get any rest. She closed her eyes and saw DuMonde.

Chapter Eight

Rome has a rhythm of its own and this morning was no different. It begins bustling early and after a fresh pastry and coffee, Roan was ready to tackle the tourist traps. Shauna, however, wasn't that convinced. Her aim this morning was to see two of the local churches, then go to the audience and follow-up with a trip to the catacombs outside the city.

Close to the hotel is the Basilica di Santa Maria Maggiore (St. Mary Major), which had recently gone through a significant restoration. Most of that work had been done inside to clean and do structural repair. Many of the churches in Rome did something in preparation for the new millenium. The Vatican itself had a major restoration, as decades of acid rain had encrusted the buildings with a thick, black soot, eating away at the Travertine marble exterior.

The amount of artwork in these churches is staggering. Sculpture, paintings, carvings—all amazingly well preserved and displayed. There are outstanding wrought iron gates and grille work. Each side chapel in St. Mary Major is enclosed by a gate or low marble wall, similar to a Communion rail. There were so many people milling around, it was difficult to see everything.

But Shauna remained undaunted and dived right into the history and architecture of the churches. She had three churches on her schedule, St. Mary Major, The Church of St. Alphonsus and St. John Lateran. Roan was just as game, so he grabbed his notepad, camera and made certain his walking shoes were tied tight.

Years ago Shauna had studied the architecture of the major churches in Rome, but had never been over to see them in person. This morning, they walked up to St. Mary Major from the back set of stairs, then walked around to the front. She looked at her notes on the origin of the original shrine, commissioned by Pope Liberius circa 360. He wanted a shrine built at the site of an apparition of the Blessed Virgin Mary, because during the apparition to a local couple on August 5, 358, who happened to be standing on the site, the snow fell, making an outline of church on the ground. The shrine was dedicated to Our Lady of the Snows and the locals drop white rose petals from the dome each anniversary during the feast Mass.

So many of the churches have been added to over the centuries and St. Mary Major is no exception. Built over the pagan temple of Cybele, it's the only Roman basilica to retail the core of its original structure, left intact even through renovations and damage from an earthquake in 1348. The present structure dates from the time of Pope Sixtus III (432-440) and contains many ancient mosaics from the time period. The coffered ceiling is from the 16th Century, gilded in gold said to be from the Incas. The medieval bell tower is the highest in Rome at 240 feet. The column in the Piazza celebrated the famous icon of the Virgin Mary in the Pauline chapel of the Basilica. It's known as Salus Populi Romani or Health of the Roman People, due to a miracle in which the icon helped keep the plague from the city. This icon is at least a thousand years old, and tradition holds that it was painted from life by St. Luke the Evangelist. There is evidence of the icon's age from materials in the basilica archives which radio carbon date the piece to be approximately 2,000 years old, and reinforces its sacred tradition.

Below the sanctuary is the Bethlehem Crypt where many significant figures in the history of the Roman Catholic Church are buried. The crypt is furnished with an altar, plus seating for the Holy Eucharist. A relic of the crib believed to be used in the Nativity of Jesus is protected within the Crypt. St. Ignatius of Loyola presided over his first Mass as a priest in the crypt on December 25, 1538. He would later establish the Society of Jesus. The bodies of St. Jerome, Pope Pius V and artist/architect Gian Lorenzo Bernini are buried there.

The Pope often uses the basilica personally and presides over the Feast of the Assumption each August 15th. A high, canopied altar dedicated to the Pope is used exclusively by him, except for a few chosen priests, including the archpriest, who is responsible for the basilica.

Roan fervently scribbled in his notebook about the paintings, sculpture and the Crypt. Now that his sight had returned, so did his passion for his art. He wanted to create something, he wasn't sure just what, but something. Shauna was taking pictures of the artwork and some of the ceiling. This was a dream come true for her and she wasn't wasting a precious moment. By 11:30, they had exhausted their time and must be ready to go over to the Vatican for the audience with the Pope. The next church would have to wait for later in the afternoon.

Today's audience was held inside for logistics sake. Because of Holy Father's frail constitution, he could only travel very short distances and it was easier to move his chair through the Vatican to a convention-sized room for the audience. Over a thousand people with tickets could attend and Roan and Shauna were fortunate to be up front with some of the dignitaries of foreign consulates. And they were close enough to see the sparkle in Pope John Paul II's eyes. It was still there, even with the trauma of Parkinson's, which had robbed him of motion. The pain was evident, too, but he bore it with such grace and love for Christ and His mother. If ever there was a role model for the world, Roan and Shauna were looking directly at him. There was such power in his warm demeanor and strength in his faith which propelled him to go forward despite the challenges. Just being in his presence was, for the Sandersons, a life-changing experience. Here is a living Saint.

Forgotten was DuMonde. Forgotten were blindness and despair. Now was the time for hope and rediscovering the amazing treasures around them. Roan was getting hungry and opted for a quick lunch after the audience, but this was afternoon and things closed down in Rome until around 4:00 PM. The café at the hotel did have a coffee bar with sandwiches, which was ideal. When they got back, they changed, put their walking clothes back on and went downstairs for a cappuccino and a sandwich.

It was a lazy afternoon and several of the pilgrimage members were there. Roan and Shauna sat with them, discussing what each had seen that day. It was odd not having Maggie with them on this leg of the trip.

Shauna turned to Roan and said, "I miss Maggie. Wouldn't she love these churches?"

Roan turned to Shauna and responded, "I can see the two of you now. You are schlepping through the churches, darting into stores, dragging through more churches and finishing up with more stores. It simply boggles the mind! It's Power Tripping at its very best."

Shauna smacked Roan on the shoulder with her brochure from St. Mary Major and squinted at him.

She pursed her lips and said, "You are a man. I am a woman and I shop. It's part of my job description. I'm finally able to do that and I am not letting that opportunity slip away. And besides, it isn't all for me, either, Roan. Right?"

"Right," replied Roan. "You are buying for others and that's great. I don't object at all. Just get something for yourself, too."

Shauna kissed Roan on the cheek and said, "If you are finished with lunch, let's go over to see "Our Mother of Perpetual Help.""

"Oh yeah, let's go," grinned Roan. "I have literally been waiting for this years. This is the icon which hangs in the Quiet Room at the apartment and you know what? We don't have a Quiet Room at the house. I think we need to fix that."

"Yes we do," said Shauna. "And I think we can begin with a new copy of the icon we can frame for the house. And let's get one for Katie and Jim, too. I'm also going to the shop on the way back to get additional posters of saints and religious themes, some for the store and some for us. There are some statues I want, too and I will get those, have them sent to the store and divide out what I want for us at home."

Roan had another idea. But before he presented it to Shauna, he got his sketch pad and began doodling. His idea for the Quiet Room meant expanding the house from the glass gallery which connected the studio to the house. He wanted to incorporate the Mary Garden into it somehow. But now they were on their way over to the beautiful Victorian-gothic Church of San Alfonso (Church of St. Alphonsus) and maybe he would get some ideas over there. This church houses the icon of our Mother of Perpetual Help, venerated in this parish named after the Marian Doctor of the Church, St.

Alphonsus Liguori, founder of the Redemptorists. They are the custodians of the shrine and picture.

Roan and Shauna walked up the steps of the church, which is just a few blocks west of St. Mary Major. Inside the doors are statues and family chapels dedicated to significant saints, including one to St. Gerard Majella, Patron saint of Motherhood. The church's soaring ceiling seemed to pull one along to the front of the sanctuary—drawing one closer to the icon above the altar. A copy of the icon is in the center aisle between the Communion rails under plexiglass to enable people to see what the icon looks like up close. There is an overpowering feeling of a mother's blessings in the church and it made Roan feel as if his own mother was right there with him. When your parents are no longer with you, there is always that presence—a comforting feeling they are watching over you and this is how Roan felt in the church. He motioned to Shauna to sit down in the front pews so they could look at every detail.

As he sat there in tears, he picked up Shauna's hand, turned to her and said, "This is almost better than Medjugorje. Can you feel Our Lady here? I can see her in everything in this church. It's not just the icon being here, it's her presence. Our home has it. The Gallery has it. I'm so overwhelmed, I'm in tears."

Shauna was just as moved. As she held Roan's hand, she looked around at the altar and at the dedications of parishioners to Our Lady.

Then she looked at Roan and exclaimed, "I feel so warm in here. You know this church isn't heated, but it feels like home. It's that feeling I got when we moved to Bemidji. It's the mother's presence and I feel it distinctly in this church. We need a beautiful copy of the icon for our home."

Roan smiled and looked over at the Sacristy. People were going in and coming out with rolled tubes of plastic with posters inside. The church's shop was in the Sacristy, so they went in to see what was available.

There were posters of the icon in various sizes, ready to be matted and framed. Shauna picked out several sizes and bought a dozen posters, along with a story about the icon. It's such an unusual and involved story, Shauna thought it should be part of their Quiet Room at the house. The story of the church was available as well, so Shauna picked up a few of them and as she walked out of the Sacristy, she began to read.

The painting originally came from the island of Crete where it had been venerated for a number of years. The earliest written account is from an old document-plaque written in Latin and Italian which was placed before the icon in the church of St. Matthew, where it was first venerated in Rome in March of 1499.

Two years before that, a merchant in Crete, who was returning to Rome, took the picture to save it from possible destruction from invading Turks, but the document says he stole it. While he was at sea, a horrible storm arose, which could have taken the lives of everyone on board. The sailors, not knowing of the presence of the icon, prayed to Our Lady for help. Amazingly, the ship arrived safely in Italy. It was obvious, Our Lady wanted this picture in Rome.

There is so much more to the story but Shauna read on. The story said Our Lady actually told the small daughter of the merchant's friend, exactly where she wanted to icon to be venerated and chose an equal distance between the basilicas of St. John Lateran and St. Mary Major. This was the Church of St. Matthew.

The young girl's mother told the Augustinian friars about the picture, who came to see it in her home and were so impressed with its beauty, they made plans to transfer it to the church. That happened on March 27, 1499. St. Matthew's became a popular pilgrimage place in Rome and the icon was venerated for three hundred years.

The story goes on to say, in 1798, French troops occupied Rome. General Massena, the governor, decided that Rome had too many churches. He probably had his eye on the valuable land they occupied, so he ordered thirty churches closed and destroyed. St. Matthew's was one of them. For sixty-eight years, nothing more was heard of St. Mary of Perpetual Help. Most people thought it had been destroyed along with St. Matthew's. The series of events which resulted in the restoration of the icon to public veneration is so unbelievable, it had to be Our Lady who wrote the script to make it happen!

The icon was moved numerous times and during the pontificate of Pope Pius IX, the Redemptorists were invited to set up a mother house in Rome. They chose a vacant lot on the Via Merulana, without realising it once had been St. Matthew's Church and the shrine of the famous icon. The church of St. Alphonsus was constructed on the site and one day at recreation, one of the fathers mentioned he had been reading an account of old shrines around Rome and it mentioned the icon had been enshrined in St. Matthews, where they now stood. A young priest, Michael Marchi, became excited when he heard about the icon. He said it hadn't been lost but that he thought he knew where it was. An old priest he served at St. Mary in Posterula told him never to forget the picture which had been at St. Matthew's for over three hundred years.

And since it was Our Lady who had set the wheels in motion for it to be preserved, then shown again, the Redemptorist Father General, the Most Reverend Nicholas Mauron, decided to bring the matter up to Pope Pius IX. He set about restoring the icon to its rightful location and on January 19, 1866, the picture was brought back to St. Alphonsus from St. Mary Posterula. On April 26th, a great procession was staged carrying the icon throughout the Esquiline region of Rome and then it was enthroned above the high altar in a specially constructed niche for it.

During the procession, people lined the streets and decorated their homes with flowers and banners. Numerous miracles were attributed to the icon as it passed, as Our Mother was obviously delighted her wishes had been understood. Paralyzed and ill children were healed as the picture passed their windows. Once word got out of the miracles, and people flocked to the shrine with abandoned crutches and votive offerings in thanksgiving for the healing from Our Lady.

Many subsequent Popes have pictures of Our Lady of Perpetual Help visible in their private quarters or near their seat of office. Pope Pius IX told the Redemptorists to "Make her known" and they have done just that. When the Archconfranternity of Our Lady of Perpetual Help was formed, Pope Pius IX blessed the project and asked his name be added to head the world-wide membership.

So many people wanted new pictures of the icon, that in 1990, the picture was taken down, inspected for damage and it was found to be in delicate condition. The wood had cracks and fungus which threatened irreparable damage and the paint suffered from environmental changes. Restoration had to be done at a minimal, because anything major would have caused more damage. X-rays, infra-red images and Carbon-14 test indicated the wood of the icon could be dated from 1325 to 1480.

Roan was truly excited about his ideas and before they left the church, Roan looked at the altar, with its magnificent paintings in the arches over the altar. The icon of Our Lady belongs there.

Roan was tired, asked if he could beg off the shopping and return to the hotel for a coffee. Shauna decided to pop into the gift store a couple of blocks from the hotel. There were more statues to see, gifts to buy for the family and get something nice for Janet before she took her new assignment. The shop was filled with posters of the saints, some framed and most just hanging from racks. The paper was heavy, coated stock, which would withstand mailing or carrying in luggage. Shauna was delighted and made a selection, then had everything sent to the house. She didn't really want to carry more gifts on the plane. She also had them add the posters of Our Lady of Perpetual Help inside the poster mailing tube as well. There was one additional shop, a few doors down from the hotel, which had been recommended to her. She wanted to surprise Roan with a papal blessing of their marriage.

Shauna stepped into the tiny shop, filled with all kinds of blessings you could order from the Vatican. She felt a marriage blessing would truly make the lake house theirs and it would please Roan. Shauna selected a beautiful ornate style and was told it would take 6-8 weeks for processing. She paid for it and left for the hotel, quite pleased with her exhilarating day.

The afternoon had flown by and there was enough time to take a nap before the evening meal at 7:00. Roan and Shauna were exhausted from walking and when Shauna got back, she met Roan in the hotel lobby. He was studying one of the brochures they picked up at St. Mary Major. He had been sketching, but didn't say what it was. Shauna was too tired to ask. They went upstairs for a rest.

Shauna untied her sneakers and laid down on the bed. The moment her head hit the pillow, she was asleep. But this wasn't the rest she had planned. She immediately began dreaming and soon, her dreams became the worst nightmare imaginable.

Shauna found herself walking into what looked like a large indoor shopping mall inside a beautiful old building. There were brightly coloured shops lining the corridors. The mall was laid out like the spokes on a wheel with a central courtyard. Shauna thought to herself, *This reminds me of the wheel of St. Catherine of Alexandria. The Emperor Maximus tried to kill her on the wheel for converting people to Christianity and when he forced her onto the wheel, it shattered with her touch. What a strange way to build a shopping mall!* As she would soon find out, this was not a normal shopping arcade.

As Shauna sank deeper into sleep, she found herself walking into store after store, looking at the toys in one shop, clothing in the next and wonderful Florentine gold jewellery in the shop next to a florist. It was a shopper's paradise until she walked into the flower shop. Thinking she would find beautiful roses and arrangements, Shauna found herself in the middle of a cold, black, forest-like room, with bare trees and a chilling wind whirling past her shoulders. There were cries for help softly emanating from the corners of the forest. She heard subtle scurrying of mice or squirrels along the moss covered paths between the rows of sickly trees. Then she heard her voice—someone calling from the depths of the blackest part of the forest.

"Shhhaaaauuunnnnaaaa," whispered the voices. "We see you Shauna, come to us."

Shauna began to shudder and roll on her bed. Roan came over from the table where he was sketching and tried to wake her but couldn't. He just sat on the end of her bed transfixed as Shauna sank deeper into her torment.

The voices became louder and Shauna tried to run out the shop door, but it was gone. Within moments, Shauna could feel someone's hand on her shoulder. She looked over and saw a bluish-white hand, as if it was from the grave, clutching her. Tiny shadowy figures tugged at the hem of her skirt and clawed at her legs.

She shouted, "Get away from me. Who are you and what do you want? St. Michael, come to my aid."

"He's not going to find you Shauna," whispered a gruff-voiced man. "Your soul is mine and there isn't anything you can do to get away from me."

This frightened Shauna even more and she screamed, "I don't know who you are or what you want, but my soul belongs to me and the only place it's going is to Heaven because Jesus is my Lord and Savior and He rules here, not you. Get away from me, you evil being."

Roan was really concerned now and left to find Father Pat. He suspected some evil presence had latched onto Shauna. Roan banged on doors until he found the padre.

He explained what was going on and Father Pat said, "I'll bring my crucifix and holy water. I think she is in the middle of someone trying to possess her and we must intervene. You know the more good people do in the name of Christ, the more people will be attacked because the evil one hates being a loser. He tries and tries through various forms to get into people's heads and steal their souls, but Shauna is a fighter and centered in Christ, so this will be a battle. We'd better get over there."

In the meantime, Shauna was becoming weary of this menacing voice. She turned around only to find DuMonde standing in front of her, his lifeless coal-black eyes staring back at her. It was his clammy hand on her shoulder.

Shauna was now well aware of who he is and snarled at him, "Ah, I see what this is all about now, DuMonde. You think you can steal my immortal soul do you? Well, I have a surprise for you."

Shauna pulled the Celtic cross from beneath her sweater and shined it in DuMonde's face.

"You see this, you evil man?" she exclaimed. "This has been blessed by Our Lady several times and it shines out through your darkness. There is NO WAY you can possess me and if you think you can harm me or anyone around me, think again. St. Michael is here because I can hear him."

DuMonde suddenly heard the flapping of wings and twisted around to see an intense light coming from the back of the trees. The rush of wind blew away the trees and left Shauna and DuMonde standing in the middle of a shimmering pastel blue lake. She grabbed the crystal rosary from her pocket and held it up to the light, shaking it at DuMonde.

"Listen up, evil one," shouted Shauna. "Only light lives here. You have no power here and if I ever see you again, the same thing will happen to you again."

A brilliant silver light streamed from the sword of St. Michael as he poised to run it through DuMonde's heart. The rosary diffused the light and took out all the little shadows left lurking around the perimeter of the room.

During this time, Roan and Father Pat were watching the scenario unfolding and drenched Shauna in holy water as Father Pat prayed over her.

Shauna's face had turned ashen, her pulse was thready and her skin clammy. It was if she were near death.

Roan held the crucifix over Shauna's forehead, as she continued to shout, "Get thee behind me, satan. Christ lives here. You have no power. St. Michael my defender. Slay this dragon and his minions."

In the flash of blinding light, St. Michael slashed through DuMonde with his sword. A loud cry came from him and as darkness faded, DuMonde disappeared and Shauna could see the face of her rescuer. St. Michael is definitely a warrior for Christ, but his face is as gentle as a small child's, with a strength only he could possess. His blue eyes sparkled like the sun dancing off the lake they were standing in. He folded his wings over Shauna as she continued to shudder, but soon, she felt safe.

Before he left her, St. Michael said, "This evil person shouldn't bother you again, but if he does, all you have to do is call me like you just did. The work you and Roan are doing is blessed and that's why you were attacked. But be warned, the more you do for God, the more likely DuMonde or someone like him will be around the next corner ready to strike again. God loves you so much, He sent me to protect you. And there is another message I bring you."

Shauna looked around the lake to see blue and silver balloons floating upward to the sky. She didn't have to ask who sent them.

She turned to St. Michael and said, "You really DO exist. You really ARE a Godsend, St. Michael. Thank you and thank my Lord, please. And you can thank the other little "angel" who is watching over us."

St. Michael left with a swoosh of his wings and in moments, Shauna was awakening. Roan and Father Pat were hovering over her as she regained consciousness.

"What happened here?" she asked.

"It's okay Honey, you had a really bad nightmare, but you are fine now," explained Roan.

Father Pat asked Roan to go downstairs to the hotel bar and get Shauna a large brandy. He would stay with her and continue saying a few prayers as he explained to Shauna what had happened.

By this time, people from the pilgrimage were at the door watching as the attack unfolded on Shauna. They were clutching rosaries and praying as she came out of the nightmare. Roan came right back up with the brandy and gave it to her.

"Here, Honey, sit up," said Roan. "You have gone through a really bad experience and this will help."

Shauna gladly took the brandy and sipped it as Father Pat explained the demonic presence which tried, unsuccessfully to take control of her soul. Shauna looked around at all her friends standing in the doorway and asked them to come in. She explained what she had experienced and asked them to pray for her.

Roan asked if someone could bring the supper up to them, because Shauna wasn't able to go down for the meal. Sister Monica said she would be glad to do it. Now Shauna could fully sit up on the bed and explain a little more.

"It was the scariest thing I have ever experienced," sighed Shauna. "But you know what? St. Michael really does exist and he came to my defense right after I called him. DuMonde is an evil spirit, he might even be the devil incarnate, but I'll tell you this. God is in His Heaven and all is right with the world right now. And Miss Lulabelle has been our guardian angel all along. She sent balloons!"

"You mean like the ones on the cart outside on the street?" remarked Father Pat. "Roan, take a look outside."

Roan walked over to the window and could see a street vendor's cart, complete with blue and silver balloons flying from strings attached to the ends of his cart.

"Yes," replied Roan. "Those are Lulabelle's balloons. I'll be darned!"

Shauna smiled and you could tell the brandy was making her fall asleep. But this time, she would get exactly that, sleep without nightmares.

"I think it's time to leave now Roan," said Father Pat. "Call me if you need me, but I think Shauna should sleep well. Make sure she eats something though because her body has gone through physical trauma and nourishment will be good for her. Good night, Roan. Nite Shauna."

Roan said goodbye and called down to the hotel kitchen to explain Sister Monica would be coming in to pick up two dinner trays.

Shauna looked over at Roan and said, "I'm sure glad that's over, Roan. I've never experienced anything like that in my life. I can imagine the hell people go through who are possessed. But you know what? I think I can paint a portrait of St. Michael now that I have seen him up close."

Roan smiled and took the glass of brandy from Shauna's hand.

"Get a little rest now, Sweetie," whispered Roan. "I'll let you know when supper is here."

Roan finished off the brandy. It had been an unbelievable experience, watching the woman he loved writhe in such agony in the dream. But he found out just how strong her faith could be when tested. He thought he knew how firm her commitment was, but this confirmed it.

In about an hour, Sister Monica brought up the supper trays The chef put food on the trays which could be eaten cold if necessary. The rest of the night went smoothly and morning would bring a delightful new day, starting with Mass at St. Alphonsus Church. They had only one day left on their pilgrimage and Shauna wanted to see St. John Lateran and the Catacombs before they left for Minnesota. Shauna felt reborn as she got ready for the day.

Roan peeked around the corner of the bathroom and gave Shauna the once over.

"Looking good, Mrs. Sanderson," Roan gushed. "Can I pick 'em or what?"

"Yeah, well, backatcha, Mr. Sanderson," Shauna replied. "My taste isn't so bad either ya know!"

Shauna felt good about today and dressed in a bright blue sweater and paisley skirt accompanied by a rope belt and brown leather boots. She wanted a few pieces of Florentine gold (the only really good thing about her dream before it became a nightmare!), but Roan reminded Shauna there is still one portion of their honeymoon to come and that's to Tuscany and Florence, where the magnificent eighteen-karat gold jewellery is made.

"Oh, that's right, I forgot," explained Shauna. "I guess I just wanted something from here, that's all. I can wait."

"No, if you really want a couple of pieces, you should get them," insisted Roan. "Let's see on the way back from Mass."

After a light breakfast, the pilgrims walked over to St. Alphonsus Church for the English Mass. Even this early in the day, the church was filling up, so Roan found a nice pew up front and they sat with the rest of the group. Father Pat had been asked to con-celebrate and do the homily. You could tell how delighted he was. His face radiated the joy in his faith. And the feeling in the church was that of immense love.

Roan sat with Shauna's hand in his during most of the service. This would be a honeymoon to remember and they both gave thanks for Miss Lulabelle's generosity and thoughtfulness. Both of them keep thinking Lulabelle was still alive, but Roan found her body on the shore. Still...

The pilgrims decided to have one last meal together before taking off for their homes. One of the pilgrims, Stephen Palmer, had found a beautiful outdoor café which could seat their group and had called ahead to make a reservation. It was good just to sit down and talk together about their remarkable two week journey of faith. Soon it would be over, but the friendships would remain.

Roan and Shauna didn't leave until the next morning, so they bid farewell to Nives and her group, then grabbed a taxi over to St. John Lateran to look around. Shauna was just about out of memory sticks, but there was enough memory for the basilica and the Catacombs later that afternoon. She would take her photographs carefully.

As they drove up to St. John Lateran, Shauna was amazed at how much the church looked like a palace. Shauna exited the taxi and took a picture of the late baroque period façade. It had been completed by Alessandro Galilei in 1735 after he won a competition for the design. It is, in fact, a basilica and the cathedral of Rome. It is the oldest and ranks first among the four patriarchal basilicas of Rome and holds the title of ecumenical motherchurch among Roman Catholics. It contains the papal throne (Cathedra Monana) and even ranks above St. Peter's Basilica at the Vatican.

Shauna was correct about the church looking like a palace because it literally was—Lateran Palace, dating from the 4th Century. Emperor Constantine gave the palace to the Bishops of Rome in time to host a synod of bishops in 313. The palace basilica was converted and extended to eventually become the cathedral of Rome, the seat of popes as patriarchs of Rome. It was dedicated by Pope Sylvester I in 324, declaring it to be the Domus Dei or "House of God" and it became the "Most Holy Lateran Church" meaning it became the mother and head of all churches in the world.

The church has been enlarged many times over the centuries, but still retains many of the older structures inside. There are also seven altars, an octagonal baptistry which provides for full immersion and numerous relics and magnificent artwork. This is a church well worth seeing.

Roan said an hour in this church was enough walking for a while and felt they could opt for a quick snack. Shauna agreed and noticed a small café across from the plaza. Several of their friends were also there and were waiting for the catacombs tour in an hour. Shauna ordered a pasta salad, while Roan got a bowl of minestrone soup, fresh bread and coffee. In no time, they were ready for the next part of this day's journey.

The catacombs tour took place just a few miles outside the wall of the city. Their guide was an American priest who volunteered his time to show pilgrims what a catacomb would look like, but without bodies. The walks were long and narrow, but gave an excellent description of how the early Christians had been buried and also how they worshiped. The labyrinth of chambers could easily get one lost, but Roan and Shauna stayed close to the group and didn't wander off.

Along the walkways were burial nooks carved out of the wall. Some were almost family sized, while others might have been the final resting places for children. There were several mock-ups of burial chambers as they might have looked in the third or fourth centuries, plus the guide also showed the pilgrims where the early Christians prayed. The faded tempera paintings and designs indicated communion sites and some even designated the burial plots of high-ranking officials and bishops. However, there are no remains left. Whatever was there, was relocated to prevent looting and vandalism. The catacombs are basically a historical reminder of what had been.

Roan looked at Shauna and said, "Isn't it sad to think people had to worship underground for centuries before they had the freedom to worship above ground—in a church?"

Shauna replied, "We take for granted our freedoms. They are freedoms these people fought for, died for and dreamed for their children. It's amazing what we take for granted when you see this."

"Mmm, you're right, Shauna," agreed Roan. "It's a testament to the strength of their faith and will to persevere against all odds."

After another hour and a half of walking, it was time to head home. A nap sounded like an excellent idea, plus Shauna had to finish packing. The plane left for Minneapolis, via Chicago at 7:00 AM, which meant a very early morning. The bus ride back took only fifteen minutes, but Shauna could see the lovely hillsides and villas peeking out from fringed gardens. Their next trip to Italy would be an amazing period of growth for Roan and Shauna—and lots of fun! Shauna smiled as she watched from her window.

There were messages at the front desk for Roan. Franco had problems with the new stoves and had to close the restaurant for two days. The supplier was working on the problem, which had been a fault in the valve system delivering the natural gas to the burners. And could the boss talk with a vendor in Rome about olives and other condiments? The numbers were scribbled on a notepad, but Roan didn't take the chance and called Franco on his cell.

It was almost 10:30 AM Minneapolis time and Franco would hopefully be getting ready for the luncheon crowd. Roan dialed the number and let it ring. It rang and rang. As he hung up, he said to himself, *that's not normal, but maybe I should try again. Someone should be there by now.* Roan tried again and this time, Franco answered, completely out of breath.

"Allo, Boss, eets me, Franco," he wheezed. "I am sorree Boss, but wee have had a fire. Eet just happened. Eet is de dam stoves again."

"Franco, slow down and catch your breath," exclaimed Roan. "How much damage was done and is anyone hurt?"

"No one hurt, but smoke and a leetle fire damage," cried Franco. "We weel have to shut down again. I am so sorry Boss."

"Ok Franco," explained Roan. "Here's what I want you to do. If your day planner is still readable, look up those numbers here in Rome and I will contact the suppliers before we leave. Second, call the insurance company and third, call the equipment suppliers and tell them to contact me here in Rome now. Got all that, Franco?"

"Yes, I weel do eet now," sighed Franco. "Goobye Boss."

Unfortunately, Roan couldn't get another word in, but he dialed the numbers Franco had given him to order specialty items. After speaking with the owners, Roan placed the order for several kinds of olives, relishes and peppers, plus spices and a rather large order of cheese, Roan sat with his notepad, scribbling down prices and order numbers. The phone rang and it was the equipment supplier.

"I'm sorry Mr. Sanderson," said the man, a Mr. Gilcrest. "There was a bad connection and we thought we had it fixed, but I guess not. I am having two new stoves delivered this afternoon and I am installing them personally. Sorry for the inconvenience."

"Mr. Gilcrest, I want your assurance this will be done correctly this time, Roan explained. "And I also want you dealing with the insurance company, who should be calling you right about now. We have a very successful restaurant with patrons waiting for their reservations and now it must be redecorated! Make sure this is done today, please."

Mr. Gilcrest responded, "Yes, Mr. Sanderson. It will be finished this afternoon. I am bringing in a plumber and an electrician to be certain it's done right."

Roan slammed the phone closed and walked over to Shauna who was checking the flight schedule at the front desk.

She looked up from her paper and asked, "What's the good news, if any?"

"There was a small fire in the restaurant, but no one was hurt. We will need to redecorate because of the fire and smoke damage," said Roan. "Can you contact Sandra and get her over there today?"

"I'll try her now and see if she can go over. Then I'll have her call me," replied Shauna. "Great way to start the week off, isn't it?"

They walked back up to their room and sat down. Roan called room service and ordered sandwiches and drinks.

Shauna looked over at her suitcase and said, "Guess I should begin packing. I'm fairly well organized and there really isn't much to pack. I did a lot of looking in Rome, but not that much buying. I surprised myself! But I'll call Sandra now and see what her schedule looks like."

Roan grumbled to himself and busied himself in his notes. The phone rang and it was the insurance agent. He had good relatively news to impart.

"Roan, this isn't as bad as it sounds," said Paul Smith. "There is a warranty on the stoves and connections, the structural damage isn't terrible and can be repaired easily. Your only down time now will be repainting and some plaster work. And, of course, cleaning the soot off everything. That's going to take the time."

"Okay, Paul," replied Roan. "Do what you need to. I have Shauna contacting Sandra and she will organise the cleaning and redecorating. Have Franco sign the claim forms to get them rolling and I will be back there in a few days to finish up the paperwork if you need me."

"Fine," said Paul. "I will call you if I need anything else. Bye."

Just then, Shauna's phone rang. It was Sandra.

"Hey Shaunny, what's cookin'?" Sandra asked glibly. "And why in the hell am I calling Rome?"

"Hey yourself, Sandra," replied Shauna. "The restaurant has had a fire and they need you over there to organise the cleaning and redecorating. We won't be home for a day or so and it will take Roan a few days to get organized, so would you be a dear and go over there now, if possible?"

"Sure, no problem," said Sandra. "I was headed over there anyway to talk with Marcel about a company party we want to arrange for one of the owners who is retiring and guess who becomes the full partner?"

"I'm taking a wild one here, but I would say you?" Shauna asked.

"Correct," responded Sandra. "And it's a magnificent offer, much of the thanks goes to you and Roan for bringing in all this business. AND, I have had almost twenty new commissions from patrons of the restaurant and the media. It's brought in over five million dollars in the last six months! Hey, how is Roan handling the blindness?"

Shauna had forgotten to tell anyone about Roan getting his sight back, but played it close to the vest.

She only said, "He's doing fine, Sandra. That was quite the adjustment, but he's had a good pilgrimage and is looking forward to getting home. He's all healed up and ready to get back into his normal routine. Oh, and I am expanding the Gallery into a Design Studio, complete with furnishings."

"Wow," exclaimed Sandra. "Any help I can offer, I will be glad to. If you need any suppliers' names and references, please give me a ring, Doll, okay?"

"You got it, Sandra," replied Shauna. "Must run. Call me after you have been to the restaurant and remember, this is a seven hour time difference here and we are leaving at 7:00 AM tomorrow morning—up at 3:00 AM. Bye now."

Shauna kicked off her shoes and put her feet up. Just then, there was a knock at the door. Food had arrived. Shauna got up and opened the door. She took the trays and tipped the waiter. She set Roan's tray on the table and she took hers to the bed.

"Ahh," said Shauna. "This is the life. Supper in bed!"

Roan smiled at Shauna and said, "It's the little things that make you smile, isn't it, Dear?"

Shauna winked at her husband and proceeded to eat her meal. After eating, Shauna walked over to the windows to look at the street scene. The little cart was still there with the blue and silver balloons. It was situated in front of a leather goods store and it got Shauna to thinking. *Gloves, I wanted gloves. I'd better get them now.*

"Roan, I'm going across the street," Shauna said. "I forgot that I wanted to buy some gloves. The shop is right behind the vendor's cart on the street."

"Okay Honey, hurry back," replied Roan. "You want to get an early evening tonight."

Shauna took her fanny pack and left her cell phone for Roan if Sandra called. She walked across the street to the shop, which had just reopened for the evening customers. The store had amazing products. There were silk scarves displayed on the counter and in cases. There were handbags, wallets and cigarette cases, plus several cases of gloves. There was a men's section, too with wallets, belts and briefcases. This is where she would shop. After all, this is where Lulabelle's balloons were and this must be a good place to be!

Shauna found several scarves for herself, Katie and Sandra. She bought a couple of handbags for herself and a large one for Katie. Roan's wallet was in shambles and she found a beautiful smooth leather one for him, one for Conor and one for Jim. There was an elegant briefcase for Stephen. Then it came to the gloves. There were gloves of every colour and style. Shauna picked out several of the same style but different colours for herself—yellow, purple, red and royal. She found a few pair for Katie and Marie. And there were small jewellery boxes for herself, Katie, Marie and Janet. Shauna's plastic did more damage in there than on the entire trip! But she had everything sent by express and took several business cards, just in case she needed anything else when she got home. The clerk was flabbergasted!

"Thank you Madame," sighed the clerk. "You will just make the last express pickup tonight and have your things in a few days. You are wonderful!"

Shauna smiled and explained, "My friend Nives told me about your store and said you had the best leather goods in Rome. I see now she was correct."

"Oh Nives, yes, she is a faithful customer every year," responded the clerk. "She brings me a lot of customers. Here, please accept a couple of scarves for your patronage."

Shauna was delighted and said, "Thank you so much. I will also be a faithful customer and I look forward to seeing you on our next trip. I'll be back here on business with my associates in a few months."

Shauna smiled and took the scarves back with her. Roan would think she only bought two things, but she would have to explain that later. When Shauna got back to the room, Roan had information for her.

"I just spoke with Sandra and the place needs total cleaning and painting. There is gooey soot everywhere. The good news is everything is covered by insurance and business interruption insurance kicked in, so we aren't out any money. Our staff will be paid and have a few days off too. We should be back in business within three days."

"Good," replied Shauna. "That will give you just enough time to get home, rest up and then go down to the cities. And by the way, we didn't tell anyone at home about your sight being restored. And I know Maggie didn't say anything. Play along when we get off the plane and then let everyone know. What do you think?"

"Brilliant idea," sighed Roan. "I want this to be a day to remember. We have so much to be thankful for. By the way, those scarves are lovely. Nives was right, they do have beautiful things over there."

Roan looked over the brightly coloured scarves, thought for a moment, then said, "I'm going downstairs to the café and see if they have a couple of cappachinos to go. Would you like anything else?"

"Oh, ah no, that would be fine, Dear," replied a surprised Shauna. "See you in a bit then."

Roan dashed out the door and across the street to the little leather goods shop. He asked the clerk what would be a nice gift for his wife.

The clerk pulled out an elegant handbag with numerous pockets, done in a rich burgundy leather. There were gloves to match and a silk scarf done in a paisley design.

"I'll take them. These are perfect," responded Roan. "My wife will love them. She just came over here and brought back the most elegant scarves. I just wanted something more for her than two scarves."

The clerk looked at him and tried to keep a straight face.

She replied, "You mean the tiny little lady with the long dark hair? She is beautiful. And she has a sweet smile and a very generous heart. These will be perfect for her. Should I have them sent by express or do you want to take them with you?"

Roan considered his options and said, "Might was well take them with me. She needs a surprise every now and again. Thank you very much. She will be delighted."

The clerk wrapped everything in tissue paper, wrote up the sale and gave him a carry-bag to take with him. Roan smiled and exited the shop. He came back upstairs with his goodies and opened the door.

Shauna looked at him quizzically and asked, "That doesn't look much like cappachino, does it?"

"Ah no, it doesn't," said a contrite Roan. "But I didn't want you leaving Rome without having a nice leather ensemble for yourself. That girl at the shop across the way is really nice and she said they would go very well with your colouring. Here Honey."

Shauna was quite stunned, but took the package and peeked inside. She opened the tissue and pulled out the handbag, then the gloves and scarf.

"Oh Roan, these are just beautiful," she sighed. "And they go with all my clothes. I can wear the scarf tomorrow and I won't have to take the fanny pack on the plane. Oooo, thank you Roan. You're the best husband in the world."

Shauna planted a big kiss and a hug on her husband, then began to pack. She put all her documents, personal items, etc. in her new handbag. There was space for her cell phone, checkbook and passport. All the little pockets were grand for her lipstick and cologne, plus space for her notebook and pen. She'd wear the paisley skirt tomorrow, with the new scarf matching perfectly. Her yellow sweater would also make a lovely completion to the ensemble. Spring was really in bloom now!

Shauna finished as Roan completed his notes. They snuggled under the covers and finished their last night in Rome with amore.

Chapter Nine

It was raining when they got up. 3:00 AM is a rather uncivilized time to wake up, but they had to make their flight and this was the only way. It took little time to get moving, as they were packed. They double checked the room for any items left behind, then brought the bags to the desk. Roan checked out and the concierge called a taxi. Within a few minutes, their taxi was waiting and they left for the airport.

It took about forty-five minutes to get through traffic and through all the security at the entrance. A porter took the luggage and checked their tickets for the proper airline. They went to the ticket counter, checked in and left the bags. Fortunately, they were early enough for Shauna to do a little window shopping along the concourse.

There was a shoe shop with beautiful sandals and comfort shoes in the window. These stores were open twenty-four hours a day and Shauna asked Roan if she could go in. She came out with three pair of shoes! Roan just shook his head and laughed.

Shauna justified her purchases by saying, "Hey, one pair matches the new handbag you bought me. And the other two are for summer. I didn't have any summer sandals, Roan."

Roan smiled and walked along the concourse.

He stopped at a window with marble chess sets in the window and said, "Hey Shauna, look at these chess sets. Wouldn't they be great for Stephen,

Charles and Jim? Why don't we get them and have them shipped?"

"Oh these are great," explained Shauna. "Let's get one for our house, too, Roan. I think Conor might like to learn to play chess. Then he and Jimmy can play something other than gameboys! This will give their brains a workout."

Roan smiled and picked out four chess sets and had them sent. Shauna had a few ideas for the Gallery and decided she and Katie should come back to Rome on a buying trip for the store. She took out her notebook and jotted the ideas down, then took one of the business cards from the store for reference.

As they walked to the gate, Shauna mentioned, "I have some ideas for the vignettes in the store. We can combine some of the Italian leather items I've seen with our native pottery and some of Lillian's photographs. I'd like to bring Katie over to Rome in a couple of months to do some buying for the store. And I want to check out some of the other areas around Rome, plus maybe look at Greece. But I want to go over these things first with her, then with you and Jim. We have lots of time to do this."

Little did Shauna know how busy she would be when she got home. There were projects to design for the architects in the Cities for their homes, the Gallery design and furnishing for the expansion, getting Charles and Marie's home ready to move into and get the restaurant back in shape. Conor would be out of school soon and there was summer to plan. And then there was a wedding to plan. Looks like Shauna had more than her fair share on her plate. But these were delightful things for Shauna. And she had worked hard for much of it.

Soon it was time to board the flight to O'Hare, then onto St. Paul. They went through security again and sat in the waiting area for another half hour. Shauna decided to call through to Katie and let her know when they would be home.

Katie was bubbly as usual for being called so late at night. Shauna had forgotten about the time differential. She apologized by saying, "Oh Katie, I did what I said I wouldn't do. I'm, so sorry."

Katie wasn't unhappy, but glad to hear her friend's voice and said, "That's okay, Shauna. It's great to hear your voice. How's everything going over there?"

"We're all good here, Katie. We have lots of surprises and experiences to share and tons of pictures. And, I think you and I need to come to Rome in July to do some power buying for the store," Shauna giggled.

"It's good to hear your laugh, Shauna," replied Katie. "Last time I spoke with you, you were about to strangle Roan. How is he, by the way?"

"The pilgrimage did wonders for him, Katie," explained Shauna. "And I dragged him all over Rome! Be prepared for some express shipments from Medjugorje. I ordered some statues and icons for the shop. I can't wait to show you what I bought."

"Remind Roan the shop next to ours is vacant and we could knock out the wall and physically expand the store into that space," remarked Katie. "What do you think of that idea, Shauna? Ask him on the way home, would you? We could become demo dollies!"

Shauna's face lit up and Roan could tell the wheels were grinding again.

He looked over at Shauna and asked, "And what, pray tell, seems to be up your collective sleeves?"

She said, "Hold a mo, Katie, Roan is asking me something."

Shauna set the phone on speaker and asked Roan about the connecting wall between shops. Since the other side was vacant and relatively the same size as the Gallery, it's ideal to expand the shop into and would if it be alright to go ahead?

Roan stared blankly at Shauna and said, "Sure, that space has been vacant for a while and I think it's a great idea. Go for it. You two really made the decision before we left and this will simply confirm it. Just have Jim or Katie call the city planning commission and see what permits we will need for demolition and remodeling."

"Did you hear him, Katie?" Shauna exclaimed. "I think we have a winner here!"

"I'm on it," said Katie. "I'll have Jim call in the morning. See you when you get home. Call me from the St. Paul airport and we will come out to get you. Bye!"

The flight was being called and Roan looked at Shauna with one of his amazed stares.

"You two are like a tsunami and a tornado rolled into one. Nothing stops you, does it?" Roan asked.

"Just gotta know how to plan things, Roan," replied Shauna. "Once you have the idea, plan it out and go for it. If you fail, at least you have tried your best, but if you succeed, it makes the effort all the sweeter."

They found their First Class seats and put their carry-on bags in the racks up top.

The flight attendant noticed Shauna's handbag and said, "What a lovely handbag. I think you must have shopped at the leather goods store across from the Hotel Bellafiore, am I correct?"

"Yes," responded Shauna. "My husband bought this for me, isn't it lovely? How did you know?"

"That's a signature handbag and I recognized it. I have it in navy and love it to bits," she said.

Shauna was delighted and ran her hand across the smooth leather. It smelled good, too!

The plane took off and the Sandersons settled in for a long flight home. The leather seats were warm and invited napping. But the champagne came first, then a nice breakfast, hot lemony towels and a movie. Shauna and Roan fell asleep after the towels!

Two-thirds of the way through the flight, a light luncheon was offered.

Shauna nudged Roan awake and blew into his ear, "Yummies are here."

Roan opened one eye and told his bride, "I think I'm in the mood for something tantalising. Oh, you mean food!"

Shauna smacked Roan on the arm and smiled broadly. The attendant brought two trays of steak, potatoes and veg. Of course, they also served champagne and coffee, with chocolate on the side!

"I'll just be glad to be home," sighed Shauna. "There is so much to do now and although we have only been gone two weeks, it seems like much longer. Home will make me feel wonderful."

Roan got up and walked around several times during the flight. It's always good to prevent DVT, which can literally kill if you don't move your legs for a long period of time. The circulation becomes impeded, so it's best to keep moving on a long flight or a drive.

Before they knew it, the captain announced they were descending into O'Hare. Time to change their watches, too. Thankfully the flight went swiftly and there were two more to go. Getting through Customs would be fun.

As they stood in line, a Beagle sniffer dog came through the passengers and stopped at Roan. It looked up at him and grinned.

Roan asked the handler if he could pet the dog and he said, "Yes, but only for a moment. His name is Boomer."

Roan bent down and patted Boomer on the head and scratched his chin.

He asked Shauna if they should have a beagle and the handler explained, "Not unless you like buying food and don't mind beggars. That's one of the reasons we employ beagles in this service. They are always hungry and can sniff out any type of food stuff from yards away!"

Roan thanked the officer and as they went through the passport check, the agent looked at Shauna's handbag and said, "Been to Rome?"

Shauna asked, "You too?"

The woman smiled, stamped Shauna's passport and said, "Mine's black and I have the matching gloves!"

The next layover wasn't very long and Roan suggested they go over to the gate area. They could get a beer and a sandwich while they waited.

It was calming to sit and watch others in a frantic hurry to get somewhere—just watching mankind go by, taking a sip of soda and a bite of sandwich. How peaceful it felt.

Too soon they were called again and Shauna took Roan's hand saying, "We are that much closer to home now. Are you doing okay with these planes?"

"You know, I haven't even thought about it most of the time. I'll know more when I get on the shuttle," he said.

Roan became very pensive and looked over at Shauna and said, "I have been so busy focusing on myself that I didn't think of those pilot's families. They must be suffering terribly with the loss of their loved ones. Maybe I should set up some kind of trust fund for their kids, pay some bills or donate to a memorial for them. They kept us from perishing in the crash, losing their lives in the process and I need to do something for them—to thank them."

"We can find out what's been done so far, Roan and maybe we can get together with the other survivors and have a memorial for them. That would be nice," expressed Shauna.

This leg of the journey took only a little over an hour and when they landed, Shauna called Katie to tell her they were in St. Paul. As Shauna walked through the airport toward her next gate, she heard a familiar voice shouting over the din of the crowd.

"Misses Shauna, Mr. Boss, eets me, Franco," he yelled.

There he was, running toward his favourite people and he practically ran them over. Roan had called Franco to meet them and fill him in on the progress of the restaurant. And he thought they should go over to see it, since they were in the cities. Shauna was less than happy, but went along with it.

"But we will miss the flight, Roan," she exclaimed.

"Not to worry," Roan said. "I have the company jet standing by and Franco will go down to pick up the luggage from the carousel. I just cancelled the shuttle!"

But as Franco got closer, he could sense something was different about his boss.

He squinted at Roan's face and exclaimed, "Can you see me, Boss?"

"Yes, Franco, I can see you," replied Roan. "I have my sight back."

Franco jumped up and down, grinning from ear to ear and screamed, "I am sooo excited, I can't stand eet. You can see, you can see!"

"Yes, I can see and I also see we need to get the bags, Franco. Can you go down and get them for us? Here are the stubs if you need them. We will make our way to the entrance and meet you there. Okay?"

"Ok Mr. Roan. I'll get the bags and the car. It's in the usual place, so give me a few minutes okay?" asked Franco.

Roan shook has head and Shauna had to call Katie again to tell her to hold on for a little while. They wouldn't be home just yet. And Shauna called the house to tell Janet about the delay. Everything was running smoothly for a change!

Ten minutes later, Franco drove up in the company SUV. He opened the door for Shauna and Roan grabbed a spot in the front seat. As they drove along to the restaurant, he talked with Franco about the clean-up. Shauna called Sandra on the phone and asked if she could meet them there. This way they could get things done sooner, rather than later.

The clean-up was going well and as they pulled up to the parking lot, Roan could see a number of service vehicles in the lot. Sandra arrived shortly after they did and everyone went in together. It took Sandra and the staff a moment to realise Roan could see. Roan gathered everyone around and asked for their attention.

"Friends. I want to thank you for all you have done to get Ristorante Tuscano up and running in such a short time. We can celebrate later, but I wanted to tell you how much your prayers helped me during this difficult time. I have regained my sight and it's thanks to your prayers and good wishes. It's so much appreciated. Thank you."

Gramma Giovanna came out from the kitchen, hair flying and yelled, "Hey, you gonna get me behind here. Oh, Mr. Roan? You can see? Praise God the prayers worked. Franco, get the tomatoes."

Roan did a walk-through the kitchen to see the new stoves. Franco gave him the invoices and insurance forms, since they had just arrived and a crew was finishing scrubbing the walls and floors. Everything was covered in a slimy film of soot. And the fire smell was still there, except that Gramma's sauce, drenched in garlic, overpowered some of it.

As Shauna and Sandra talked, Roan looked at his watch and asked Franco if the house had food in it.

"Yes, Mr. Roan, the house is ready to go if you need it," explained Franco. "I know eets getting late, so you ask Misses Shauna to stay overnight?"

"I think so, Franco," said Roan. "Let me ask her."

Roan caught Shauna's eye and she walked over. She had a feeling what he was going to say and beat him to the punch.

"You probably want to stay over at the lake house tonight and you know what? That's just fine with me," she said. "We can go home when we want tomorrow and I am so tired, I just want to put my feet up and get some rest."

Roan smiled, shook his head and said, "Get the car warmed up, Franco. I'll take the car out to the house and we will just fly out in the morning. Maybe we can get over the jet lag faster this way."

They said goodbye to the staff and Sandra, then drove out to the house. It was good to see the house in the afternoon sun. It was like an oasis in the urban jungle and the moment they walked in, they were at peace again.

"I want to take a shower," exclaimed Shauna. "That's all I want to do. Then I want to put my feet up. That's it…end of story."

Roan called the house to tell Janet they would be staying over one night. Then he called Katie and explained why. Roan set his keys on the kitchen counter and looked in the fridge, which was fully stocked with favourite foods. Franco probably figured they would stay overnight. The boy was certainly thoughtful.

Shauna dashed upstairs, threw her clothes off and turned on the rain shower. The steamy water felt good and she washed the grime out of her hair and off her skin. Thank goodness she had clothing and personal care products at the house. When she finished, she put her bathrobe on, blew her hair dry and went downstairs. Roan had made a surprise for her.

There was a plate of smoked salmon, cottage cheese and crackers. There was even fruit for the plate. And Roan had opened a bottle of Chardonnay, readying a glass as she walked into the kitchen.

"Ooo, this is wonderful, Roan. Thank you," she said. "Oh, maybe we should wash some of our clothes before we go home. I want to wear my blue sweater and it's a little grubby."

"Sure Sweetie," replied Roan. "I'll get the cases from the garage and you can go through them, pick out what you want to wash and we can start the washer."

Shauna took the food into the living room and sat in her favourite over-stuffed chair in front of the fireplace. It was still chilly enough for a small fire, so she lit the gas starter and put a few logs on. She ate the food slowly, sipped her wine and promptly fell asleep in about ten minutes.

Roan came in and said, "Shauna, I have your things ready for the washer. Shauna?"

He took the wine glass out of her hand and placed it on a coaster on the end table. Then he grabbed the laundry basket and put their clothes in the washer. He fixed a plate of food for himself and sat with his glass of wine on the opposite chair, enjoying the fire. Before he realised it, the buzzer went off on the washer.

Oh great, here we go again—back to life in the fast lane, Roan mused. He put the clothes in the dryer and returned to the living room. Shauna was fast asleep and looked like a little doll, cuddled up in her chair. This was a good way to get over the jet lag.

Soon his task was done and the clothes were ready to wear. The rest could be packed. He left that decision to Shauna. All he cared about was clean underwear!

At 10:00 PM, Roan put out the fireplace and gently nudged Shauna awake. They walked up to the bedroom and both fell fast asleep. They awoke at 9:00 AM when the phone rang. It was Franco asking when they wanted to leave. Roan said 1:00 would be good and could he come out and pick them up.

Shauna smelled the coffee brewing in the kitchen, grabbed her robe and went downstairs. There was toast and jam, fresh orange juice and milk. It was a perfect start to her day. Roan followed after his shower. It was so good just to take things slowly now, because the pace would soon speed up. Shauna thanked Roan for doing the laundry.

Shauna put on her new shoes, her blue sweater and paisley skirt with matching scarf. She looked beautiful. The blue brought out the sparkle in her eyes. And the new gold necklace and earrings she bought in Rome added the perfect touch of class.

"Ready for my close-up, Mr. DeMille!" Shauna laughed. "Let's get out of Dodge and home to the range, Rover."

"I see the sleep did you some good there, Mrs. Sanderson," mused Roan. "You are ready to tackle the world again."

They cleaned up their dishes from the evening before, swept the house for left-overs and piled the bags into the car. Now they just waited for Franco to get there.

Shauna pulled out her planner and looked at the schedule for May-June. The dates were becoming full and she didn't know when Maggie and Tim would be married. She penciled in the Gallery demolition, the meeting with the architects and some time for Charles and Marie to get their wishes for the house décor. It left little time for anything else.

Franco and Marcel pulled in the driveway and honked. Marcel waved, then dropped Franco off. It would take about 45 minutes to get to the private airport, but that was fine. The trip back wouldn't take very long in the company jet. Everything was ready to go when the Sandersons got there. Shauna called Katie right before they boarded and told her they would be coming in at the private section of the airfield.

The pilot, Bob Marks, greeted Roan and asked, "Are you alright flying in this plane, Sir?"

Roan replied, "I have to be, Captain Marks. Not every plane crashes and I need to get over my fears. I've just been half way around the world, so I think this should be a piece of cake. Avanti!"

It was good to be on the "Shauna" again. This jet was extra quiet and allowed a smooth ride home. Time passed swiftly and soon the familiar shoreline of Bemidji came into view. Captain Marks flew over the lake house and wiggled the wings of the plane to signal Conor his folks were home.

Conor saw the plane dip its wings and called to Janet, "Hey Janet, did you see that? Did you see it? The pilot dipped the wings of the plane over the house. WOW!"

Janet smiled and said, "Your folks will be home in a few minutes. Did you clean up your room yet?"

Conor grimaced and shot upstairs, while Janet finished putting out fresh flowers Katie brought over. She also called downstairs to Marie and told her the Sandersons would be home in about ten minutes.

Katie and Jim were waiting for the plane to descend and park. The steps came down and Roan was the first to come out. He didn't have his cane and he didn't wear his glasses. Katie realised Roan could see and she began to cry.

"Oh my Lord," she cried. "You can see again Roan. Oh thank God."

Katie ran up to Roan and hugged him. Jim also came up and gave Roan a hug. Shauna was right behind and Katie couldn't contain herself. The friends hugged for a long time, as if they had been apart for years.

Jim gave Shauna a kiss on the cheek and said, "That must have been some pilgrimage."

Roan remarked, "You have NO idea what we went through. This was the most amazing two weeks we have ever experienced. Just wait until we tell you."

Jim loaded the bags in the car and drove everyone to the house. Conor was waiting on the front deck for his folks and ran out to see them. He stopped dead in his tracks when he saw his Dad looking straight at him.

"Dad, you can see? You can see me?" he queried. "Is this real, you really can see me?"

"Yes, son, the miracles have happened," replied Roan. "And they keep on coming."

Conor hugged his parents tightly. As they all walked inside, Janet and Marie met them at the door. Marie was already in tears and Janet was delighted to see Roan's vision had returned. Jim brought in the bags and Mickey came running up to his Mom, almost getting caught in her feet.

"Mickey, you old dog. How are you?" Shauna asked. "Where are the rest of our little house trolls?"

"Oh they are around," explained Janet. "Just give them time."

Roan asked everyone to gather in the living room, as he wanted to explain the last two weeks and tell them what the next few would be like.

He began, "The pilgrimage was filled with many prayers, spiritual growth and a release of pain that had been pushed down into my soul so far, I didn't even remember it was there. But that's all gone now, my sight has been restored and our friend Maggie is engaged to an old friend she reconnected with in Medjugorje. Our tour of Rome was excellent and we will explain in more detail later. There has been a fire in the restaurant, so I will have to go back in a couple of days to make sure it's cleaned up properly and we can open as scheduled. Shauna and Katie are expanding the business, Janet is leaving for a new assignment and I'm going to work on some pottery for the shop. THEN, I am going to find a way to serve the church, possibly as a permanent deacon. That's it in a nutshell!"

"I'd say that's quite enough for a couple of weeks, don't you all?" replied Shauna.

Katie was delighted and said, "We are ready to take on the world now. It's all so exciting!"

"Well, give us a couple of days to get our feet back on the ground, would ya?" exclaimed Shauna. "Roan and I really need to settle in, get organized and see where we need to be. We want this organized to make our time used most efficiently and right now I could use some supper and a glass of wine".

"That's our cue to leave," said Jim. "We can get in touch in the morning. Come on Katie."

Marie said there was a meal prepared for them in the oven and Janet said she would be leaving tomorrow afternoon for her new assignment. Time was moving ahead as it should.

After everyone disbursed, Shauna, Roan and Conor sat down to get reacquainted.

Conor was curious about Roan's vision and asked, "What was it like to get your sight back, Dad? Did it happen all at once?"

"It went in stages, son," explained Roan. "There was a series of events and it actually hurt so badly I had to go to the clinic in Chitluk to get some drops for my eyes. Then, when we were having coffee before Mass, I got my sight back—just like that and I could see the sun spinning. It was more than a miracle, son, it was simply amazing."

"Gee Dad," Conor exclaimed. "That is a miracle. I'll have to tell Jimmy about it tomorrow at school."

"By the way, young man," asked Shauna. Why weren't you in school today when we got home?"

"In-service day, Mom," Conor explained. "We have a couple of those in the next few weeks and there is a parent-teacher conference next week, so I'm glad you're back."

About that time, Tyler came strolling in with the tail of a mouse hanging out of his mouth.

"Oh that's gross, Tyler," screamed Conor. "Get rid of the mouse."

Tyler did exactly as he was told and opened his mouth. The mouse fell out and ran away. It ran directly into Flash's house, took one look at the HUGE rodent sleeping in a little bed and ran back out into the living room. Tyler glared at the mouse, as it ran to the doggie door and out of the house.

"Hmm, well, time to eat and then we can unpack," Shauna said with a yawn. "Okay, Conor. Let's chow down. Call Janet and we can get started."

Janet came downstairs, all dressed up and said, "I'm sorry but I can't stay for supper because I have a date with a doctor I met when I applied for my new job. He's taking me down to Minneapolis tomorrow afternoon."

"Oh ladeda," giggled Conor. "Janet's got a boyfriend. Janet's got a boyfriend!"

"Have a nice time, Janet," replied Roan. "It's a lovely night out there and I'm sure you will have a good time."

The doorbell rang and a very handsome young man asked for Janet.

Roan gave him the once over and said, "You take care of our Janet, please. She's very special to us, so show her a good time."

"Yes, sir. I will," blushed the young man. "Good night, Sir."

Roan walked away chuckling and you could see the look on Conor's face. He must have said to himself, *I hope Dad doesn't do that to me when I start dating.*

They ate quietly, then everyone went to bed early. But Roan went out to the office to go over his notes for the next morning and send a fax to Inspector Cresswell in Rome to relay the events of the past two days. So far, so good. He was learning the importance of good organization from Shauna. He turned on the computer to get his messages and noticed one stood out. It read, *This isn't over.* Roan quickly forwarded this to Inspector Cresswell and deleted the message, so Shauna or Conor wouldn't see it.

He went to bed troubled over the message, but had other things on his mind which demanded more immediate attention.

Conor was up early to get to the school bus. Janet was packed, ready to leave, while Shauna was making breakfast. The express driver knocked on the front door with the cartons from their trip.

"Well, you are certainly early, Bob," sighed Shauna. "I expected you a little later. Would you like a latte to go?"

"Oh yes, Mrs. Sanderson," replied Bob. "That would be great."

Shauna gave him the coffee/white and decided she'd better open the boxes. The craft knife was in the kitchen, but she was too excited about the contents. Janet was leaving and she had to give her those gifts first. Shauna opened the carton from the leather goods store and picked out the jewellery box and scarf she's selected in Rome. She added those to the items she bought in Medjugorje, put them all in a lovely little bag and tied it with a silver ribbon.

Roan walked in the room and remarked, "Oh, I see the boxes have arrived. That was quick."

He looked at the bag and asked, "Is that for Janet?"

"Yes," replied Shauna. "I got her things ready since she's leaving today. I'll really miss her."

The phone rang and Roan answered it, "Oh, right. We can do that. Charles, Marie and I can meet you there about ten, if that's okay?"

"Who is that, Roan?" inquired Shauna.

"The insurance agent and contractors want Charles and Marie over at the construction site to do a walk through," replied Roan. "Then you and Katie can get to the decorating part. They could be ready to move in within two weeks."

Roan called Charles and Marie on the intercom and made arrangements with them to be over at their house at ten. Shauna finished uncrating her gifts and took the items into the bedroom. After breakfast it was time to go into town to meet Katie at the Gallery. And she had to take her memory sticks in to make CDs to send out photos for family and friends.

Roan drove up to Charles and Marie's reconstructed home, pulled into the driveway and got out to a warm reception.

Charles greeted Roan saying, "Welcome home, Roan. It's a miracle you can see again. And since you CAN see, you will notice how beautifully the house came out. Gone are the ashes and devastation, here is my lovely four-square home again, only better."

"Hey, it looks super, Charles," sighed Roan. "I'm so please it came out the way you wanted. Have you seen inside yet?"

"Yes, it's magnificent," exuded Charles. "Just look at how much bigger and better the house is now. And the additions you insisted upon really give us the room we need. Come on in and check out this kitchen. It's better than the restaurant!"

The kitchen has an eight-burner professional stove, a large, upright freezer, a double refrigerator and two dishwashers. There were scores of limed oak cabinets, tiled walls in a terra cotta colour and earth-toned tile on the floor. The Belfast sink was white enamel, which came along with the latest faucet, plus instant hot water and spray attachment. And, to top it off at the stove, there was a swing faucet to fill pots without having to bring them over to the sink. The double built-in ovens were next to the stove and a large microwave oven stood on its own counter with space for pans beneath. This is the kitchen a professional chef (like Charles) would give his eye teeth for.

The hallways were painted in a deep mink brown, with white wainscoting and ceiling medallions. Period Victorian fixtures and sconces adorned the walls and ceiling. The living room was painted in a light beige with a feature fireplace of limestone along the west wall. Sconces flanked either side, with bookcases along the lower half of each wall. The dining room was separate from the living room and the French doors on the South wall led to the conservatory. The family/great room was on the East portion of the house behind the kitchen, with a passthrough to the breakfast nook. Each room flowed into the next. And since the painting had been finished, it was time to select furnishings.

Charles showed Roan the state of the art security system, which connected directly to the fire department and rescue squad in case of another incident. The panels could be accessed from any room in the house, including the conservatory. It also controlled the environmental systems, including air exchange, air conditioning and the radiant heat flooring. It raised and lowered the outside light levels, turned on other systems and even controlled the stereo! The security cameras, strategically placed around the house, kept intruders at bay and helped Marie keep tabs on the children when they were outside playing. If it was new, Roan had it installed. Seeing all of these new electronic inventions gave Roan an idea.

The contractors followed Charles into the house, along with the city inspector. It was time to sign off on the house, as all the mechanicals and structure had passed inspection. Charles finally had his keys and the look on Marie's face was priceless. The landscapers were next and due within a few days to lay the lawn, plant new trees and complete the raised flower beds around the perimeter of the house.

The insurance agent had Charles and Marie sign their new policy and Roan gave the agent a check for five years' fees. That way, Charles and Marie didn't have to worry about that part of their lives and could rebuild financially without worry. Stephen Brennan had also paid the taxes on the house for five years for the same reason. Or maybe we should say Miss Lulabelle paid everything.

Roan spoke up and said, "Okay, you two. It's time to go down to the Gallery. Shauna and Katie are ready to get started on decorating this palace and they have some fantastic ideas. And, now, with them going into the decorating business with furniture, too, they will have some great designs to show you. Now get going and congratulations."

Marie hugged Roan and walked outside with Charles. Roan asked the contractors to hang back, because he wanted to discuss the quiet room addition and some security concerns, which needed to be addressed immediately. He wasn't taking any chances with his family's safety in light of the e-mail he received.

Roan asked the contractors to come back to the house with him, because although the addition could wait, he wanted the security system installed right away.

He said, "Listen, fellas. I don't want Shauna to know about this yet, but just say (if she asks you about it) that when I saw Charles' new system, I wanted one, too. That's the truth and let's leave it at that, okay? And while you are at it, give me a bid on demolishing the west wall at the Gallery. We are expanding. I'd like the same security system in the Gallery as well."

Once they arrived at the lake house, Roan showed the contractors around and explained he wanted the same system they had just installed, but with several additions.

"We need to make this self-sufficient," explained Roan. "In other words, if the electricity went off, an interior back-up system could kick in without interruption of service. And I also want bullet-proof glass in the addition. All windows, doors, entrances and exits in the house need to be securely alarmed."

"But Roan," remarked one of the men. "Why do you need this heavy security on the house? Your folks never needed it."

"We've had a significant threat on our lives recently and we don't know who it is," explained Roan. "I just don't want to take any chances, understand?"

"Yeah, sure," replied the contractor. "I'll get on it now."

Roan dialed his cell to tell Shauna and Katie that Charles and Marie were on their way down to the Gallery.

Shauna was excited and said, "We are all ready here, Roan. We have books, swatches, paint colours we can match to. You name it, we probably have it. Katie has been gathering all this information while we were gone and we are just waiting for them to get here. This is so exciting!"

"I have some calls to make about the restaurant, so I will see you when you get home, Honey," replied Roan. "I will probably have to go down to Minneapolis to check on the progress in a day or two."

"Okay, Dear," responded Shauna. "See you at home."

He had another call to make. This was to a friend of his in the executive security business in Arizona. It might be a good idea to fly down there to meet with him about hiring an under cover agent to work in the Gallery or as an assistant at the house.

Roan dialed the private office number.

A man answered and said, "JB here. Roan, is that you?"

"Yes JB, it's me," Roan replied. "I have a matter I need to discuss with you and it's rather urgent. What's your schedule like in the next couple of days?"

"Oh, a little bit of this. A little bit of that. Nothing really major. Feel like a round of golf?" asked JB. "I can arrange my time any way you need me to, Roan. This sounds serious."

"It is," Roan responded. "But I don't want to talk on the phone. How about seeing you on Wednesday. I'm flying down in the company jet. And I'll arrange for a vehicle while I am there."

"Great Roan," exclaimed JB. "It'll be super to see you after all these years."

Roan called the restaurant, then his pilots and the car rental company. The wheels were in motion for this next portion of the trip. He would tell Shauna about the e-mail at supper tonight.

There were some e-mails on the computer waiting for a response. Roan looked at the list and saw nothing of concern. He did see one from Inspector Cresswell and opened it.

The contents read, *'DuMonde seen in Paris yesterday. Assume he is on an assignment. Am having him followed where ever he goes if at all possible. Will keep you informed. Cresswell.'*

Roan sent a response telling the Inspector about the security plans being installed immediately and that he is considering having executive protection in the house until this is over. And since Shauna and Katie will be going to Rome for a buying trip, it would be wise to keep the Inspector aware of their schedule before they arrive. Soon it was time for Shauna to get home, so Roan took out some meat from the freezer and looked in the pantry for something to go with it. Just then, the door opened. It was Conor coming home from school. Jimmy was with him and they were hungry…they were always hungry!

"Hey Dad," yelled Conor. "We're hungry. Can we order a pizza and stuff?"

Roan put the meat back in the freezer and replied, "Okay you guys. What do you want on it?"

"Everything and better make it two. We had practice today," said Conor.

Roan mumbled to himself, *Practice? Practice of what? I've been away two weeks and my son has 'practice'? I'm getting too old for this!*

"Okay, everything, sodas, salads and what else guys?" asked Roan.

"See if Mr. Young has any chocolate cake today. We LOVE his chocolate cake," giggled Conor.

Jimmy was already in the media room watching tv, with Conor coming in a fast second. Roan heard the garage door open and heard Shauna coming in with Marie and the kids.

"I just ordered pizza from Mr. Young's. I didn't even think about you, Charles and the kids, Marie. Sorry," Roan explained.

"We aren't staying Roan," said Marie. "Charles has a party booked for tonight and the kids will stay in their little play room at the back of the restaurant. We will eat there. But thanks for the offer."

Shauna waved at Marie and she and the kids left.

She could sense something was up with Roan and said, "Okay give, Mr. I know those wheels are spinning around in that head of yours. Is there something I should know?"

"Sit down for a second, Shauna," Roan explained. "We had a threatening e-mail from DuMonde. I don't know how he got the e-mail address here. I have NO idea what's happening, but I am increasing the security in the house—getting a system like Charles and Marie have, plus I am talking with someone in Arizona on Wednesday and have forwarded all of this information to Inspector Cresswell at Interpol."

"Oh, is that all?" cracked Shauna. "So glad I asked!"

"No that isn't all, Shauna," remarked Roan. "I've also decided to put the same type of system in the Gallery. It's probably a good idea anyway with the expansion of the shop and the new merchandise. And, if you think about it, the system can turn on the lights, handle the computer operation, regulate the heating and air, plus a lot more."

"That's a smart idea," said Shauna. "I definitely have no problem with that. Although I take some of this seriously, I can't let it run my life. But the added security for the shop will be very welcome. By the way, did you speak with the contractor about knocking out the wall?"

"Yes, I did," replied Roan. "He can get to it later this week and get all of the electronics added at the same time. It's a smart plan and while they are installing the system here at the house, the contractor will be working on the Quiet Room addition. I'll show you my ideas later this evening. I think the pizzas have arrived."

Mr. Young brought in two very large pizzas, two large bottles of soda, four salads and a beautiful chocolate cake. The boys bolted in from the media room without being told food was there.

Mr. Young delighted in seeing the boys and said, "Look at Conor now. He looks great. And look how he's grown—both of them. It's hard to watch them grow up so fast. Well, enjoy, folks."

"Thanks, Mr. Young," said Shauna. "Okay boys, let's eat!"

The evening went normally, with Shauna handing out gifts to Conor and Jimmy. Franco called from the restaurant, explaining the work was going well and they could be open as soon as Wednesday. Roan told Franco he would be down in the morning to inspect the work, arrange for a security system at the restaurant and the lake house down there, then would be going to Arizona on business for the day. Roan showed Shauna the plans for the Quiet Room, which she whole-heartedly approved.

Morning came as usual with the contractors there to install the new system. Shauna went into work until Roan left, then returned to supervise. Katie picked out furniture with Charles and Marie, along with their accent pieces, wallpaper and carpeting for the bedrooms. All was rolling along well. Friday, the contractors would tear down the dividing wall between the shops, install the new security system and begin on the Quiet Room. That's a lot of activity for three days!

Roan flew into the Phoenix airport to meet with JB Foster, the security expert. As the jet touched down, Roan felt a little more at ease knowing his family would have the best protection available. He went to the car rental counter, got his vehicle and drove into town. He went into SSS, Serpentine Security Systems and JB met him at the front counter.

"Roan, old friend," exclaimed JB Foster. "Glad to see you my man. Tell me, how is that new bride of yours? I seem to remember her from college—quite a looker if that's who I think it is."

"Yes, she is absolutely the most beautiful woman I have ever met, JB," explained Roan. "She's funny, smart as a whip, spiritual and really lovely. And she's a great mom. I'm a very fortunate man."

JB shouted at his receptionist, "Hey Judie. I'm off to the course with Roan. You need me, call. But don't. Okay?"

"Yes, sir. Got it," added Judie.

As they drove away from the office, Roan began to explain the problems they encountered with DuMonde in Bosnia and in Rome. There was no reason for someone like that to be stalking the Sandersons.

Roan asked JB, "Do you have any idea why this person would be stalking us? You know me well enough to know my past is an open book and I'm a pretty boring guy when you get right down to it. But it concerns me enough to come to Arizona to talk with you."

"I know Cresswell and he's the best Interpol has," explained JB. "If he is handling this, you can be assured everything is being done. However, if you feel you would like an added layer of security, my senior vice-president is a top notch Intel/Anti-terrorism Specialist, is anxious to get back into the field and out from behind a desk. I can loan her to you for a period of time. She could pose as your personal assistant. You said you have a lot going on these days and she is proficient in computer applications and research. She cooks well, is a fantastic photographer and makes a great cup of coffee. But she doesn't come cheap."

"Hey, money is no object these days, JB," said Roan. "Would she like to work with us for a few months?"

"Well, let's go ask her. You didn't really want to play golf in this heat anyway, did you?" responded JB. "But first, let's get some lunch. You'll like that."

The friends went to downtown Phoenix for lunch. The Mexican menu is always fresh at this local cafe and Roan was pleased to just sit without distractions, except for senoritas in their brightly coloured blouses. After a short lunch, they returned to the office to talk with JB's senior VP, Alexandra Simpson.

As they walked in, JB called to Ms. Simpson, who was interviewing a new recruit for their anti-terrorism unit. The company had contracts with independent contractors who supply protection specialists to executives and dignitaries in Iraq and the Middle East. They operated in the hot zones and sometimes, operatives didn't come home to their families. It takes a special type of person to have the commitment and training to accept assignments like these.

Roan was astonished at how petite Ms. Simpson is. As she walked over to meet him, she looked as if she couldn't even hold a gun, let alone fire one. But she indeed, was a Certified Investigator and Protection Specialist. As a matter of fact, she was one of the first women to be certified in this field in the country.

"Did you need me for something, JB?" asked Ms. Simpson. "I have that new recruit over there I need to finish interviewing."

"Alex, I want you to meet an old friend of mine, Roan Sanderson," explained JB. "He has a problem with the "Ghost" and I think this is an assignment you would really enjoy. Maybe Dennis can complete the interview?"

"The 'Ghost', are you kidding?" replied Alex. "That man has been the bane of my existence and I would love to put him away permanently. You bet I'm interested. Let me inform Dennis where we are and I'll be right back. Nice to meet you Mr. Sanderson."

After a few moments, Ms. Simpson returned and they went into JB's office to confer about the problems. Alex grabbed her coffee and sat in front of the desk, next to Roan.

"Let me tell you what's happened in the last two weeks," explained Roan. "For unexplained reasons, we have been stalked by this character DuMonde. He tracked us from Zagreb to Medjugorje, then onto Rome. My wife had a nightmare, which seemed VERY real, featuring this "Ghost" and now I have received an e-mail from him telling me it isn't over. Since you have had dealings with him and understand his methodology, do you feel I have valid concerns for my family and our safety?"

Alex looked directly at Roan and said, "Yes, you are right to seek help. The man is unpredictable. He pops up without warning and disappears the same way. We know he has killed and has no compunction about killing again. He gets a 'high' from the kill and from stalking his victims. Tell me, Mr. Sanderson, what have you done so far to protect your family?"

Roan quickly responded, "We are installing a state of the art security system this morning, both at our home and our store. We are expanding our store, so it's the right time to add a security system anyway, but we also are providing one for our restaurant, our home in the Twin Cities and the small house I own on the lake. We never needed anything before, but now it's essential. Everything will have an internal back-up system, controlled from the house, just in case the power is cut for any reason. Our generator has the capacity to handle much more than we have on it now anyway."

"That's an excellent beginning, Mr. Sanderson," expressed Alex. "But why do you want me to come out to assist? You really don't know anything about me or that I can actually handle this type of job. But here's my resume to read over. It assure you I am totally capable of this kind of assignment."

JB interrupted and explained, "It might be good to keep a low profile on this one, Alex, because Roan is gone a lot these days getting his restaurant up and running. And, with the business his wife has, her needs for protection must be met. Sometimes they can't be in the same place at the same time. And they have a teenage son to consider as well. If you went under cover as his personal assistant, that wouldn't attract attention, giving you access to every part of their lives and I think you would enjoy the change of pace from this nutty office. Besides, this is your area of expertise and you haven't been able to use it lately."

"This sounds good, JB," expressed Alex. "But I would need some time to tie up loose ends, deal with the house and the dog, etc. When are you considering my 'appearance' up in Minnesota?"

JB continued, "I think it's safe to bring you up there in about two weeks. Their nurse just left, as they have had a series of accidents over the past six months. That had nothing to do with this, but their work load has gotten pretty heavy and being an assistant would be an ideal cover. Your benefits here will continue and we'll take care of the apartment, the dog, etc. I'd say it's a nice assignment and you can make a difference. Just think, you might be the one to bring down DuMonde."

"I like the idea a lot," expressed Alex. "But what about the money? What's on offer?"

Roan always loved this part and said, "I was thinking around $80,000 for your part and $40,000 to the agency for supplying you. Is that fair for both of you?"

"How long I am going to be up there?" asked Alex.

"About two to four months, depending on how the threat diminishes or if you catch the bastard," explained Roan. "And who knows, I could steal you away from JB for my own company. What do you think of that?"

"Oh I don't think so," replied JB. "She's mine and I couldn't run this place without her. Alex, here is a dossier on Roan and his companies for you to review. It will give you a detailed background on what he's been doing the past few years. If you are satisfied with the background and the other details, I assume we have a go ahead."

"Is that a deal then, JB and Alex?" asked Roan. "I hope I can count on you."

Alexandra nodded her head in approval and they all shook hands on it.

"I'll draw up the contract for you to sign, fax it to you in Bemidji and in two weeks, you will have a new assistant," said JB.

"Great," said Roan. "I look forward to working with you Alex. Is that what you want to be called, Alex?"

"Yes, that's fine," she replied. "But just in case, I will use a different last name, say Baker. And remember, I will have a fire arm with me. I will need a place to lock it up, say, in a closet safe, if possible."

"I have a place all set up at the house," explained Roan. "The house is very large and you can have your pick of location in it. Whatever you need is probably there now and if not, I'll make sure it is."

"Then thank you Roan," agreed Alex. "I look forward to working with you and your family. It will be a nice respite from this chaos!"

"Oh, one more thing, Alex," Roan asked. "Do you have a current passport, because there will be International travel involved in a couple of months. You'll get to meet Inspector Cresswell from Interpol, too."

"Yes, I do. It's always with me," responded Alex. "I know Cresswell a little. We worked on an assignment in Beruit a few years back. Good man."

"Fine, then I need to get back home to the business," said Roan. "It's rather wild there this week."

Roan departed and drove directly to the airport. Captain Marks was ready to leave, as a storm front was moving in and he wanted to beat it. That was just fine with Roan, as he had no desire to be in another plane crash, especially in his own plane.

Upon arrival, Roan went directly home. The family had eaten supper and Conor was ready for bed. It was a good time to talk with Shauna about hiring Alex.

Roan walked over to Shauna, who was at her desk in the studio and said, "I hired an Intel/Anti-terrorism Specialist named Alexandra Simpson. She's JB's right hand at SSS, actually his senior VP and the first woman in the country to be certified as an executive protection specialist. She will be well suited to the task of my 'personal assistant' and I don't want anyone else, except Stephen to know who she is. Not Katie or Jim, nor Conor or Jimmy. This must not get out, because it will compromise her cover if anyone else knows."

Shauna replied, "I agree. No one else will know. And right now, you really DO need an assistant because I am certainly going to be busy with all my contracts here and in the Cities. Don't forget I have those designs to do for the architects' homes, too. When will she be here?"

"I have scheduled her to be here in two weeks, so she can tie up her projects there," replied Roan. "And she will be going with you to Rome and wherever when you and Katie go on your buying trips for the store."

"That should be fun for her, too," said Shauna. "This will work out well."

Roan began to yawn and explained, "I need sleep. This has been a long day. Oh, by the way, did they finish the security system today?"

"Tomorrow," replied Shauna. "They needed additional cables or something for the Quiet Room addition. The store will be finished on Friday and the little house on Saturday. I figured you really wouldn't sell it and that house is serving us well when we have lots of guests."

"Lets get some rest, Honey," said Roan sleepily. "I'm done in."

They went to bed with more confidence in their security. Shauna set the portion of the system which had been completed, then joined Roan for a restful night.

Chapter Ten

The tapping of rain on the bedroom's French doors woke Roan at 4:30 AM the following morning. He rose quietly from the comfort of his bed and walked out into the living room. The binoculars were on the end table, so he picked them up to search the lake for any activity. Just as dawn was breaking over the Southwestern beach, Roan spotted a diminutive figure—a child he thought. But focusing a little closer, he could see a slight woman, barely a wisp of a thing. A tiny white animal bobbed up and down next to her as she walked along the beach.

That's her—she's the one, Roan murmured. He almost dropped the bins, raced to change into his sweats, picked up his security remote and ran out the front door. As Roan ran down to the south shore, he eventually slowed, as not to frighten the woman. He got close enough to see how frail she was. The fragile lady was clad in a white turtle neck with navy pullover, white slacks and walking shoes. This morning she used a cane to steady herself against the morning dampness. She seemed unremarkable to Roan and yet...

As Roan approached, the little dog ran to him and wagged its tail.

Roan bent down to say hello, "Hello little one. Out walking with mommie?"

The woman spoke sharply to the little dog, "Trixie, get back here and don't annoy the nice man.!

"It's fine, Ma'm," said Roan. "She's a playful pup. Must smell my animals on me."

As the dawn shown clearer and the rain vanished, he could see the sparkling blue eyes behind the scowl.

Roan suddenly realised he was staring and blurted out, "Oh, I'm so sorry for staring at you. It's just that you remind me of someone who meant a great deal to me and I miss her. Someone said they'd seen her on the beach, but…"

Almost on que, the sweet lady looked up and exclaimed, "I get a lot of that lately."

Roan was stunned. Unable to put two thoughts together, he simply stared, then caught himself again. This time, he turned beet red.

"Well, let me tell you who I am not…" she continued. "I am NOT Lulabelle Lavinia LaFontaine. Who I AM is Millie Forsythe—Lula's twin sister."

Roan nearly fell over from shock.

"I know," she said. "Quite a surprise, isn't it?"

"But, you're so different, except, somehow the same," gasped Roan.

"That's how twins are, Roan," she explained. "Yes, I know who you are and that's why I didn't walk away from you just now. I've lived on this lake a long time and knew your parents very well. I watched you grow up and become the man you are today. And I watched the video of you and Shauna being married. She's a wonderful woman, so much like your mother."

Roan walked over to a retaining wall and sat down. Millie joined him and continued the conversation.

"There were three of us, Lulabelle, Emmeline and me," she explained. "Emmie was the oldest and passed away a few years ago. Then Lula and I remained and we lived together for a couple of years after her husband passed away. I never wanted to interfere with her success, because she earned it. Her flamboyant style was not mine, although I am also a writer. I do historical fiction and non-fiction, write for universities and encyclopaedias. I live in Ireland much of the year, but like the summers here in Minnesota best."

"But why haven't I seen you before now," asked Roan. "Surely our paths must have crossed over the years."

"Oh they have, they have," remarked Millie. "You just weren't aware of me. After all, you probably thought I was Lula. Children don't always make that distinction, you know."

Roan was still in shock seeing this woman who was remarkably like his dear friend.

He smiled and said, "Would you like to come up to the house for coffee or lunch sometime, Millie?"

"Yes, Roan," she replied. "That would be lovely. I want to meet your family in person, too. I think Shauna will be in for the same shock you were! Here's my business card and you can give me a call when your schedule permits. I know you have a restaurant to run these days."

How did she know that? thought Roan. *Well, it WAS in the papers and on tv I guess.*

"I'll take Trixie back home now," Millie replied. "I don't want her getting a chill."

"Goodbye, Millie," said Roan. "Good to meet you. Please come by soon so we can continue our conversation and you can meet my family."

Millie smiled as she walked back up the beach and Roan went back home to tell Shauna who he'd met. He pushed the button on the remote and walked inside. Shauna was making breakfast and a little concerned when she couldn't find her husband.

"Oh sorry, dear," remarked Roan. "The rain woke me up and I saw someone on the beach. You will never in a million years guess who I met this morning. Her name is Millie Forsythe and she's Lulabelle's twin sister."

"Who?" asked Shauna. "Lulabelle's twin sister? I didn't think she had any family at all and now you are telling me she has a twin?"

"Yes, and you will be meeting her soon because I invited her for coffee when she's free one day," explained Roan. "She's amazing and so much like Lulabelle, but also very different from her. It's like a Ying and Yang combination."

"Whew, this is amazing," remarked Shauna. "I can't wait to meet her and get to know her. How long has she been around here?"

"Apparently all my life and probably more," explained Roan. "She watched me grow up, knew the folks and also lives part-time in Ireland. Like I said, an amazing woman. Did you know, there were actually three sisters?

Emmeline died a few years ago, leaving 'Lula' and Millie. I'm just astonished."

"Maybe this clarifies why it seems as if Lulabelle is still alive," mused Shauna. "Maybe Millie is responsible for some of the activity we have accredited to Lulabelle?"

"Well, maybe," explained Roan. "But I kind of doubt it. Millie seems to be her own person and said she never wanted to steal Lulabelle's thunder. I'll tell you this, though, I want to know all about these two women. It might answer a lot of my questions."

Shauna set the breakfast on the table and explained about the designs and furnishings they picked out for Charles and Marie.

"I'm really excited for them," she said. "Even the wallpaper for the kids' rooms is great. Marie has a wonderful sense of style and everything goes so well with the paint they chose. The richness of the wood floors and oriental carpets, plus the symmetry of the accent pieces all blends so beautifully, I think they will love the results."

"Great," exclaimed Roan. "I can't wait to see the finished product. You know, there are two apartments above that store as well and neither is rented. If we kit them out, we can use those as guest apartments when we have visitors. I'm thinking about when Conor graduates, during the Holidays or for business guests."

"Oh I think Katie would love to have a go at those, Roan," said Shauna with great glee. "I'll let her know she has a free hand! Oh, and Jim's web site for the Gallery? He should have that up and running soon."

"Fantastic," replied Roan. "This is all coming together well. I'll be here to finish up the security system with the contractors and get the house ready for them to begin the construction of the Quiet Room. If they get done by afternoon, I'll come down to the store and help you and Katie."

About an hour later the contractors were ready to finish the installation and allow for connecting cables once the addition was completed. By eleven, Roan was ready to go down to the Gallery and look at what Katie and his friends had picked out for their home. The new statues and other items Shauna bought in Medjugorje and Rome had arrived. They were beautifully displayed in the store windows. The colours were rich and bold. They made quite a statement. There was a small sign indicating the Gallery would be expanding in the next week and to come in a visit the new design studio. Katie was in the basement framing some of the posters. This certainly wasn't a hobby, but a thriving business, due to the talent and drive of two very determined ladies.

Jim had moved some of the furniture back from the connecting wall and relocated the cash register and phones. Luckily the counter was modular and disassembled easily. Now all they had to do is take out the wall, clean up the mess and clean the other side. Katie had ordered the blue stone tiles for the floor, paint and light fixtures. There were two structural posts inside the wall and once the remaining sections had been taken out, the posts would be made into an arch, as a decorating feature, keeping the support in place.

The security system installation team was working on the existing structure, ready for the next phase. They put in all their control pads and wiring, then went upstairs to the apartments on both sides and installed those systems. It was like an army of cables, wire and workers. There were three women on the team, as well. Shauna had coffee and donuts available for everyone when they took breaks. Only Katie, Jim, Roan and Shauna would know the security codes, because they would be set after installation. Additional generators were installed in the basements and electrical needs were assessed to be certain the new load could be handled effectively. Roan was very satisfied.

Stephen Brennan came by to say hello. He hadn't seen Roan since his eyesight had returned. He was thrilled to see Roan so involved.

He expressed himself in his usual manner, "You old salt, you. You look fantastic. See, I told you so."

"Hey Steve," laughed Roan. "What do you think of our expansion here? Quite the production, I'd say."

Stephen replied, "Oh yeah, it is. But it isn't unexpected. These ladies are amazing."

"Steve, I met someone this morning I want to ask you about," said Roan. Her name is Millie Forsythe and I could have sworn she was Lulabelle. It really took me aback."

Attorney Brennan put on his poker-face and said, "I have heard of someone who resembled Lulabelle, but I don't know if I ever met her. That's kind of weird, isn't it?"

"Well, the best part is, she's Lulabelle's twin sister," Roan explained. "And the strangest part is she knew my parents and watched me grow up. I wonder why I have never heard of her before and why didn't she inherit the estate?"

"Oh that is strange," said Brennan. "And you spoke with this woman for a while?"

"Yes, I did," explained Roan. "She's coming up to have coffee with us soon and I want to get to know her. She's so much like Lulabelle, but then again, very different. She's very much her own person and not like our scatterbrained Lulabelle."

Stephen Brennan couldn't tell Roan he knew Millie. And he would never tell Roan her involvement in Lulabelle's life. Only he knew the extent of her association with her sister's legacy and wasn't about to tell Roan, although he was bursting to do it. Sometimes secrets must be kept and although the attorney-client privilege didn't exist anymore, his with Millie did. He was bound by oath not to say anything, but with Roan, he would find out at some point. Stephen had to be on his guard not to let it slip.

Stephen spotted Shauna in the back of the Gallery and went over to say hello.

He grabbed her and gave her a big hug, saying, "Ooo, if you were still single, I'd take you away to my grand cabin in the woods!"

Shauna replied, "Grand cabin? I thought it was a shack where the deer and antelope play rock music and the bears eat your food and dump on your yard!"

Brennan pretended to be stabbed in the heart and clutched his chest, exhorting, "You cut me to the quick, my lady. I, but a poor attorney, wouldst sweep thee off thy feet and take thee to the land of eternal bliss."

Shauna looked as if she would hit him, then composed herself for a reply.

"Naah, I don thin so buddy boy," responded Shauna. "You are one silly man, Stephen. We need to find you a good woman!"

Mr. Brennan shook his head, took a bow and went back to work.

Roan came over to Shauna and asked, "So what was that all about? He was unusually cheerful, wasn't he?"

"Yes, too cheerful," replied Shauna. "He's hiding something."

"One of your hunches, Shauna?" asked Roan.

Shauna tapped her chin with a pencil and said, "Yes, call it a hunch. I'll let you know more when I get a sense of what he's up to. I just know there is something he doesn't want us to know."

Roan shook his head and explained he would go back out to the house. He needed to make some calls, then start supper.

"Pork chops okay with you for tonight?" Roan asked. "I can do some shopping too, if you need me to."

Shauna rummaged around in her purse and gave Roan the shopping list.

"Here you go, Sweetie," smiled Shauna. "That way I can spend the time here and finish up the installation. I'll be home around 4:30. Thanks."

Roan waved goodbye and drove to the market. He picked up the items on the list, added some wine, extra chocolate ice cream and went home. He arrived to find the contract in the fax machine and some e-mails which needed to be attended to. One of them was rather disturbing. It was from DuMonde again.

It read, *'I know what you're doing, what you have planned and who you have contacted. It won't work. Your life is in my hands. Be afraid. Be very afraid. MDM.'*

Roan didn't take this lightly and forwarded the e-mail to Cresswell, suggesting they communicate in another way. Maybe the phone and Internet lines had been hacked. Possibly someone on the inside was forwarding information to DuMonde, but who? Maybe this was simply a blind threat. DuMonde didn't know anything, but was calling his bluff. Was Cresswell corrupt?

This is getting too complicated and I don't know who's doing this or why, thought Roan. *I'll save this and show Shauna tonight.*

Roan put the groceries away and began making supper. Conor came in from school and opened the fridge.

"Hey hey, son, get some fruit," yelled Roan. "And don't leave the door open."

"Aw Dad, come on," replied Conor.

"You will be eating in about half an hour when your Mom gets home. You can wait that long," expressed Roan. "Restraint is something you need to learn, young man."

"Yes, sir," responded a dejected Conor.

Just then, Shauna drove into the garage.

She burst in with a huge smile on her face and said, "We just got an inquiry from the university to redecorate the girls' dorms and several of the office buildings. Katie is going over Monday to survey the buildings, meet with the board of directors and take some photographs. We can make up a bid and should know in a few weeks if it's been accepted. Isn't that fantastic Roan?"

Roan kissed Shauna and said, "Looks like you are really on your way, Honey. That's great."

In about ten minutes, Roan called his family for supper. Conor was impressed with pork chops. He hadn't had those yet.

"Hey good grub there, Dad," laughed Conor. "Got any more?"

"The boy is still a bottomless pit, I swear," exclaimed Roan. "Yes, here are a couple more, some corn and more potatoes. Is that enough?"

"Sure, but what's for dessert?" asked Conor.

Shauna couldn't keep a straight face and said, "Welcome to parenthood, Roan!"

They finished eating, while Conor went to his room to study. Roan asked Shauna to come out to the studio for a bit. He wanted to show her the e-mail he received. They took their wine and walked into the living room of the studio. After they sat down, Roan handed Shauna the copy.

Shauna read the e-mail and handed it back to Roan saying, "Do you think this is a blind ruse or do you think this is actually from DuMonde? I think there are more people involved in this than just one man. Could this be someone in Interpol who has access to the information about us? But why? We have no enemies. I really don't get it, Roan."

"Let's go outside for a little walk along the beach," Roan said.

As he said this, he motioned for Shauna not to say anything. He imitated a phone caller, a bug—anything to indicate to Shauna the house might have a listening device in it. They walked out to the beach and Roan made his concerns known to Shauna succinctly.

"I think the house is wired for more than security. And those GPS buttons Cresswell gave us in Rome? Let's get rid of them, because they could have been switched into more than a tracking device. Is there anything new in the house other than the things we brought back from our trip like flowers or strange food stuffs?"

Shauna thought for a moment and responded, "Katie brought flowers for our return, but those were from the grocery. We can look at them if you want. But that's it. Maybe you should contact JB and have Alex bring up some sweeping equipment with her, just in case something IS in this house."

"I have another thought," said Roan. "Take your cell phone apart and see if there is anything inside which could be a device. I'll do the same. And let's walk around the house and look at all the phones, the lamps, under tables— anywhere you think someone could have planted a device of any kind. If we have to wait for Alex, let's use the time wisely."

"Don't give out a clue to anyone else, especially Conor or Katie," said Roan. "They don't need to know anything now, because we don't have anything concrete to tell anyone. If it's Cresswell on the graft, we have to catch him at it. And if it's someone else, we need to find them. I know Alex will help us, but this is the time to be proactive. And this business with Stephen? I'm beginning not to trust anyone."

They walked back inside, popped some corn and put on a movie. Shauna brought her phone over to Roan, who pulled it apart and found nothing. He did the same with his cell phone. Nothing again. Then Shauna brought out her fanny pack, tore open the lining and pulled out the small disc Cresswell had given her. She put it inside a small plastic craft bag and gave it to Roan. He checked his jacket and did the same with the one in the lining. He locked them up in the safe to give to Alex when she arrived. The sound of the movie muffled them walking around the rooms looking for devices. When it came to the computer, Roan found something that didn't belong there. He waved at Shauna from across the room and motioned for her to come over.

Roan wrote on a pad of paper, 'Look behind the computer tower. There is a small, round disc, like the ones from Rome, stuck on the back by the Internet connection.'

Shauna looked at it, peeled it off and took it back to the studio, placing it in another plastic bag.

She took the pad of paper and scribbled, 'It looks like there could be more of these throughout the house. I will look in the morning after Conor goes to school. I'm guessing someone who didn't belong to the security company must have put these in here.'

Roan shook his head and they settled in to watch the movie.

Jim called from the shop the next morning at 8:00 to tell Roan the wall was about to be knocked out. Roan said he would be right down, but Shauna had something to do out at the house. She would be in tomorrow morning.

Shauna got dressed and proceeded to look for more buttons after Conor left for school. It didn't take her long to find more. A lot more.

Then Shauna got the bright idea to look for surveillance cameras. She knew the ones for the outside were pointed in specific directions. The ones inside were aimed at general areas of the house. However, she wasn't comfortable not knowing if there were some which were not connected to their system, but to somewhere else. And she found what she was looking for.

Hidden in several places in the living room, behind plants and inside the china hutch were tiny spy cameras. Shauna put duck tape over the lenses and pulled them out to see what type of wires were attached. The lines were green and red. The ones on the system were white, blue and yellow. She kept looking and found one in their bedroom, one in Conor's room. In fact, there were spy cameras in every room, including the bathrooms, downstairs in Charles and Marie's rooms, even in the wine cellar. Shauna taped every one of them, wrote down their location on the pad and waited for Roan to call. When he did, she was very cryptic about her conversation.

"Oh hi Dear," said Shauna gleefully. "How is everything going at the demolition?"

Roan said, "Fine Honey. Are you coming down this afternoon?"

"No, Roan," explained Shauna. "I found some ants in the kitchen and am waiting for the exterminator to get rid of them. Maybe you would like to talk with him. He should be here in about an hour."

Roan picked up on the word 'ants' meaning bugs and replied, "Sure, they don't need me here right now, so I can come home."

"Thanks, Honey," Shauna responded. "You are so much better at this than I am. I hate these creepy crawlers."

"See you in a bit," acknowledged Roan.

When he got home, there were thirty buttons in plastic bags and twenty spy cameras with duck tape on them. Shauna had already written her descriptions of where she found them and how many, but she wasn't sure she found them all. Just then, they heard a vehicle drive up.

Roan looked out the window and exclaimed, "It's a man from the security company. Hide these bags. Say nothing and go into the media room. I'll switch on the video cameras and see if they get a picture of this guy. If he's legit, that's fine, but if not, at least we have a record of who he is."

Roan switched on the cameras, activated his security code and followed Shauna into the room. The man knocked on the door, called out the Sanderson's name, trying the door—hard—then walked away, possibly trying to find an open door. The telephone rang but the answering machine picked up on the first ring. Roan could see the man walking around the perimeter of the house, checking doors, peering in the windows. His uniform looked right, but Roan didn't recognize him. He was a heavy set man, maybe in his 50's, with what looked like a dark blond wig and thick glasses. He was tall, about 6'1" and had broad, hunched shoulders.

Once the man was gone, Roan pulled the video tape and called the owner of the company to verify the man had been sent out for a reason.

Frank Smart, the owner of the security firm came out immediately after Roan's call. Roan asked to go over the invoice with him and since he trusted this man, Roan asked him to view the tape.

"Frank, I have known you a long time and I want you to tell me why someone from your firm would be coming back so soon without calling us to arrange a time," remarked Roan. "Please look at this tape and tell me if you know the man on it."

Mr. Smart looked at the tape and said, "Roan, I know all my men and I have never seen this one before. I haven't hired anyone recently and all my men have been with me for years. You know most of them. What's going on Roan?"

Roan showed Frank the additional cameras placed throughout the house. The man probably couldn't get reception on them, so he came out to check out why.

Frank shook his head and said, "Let me go out to my car and get some testing equipment to see that everything is working properly. That will tell us if there is a problem with the system, Roan."

Shauna came out of the media room with a few additional bugs and Roan put his finger up to his lips. Frank came back with scanning equipment and it detected listening and video devices which were not part of their security plan. As each was detected, Frank pulled it away from its hiding place and put it in a jar filled with oil. He spent almost three houses looking over the house. Once he was satisfied all the bugs were removed, he felt free to talk.

"This is a real mess, Roan," explained Mr. Smart. "Someone has gone to extraordinary lengths to compromise the security here. This is the kind of crap Interpol used in the past—several years ago. They certainly aren't ours."

"Interpol?" asked Roan. "Would they double up on the system here?"

"Roan," continued Mr. Smart. "Our company has the highest government security clearance possible, because we do systems for the Defense Department, Bureau of Indian Affairs and the CTB, the private government security contractor. No, Interpol wouldn't do this kind of job."

"But could someone with past Interpol connections or training pull this off?" asked Roan.

"Possibly," replied Smart. "This is some nasty stuff, Roan. I'll take a copy of the tape and see if my friends at the CTB can identify the man on it."

Roan quickly copied the tape and gave it to Mr. Smart.

"I'll call you when I get something," Smart retorted. "In the meantime, act normally and don't say or do anything to make them suspicious. Bye Shauna."

Roan made two copies of the tape and placed each in a separate safe in the house. He placed the remaining bugs in there also, locked the doors and stared at his wife.

"Have we stumbled onto something we have no control over?" Roan whispered. "What the hell is going on here?"

Conor was spending the weekend with Jimmy, so he wouldn't be suspicious anything was wrong. Roan went into the bedroom and spotted something Shauna missed. It was a projection camera, obviously remote controlled. But he left it alone and asked Shauna to come into the bedroom.

He motioned for her to come into the bathroom and said softly, "Look at the top of the armoire and you will see a video camera. I have a feeling you will be experiencing a nightmare tonight."

Shauna walked through her bedroom and put a sweater away in the armoire, glancing up the top as she closed the doors.

Roan followed her back to the kitchen and Shauna became frightened, saying, "This really isn't funny now. It's getting serious and I'm concerned for our safety. Is there anything we can do?"

"Let's see what they have in store for tonight and hopefully it isn't a two-way camera. I'd just love to have signs made up, have them under the covers and pull them out when their 'nightmare' is over—give them a rating! It would just piss them off more and we'd be in bigger trouble, but just once, I'd like to stick it to them."

"Rambo Sanderson," Shauna giggled. "I know, I know, not funny."

Shauna ordered lasagne from Mr. Young and they ate a quiet dinner. The next few days would be peaceful. There were no e-mails from Mr. DuMonde. There were no strange people or phone calls. Nothing. Not even a nightmare. Shauna went into work the next morning and helped Katie clean up from the demolition. Mr. Smart was also there to "check the system" and found what he was looking for. Now he called in the CTB.

Monday morning, Mr. Smart set an appointment with Roan, Shauna and a CTB agent, who had connections with Interpol and MI-6 in the UK. He had viewed the tape and had a theory. They met at the apartment upstairs from the shop and would use it as a base of operations.

"Mrs. Sanderson, Mr. Sanderson. My name is Parker, Parker Fitzgerald. I'm with the International anti-terrorism squad of the CTB, *Counter Terrorism Bureau* and I want to give you what I know," he said with authority. "The man in the tape is obviously wearing a disguise. We know it isn't DuMonde. DuMonde is taller by three inches or more. It was difficult to tell because of the angle on the tape, but this man is smaller. The features have been altered to make him unrecognizable. But if you look on his left hand, there is a gold Irish Claddagh ring—maybe a wedding ring. It's all I have to go on, but it might be enough to identify him."

"Are you considering IRA involvement at all?" asked Mr. Smart.

"Most of our family and friends are of Irish/American heritage, Parker, but this doesn't make sense," explained Roan. "It must just be co-incidental."

"Whether it is or isn't hasn't been proven yet," Mr. Fitzgerald said. "I seem to have my work cut out for me and I would like to use this apartment for my team if I may? We'll pose as decorators on the project downstairs as our cover. I myself swing a mean hammer!"

"Oh yes, sure," responded Shauna. "Anything you need, we can supply."

Roan interjected, "We have someone coming in from SSS in Phoenix to work under cover in a little less than a week. Will you have problems with her being around?"

"No, that isn't a problem," he replied. "In fact, that's brilliant. Who is it, by the way?".

"Alexandra Simpson," Roan replied. "Are you familiar with her?"

Parker looked at Roan and said, "Yes, we have worked together in the past. She's an excellent operative and I have every confidence in her as an agent."

"Thanks," said Shauna. "That makes me feel better, too."

What Parker didn't tell anyone was that Alex had actually been his Fiancée years ago in college. His parents had broken them up because they didn't want their son marrying someone they hadn't picked out for him. The love was still there, only the years had gone by. He only knew she was with SSS and her reputation was sterling. Just the sound of her name brought up the old feelings. But he had to put his own memories aside to help this family.

Shauna had to figure out something to tell Katie about the extra 'workers', so she decided to tell her the wallpaper company had sent them to assist with placement of their displays and colour co-ordination on the walls to highlight their samples to their utmost advantage. That should do it. These men turned out to be a laugh a minute and they would make the task much more enjoyable. Only the Sandersons knew who they really were.

Roan made arrangements to have food and household items sent over to the apartment, while Shauna made certain the laundry was done, fresh towels placed in the bathroom and the apartment was aired out. And Roan offered the men the use of his office upstairs, as it had an additional bedroom.

Because the apartments over the vacant store hadn't been used for a few years, Roan decided it was wise to check the status of the appliances, wiring and plumbing. He found them woefully inadequate and had the contractors bring everything up to Code when they put in the new alarm system. He ordered a new refrigerator, stove, oven, microwave and laundry duo for each apartment, then checked with the other four tenants above the other stores to see about their appliances.

He realised he had been somewhat of an absentee landlord over the years and wanted to rectify that immediately. Tenants also told him some of the windows needed replacing and the heating systems weren't up to snuff. That's all it took for Roan to call the heating contractor and put in all new heating and air systems in all the apartments. And since the contractors were at the Gallery, he went down to talk to them about putting in all new windows, additional blown-in insulation if needed, check their mechanicals and go up on the roof to see if a new roof was needed. The entire building was checked out, refitted and made safer for his tenants.

And Roan had one more thing installed—a panic button. The tenants were mostly hold-overs from his parents' friends and some quite elderly. This way, if there were a medical emergency, they could hit the button and summon help immediately.

Now to the tasks at hand. The CTB moved in under the guise of decorators, with the equipment inside crates marked "Fragile—Display Units" or "Wire Racks." It was perfect. The elevator took them upstairs without anyone suspecting what was going on. There were two apartments to work on, the store expansion and no one would even notice them…unless it was Katie.

Soon there was another visitor to the store. Maggie had returned from Medjugorje and was excited to share her news. She and Tim had set a wedding date For December 20th in Bemidji, but they would be living in Edina where Tim worked.

Shauna embraced her friend and offered her some coffee. Maggie was amazed at the progress on the store and excited about all the activity.

Shauna gave Maggie a cup of coffee and asked her to step outside to the benches with her saying, "I am so happy for you Maggie. Tim is such a great guy and to find each other after all these years? Wow. Listen, I need to tell you about this business with DuMonde. It's escalated and we found listening devices all over the house. Katie and Jim must not know about this right away because we don't want them in danger. We have a specialist coming in next week to help out, plus the men who seem to be decorators—aren't. So until we say okay, keep this one under your smock, okay?"

"Tim is keeping his eye on this at the other end," explained Maggie. "He will let me know if DM's activities are stepped up. Don't worry about a thing. This will all work out."

"Oh, and another thing," said Shauna. "Roan met the most extraordinary woman yesterday. She's Lulabelle's twin sister Millie. Did you know about her?"

"Yes, I did, actually," responded Maggie. "But I thought she was dead as well. There was a third sister, too—Emmeline Rutherford. She has been dead for years now though. I know about her. She wasn't very nice—very bad tempered woman, not at all like Lulabelle. Something must have happened to her to make her so bitter. Could have been jealousy over Lulabelle's success. She didn't talk with her family much. I believe she had a son who would be around Roan's age. But he disappeared right after his mother died."

"Fascinating," exclaimed Shauna. "Would you tell Roan about this tonight. Do you have plans for supper?"

"No and my fridge is empty," said Maggie. "I'd love to come out, say 5ish?"

"Great," Shauna said joyously. "I'm so happy you are home."

Maggie left to unpack and get herself ready for supper. Shauna spoke to Roan about Maggie's information and he wanted to know more. Thankfully, it would be the three of them, because it being Saturday, Conor was still at Jimmy's. And Maggie had a couple of favors to ask of the Sandersons.

At 4:00 PM, Katie and Shauna closed the store to continue the renovations on Monday. Everything had been delivered upstairs, so the "decorators" were set and Shauna could go home to begin supper. As Roan and Shauna walked out of the Gallery, Mr. Fitzgerald stopped them.

"Who was the chubby little woman you were talking with?" Parker asked.

"Oh, that's our friend Maggie McManus," explained Roan. "She is engaged to a police officer on assignment to Medjugorje and was there when DuMonde popped up. She knows what's transpired, but not everything from here. She can be trusted with anything, so if you need her, simply ask."

"Thanks," he replied. "Sweet little lady. She has a glow about her."

"There's a reason for that," explained Shauna. "She set her wedding date with that officer, who is an old friend and was the best man at her wedding to her late husband over thirty years ago. It was love at first reunite! It just goes to show you can rekindle the love you once had and make it even better. Roan and I are proof of that, too. I'll tell you about it someday. See you Monday, Parker."

Roan and Shauna walked hand in hand to their car. As they drove home, Shauna told Roan about Maggie knowing Millie and her other sister Emmeline. She would tell them about these women at supper.

"Good," said Roan. "Maybe she can shed some light on Millie. I'm still a bit shell-shocked over meeting her."

Roan pressed the garage door button and drove in.

Then he pressed the button on the security alarm and said, "I'm just going to keep pushing people's buttons for the rest of my life!!"

They laughed and went inside. Flash and Tyler toddled over to greet their owners, then sped off in some imaginary quest. And Mickey, well, he was still asleep in Conor's room. Shauna went through the groceries and decided on a nice baked chicken recipe she got in Rome. A fresh salad, some wine. That would make for a lovely evening.

While Shauna was working on supper, Maggie's memories were working overtime. She had scrapbooks with news clippings from the last thirty years. It had been Paul's hobby, then hers and when she talked with Shauna about the three sisters, it got her thinking about those clippings. She went through a box of old albums and found one about Emmie's death and funeral. As she browsed the headlines, she came upon something which could change the face of the investigation.

Maggie grabbed the album and walked out the door. As she got into her car, she couldn't help feeling someone was watching her. It sent a chill up her spine, but she pressed on and drove away. Instead of driving into Heather Lane, Maggie drove past the house to the side road, which only 'townies' knew about. She pulled into the side driveway and ran into the house.

"You guys, someone was watching me just now," wheezed Maggie. "I know someone was out there and I have something I need to show you. Come over to the table."

Maggie opened the album to show information about Emmeline Forsythe Rutherford, her biography and clippings from her obituary. It said she was survived by two sisters, Lulabelle Lavinia LaFontaine, the noted romance novelist and Millicent Forsythe, also a writer of historical fiction and noted lecturer on Irish history. And there was a son, Ronald B. Rutherford, 39 of Maam Cross, County Galway in Ireland. The obituary was dated September 25, 1991. Emmeline's husband, Ronald, Sr., preceded her in death in 1986. There were photographs of the sisters together. You could barely tell Lulabelle and Millie apart, but Emmeline stood out because of the scowl on her face.

There were additional photographs but one was of particular interest. It was of Ronald at his mother's funeral and on his left hand was a gold Claddagh ring, similar if not identical to the ring on the surveillance tape. The detail was grainy, but there it was. Roan was so excited, he ran to the phone to call Agent Fitzgerald.

"Can you get out here Parker," Roan said excitedly. "I have something you need to see now."

"Sure," replied Parker. "But how to I get out there?"

Roan explained the directions and Parker said he would be there directly. He took a sample book of wallpaper with him to continue the pretense, in case he was being watched—or the house was being watched. He was there in twenty minutes.

Fortunately Parker didn't look like your normal buttoned down CTB agent. He was tall, with green eyes, longer golden-brown hair and wore a Henley with shorts, boat shoes with no socks. He looked like a jock! And he wore a gold earring in one ear. He walked to the front door, rang the bell and Shauna answered. Maggie's mouth flew open. You could just hear her say to herself, *'Look at that gorgeous man, I gotta stop droolin'!*

"Maggie," said Shauna. "I want you to meet Agent Parker Fitzgerald, with the CTB."

"Hello Maggie," Parker said in a deep base voice with just a touch of an Irish lilt. "Just call me Parker."

"Oh yeah, I can do that—oh, I mean, it's nice to meet you, Parker," replied a very nervous Maggie. "I have an old scrap book that may have some insights into your local stalker. I think I know who it is."

They sat down at the table and opened the scrap book to the page with Ronald's picture on it. You could almost tell his height and body build from the picture and the ring was definitely standing out in the photo.

"Roan, can you roll the tape again?" asked Parker. "We can compare it to the ring the repair man was wearing and maybe get a sense of the man's height."

Roan got a copy of the tape and put it in the living room VCR. As he ran it, Parker could see the same ring and the same man in the album. Before he could say anything, Parker saw a shadow running away from the front window of the house.

"Stay here, folks," whispered Parker. "We have an uninvited visitor."

Parker ran out the front door just in time to see a man running away, get into a beaten up old van and drive away. He couldn't see the face, but the height was right. Was Ronald Rutherford back? Was he the one stalking Maggie and threatening the Sandersons?

A few minutes later, Parker came back in and said, "I think we have a match and he knows it. The threat will be greater now that we know who he is. I want you to stay here tonight, Maggie, while I go back and work on a profile of Ronald Rutherford. Is that okay with everyone?"

Roan spoke first, "Sure, Maggie can always stay here and if you can wait a minute, I may have an old yearbook in the basement with his high school picture in it. Of course, it isn't recent, but it will give you the facial structure you can age and get an idea of what he looks like now. Just a minute."

Maggie ran over to the brandy and poured herself a stiff one.

She sat back down and said, "This is just too weird. I get home and am right in the middle of it. Tim will never believe it!"

"Well, you can tell him when this part of it is over, Maggie," replied Parker.

Roan came back upstairs with two old year books, gave one to Parker and both thumbed through the pictures.

Parker found one first and the caption read, 'Ronald B. Rutherford, Jr., President of the Latin Club, Science Club and Physics Club. Class of 1971.' And there was his photo. He resembled his mother with a semi-scowl, wild hair and thick glasses. His eyes sunk deep in their sockets and it made him look somewhat sinister. And the dark red circles around his eyes made him look evil.

The other year book had several photos, too. But most of them were from a distance. It showed Ronald to be tall, thin and gawky. His thick black glasses stuck out as if they weren't part of the photograph. Parker was fairly sure they had the right person.

"May I take these things back with me to work on?" asked Parker.

"Sure," replied Roan. "But first, let me scan the photos in and make copies because things happen around here and I don't want these lost."

"Good idea," Parker remarked. "I can wait a bit."

By now Maggie was almost sloshed, but sat calmly in her chair. Once the copies were made, Parker said goodnight and went out to his car.

He put the key in the ignition and turned it to hear a 'click, click, click'. Parker jumped out of the car, grabbing the books as he ran away from the vehicle just as it exploded, BOOM, throwing Agent Fitzgerald into the air and scattering the papers. The hood made a hissing sound, like a bottle rocket taking off as it goes skyward. The blast also broke windows in the house, set off the alarm, destroying the garage, with three cars inside. In moments the garage was a blaze and Agent Fitzgerald lay on the ground bleeding from shrapnel wounds.

Roan scrambled to his feet and told the women to stay put. He ran outside to see his house on fire and Parker in the bushes at the side of the house. Roan ran back inside and called the police, who had been alerted by the alarm. They were already on the way with the fire department. He grabbed the tape, discs with the photos on it and ushered the women out onto the lawn, grabbing a blanket from the back of the sofa as he left. He rushed to Parker's side and covered him with the blanket. Roan used his cell phone to call the paramedics and advise them of Parker's condition, then saw his neighbors running to his aid.

Because Maggie consumed the brandy so fast, she'd passed out on the front lawn. Shauna stood and watched the garage burning, while Roan attended to Parker. Soon the sirens could be heard and the fire trucks pulled up outside the stand of trees on the road. They had to drag their fire hoses through the trees to get to Heather Lane, because the hydrant was on the county road side.

They turned the water on immediately and put out the fire from the explosion, then the garage. Fortunately there was a fire wall in between a portion of the garage and the house, so that fire didn't spread. But the house suffered numerous broken windows in the master bedroom, bathroom and living room. Some of the door jams weren't straight and threw the doors off their hinges. The pantry was destroyed from the blast and Mickey's doggie door was gone. The kitchen window had shattered and there was glass all over the supper, the counters and floor.

As the firemen checked through the house, they shut off gas valves. They checked the entire house and gave the all clear. The paramedics were attending to an unconscious Parker. He was cut everywhere from flying glass and metal, but Roan intimated he didn't think Parker had any broken bones. Just then the CTB van drove up to the scene and two other agents got out. They rushed to Parker's side and one man got into the ambulance with him.

The other agent, Michael Keller, came over to Roan and asked, "What happened here, Roan?"

Roan handed the agent the photocopies of the year books, along with Maggie's scrapbook and said, "We made copies of pictures of Ronald R. Rutherford, Jr. We think he is the man you are after and he would have knowledge of chemical interaction, enabling him to make a bomb. Parker saw someone matching this description running away from the house just before his car blew up. Rutherford was supposed to have gone back to Ireland long ago, but we think he's back and out for some kind of revenge against us. I don't think you are dealing with only one threat. I think there are two."

Agent Keller walked around the house and looked over the damage with Roan.

He said, "Well, it looks like you can't stay here tonight. I'm sure the police can help you board up the house while they do the investigation, but the house isn't in any condition to be lived it. You don't have any gas for cooking or heating water. I'd say get what you need and find a place to stay."

"We can stay at our cottage down on the beach," explained Roan. We can pack up some things and go down there. It's just been alarmed and there is room enough for the four of us. Maggie will be spending the night. Boy, she's going to be mad when she wakes up and realises she missed all of this!"

Roan called the security company and asked for some guards to patrol the area around the house and by the cottage. Rutherford might not try for a second attempt tonight, but Roan didn't take any chances. Then he thought about the media. They didn't know about the little house and he would keep it that way. He asked Agent Keller to handle the reporters when they got there and Agent Keller agreed.

"Oh what about Charles, Marie and the kids?" asked Roan. "They need a place to stay because their house isn't finished yet."

Just then, Jim and Katie walked up and crossed the yellow tape.

Jim said, "They can stay with us for a few nights, Roan and so can Conor. What's going on Roan?"

Agent Keller just shook his head and remarked, "You'd better tell them now, Roan. The cat's out of the bag anyway."

"When we were in Medjugorje, someone began stalking us," explained Roan. "The man came to Rome and stalked us there, so we worked with Interpol to try to identify him and track him down. Unfortunately, when we got home, someone else was after us. We think it's Ronald Rutherford."

"You must be joking, Roan," Jim said. "I vaguely remember him as a geek with thick black glasses."

"Well, we think he's the same person, Jim," replied Roan. "I hesitated to get you both involved, because the CTB told me not to. So now you know those decorators aren't who you think they are either. But say nothing about this to the boys or the press. We could get eaten up alive by them. Remember what happened with Lulabelle."

Shauna walked over to Maggie who was just coming to. Tyler, Flash and Mickey were huddled up against her, shaken from the blast.

Shauna helped Maggie to her feet and said, "You will always have a blast here at the Sandersons!"

Maggie looked around and asked, "Did I miss something? Oh my goodness, I did. I DID miss something. Shauna, your garage is gone and so are some of your windows. What the hell happened?"

"Parker went to start his car and it exploded," explained Shauna. "The explosion caught our garage on fire and we lost the cars, some windows and a little structural damage. But we got out okay and you will be staying with us at the cottage tonight. I don't want to take the chance of you being attacked in the middle of the night by this nutcase."

"Oh yeah, I agree," replied Maggie. "If the bomb squad is here, maybe they can check over MY car, too."

Shauna walked over to the police captain and asked if Maggie's car could be checked out as well, since the person who did this, must have been the one stalking Maggie at her house.

Maggie was concerned she didn't see Parker with the group of agents and said, "What happened to Parker? I don't see him over there."

Roan came by and explained to Maggie, "Parker was thrown in the blast. They took him to the hospital. He took a pretty good shredding from the glass and metal of the car, but I think he should be okay."

Maggie was holding her head and grimaced, "Shouldn't have had that brandy on an empty stomach. Oh, I feel sick."

As Maggie ran off to be sick, Shauna walked over to Katie and said, "Katie, let's get some food in the cottage and also explain to Conor about the explosion when you get home. Just tell him everyone is okay, including the pets."

"Sure," said Katie. "I just wish you had been able to confide in us, but I guess you couldn't. I understand. You had our safety in mind."

"Thanks. I didn't want NOT to tell you. The CTB told me I couldn't. You can see this is a very serious matter, Katie," explained Shauna.

Shauna continued, "We are going to stay at the little house for as long as we need. Thank goodness the contractors have already been scheduled. They will just have a little more to do now!"

The insurance company representatives were now on site, along with Roan's contractors. Even Mr. Young heard the explosion and came to see what he could do to help.

"Roan, can I supply some food?" he asked. "Have you folks eaten yet?"

Roan realised they hadn't had supper because it was covered in glass.

"That would be wonderful, Mr. Young," expressed Roan with a smile. "Katie went to the trading post for groceries, but we do need supper. There are four of us and I think we may need a couple of pizzas and salads, maybe some soda and your famous cake. Conor isn't with us tonight, but this is making me so hungry. Oh, we are staying down at the little house tonight and should be there in a few minutes."

"Done," said Mr. Young. "I will be back down there in about half an hour?"

Roan smiled and said, "Thanks. You are coming to the rescue again!"

Roan rounded up all the people involved and told them if they needed him, he would be down at the cottage. Shauna packed some clothing and essentials, including her jewellery, got Roan's things, a few movies and their wedding photo and went outside. She also picked up the remotes for the main house and the cottage, then closed the door. The fire department was boarding up the house, but suggested they leave the lights on.

Maggie staggered in to get her purse and walked down to the cottage with Roan and Shauna. Shauna had never been in this house, but felt comfortable with the decision, since this had been Lillian and Roddy's first home on the lake.

The police went in first, turned on the lights and searched the entire place, including the basement and garage. Everything was locked down tight.

No one had lived in the house since their wedding five months ago. The house had four bedrooms, a dining room, decent sized kitchen, two full baths and a small studio. And there was a great room with a beautiful stone fireplace, a laundry, small pantry and garage—kind of a mini-version of the bigger house. Roan kept it move-in ready just in case guests dropped in unannounced. Shauna looked through the bedrooms and found one with a queen sized bed for them. Maggie was right behind her and picked out one with a double bed. Shauna then opened the windows and let some evening air in. But the odor of fire and burning fuel was still strong, so she closed them quickly.

"Guess we should turn the air conditioning on for a little bit to clean the air," Shauna said. "It's a little musty in here and the air outside is pretty foul."

Roan agreed and within a few minutes, the home was refreshed. A knock at the door startled Roan. He went over, peered through the peep hole and opened the door. It was Jim and Katie, Mr. Young and the security company owner, Mr. Franks. Everyone came in at once. Katie found the kitchen and began putting away the food. Mr. Young dropped off the pizzas and Mr. Franks showed Roan how to operate the systems for the house and assured Roan men would be posted around the house 24-7.

Katie asked if she could do anything else and Maggie said, "Yes, please Katie. Can you take me home for a few minutes so I can get some clothes and things for the next few days?"

Jim replied, "We can take you with us Maggie and bring you back. We have no idea if this man is close to your house now or not and we need to be safe rather than sorry."

Maggie sighed with relief and said, "Thanks Jim. I appreciate it. The quicker we get out of here the quicker we can get back."

Shauna gave Katie a hug and sighed, "I think I can come in on Monday, but I don't have a car. I suppose we should go shopping for one tomorrow afternoon—but we also have no way to Mass in the morning either."

"I can stop by the Ford dealership on the way back into town and ask Morris if they can bring out a couple of loaners until you can pick something out if you want me to," said Jim.

"Great Jim," replied Roan. "That would be a big help. I think we are going to be here for a week or so until the house is attended to."

Mickey and Tyler ran around inside, but Flash wasn't so sure about this place. It didn't have his house, so he went back to his own place and slept there. He watched carefully from his 'living room' as people came in and out of the big house. Men in big yellow pants and over coats had huge pieces of plywood, nailing them on the windows. And some man was sweeping up the food from the floor. No grub for Flash tonight.

As night had fallen, a sliver of sunset could be seen from the front porch of the cottage. Shauna still felt like a newlywed and wondered what Lillian might have thought when she moved here.

Roan turned off the air conditioner and searched the food Mr. Young brought. He opened the pizza and placed a couple of slices on a plate, then sat in the living room. Mr. Franks, Katie, Jim and Maggie had left and Roan felt a little chilly, so he checked the flu and put a small fire in the hearth. Shauna, too, put some pizza on her plate and sat with Roan.

"What do you think of this little cottage, Shauna?" asked Roan. "My folks loved it here. It was good for me when I came home, too."

"It feels good here, too, Roan," remarked Shauna. "Thank goodness we have it."

Roan's cell phone rang and it was Jim calling from the Ford dealership. He almost missed closing time, but Morris was still there and would come out with his wife and a couple of cars for them to use until they could select something permanent.

Roan thanked Jim, then went back to eating. About half an hour later, Jim and Maggie returned with Morris and Sally Miller, the dealership owners and the loaner cars.

They handed Roan the keys and Sally said, "These are yours for as long as you need. Then we can discuss what you would really like to have!"

Roan thanked the Millers and Jim took them back to town. Maggie took her suitcases up to her room and came back down for some pizza. Roan set the alarm and everyone felt safe at last. Four guards were outside and about 9:00 PM, it was time for sleep.

The next morning at 5:00 AM, Roan got up, made the coffee and set upon his rounds as usual. The security men were still outside, so he offered them some coffee. Roan asked if anything unusual happened during the night and they said no. But within a few minutes, Millie came up the path and a security guard stopped her.

"It's okay, Harry," said Roan. "This is a neighbour and she's fine. Come on in Millie."

"I'm sorry to come up so early Roan, but that's what I do. I'm an early bird," said Millie. "I saw the explosion and had to find out what happened. I figured you would be here. Any idea who did this?"

"Yes, I'm afraid we do, Millie," explained Roan. "Won't you have some coffee?"

"Yes thanks," she replied. "The house looks like it did when Lillian and Roddy were here. We had some good times in this cottage."

"Millie," asked Roan. "Have you heard from your nephew Ronald recently?"

Millie thought for a moment and said, "Oh heavens no. He's been gone for years, since Emmie's funeral. He went back to Ireland and I haven't heard from him since. He could be dead for all I know."

Roan measured his words carefully and asked, "Did he wear a traditional gold Claddagh ring on his left ring finger?"

"Why yes, it was his father's wedding ring," Millie explained. "Why do you ask, Roan?"

"I'm sorry to tell you this, Millie," explained Roan. "But your nephew was the one who threatened us, bugged our home and blew up a CTB agent as he got in his car. We have him on security video."

Millie set her cup down and sat back in the chair.

She thought for a moment and said, "Ronald was always a tormented child. A recognized genius at twelve, no one knew how to handle him, not even his parents. I think Emmie died of a broken heart after Ron Sr. died. She was the most bitter, nasty person at times because she couldn't deal with the heartbreak or with Ronnie's ever changing temper. Ron Jr. was distraught when his mother died and he returned to Ireland, becoming a forensic scientist for Interpol in Dublin. I assumed he was still there."

"No, he's here, Millie," explained Roan. "And he almost killed a man and tried to blow us up. He's in very serious trouble."

Just then, Shauna walked into the room. She did a double take when she saw Millie.

Shauna's brow knitted up and she extended her hand in friendship saying, "Hello Millie. I'm Shauna. Sorry I look so surprised, but it's just so uncanny. You look so much like our beloved Lulabelle."

Millie shook Shauna's hand and explained, "We were identical twins, you know. Most people couldn't tell us apart. Then Lula began exhibiting strange behavior and morphed into the character you knew. She had dementia, poor girl. But she never had heart problems, of that I am certain. That's why her death came as such a shock to me."

Roan explained he thought that might be the problem, but Lulabelle never acknowledged an illness. She was just—well, Lulabelle.

"But why didn't you come forward about this when she died, Millie?" asked Shauna. "There might have been another reason for her death—like she might have been over-medicated—or murdered."

Millie was silent for a moment, then said, "I was in such a state, I left for Ireland right after the funeral. As far as I was concerned, her time had come. I bundled myself in my little cottage and didn't leave until a couple of weeks ago. I couldn't bring myself to come back here. A friend sent me the video of your wedding and I knew I shouldn't stay away."

"Millie," asked Roan. "Would you feel comfortable talking with the police about Ronald?"

"Yes, I suppose so," she replied. "I'm not sure I can add much, but I will try."

Roan picked up his cell phone and called Agent Keller, who was at the hospital checking on Agent Fitzgerald.

"Agent Keller will be right out, Millie," said Roan. "He's very nice and just wants to ask you about Ronald, what kind of person he is, his background, etc. Stay and have breakfast with us."

Millie agreed and in a few moments, Maggie also came down for breakfast. She took one look at Millie, blinked and went back upstairs.

Maggie poked her head around the banister and said, "Lulabelle? No, it can't be."

"Hello Maggie, don't be afraid," explained Millie. "You must not remember me. It has been a number if years."

Maggie approached cautiously and said, "The resemblance is uncanny. No, I'm sorry. I don't remember. Have we met before?"

"Yes," explained Millie. "We met after Paul died and I came to your house. I was the one who consoled you—not Lulabelle. I'm sorry if I confused you then."

Maggie was speechless and sat down on the foot stool by the fireplace. Shauna got her a cup of coffee and Maggie said nothing. The doorbell rang. It was Agent Keller and the police chief. Roan opened the door and asked them in. Roan introduced them to Millie.

Agent Keller spoke first, "Ms. Forsythe, you are the aunt of Ronald Rutherford, am I correct?"

"Yes, I am," she replied.

"Have you seen him recently?" asked Agent Keller.

"No. It has been more than ten years since I have seen him," she said.

Agent Keller took the photograph from his briefcase and showed it to Millie.

"Is this Ronald?" inquired Agent Keller.

Millie sat again in silence as she stared at the photograph of her nephew.

She cupped her hand to her mouth and cried, "Yes, that's Ronnie. He looks so old and may be wearing a disguise, but that's definitely him."

Michael Keller said, "Thank you, Ms. Forsythe. I know this wasn't easy."

Roan asked how Agent Fitzgerald was and Agent Keller explained how he was doing.

"He's very bruised and cut up," explained Agent Keller. "He has a severe concussion and hearing loss, but that should come back in time. Right now, he's in a lot of pain. We found the residue of a home-made bomb under the front seat of the car. It was rigged to the ignition switch and when Parker turned the key, the bomb exploded. It's a miracle he wasn't killed."

"May I go up to the house and see what he did, please?" asked Millie.

Roan said, "We should all go up and see what's left. I have no idea how much damage was done to the neighbor's homes either. That blast was pretty powerful."

Agent Keller felt they should all go together and left the security guards in charge for a moment. As they walked up the path, Roan noticed the cars left for them in the driveway. There was a silvery blue Ford Fiesta 3-door hatchback and a metallic teal Ford F-150 extended cab truck. When they got up to the house, they could see the boarded up windows in the living room, the crater where the car had been and the decimated garage. All the cars had been towed away, plus the lodge pole pine trees next to the house had to be cut down because most were broken in half from the blast.

Gone was the bedroom deck and water feature. The birdhouses were flattened. Suddenly Shauna thought about Flash. She walked quietly around to the other side of the house to see Flash sleeping in his little house.

Shauna whispered to him through the little door and asked, "Flash, do you want something to eat. Mommie is here, Sweetie."

Flash opened his eyes, made a little squeak and rolled out the door into waiting hands. He nuzzled in Shauna's shoulder as she took him in the house to see if she could find some nuts in a cabinet.

Shauna made her way through the broken glass, still holding onto Flash. She found a box containing granola cereal, which would have to do. She took it back out to Flash's house and poured some in his dish. He was so delighted to have some food at last, he chirped his thanks.

Shauna unlocked the door to the studio and set the box inside, then locked the door again. She could see a light on the answering machine in the office and decided to go back in and get the messages. Shauna took the tape out and put it in her pocket, then went back outside.

Her heart sank as she looked at her battered house. But she also knew it would be made new again. Some of the neighbors came out to look at the house and talk with Roan about the explosion.

Roan felt he should be honest about what had happened and explained, "We think we know who did this, but not why. We have the man on the security tape and have identified him."

One of the neighbors spoke up and asked, "Was he tall, thick glasses and somewhat skinny? This guy had sort of wild, gray hair, too, if I remember right. We saw someone like that watching the house for several nights last week. It weirded us out a little, but we didn't call the police or anything. Maybe we should have now that I think about it."

Agent Keller asked if they would come over and look at the photograph he had with him.

"Yes, that's the one," replied the neighbor. "He looks a little different in this picture, but that's him."

Another neighbor identified the man, then another. All had seen him while Roan and Shauna were on their trip.

"I'll put out an APB on him," said the captain. "No time to waste before he hurts or kills anyone."

Millie began to cry and Roan asked if he could escort her home. Shauna hugged her and told her to come by anytime. They walked away silently down toward the beach.

The police had kept the media away from the scene and with it being cleaned up, there wasn't much to see. Somehow they lost interest in the Sandersons and congregated outside the hospital, waiting on news of Agent Fitzgerald.

Roan and Millie finally got to her cottage and she asked Roan to check on her in the morning.

"Sure, Millie, I will be glad to," replied Roan. "I will come down early around 6:00 if that's okay."

"Splendid, Roan," Millie said. "I appreciate your kindness. I can see why Lula loved you and Shauna so much."

Millie went inside and closed her front door. Roan took a quick look around the house and went back to his own cottage. There wouldn't be time for Mass this morning, but he knew God would understand. Roan asked a security guard to have someone stationed at Millie's house in case Ronald decided to go there.

Shauna was looking at the vehicles in the driveway. She was especially interested in the truck.

"Oh Roan, I like the truck," exclaimed Shauna. "Look at the cab. It has a CD player and everything. I don't think I need to look very far for another vehicle."

"What makes you think the truck is for YOU?" Roan exclaimed. "This is the one I like. Keep your mitts off!"

Agent Keller needed to leave but had something for Maggie.

"Here are your keys, Maggie," he said. "Your car was not wired, but you have a shattered windshield and some broken windows. You'll need to have it towed to the garage."

"Oh thanks," sighed Maggie. "Just what I need now."

"Don't worry Maggie," remarked Roan. "I think I have a solution for that."

Roan handed Maggie the keys to the hatchback, since he had decided to buy another truck AND a family sedan. He got the phone number for the Millers from the key fob, called them and asked if there was a burgundy F-150 on the lot and if there was, he would buy all three vehicles, plus a silver four-door for the family. The exact cars were there and within half an hour, two additional vehicles were delivered.

Sally Miller drove the burgundy truck out and parked behind the teal F-150.

She got out and looked over at the Sanderson's house and remarked, "What a mess. Roan, do you know who did this?"

"We do now," explained Roan. "It looks like Ronald Rutherford."

"You mean Ronnie from the science club in high school?"

"I'm afraid so, Sally," replied Roan. "He's been positively identified by more than one person. But we still don't have a motive. I never did anything to harm him. Oh, listen, when you are making up the paperwork on these, I want to pay for all of them, including the hatchback. Have Maggie's name put on the title, would you and Shauna's on the teal truck. The other truck will also be a business expense, so please title that one to me. We can deal with the insurance reimbursement later."

"The teal truck?" asked Sally.

"Yes, the teal truck," replied Roan. "She loves trucks, I suppose because she hauls so much around with her. You might also look into getting a customized topper for it, too. The store will need that for deliveries. The colour is perfect for the store."

"Oh right," smiled Sally. "I heard you are expanding into a design shop and will offer specialized furnishings. That's exciting. I need some new things, so I'll come down."

"THAT'S what I forgot," Roan sighed. "Do you have a Ford Explorer or some type of family van for Charles and Marie? Their family car was destroyed in their house fire and for some reason, their insurance didn't cover getting a new one. Do I get a fleet discount for these?"

Sally laughed and said, "I definitely will have to give you special pricing on all of these vehicles, Roan. Oh there's the other half now."

Morris Miller brought over the most beautiful silver four-door sedan Shauna had ever seen. It was fully loaded with all the new GPS tracking systems, backup camera and tilt everything! And it being silver, was a true salute to Lulabelle. Maggie and Shauna looked over every inch of the car, felt the glass-like finish and rich blue leather interior.

"Oh yeah, awesome," exclaimed Maggie. "This is the real deal here folks!"

"Roan wants another vehicle for Charles and Marie. Can you pick out a family van for them and put it in their driveway with a big bow on it?" asked Sally.

"Is this a fleet, Roan?" remarked Morris. "I'll have to give you the BIG discount on all these."

"Hey, we had the coffee and forgot the breakfast. Who's for breakfast?" Roan yelled.

Everyone waved wildly and opted to go into Clifden's for Sunday brunch. Shauna called Katie and Jim to join them and bring the boys. Hopefully it would be a relaxing Sunday for everyone.

Conor ran up to his folks in the parking lot and hugged them. He had heard about the bomb and wanted to know if everyone was okay.

"Gee Mom and Dad, you had me worried," cried Conor. "Is the house like gone?"

"No, just the garage and a there's a huge hole in the driveway," explained Roan. "There are some broken windows and structural damage but nothing that can't be fixed and look at what's in the driveway here? See the teal truck? That's your Mom's new car!"

"Oh no way, Dad," shrieked Conor. "Oh wow, that IS totally awesome. Hey Jimmy, come over here and look at Mom's new truck."

Jimmy walked around the truck with his thumbs up.

Since he was now into one word sentences, he uttered, "Smooth!"

Everyone laughed and went into the restaurant. After brunch, they drove over to Charles and Marie's new home. They had been spending their free time there and Katie wanted to bring them some of the heavenly banana muffins from Clifdens.

The beds had been delivered for the children's rooms, along with a few other pieces of furniture. The dining room table and chairs were set up, along with the kitchen furniture, patio furniture and living room set.

Morris Miller had left early to get the van for the family and turned into the driveway without mussing the big red bow on top. He came in separately and joined in the group without saying a word, except 'hello.'

Charles gave the grand tour, while Marie showed off the curtain samples. Cookie even had her own little hand-made house in the corner of the family/ great room. The house was magnificent and it was the first time the Millers had seen the inside.

"Hey folks, we need to go," explained Morris. "Can we hitch a ride, Roan?"

Realising there were a few too many people for the cars they had, Roan said quietly, "You will have to squeeze into the back seats of the cab. Thank goodness it's an extended cab!"

Katie and her family left as well and as they all walked out, they waited for Charles and Marie to come out to say farewell. All of a sudden they realised there was a brand new van in their driveway with a huge red bow on it.

Everyone clapped and yelled, "Welcome Home friends."

Everyone drove away with smiles on their faces. Roan decided to take Conor home then and show him the damage to the house. He dropped the

Millers off at the dealership and drove directly to the house. Conor needed to pick out his school things anyway to take down to the cottage.

When they arrived, a police officer greeted them saying, "We've had a sighting of Rutherford. I'll take you inside to get a few things, then I want you back at the cottage ASAP and locked inside until I say it's okay to come out."

"Alright, everyone come in quickly and get what you need," said Roan quietly. "Conor, get only what you will need for the next week—school things, books, whatever you need and come right back down."

Shauna got out another bag with some additional clothes, opened the armoire and threw a scarf over the video camera. That was the only link inside the house. She went into the kitchen, got a couple bottles of wine, her spices and some utensils, piled everything in the bag and left with Conor. The officer locked the house again and activated the security system with the keypad.

Maggie chose to wait in the truck because she had everything at the cottage. She tapped nervously on the window until the officer came back. The Sandersons got in and drove to the cottage. They all hustled inside and turned on the security system.

Shauna showed Conor the remaining two bedrooms and let him choose which one he wanted. Mickey had already chosen one for him, as he was lying down on the comforter in the room facing the lake. The dog jumped up and ran toward his human. Tyler came bouncing in, too. Flash was the only one missing.

"Hey Mom, where's Flash?" inquired Conor.

"He's back at the house in his own little place," she explained. "He has been fed and taken care of. I don't think he understands what's happened and he's safe in there."

"Cool," replied Conor.

The folks watched movies, popped corn and played some card games. Shauna poured over her planner to schedule in the renovation of the store, the house and finishing details for Charles and Marie. Roan called Franco at his house to let him in on what had happened before he saw it on television. Then he called JB at home to explain the past 24 hours. Alex was ready to fly in immediately and Roan said he would meet her at the airport tomorrow afternoon.

After a quick supper, everyone went to bed. Something kept nagging at Roan and it prevented him from sleeping well. He got up the next morning at 4:30, took a shower and got dressed. He took his cell phone with him and his remote. And he told the officer on duty where he was going. The officer radioed the man on duty at Millie's and got no response.

"Listen," shouted Roan. "Get a squad down there now. I think Rutherford is in the house. Go, do it now."

Roan ran down along the beach and finally got to Millie's. He could see Trixie running around inside, trying to get someone's attention. And he could see Ronald back handing Millie across the face as she was tied to a chair in the kitchen. He was screaming at her and when he saw Roan, he fired a gun at him through the sliding glass door. Roan ducked behind the retaining wall and called the police on his cell phone.

"Shots fired at Millie Forsythe's home on the lake.," shrieked Roan. "Rutherford inside doing the shooting, this is Roan Sanderson. Hurry."

Ronald shot three more times at Roan, but he missed each time. Roan's heart felt as if it was beating a thousand beats a second.

Ronald was throwing things around inside and at Millie. Her back was to Roan with her head slumped on her shoulder and he couldn't tell how badly she was injured. Suddenly, the sirens could be heard in the distance and Ronald looked out the window toward the noise, then looked straight at Roan. If stares could be bullets, Roan would be dead. Ronald yelled an obscenity, kicked the dog in the ribs and ran out the side door.

Roan ran inside the house through the plate glass window, which had been shattered by one of the bullets. Millie was tied very tightly. Her mouth was bleeding and she had bruises on her face and around her eyes. There was a gash in her head, which would need stitches. The little dog was moaning in the corner and Roan went to check on her after he had untied Millie.

The police burst in and yelled, "Freeze Rutherford."

Realising it was Roan, they put their weapons down and began searching the house. They found their officer face down in the front garden with his head caved in. A bloody shovel lay on the ground next to the fallen officer. The front door had been forced and when they reached Millie, she was barely conscious.

Roan waved to the paramedics and ran to her side.

"Millie, can you hear me? It's Roan," he said anxiously. "Millie, hang in there, I'll get you to the hospital."

Roan called Dr. Drummond at home, explaining what happened. The doctor got dressed, drove straight to the hospital trauma unit and had everything ready when the paramedics got there.

Roan rode in the ambulance, holding Millie's hand. Once they arrived, Roan called Shauna, who by now was aware of what was happening. He asked her to take an officer down to Millie's and get Trixie to the vet.

"Listen, Honey, when you get back with the officer, whatever you do, keep that house locked up," Roan said excitedly. "Call the school and keep Conor home today. Do not go out until I tell you it's safe."

Shauna was really shaken up now and sobbed, "Please be careful Roan. I'll do as you ask and let Katie know I will be a little late. She has that bid to prepare for the University. Maybe she can reschedule in light of what's happened."

"Go get the dog now, please, Shauna. I love you," pleaded Roan.

Shauna asked an officer to go down to the house to get Trixie. The others called for reinforcements so two could be inside the house, while four guarded the outside. Now Rutherford was armed and extremely dangerous, having killed one of their own.

Roan met Dr. Drummond as they entered the trauma bay and said excitedly, "Millie has been beaten within a whisper of her life. Do what you can, she needs to tell me why her nephew beat her like this."

Roan paced the waiting room floor and began praying. He knew what it meant to lose people he loved and now that he found Millie, his connection to Lulabelle was fading fast. If only she could hold on.

An hour later, Dr. Drummond came back to speak with Roan.

"I wish I had better news, Roan, but she is still in a coma," explained the doctor. "Whoever beat her used an iron—a steam iron. You can see the marks on her face. And he beat the daylights out of her. When I was treating her, she did come out of the coma long enough to say, 'Golden Boy'—hated you—kill you' and then she lapsed into the coma again. Does that mean anything to you?"

"No, nothing," replied Roan. "Can I sit with her for a while?"

"Sure," said the physician. "And by the way, glad to SEE you. I knew it was only a matter of time, Roan."

Roan smiled, then walked into the hospital room and took Millie's fragile hand. It was so warm and soft. Roan began to cry. Millie must have heard him, because she opened her eyes and turned her head toward him.

She began to whisper, "Thank you Roan, you dear man. I knew I was right to entrust the money to you. I love you so much. You do know, I AM Lulabelle."

With those words, she was gone. The machines began to whine and the monitor showed a flatline. The nurses tried to revive Millie but it did no good. Roan walked out of the room with his hands covering his face in sobs.

The officer with Roan came over, put his hand on Roan's shoulder and asked, "Did she say anything about her nephew? Why did he do it?"

Roan looked up at the officer and said, "She didn't say a thing just now, but earlier she said something about golden boy, hated you and kill you. I don't know what that means. But she didn't say anything, no."

Roan walked slowly to the squad car. They drove back in silence. When they got to the house, Shauna was home. She walked up to Roan, put her arms around him and held him for a moment.

"The dog didn't make it either," wept Shauna. "We need to go inside, Honey."

Roan sat down in the leather chair by the window and cried. Shauna knelt down beside him and let him weep. Maggie got him some coffee and set it on the table. Finally, Roan looked up and explained what happened that morning.

"I was to check on Millie this morning and I did, but something told me things weren't right," sighed Roan. "That's when I had the officer check on his man down at Millie's. Ronald had killed him and broken into Millie's house. He beat Millie with a steam iron of all things, while she was tied to a kitchen chair. He shot at me, four times. He yelled some obscenity and kicked the dog so hard she flew against the wall. He'd ransacked the house, too. Right before the police got there, Ronald fled out the side door. We took Millie to the hospital but her age and extent of the beating were against her coming out of the coma. She came out of the coma long enough to tell me thank you, she loved me and she was proud of me. She died while I was holding her hand."

Roan continued to cry, when Jim's brother Alan came to the door. He had been at Millie's house and had some papers for Roan in a sealed manila envelope with his name on it.

"I think these must be important, Roan," explained Alan. "I thought you should have them right away."

Roan shook his head and Shauna took the envelope. She placed it in front of Roan, but let him continue grieving. Before too long, the police chief, along with Agent Keller, came back to the cottage.

Shauna asked the agent, "Agent Keller, Roan's personal assistant is coming in on the afternoon commuter flight and someone needs to pick her up. Could you do that for us and fill her in? Her name is Alexandra Baker."

"Certainly," replied Agent Keller. "I'd better get going because she will be here in about an hour. I'll bring her here, then."

Roan spoke with the Chief Reynolds about Millie and what he witnessed as she was being beaten by her nephew. He painfully recounted what he'd seen, but kept his conversation with Millie private. After the chief left, Roan took the envelope and went into the studio to look at the contents.

He noticed the handwriting looked like Lulabelle's. He chuckled as he opened the flap. Inside were notes for Roan, Shauna, Maggie and Stephen Brennan, plus a letter to Roan explaining the contents. There were also four zip discs with new books on them, ready to be sent to the publisher. And there were personal photographs and a copy of Millie's Last Will and Testament enclosed. Roan pulled out the letter of explanation first.

Millie had typed the list, then a short reason for each enclosure. The letter, dated the day before she died, read as follows:

"My dearest Roan,

The letters enclosed are for each of you, Shauna, Maggie and Stephen. Each explains gifts to them in my will and in Stephen's case, instructions to disburse these gifts. The discs are my latest books which need to be sent to the publisher, their address is on each disc. It will, however, be up to you to promote them (so you'd better read them first!).

As you have probably guessed, Lulabelle and I could have been one person and basically for the last five years or so, we were. I wrote all of her romance novels, everything except for the children's books. Those were actually hers and she deserves the credit for them. The Alzheimer's robbed her of her ability to write and since I had been doing the series for so many years, I simply continued. I earned the money and put it in the trust her husband had established with his earnings. She never wanted for anything, but I continued to control her income. When she turned up dead, I felt the money should benefit others rather then me, so that's why you were my choice to distribute it as you deemed fit. In your letter, I will explain why I chose you and Shauna.

The letter to Maggie is also personal and there is an additional bequest to her now that she is to be re-married. Paul was a dear friend of Emmie's husband, Ronald, Sr., and assisted him during the later years of his life. Without Paul's help, Ron's years would have been greatly diminished and he was able to live in dignity without encumbering Emmie, whose depression over Ronnie turned her personality inside out. Ron, Jr. had no interest in his parents, their needs or cares. All he ever wanted was their money—and he never got a penny. It's a possible motive for him coming after you. This is the trust I set up for Maggie years ago, letting her think it came from Lulabelle, when it was, in fact, Ron and Emmie's estate. The bequest is the balance of this estate, some of Emmie's jewellery, including our Mother's wedding rings and family items Maggie had always admired.

Although I didn't get the chance to know Shauna well, I wanted to give her the bequest of my jewellery, some of the photographs of Lulabelle and myself with your parents. Maybe you can frame them and keep them as a momento of our friendship. Shauna reminds me so much of Lillian with her grace, style and dedication to the faith. And she has raised a wonderful young son under very difficult circumstances.

Please don't be too hard on Stephen. He has had to maintain attorney/ client privilege for many years because of this duality between Lula and myself. But everything has been done legally and above-board. We made certain it was. He was never able to tell you about our little deception and when Lula died, we kept up the pretense. Yes, when you saw silver and blue balloons, I did it. And when things popped up as if Lula had done them herself, I admit, I did it. But in her lucid moments, Lula told me what she wanted for you—she just wasn't able to accomplish it herself. So I became

Lulabelle Lavinia LaFontaine. However, you must always remember, she did love you and was always grateful you cared enough to look after her all those years.

My will also states the division of my own property and goods, plus my funeral arrangements, which are much less grandiose than Lula's. A simple Mass of Christian Burial at St. Philip's, a small graveside ceremony at the cemetery, no reception or fuss. Just put me with the rest of the family, except for Lula, of course. Keep her on your mantle! She'd want that. Yes, Roan, I am now and have always been a practicing Catholic, as were Lulabelle, Emmie and Ron. So maybe you can have a priest say a blessing over Lula's ashes. I'm not quite comfortable with her funeral rites!

There are bequests to the church, some other organizations and instructions to give the balance of my estate to you and Shauna equally. I advise you to put this into the trust we established earlier, as it will help the money grow faster and replenish itself. My boy, you aren't spending fast enough!

I have followed your career from the time you were a small child, Roan. I was always there as you grew up. I saw you have your first communion. I was there when you graduated from high school and college, then when you married Mary…and afterward. I was always in the background. I was your mother's best friend from the time we were in Catechism class at St. Philip's all those years ago. So you see, you could have been my son and I will always think of you in that way.

I don't know how many years I have left on this earth, but if you are reading this now, it means Ronald, Jr. has probably come after me to do me in. I'm the only one left, but I do feel he bears you a huge grudge all the way from high school. You could do no wrong and he was always the one left out. Funny, how the years grind away at a person's soul like that. And now that you have the family money, it makes you an even bigger target for his demented mind. You know, it wouldn't surprise me if Ronnie blew up Lula's house and killed her just to get her money! The boy needs help, Roan.

So there you are. Please give each person their letter now and think of me every once in a while. Read the discs, because two of the books are the trashy Lulabelle novels and two are new works of historical fiction. I'd rather you don't have any surprises and oh, please tell Katie, those books at the

Gallery? I'm responsible and there are more at the publishers! But tell her to keep it quiet, okay?

My very best to you and my loved ones always,

Millie."

Roan rose from the table and walked into the living room. He handed the letters to Shauna and Maggie to read in private. He saw Stephen Brennan coming up the path and the moment he entered the house, Roan scowled at him and handed him the envelope.

"Oh, so you know already," remarked Stephen. "Sorry, Roan. Don't hit!"

Roan tucked his own letter in his pocket and went into the kitchen for a hot coffee. Stephen got one too, then put his briefcase on the dining room table and opened it.

Inside were four keys, each to a safety deposit box. Each key was in a jacket with a name on it. Stephen handed Maggie her key, Shauna hers, Roan his and kept his own key. He asked each person to read their letter now, as it would explain the keys.

Shauna read her letter. It was relatively short, but told her about Millie's bequest and for her to pick up the items at the bank. She indicated Roan would have a surprise for her in his letter.

Maggie sat in disbelief when she read hers. Millie had left not only personal items, but the rest of the bequest, twenty million dollars set up in the trust. It was hers to do with as she saw fit for her personal use. The trust was administered by the bank, as usual and taxes would be paid by them, per agreement from years ago. Maggie had no worries unless it was how to enjoy the money. Millie also gave her the lake house and whatever was inside.

Roan's letter was a little more specific, going into more detail about the relationship with his folks. She also gave him her cottage in Ireland, called "Roselyn Cottage" in Ardmore, County Waterford. She wrote most of her books there and always knew she would leave it to Roan. The cottage was freehold and the taxes had been paid well in advance. This was her favourite spot in the world and Millie knew Roan and Shauna would take excellent care of it, then hand it down to their children.

"Now, if anyone has questions, please feel free to ask," said Stephen. "I know this is a lot to take in all at once, but I can help."

Maggie spoke first and asked, "Maybe we should go down to the bank now, if you would go with me, Stephen. With Ronnie out there, no one is really safe until he is locked away for good."

"Sure Maggie," he replied. "We can go now. I think I hear another car coming up, so Roan, if there isn't anything immediate, I'll take Maggie to the bank and bring her home."

Agent Keller and Alex exited their vehicle and passed Stephen on their way in. Stephen gave Alex the once over and you could almost hear him say, *nice, very nice*!

The front door was still open and Alex walked in with Michael behind her. Shauna was surprised to see such a petite woman in a three-piece suit walk in.

Roan got up and introduced her, "Alex, this is my wife, Shauna and our son, Conor. Family, this is Alexandra, my new personal assistant."

"Alright Dad, when do I get one of these," exclaimed Conor. "Hey Alex, I'm Conor."

"Please forgive the twelve year-old, Alex," replied Roan. "Hormones, you know."

"Pleased to meet you all," said Alexandra. "I'm assuming from what I just saw up the road, these are temporary quarters for you until the house can be restored. Agent Keller has informed me what happened this morning."

"Conor, would you take Alex's luggage up to the extra bedroom for her?" asked Roan.

"Sure Dad," he replied. "Happy to."

"Well, Alex, this wasn't exactly the welcome we had planned for you," explained Roan. "But we have had a bit of a problem here named Ronald Rutherford, Jr. He's just killed a police officer and his aunt, plus blew up a CTB agent and our home as you have seen. Busy boy, our Ronnie."

"Would you like some coffee, Alex? May I call you Alex?" asked Shauna.

"Yes, that would be fine, Shauna," replied Alexandra. "I tend to be informal at the house, but with clients in public, I am all business. I'm looking forward to seeing how I can help with all these details you seem to have 'inherited'."

"Right now we are somewhat in a lock-down situation, Alex," remarked Roan. "There has been a sighting of Ronnie in the area and with this latest murder, and us being targets, we feel it's best to stay inside and be safe."

Agent Keller excused himself by saying, "Sorry folks, but I need to get over to the hospital to see how Agent Fitzgerald is doing. I hope his hearing has come back. Bomb blasts are pretty concussive and I'm sure he is in a world of hurt right now."

"Is that Parker Fitzgerald?" asked Alex. "He was the one severely injured?"

"Yes, do you know him, Alex?" replied Keller.

"Mmmm, yes, we are friends or at least we were years ago," said Alex.

She glanced down at the floor, thoughtfully remembering her past life, then looked back up. More officers were at the door to speak with the men inside.

"Shift change, I expect," explained Roan. "This has been a very long day. Maggie should be back here soon."

"Say Conor," asked Alex. "Can you show me to the room I will be using. I need to unpack and check in with my service to let them know I arrived in one piece."

"Sure, follow me," replied Conor. "Up the stairs and to the left."

Katie called from the store and asked for Shauna.

When she came to the phone, Shauna said, "I'm here Katie, were you able to reschedule the bid at the university? It has been so wild here, I haven't even had the chance to call you."

Katie replied, "Yes, I rescheduled for Friday. How on earth are you all doing out there? Jimmy said Conor couldn't come to school today and now Millie is dead? This is really serious, isn't it, Shauna?"

"Katie, you have no idea what we have had to endure," explained Shauna. "Ronnie killed Millie, shot at Roan and also killed a police officer. And he blew up the CTB agent, our garage and lots of the neighbors' windows. This guy is out of his mind and extremely dangerous. Please, Katie. Watch every worker at the store and be certain the alarms are set everywhere. The police lost track of Ronnie this morning and he is out there, armed and extremely dangerous."

"Jim has a couple of days off," replied Katie. "I will have him work at the store, just in case. Oh, and the decorator? He's really good. I hope we can keep him."

"That 'decorator' is a CTB agent, Katie and no, we can't keep him no matter how good he is!" responded Shauna.

"Oh you really aren't kidding aren't you?" asked Katie. "A CTB agent? You told me that yesterday but I didn't believe you."

"They all are," replied Shauna. "I just hope Parker is okay. He was severely injured in the blast. Maybe you and Jim can come out for supper tomorrow night, meet Roan's new assistant and see the damage in the daylight. It's simply unbelievable."

"Sure, we can come out. Do you need more food? I only brought you one bag of it yesterday and you must be out by now." said Katie.

"We are, but we'll order a bunch of it and have it delivered," replied Shauna. "It looks like we all might be here for about a month or at least until Ronnie is captured. I have no idea how long it will take to get the house back together. The blast did structural damage, as well as blew off the garage, so I don't know at this point."

"Okay, well, I will talk with you tomorrow and we will bring Jimmy out after work," Katie said with a sigh. "I just wish this hadn't happened to anyone."

"I know. Roan is in a terrible state because he was with Millie when she died," explained Shauna. "Look, I need to go now and make up the food order and get supper on the table. I have a bunch to feed. See you tomorrow. Bye."

Shauna got out her planner, started writing out a list and pulled out the tape from the answering machine from her pocket.

She handed it to Roan and said, "I almost forgot to give you this. I saw the machine blinking when I went to feed Flash last night and took the tape out. I don't even know what's on it."

Roan took it over to the machine in the studio and pressed play. There were short messages from friends and one from Ronnie. It said he was going to kill everyone who knew Lulabelle. No one was safe. He blew up her house, killed her, making it look like a heart attack and Roan was next. Roan quickly gave the tape to an officer on watch and told him to get this down to Agent Keller immediately.

After a short while, Conor turned on the television and the story was all over the news. It identified Ronnie, his Aunt Millicent Forsythe, the

Sanderson's home, with all the damage and the dead police officer, his family and all the nasty details. They all sat transfixed at the reporter, who struggled with her words as she spoke. The police had issued a warning to residents to stay in their homes and be aware of who was around their houses. Ronnie Rutherford was armed and deadly. He had killed and would kill again without provocation. County, State and Federal law enforcement agencies had been called in to patrol the area in and around Bemidji. Because Rutherford was a native of the area, he knew where to hide and it would be difficult to locate him, but not impossible.

Shauna walked away from the news broadcast and called the grocery store in town. She gave them her list and asked if they could deliver in the morning. Then she called the florist across from the Gallery and ordered flowers for Millie. She ordered white roses and lilies, with silver and blue ribbons.

Roan took her cue and called the publisher's number on the discs. He advised them of the situation and explained he would be sending them on for publication. Then he called the church and left a message for Father Miller. Soon Stephen and Maggie would return, so Roan went to the basement and brought up the big leaf for the dining room table. There would be about ten for the evening meal.

Roughly ten minutes later, Maggie came in with a box containing Millie's family treasurers. While Shauna made supper, Maggie explained what every thing was, showed off the beautiful family jewellery which had been Emmie's and pointed out the people in the photos, including her late husband, Paul. There were lots of memories in that box. You could tell Maggie had been crying.

By 7:00 PM, Shauna had supper on the table. They all said grace and gathered around the table, saying an additional prayer for the fallen officer and for Millie. Stephen was glad for a home cooked meal and Alex was getting to know the family and friends who made this circle go 'round. The security men were also fed, then it was more quiet time at the Sandersons. It was beginning to rain and as a thunderstorm moved in, a shadowy figure moved in and out of the trees near the lake. Was it Ronnie? Or someone else? A shot rang out.

Chapter Eleven

One of the rookie officers shot at the figure down by the lake.

He missed, but another policeman came over and admonished him, "You idiot. That could have been a neighbor out walking his dog. Yes, of course it could have been Rutherford, but never, ever discharge a firearm without a clear target. Understand?"

The officer shook his head and went back to his post. Now Alex was well aware of the tension surrounding the household and those protecting it. She said she'd had a long day and was going to bed. Maybe the rest of the family should think about it, too.

Stephen said goodnight and would call them in the morning. He left and Roan turned on the security system. The porch kept the rain off the men outside, but they were now extra vigilant with Rutherford on the loose.

Alex closed the door and turned the lights off in her room, took her binoculars and surveyed the lake area. The night was pitch black and the rain pelted down. The occasional flash of lightning lit up the sky and gave the lake an eerie feeling. She couldn't see anything moving until a short flash of sheet lightning hit on the other side of the lake. And there, standing with a rifle in his hand above his head, was Ronald Rutherford. He stood motionless as if defying authority, baiting police and begging them to capture him.

Alex pressed the button on her walkie-talkie and whispered, "Suspect down at the lake. Armed with rifle. Taunting you. Close in sides."

She continued to watch as State Troopers, Agent Keller and local law enforcement moved in a line toward the lake. The snare of the net was closing in on Rutherford. He had nowhere to go except into the lake. Suddenly, flood lights shined in the middle of the crescent they had formed and right in the center was Rutherford. This time, he had been outsmarted. He raised his rifle, ready to shoot, when a deputy reacted and shot Rutherford, grazing him in the leg. He fell and fifteen officers with weapons drawn converged on the assailant. A trooper kicked the rifle away, flipped Rutherford over (as he screamed in pain from his leg wound) and handcuffed his wrists behind his back. Within moments, the hunt was over. Rutherford was in custody and the city of Bemidji could relax. No one would be happier than Roan and Shauna.

During all of this excitement on the beach, Conor was watching from his window.

He ran across the hall and yelled, "They got him. They got him. A deputy shot him in the leg, then they handcuffed him and took him away in a wagon. They got Rutherford!"

Roan, Shauna and Maggie rushed to Conor's window just as there was a knock at the door. Roan ran downstairs, turned off the security system and opened to find the police chief standing there with a huge grin on his face.

"We got the bastard," said Chief Reynolds. "Tom shot him in the leg, but we got him. You can all sleep soundly tonight folks."

Alex also came downstairs and winked at Chief Reynolds. He left and Roan asked if anyone wanted coffee.

"No thanks, Roan," said Maggie. "But I'll have a small brandy—I said SMALL."

"Okay Maggie, you got it," replied Roan. "But I'll put the coffee on for the rest of us. Thank the good Lord they have him in custody alive. I didn't think Ronnie would let them take him in one piece."

Conor asked Alex if she'd seen all the activity and she explained, "No, I didn't Conor. I was fast asleep. I hate to fly and I was so tired, I just fell right to sleep. Guess I missed a show, huh?"

"Man oh man, did you, Alex," replied Conor. "Hey Dad, is there any chocolate cake left? I'm starving."

The 10:00 PM news was just coming on and Shauna turned the television on to see if there was anything about the capture.

It was the lead story and the reporter began the news, "This just in. Fugitive Ronald Rutherford has just been captured outside the home of Roan and Shauna Sanderson, down by the lake. Fifteen officers from local, county, Federal and state agencies set a trap for him and closed in about twenty minutes ago. Oh wait. Here's Rutherford being taken into the jail. Our reporter at the scene, Adam Breslin has the police chief with him now."

"Chief Reynolds, what can you tell us about the capture of Ronald Rutherford?" asked Breslin.

"Well Adam," replied the Chief. "It was excellent detective work and fantastic cooperation from all areas of law enforcement. We knew Rutherford would make a big mistake by staying too close to the house. We counted on that and it paid off. We closed in on him about 9:30 this evening and were able to bring him in. Deputy Tom Delaney had to shoot him in the leg to bring him to the ground, but that's the only injury sustained in the capture."

Adam Breslin looked directly into the camera and said, "That's live from the County Jail and now back to you in the studio."

Shauna turned the television off and sat down on the leather couch.

As she sipped her coffee, she looked out the window at the lake and remarked, "One down and one to go I think. But for now, we should concentrate on Millie and the sheriff's deputy who was killed. Let's say a Rosary for them now before we get interrupted again tonight. Alex, I know this may not be something you are used to, but you can stay and listen if you'd like."

"Yes," she replied. "I'd like that."

Shauna put the Rosary CD on the stereo and began the Glorious Mysteries in tribute to the two souls who were on their way to Heaven. Conor got to use his new rosary from Rome and Roan broke in his new one from Medjugorje. They were just about finished when the phone rang. It was Stephen Brennan. Rutherford wanted to talk with Roan.

Roan came over to the phone and told Stephen, "I'm not coming down there now, Steve. I'm too tired and going back to bed. If he wants to talk with me, I can come down in the morning. Goodnight."

"But Roan," explained Stephen. "He wants to tell you something—about DuMonde."

There was a moment of silence on the phone.

Roan finally spoke, "Alright Stephen. If you are going to be there, I will come down now. If he has anything to tell us, I want witnesses and plenty of them. Tape the conversation. I want this documented."

Roan hung up the phone and told everyone, "Stephen says Rutherford has information about DuMonde and wants to speak with me now. I'm getting dressed and will go down for this little 'chat' just to see if he's blowing smoke or if he has some real information. Alex, would you come with me please."

Alex nodded and ran upstairs to get dressed. She came back down dressed in jeans, sneaks and a navy sweatshirt with the serpentine logo written in orange on the back. Her ever-present briefcase came along. In minutes, they were out the door. Roan got to drive his new truck for the first time.

When they got to the police station, Roan met Stephen and Chief Reynolds at the holding cells. Rutherford seemed agitated but relatively subdued as he fidgeted in his cell. He was mumbling to himself as Roan and Alex walked in with Stephen. Alex turned on a tape recorder and they sat down on the bench across from Rutherford's cell.

"You wanted to see me, Ronnie?" asked Roan.

"Oh there you are," screamed Ronald. "Mr. Fancy Pants all monied up like you owned the world. Who's the broad with you? Your mistress, huh?"

"That's enough. I'm outta here," said Roan.

"Wait, wait," yelled Rutherford. "I want to tell you something about my friend, DuMonde. Yeah, that's right. Your wifey's nightmare buddy? And who do you think put him up to it, huh, Roan? He's still out there waiting for you. Look around and you will see him staring back at you with those nasty black eyes. Want to know how I know him?"

Roan turned around and looked straight at Ronnie and said, "Okay, tell me all about your friend, DuMonde."

Ronnie replied, "I met him at a prison in France a few years ago. I was doing the forensics on a kill he'd done. See, I was on loan from Interpol in Dublin. We started talking and kinda clicked, you might say. I figured a way for him to get free without being tied to it and he said if I ever needed a favor, all I had to do was let him know. He disappeared without a trace and no one ever knew it was me who helped him escape. And we kept in touch over the years…just in case."

Ronnie cleaned his glasses and continued, "You had been on the news all over the world with your new restaurant and the plane crash and all. Oh pity poor Roan. I wanted revenge on you for stealing my money and for being Mr. Perfect in high school, so I hacked into the Interpol computer system and stole your information from right under Cresswell's nose—that pratt. That's how I got your home phone number and Internet address. And you didn't have a clue. But now DuMonde does. He knows where to find you and when you least expect it, he'll be there—watching. Stalking. And he's ready to eliminate you and that pretty little wife of yours."

Roan couldn't believe what he was hearing and looked directly at Ronnie.

Roan said quietly, "And you decided to take revenge for some misguided idea you had about me? What did I ever do to you, Ronnie?"

"You were the Golden Boy of Bemidji with your good looks and talent," explained Ronald. "You had parents who adored you, friends like my Aunt Millie and Lulabelle who thought the world revolved around you. You had it all and I had nothing. I was the genius—the geek in the thick black glasses who no one looked at except with contempt. My mother had a nervous breakdown because of me. I didn't have any friends and I never went to the Prom. Girls used to run from me. And you want to know why I hold a grudge? You make me sick, Roan. I'm sorry I didn't kill you when I had the chance. Now maybe DuMonde will have the pleasure."

Alex turned off the recorder, put it back in her briefcase and walked out the door. She went to the sergeant's desk and asked to use the phone. She looked up Cresswell's secure number and called. It took a little while, but he finally answered.

"Inspector Cresswell? This is Alex Simpson with SSS," she said succinctly. "You've been hacked by Ronald Rutherford. He's in custody here in Bemidji but he has had contact with DuMonde. I am overnighting a copy of a tape we just made from Rutherford informing us of DuMonde's activity, how he was able to get Roan's information from your computer system and stating that DuMonde now has it. I'm also making a copy of the tape for the CTB and local authorities. Rutherford has killed at least three people we know of locally, but you might be able to trace him through your own records. He is, after all, one of your own."

Cresswell was stunned and replied, "One of our own? But I don't remember anyone by that name on our team."

"He was with the Dublin branch, forensic scientist," continued Agent Simpson. "He had contact with DuMonde in France. That's how they met and DuMonde is returning a favor for Rutherford's help in escaping. It's all on the tape. You systems aren't secure there, Cresswell. I'll contact you again when we get more information out of Rutherford. Until then, analyze your computer system. DuMonde might have been getting into them for years without your knowledge thanks to Rutherford giving him the codes."

Alex concluded the call and went back inside. Stephen had been asking Ronnie about Lulabelle's death and he admitted to blowing up her house, making it look like the storm did it. And he's poisoned her with a non-detectable poison which made it look as if she'd had a heart attack. She simply ran outside and died right there on the beach at Roan's house. Roan couldn't take any more and walked out.

"You selfish, self-centered bastard," screamed Stephen. "You'll rot in hell for this."

Rutherford stuck his tongue out at Stephen and yelled back, "Naaner naaner naaner. DuMonde's gonna get 'cha. You're so dumb!"

Although now it was after 1:00 AM, Stephen suggested they find a coffee shop and discuss what had just happened. There was one close to the Police Station and they went inside. Alex took her tape out and made duplicates on her machine. She gave one to Stephen, one to Roan, then made three more for the CTB, Cresswell and Police Chief. She kept the original for the file. They ordered coffee and sandwiches, then began discussing what had just happened.

Chief Reynolds came in for a break and Alex went over to give him the tape.

She also told him, "From what I have been able to learn from Ronnie's background, he is an expert at chemical compounds and he could have something on him he could take to commit suicide. I suggest you hose him down and check all orifices, including his hair and glasses for anything he could consume. Put him in a jumpsuit and order a suicide watch."

Chief Reynolds was extremely impressed with Ms. Simpson's command of police procedures and asked how she got that way.

"Years of education and practical application, Chief," explained Alex. "I am a highly trained private investigator, protection specialist and certified body guard. My weapon is a Lady Smith and Wesson 9 mm, which I carry with me. If you need my permit, just ask. I am senior vice president of SSS—Serpentine Security Systems in Phoenix, Arizona and am here working under cover as Roan's assistant. My name here is Alex Baker. So don't blow it, okay, Chief?"

"Ah, no ma'm, I won't," sighed Chief Reynolds.

Alex returned to the men and began eating her ham and Swiss sandwich. Stephen was also impressed with Alex's presence in Rutherford's jail cell and was amazed at her unruffled demeanor when he was being so belligerent.

Alex just looked at Stephen and said, "You get used to some of this Stephen. I work where there is drug and gang crime every day. Our officers are out in that on a 24-7 basis and we have to be alert to every threat, dealing with them efficiently and effectively. It isn't pretty but it's a necessary evil, I'm afraid. Sometimes it makes us hardened to people around us, but it's necessary to preserve that private space away from our daily duties."

The exhaustion was evident in Roan's face and Stephen said they should go back to the cottage. There would be plenty of media there in the morning and Roan needed as much sleep as he could get. And there was a funeral to finalise for Millie.

"Okay, if you are all finished, we should go home," said Stephen.

Roan and Alex agreed. They drove back in silence and got to the cottage within twenty minutes. Roan went straight up to bed, while Alex jotted some notes in the dining room. It was 3:00 AM and time to get at least a few hours' sleep.

Conor got up for school and ran down to catch the bus. Shauna was up making breakfast, as Maggie brought her bags down.

"I'm going home," she said. "No need for me to stay here any longer. I want to go over to Millie's house and see what condition it's in after Ronnie wrecked it. There must be some windows and doors which need replacing. Tom Delaney said he would go over with me later this afternoon."

"That's a good idea, Maggie," replied Shauna. "You need to get back into your own routine anyway, just like the rest of us. I have to get down to the Gallery, too."

They finished breakfast and let Roan sleep. Alex was on her cell phone making arrangements for the delivery of the tape to Agent Cresswell in Rome, plus she called Agent Keller to arrange a time to bring in his copy. She wanted to see Parker at the hospital. Maybe a familiar face from the past would cheer him up.

"Shauna, may I borrow the car to go into town for a bit?" asked Alex.

"Sure, the keys are on the hanger by the back door," explained Shauna.

Soon the contractors were at the door asking to get into the house. Alex said she would unlock it on her way into town. A few minutes later, a little face popped up at the front door of the cottage.

Flash toddled in the open door and Alex asked, "Is this yours? Is this Flash?

"Oh yes, this is our little pal, Flash, Alex," replied Shauna. He's Tyler's best friend. We just love him to pieces. Hey buddy, you hungry?"

Flash looked up and yawned. He followed his Mom into the kitchen and looked around at the strange place, but spied Mickey's food bowl and ambled over to it. Flash sneezed and looked up with disgust. Shauna took some granola out of the box, put it in a little dish, added some fruit and gave it to Flash. Now that was a meal.

Alex didn't much care for rodents. She thought to herself, *my dog would make a scoobie snack out of that chipmunk.* She went over to get the keys and left for town.

Roan finally woke up just as Alex left.

He came down to see an empty house, except for his wife and said, "Are we finally alone? Oh good, I can kiss my wife without someone shooting at me!"

Shauna explained the contractors were at the house and he was needed up there. Alex was unlocking the house on her way to mail the tape in town, plus check on Agent Fitzgerald. Now that Roan was awake, Shauna could go into work. She gave Roan his breakfast and kissed him goodbye.

Roan finished up, got dressed and went up to the house to talk with the contractors. The damage on the garage side of the house was the worst, but there was also structural damage on the front in the living room. Since the insurance covered everything, Roan gave the go ahead for whatever needed to be done. The other team was working on the addition, so Roan walked over there to see how they were coming along with the footings. He arrived just in time to see a worker raising a sledge hammer to demolish Flash's house.

"Whoa, don't do that," yelled Roan. "You have to save the little house. It belongs to one of our pets. We can move it and make a new entrance for it. We went to lots of trouble to find that little house for him and he loves it."

"Sure, Mr. Sanderson, we can find somewhere else for it," replied the worker.

Roan unbolted the house, took it over to the front deck where no one was working and placed it against the house. He added a note to it saying not to move the birdhouse—occupied.

Roan walked inside to see all the broken glass all over the house. He knew if Shauna saw it, she would be extremely upset, so he looked up the number of a cleaner in town, called her and made arrangements to have the house cleaned inside while the contractors were there. It was also easier for them to walk around inside if the glass was gone.

Roan looked out the front door to see neighbors coming up the path. He walked out and chatted with them for a while. One of the residents, who lived right by the beach was still in shock. The police were outside her window last night and it scared her to pieces. She was still a little shell-shocked. Folks walked around the house to see the damage. The insurance agents were out in force to fill out claims from blast damage. They went door-to-door or met up with the neighbors talking with Roan. Stephen rolled in to tell everyone about Millie's funeral on Thursday.

Meanwhile in town, Alex parked at the hospital and found Parker's room. She saw Agent Keller there and gave him a copy of the interview tape. She looked at Parker, lying in the bed covered in gashes and slashes. He was awake and squinted to see Alex clearly.

As she walked over to his bedside, Parker asked, "Am I dreaming this? Is that really you Alex? Keller told me you were here but I didn't want to hope. I've missed you. It's been a long time."

Agent Keller made a discreet exit for the coffee shop.

Alex felt her knees buckle. The hard-nosed agent was turning back into a college sweetheart at the sight of the man she loved, lying shredded on the hospital bed.

"Hello Parker, yes, it's me," Alex gasped. "I never thought I would see you again and now we have to meet like this. I have to say, you look like hell!"

"I know I do, but I'm still me under all this shrapnel!" Parker whispered. "My hearing is just coming back, so I don't hear very well yet and I can't tell how loud I am. My head hurts worse than when we trashed McGinty's Bar over St. Patrick's Day in '79? Do you remember that?"

"You were so wasted," laughed Alex. "I had to get two burley friends just to get you back to the frat house. Your head hurt for a week. That should teach you not to drink shots so fast."

"Didn't have any after that. Never again. Now I only drink wine, a beer or an occasional sherry," said Parker.

Alex came closer and looked into Parker's sparkling green eyes and said, "I see your eyes in my dreams, Parker. I feel your arms around me at night and remember all the good times we had. And I remember how it felt to love you. I never understood why your parents hated me so much, but I guess my blood wasn't blue enough for them. I didn't have the right pedigree."

Parker thought for a while before speaking. He simply looked into Alex's huge brown eyes and finally explained why his parents broke them up.

Parker choked back the emotion and said, "Their plans for me weren't the ones I had for myself. My parents lived vicariously through their children and they wanted something they never had, whatever 'it' was. But maybe in a way I was a disappointment to them because I never married to give them grandchildren. I made the CTB my family and it really pissed my mother off! But I told them money wasn't the be all to end all and I was going to make my own way. So, they disinherited me! Go figure. What about you. What did you end up doing?"

"I did a lot of different things in law enforcement," continued Alex. "I was a dispatcher for years, then got my investigator's license, went for my Master's in criminology and became a certified body guard specialising in executive protection and anti-terrorism. In the meantime, I found the time to get married, have one daughter and get divorced. Now I'm a grandmother of a seven year old named grandson named Morgan. Time really flies."

"We will have to catch up over dinner once I get out of here," said Parker. "This is an interesting assignment and I hope we will be able to work on it together."

"So do I," she replied. "It's good to see you, Parker. Really good. I will come by and see you again before you get out of here. I need to get back to the family now."

Alex waved goodbye to Parker and Mike Keller, who had returned from the coffee shop. She stopped at Clifdens to pick up some muffins for the family on the way home. Alex also went into OfficeMax to pick up office supplies she'd forgotten. Alex liked Bemidji, but wasn't looking forward to cold weather. Being from Arizona, warm weather was just right for her. The assignment would be over with by Fall anyway.

The builders were out in numbers. There were lumber trucks in the side yard of the house. Maggie's car had been towed and the tree trimmers were trying to make sense of the pines which had been blown to toothpicks by the blast. Some of the decking had been salvaged to use in another project, but Roan had chosen a new composite material made from ground up plastics and wood shavings. It wouldn't rot or mildew, plus it would last years longer than wood. This renovation would make the house stronger and more efficient. Roan could try some new materials and building techniques which weren't available when the house was originally built. If these were successful, he would implement them in the cottage. There was room to expand the kitchen and garage, plus put an L-shaped sunroom on the side facing the lake. Shauna would love that.

Roan asked the contractors to extend the house four feet and add the sunroom, put a radiant heat flooring system under the sunroom floor and balance out the house with the quiet room addition.

Meanwhile at the store, Shauna and Katie were getting information together on commercial renovations for the University. At least when Katie goes over to discuss the work, she will have some idea of the technical aspects of their needs. The remodeling was moving right along and cleaning with the shop vac as they went made a world of difference. The contractors were building the arch, the flooring was going down and Jim had put the counters back together. Soon the furniture would be there, along with the accessories and samples. "Whistling Winds Design Shop and Gallery" was on its way. Now Millie's books could be added to the stock, along with Lulabelle's.

Shauna ordered new stationery, business cards and polo shirts with the new logo on them. Katie and Shauna would have forest green or navy shirts and the guys could pick from tan or black shirts. Shauna also ordered baseball caps, sun visors, ballpoint pens, multi-coloured balloons and coffee mugs with the new logo.

Alex pulled into the driveway of the cottage, then walked over to the big house. She spotted Roan and asked him to go over the schedule for the next two weeks with her. The woman was more organized than Shauna! Then she decided to go back into town and speak with Chief Reynolds. As she drove back, she couldn't get Parker out of her mind. Could there be a way to salvage their relationship and make it an even better one, now that his parents weren't in the picture?

As Alex walked into the cop shop, several officers gave her a wolf whistle.

She whirled around and glared at them and said sharply, "What section of the regs does sexual harassment come under in Bemidji?"

The men shut up and Chief Reynolds quickly ran over to Alex to ask what he could do for her.

"I'd like to know if you found anything on Rutherford which could help him commit suicide," asked Alex. "Any traces of poison, perhaps?"

"As a matter of fact," explained the chief. "We confiscated his glasses. Inside one of the bows was a capsule which, if swallowed, would cause death instantaneously. I think it's some kind of curare derivative, but we weren't sure, so it's at the lab in Minneapolis. We stuck a vitamin pill in there in its place!"

"Glad my theory worked," replied Alex. "Did he say or do anything to implicate anyone else or the whereabouts of DuMonde?"

"No, but he fidgets a lot in there," remarked the chief. "He's super nervous."

"From what I've learned, he's always been like that, Chief Reynolds," said Alex. "However, he IS a genius and he could have something planned no one would ever expect. My advice is to have him audio monitored 24-7, record every word coming out of his mouth, because there could be one word which will help us avoid injury or death."

"Right you are, Ms. Baker," sighed the chief. "I just wish…"

"Wish what, chief?" replied Alex.

"Oh nothing, I guess," said Reynolds. "He's really tormented by his demons. I just hope he doesn't plea to insanity and find a way to get out of incarceration. I'd hate to have him in a facility he can escape from."

"Sometimes life grants us no assurances," Alex replied. "We get no guarantees and with Rutherford, who knows where this will lead. Well, see you later Chief Reynolds. Keep those boys in the office in line, would you?"

Chief Reynolds was really intimidated by the petite Ms. Baker and for good reason. She was a highly-skilled operative and no one around there had ever seen anyone like her—and probably wouldn't ever again.

Alex stopped in to see Stephen Brennan at his office to discuss Rutherford's legal defense. She was curious to know who his defense attorney would be.

"None to my knowledge," explained Stephen. "He wants to be his own attorney and refuses anyone who tries to help."

Alex wasn't surprised and asked, "If you were Rutherford, insane though he may be, planning something in addition to what he's already accomplished, wouldn't you like to drag this out with a variety of pleas, extensions, etc.? He's off the street, has three squares a day and shelter, no one bothers him and he can plot all he wants? I think there is more method than madness with our Ronnie."

"You think DuMode will surface here and bring help with him, perhaps?" Stephen asked. "Maybe we should do some in-depth background on Ronnie, his job with Interpol and any cases he might have worked on, plus any friends he made during their progress. You might be on to something here, Alex."

"I'll begin the process from my end," explained Alex. "I have a vast network in place which will get the answers faster and in more detail than regular law enforcement. Actually, we are better at it than the CTB, CIA and Interpol combined. MI-5 and MI-6 are pretty good at it, though. That's why we have the big contracts and make the big bucks!"

"I'm doubly impressed, Alex," responded Stephen. "I never realised a private security firm had such connections. You learn something new every day up here in the North woods of Bemidji."

"If you get wind of any type of defense or change in plea from Rutherford, let me know," said Alex. "I am having him monitored 24-7 and if he says or does anything which will give us a clue to his next move, we'll be able to jump on it."

"See you later, Alex," smiled Stephen. "I'll be out later with more details about the funeral and I have some papers for Roan to sign."

You could tell Stephen was a little smitten with Alex—most men were, because she was beautiful, highly intelligent, witty and deadly. That's a combination you don't find often.

The television trucks were set up near the Courthouse for the arraignment and one rookie reporter caught a glimpse of Alex as she walked across the square from Brennan's office. He decided to follow her and try for a story. Alex was about to make the man want to change professions—or underwear. She put on her dark glasses and stopped dead in her tracks. She turned around, as the man almost ran into her.

His videographer was following him with the camera rolling with a live feed and without missing a beat, Alex cooed like Marilyn, "Oooo, hi there sexy. Aren't you just the cutest thing? Wanna play?"

The reporter was blind-sided and turned to his operator to motion 'cut', then looked for Alex and she was gone. She had gone into a store, opened her brief case, put on a blonde wig and turned her jacket inside out, changed to another pair of sunglasses and added a scarf. Alex easily walked back across the square to her car and the reporter simply stood there. She chuckled all the way home.

Work was moving ahead on all fronts and Roan had gone back to the cottage to work on his eulogy for Millie. He really hated doing this, but seemed to be doing so many recently, it was almost a rote task. Alex arrived to find Roan at the dining room table, next to a huge stack of crumpled up paper, with a disgusted look on his face.

"Having problems with the eulogy, Roan?" she asked. "Never liked writing them myself but we have had to give a bunch of them lately, with operatives who didn't come back from Iraq or assignment. It's one of the toughest jobs we have."

"I just can't wrap my mind around it, Alex," Roan sighed. "You know someone, but you don't really. You care deeply about them, but didn't know them well. I'm sure the right words will come eventually."

"Maybe you can quote something from Scriptures which would be appropriate, Roan," explained Alex. "That's always comforting and it helps bridge the gap when you can't think of anything else to say. And besides, it sounds as if Millie would like Scriptures read at her funeral, other than the readings at the service."

"Great idea, Alex," replied Roan. "I'll get my Bible and see what fits in the best."

Roan realised his Bible wasn't there, but up at the big house, so he went over to the bookcase and searched the volumes on the shelf for his parent's Bible. He found exactly what he was looking for and as he thumbed through the pages, he found several photographs of himself as a child, with his parents. And there was one with Lulabelle, her husband and Millie. He thought about having that one blown up and displayed at the service. The passage it marked was also a favourite, so he felt because the photograph was marking that spot, he would use both in the service.

The afternoon drifted away and when Shauna got home, the eulogy was finished and Roan was ready to sit down and relax. That's when Stephen came by with the papers for Roan to sign.

"Hey ho, everybody. Steverino here," shouted Stephen as he walked up the pathway. "Mother put the kettle on, I'm coming in."

Brennan was such a goofball, it was hard to realise what an excellent attorney he was. But he came in, looked at Alex and gave her a 'Hi-five'— and a butt bump.

"Work it sister," he laughed. "That was some switcheroo you did on that reporter this afternoon. I thought he was going to pee his knickers when you cooed like Marilyn Monroe into the camera. Dang, that was funny. And then you disappeared? Wow, you're good."

Alex was still laughing and had to explain about being followed by the reporter. She wasn't about to be compromised by anyone, especially a wet-behind-the-ears reporter who thought he had a story.

Roan and Shauna were duly impressed and sat down with Stephen to look over the details for the funeral, while Alex wrote up some notes. Conor came rushing in to find food and Mickey came in carrying a dead frog (which had been dead for weeks by the smell of it), dropped it in the middle of the floor and let go the most horrendous fart anyone had ever heard. It was nuclear!

"Oh good God help us," screamed Alex. "Get a gas mask, get some air freshener—something. I can't breathe!"

"Oh, that's just Mickey welcoming you to the household," laughed Conor.

"Hey Mickey, you raunchy old dawg. How's it hangin'?" howled Stephen. "You have to be a champion stink pot to get that kind of reaction and look, the dog's grinning at me."

Mickey's gasseous anomaly broke everyone up and gave the folks a good belly laugh—something they hadn't done in a long time. If you ever need comic relief, look no further than a certain Boston Bulldog named Mickey McGuire.

Shauna and Alex whipped up an excellent dinner of meatloaf and gravy, smashed potatoes and a Greek salad with fresh dressing (with anchovies, no less). Alex hadn't really cooked for anyone for a while and enjoyed it immensely. Stephen invited himself for supper and the evening turned out to be quite enjoyable. Stephen got to know Conor a little better and said he would even play chess with him on the new chess sets they each received from Rome.

"Roan, that was a great gift," said Stephen. "I didn't have one and it's super. Thanks. Oh, and the briefcase? Shauna, that rocks."

Shauna smiled and sat contentedly after such a good meal. After a while they all decided to go up to the house and take a look at the progress. It was amazing how fast the builders were getting the house repairs and the additions put on. When they began looking around, Shauna had a question.

"What's this footing over here, Roan?" she asked. "I don't recognize this in the plans. Oh, and why is the house extended? That wasn't in there either."

Roan had to come clean and explained, "Since they were already working on the house, I just had them add a little here and there to make the house symmetrical, that's all. Now you will have a huge new kitchen to work with, since we seem to have so many guests. And a sunroom/four seasons room we can open up during the summer to eat outside or close it in the winter and enjoy the snow from the comfort of our own home. We will have two glass extensions on the house, which provide excellent views of the lake and take advantage of the sunshine. I can't think of a better way to balance out the house."

Conor was delighted and said, "Sweet."

"Oh, and Conor," expressed Roan. "There is a bonus room over the new garages for you to use as a game room or to watch tv with Jimmy and your friends. You guys can hang out up there and will be as you say, 'Sweet'."

"And what's in it for you, Roan?" asked Shauna.

"There is a pottery shop on the side of the studio extension, so I can make pottery again," explained Roan. "There will be a wheel, a couple of kilns and storage, plus enough light to work by. I'd say we all benefit."

By now it was around 9:00 PM and the light had faded. Conor had only a few weeks of school left, but had to be up early for a field trip to some cave paintings near Bemidji and Stephen had court in the morning, so he said goodnight. Shauna found Flash sitting in his house very confused.

"Come on, little friend," whispered Shauna. "Let's take your house down to the cottage for a little while and you won't feel so alone."

She carried the house with Flash inside, down to the cottage and put it down on the deck outside the front door. Flash looked around and waved his little arms around in agreement. Although there was no door to the inside from there, the position was only temporary and a new doorway would be built into the quiet room addition.

Tomorrow would be the arraignment for Ronald Rutherford and Stephen was ready. As time drew closer, Stephen ran over his notes and watched, as Ronnie was brought to the courthouse in shackles and leg chains. Everything was linked to a central chain around his waist. This is the time he would enter his plea. But would it be guilty, by reason of insanity or not guilty, by reason of insanity. Everyone felt the insanity plea would be used no matter which one he picked.

The following morning, as Ronnie stood before the Federal judge, brought in to hear this case, he asked Ronnie to make his plea.

"Guilty or not guilty?" asked the judge.

"Guilty, your honor," said a stone-faced Ronnie. "I plead guilty."

There was hushed mumbling throughout the court and Ronnie stood there grinning at Roan.

"He's got something tucked up that jumpsuit sleeve," grumbled Stephen.

The judge continued, "Trial will commence on August 29 at 9:00 AM. Does the defendant wish to have an attorney appointed?"

"No, your honor. I will be defending myself at that time," expressed Ronnie.

"So ordered," said the judge. "Defendant will be remanded to the county jail until trial. Bail will not be set as this man is a flight risk and dangerous to the public and himself. Court dismissed."

The people rose and Stephen looked at Roan in disgust.

"He's up to something big this time. I can feel it, Roan," said Stephen. "We have the summer to figure it out. Get in contact with some of the professors of psychology at the university and see if they can profile this guy. I'm thinking he will go with 'special circumstances' at the trial and if he does—and does it right, he could get himself off. We are going to have to stay one step ahead of him."

"We have the experts we need at our disposal," explained Roan. "Anyone we need, Alex can find. But what would be the 'special circumstances' you are talking about?"

"He might try to say his parents drove him into madness because they hated him," replied Brennan. "Or that because he is a genius, no one understood him and it drove him to do terrible things. You can bet your 50 year-old Scotch he will use some type of psychological defense here and even bring in witnesses from the town. Just watch. We need to go over the clubs and groups he was associated with in high school and see how many of the members are still around. Even teachers might be called to testify."

"There are enough of us around, I'm afraid," explained Roan. "And you're one of them, don't forget."

"Okay, well, let's concentrate on the funeral tomorrow and get that completed, then your house and we'll have time to deal with the legal stuff," said Steve.

Roan went back to the house and Alex asked how things went. She didn't want cameras around her because it could compromise her cover in that type of media frenzy. She told Roan she needed to get the appropriate clothing for the funeral and asked if she thought Shauna could show her around this afternoon.

"I'm sure Shauna would love to show you the stores here, Alex," replied Roan. "It's most of the usual chain stores, but there are some nicer local stores which carry petite sizes. You've seen Shauna is only a size three, which is really tiny like you are, so I'm sure she knows where to get the right things. Just put them on my account."

"Thanks Roan, but I will buy them myself," responded Alex. "You are paying me an excellent salary and I think I can afford this little expense."

"Which reminds me," said Roan. "I need to pay you for the first month. I should make it out to Alexandra Baker or Simpson?"

"That's actually my entire name," she replied. "My initials are ABS—go figure! But I will need to establish a local bank account. I'd say, Alexandra Baker for the cover. Would Stephen help me do that, since he is corporate counsel for the bank?"

"Sure," smiled Roan. "We all bank there anyway, so it's a no-brainer. Just take the check down to the bank, I'll call them to explain you are my personal assistant and use this address, not the main house as your mailing address."

Roan wrote out a check for $20,000 and gave it to Alex.

She smiled and folded it up, put it in her briefcase and said, "One more run to the city. I'll call Shauna and meet her at the Gallery. I can stop at Stephen's and tell him I am establishing the account under my middle name and then we can go to the bank. And we can find something for the funeral."

Alex called Shauna and made plans for the afternoon. She grabbed a quick lunch, changed her clothes and drove to town. Roan stayed to go over the service for Millie, called the bank and the funeral home. Then he contacted Father Miller at St. Philip's to finish the details.

After all the formalities were completed at the bank, Shauna took Alex to several shops, then out to the mall. They both decided on new clothes for the funeral, as Shauna was sick of the same black dress she'd worn for the past ten years. She found the most fantastic dress with two jackets, which could be worn for business or formal occasions. It had a plain, suit jacket and one with beading. Shauna bought stockings to match and simply HAD to have a new pair of black shoes to go with! Alex found something similar in navy, then found several summer dresses she liked and shoes to match. They walked over to the hat section of the store and bought several summer skimmers, scarves and sun glasses.

"I can see you and I are going to have things in common," exclaimed Shauna. "Like SHOPPING! Oh, and don't forget cooking."

"You know, Shauna," replied Alex. "I have been stuck inside at that office for so long, I never get the chance to shop. I'm simply too tired. And if I go out on assignment, I'm in BDU's or all black. I even wear cammo. Talk about androgynous! My underwear is industrial strength! My wardrobe is sorely lacking normal people clothes. We may have to do a lot of shopping. I don't even have perfume, jewellery or fun things like that!"

"Wait until we get to Rome," Shauna said gleefully. "Katie and I will be going over on a buying trip for the store and Roan wants you to go with us for protection. I've seen some delightful places and their leather goods? Oh my, they are wonderful. Katie is as daffy as I am when it comes to shopping."

"As Conor would say," said Alex. "Sweet!"

The women laughed and toted all their packages back to the car. Shauna stopped at the Gallery to check in with Katie, then drove her truck back home, with Alex following. Chief Reynolds was waiting for them at the cottage.

Shauna was pleased to see the chief making a house call and said, "So, Chief Reynolds. To what do we owe the pleasure of your company today?"

"I wanted to check in with you because Ronnie has become different," he explained. "He is quiet, almost placid. He stopped pacing in his cell. He smiles and says 'please' and 'thank you.' He wants some books to read and has requested a Bible. I'm not sure what to make of him."

"Maybe he has a split personality," replied Alex. "I'm not saying this is a real change. He could be faking it, but that could be one of the special circumstances he was rambling on about. If it is, he could have been treated for any type of disorder and we would need to subpoena the physician who treated him. This could be locally or it could be in Ireland, where he's been living. We need to get more background on him and go from there."

"See you tomorrow at the services then," said the chief. "I didn't know Millie, but I did know her sister Lulabelle. Nutty old broad, but she was a sweetie. And did she ever love kids. Too bad she never had any. Well, I'm off."

Shauna busied herself putting away her new clothes, as did Alex, then they came down to prepare supper. Conor came in wearing a karate gee.

"So, what do you think," yelled Conor. "Do I look like Chuck Norris yet?"

"This must be the practice you referred to," said Roan. "Are you and Jimmy taking Karate lessons now?"

"Yep, we sure are, Dad," replied Conor. "You keep forgetting, I'm twelve now—almost thirteen and Mom signed the consent form weeks ago."

"Oh please, don't remind me," roared Roan.

Alex spoke up and asked, "Would you like a work-out partner, Conor? I need to keep fit and there isn't a gym handy here. I'm a third degree black belt, so that should help out a little."

"Third degree?" sighed Conor. "Nuh-uh, you're way too good for me!"

Alex laughed and continued making the salad. After they'd eaten, Alex made some notes for making calls tomorrow and Shauna went up to double check her clothes for the funeral.

The next morning was slightly overcast. It was a perfect day for a funeral, if there was such a thing. Conor looked smart in his black suit. Roan was resplendid in his charcoal suit and Shauna was beautiful as always in her new dress and jacket. Her black hat matched perfectly. Alex came down wearing her new dress and jacket, hat and gloves, but without her briefcase. Roan picked up his notes and they piled into the sedan.

They arrived at the church a little before the casket. Hopefully there wouldn't be more than a handful of mourners at the service, so Millie could be buried with dignity, not in the middle of a circus. Father Miller met them at the doorway to the sanctuary.

"Good morning, folks," said Father. "I think it will be a small group this morning and rightly so. Millie was such a private person, very few knew her."

Several gentlemen came in and sat in the back pews.

Roan walked over and asked, "Are your friends or business acquaintances of Millie's?"

"We are her publishers from New York," remarked one of the men. "We felt it only fitting to be here for her."

"I'm Roan Sanderson and I'll need to speak with you shortly after the service, as I have some of her new books for you. She wanted to be certain they were published."

"Thank you, Roan, we know," said the second gentleman. "You can send them as soon as you've read them. We know of her wishes."

Katie and Jim came in with Jimmy. A few of the ladies from the parish were there, as well as several of her friends. But that was all. This is exactly what Millie wanted.

Father Miller began the service at the back of the church with the sprinkling of the body with holy water:

"I bless the body of Millicent Evangeline Forsythe with holy water that recalls her baptism of which St. Paul writes: All of us who were baptized into Christ Jesus were baptized into his death. By baptism into his death we were buried together with him, so that just as Christ was raised from the dead by the glory of the Father, we too might live a new life. For if we have been united with him by likeness to his death, so shall we be united with him by likeness to his resurrection."

The white pall, which is a remembrance of baptism, was placed over the casket by the pallbearers, Stephen, Jim, Roan and Conor and these words were recited:

"On the day of her baptism, Millicent put on Christ. On the day of Christ's coming, may she be clothed in Glory.

The Lord will open to them the gate of Paradise, and they will return to that homeland where there is no death, but only lasting joy.

Lord God, almighty Father, you have made the cross for us a sign of strength and marked us as Yours in the Sacrament of the resurrection. Now that you have freed our sister, Millicent from this mortal life, make her one with your saints in heaven. We ask this through our Lord Jesus Christ, your Son, one God, forever and ever."

Conor got up to do the first reading, which was from the Old Testament book of Job 19:1, 23-27:

"A reading from the book of Job. Job said: 'Ah, would that these words of mine were written down, inscribed on some monument with iron chisel and engraving tool, cut into the rock forever. This I know. That my Avenger lives and he, the Last, will take his stand on earth. After my awaking, he will set me close to him and from my flesh I shall look on God. He whom I shall see will take my part: these eyes will gaze on him and find him not aloof.' The word of the Lord. Thanks be to God."

The service continued until the Gospel. This was one of Millie's favourite readings. Roan got up to read and said the Gospel Acclamation:

"Alleluia. Benedictus es, Pater, Domine caeli et terrae, quia mysteria regina parvulis revelasti. Blessed are you, Father, Lord of heaven and earth, you have revealed to little ones the mysteries of the kingdom. Alleluia.

A reading from the holy Gospel according to Matthew. 11:25-30. Glory to you, oh Lord.

Jesus exclaimed, 'I bless you, Father, Lord of heaven and of earth, for hiding these things from the learned and the clever and revealing them to mere children. Yes, Father, for that is what it pleased you to do. Everything has been entrusted to me by my Father, and no one knows the Son except the father, just as no one knows the Father except the Son and those to whom the Son chooses to reveal him.

Come to me, all you who labour and are overburdened, and I will give you rest. Shoulder my yoke and learn from me, for I am gentle and humble in heart, and you will find rest for your souls. Yes, my yoke is easy and my burden light.' The Gospel of the Lord. Praise to you, Lord Jesus Christ."

The congregation sat down, Roan made the sign of the cross and continued, "In the name of the Father and of the Son and of the Holy Spirit, Amen. I knew Millie Forsythe for only a short time. But from what I understand, she knew me all of my life. It turned out to be quite complicated, but in the short time I knew her, I loved her as a child loves a parent. It's as if I knew her my entire life. Her warmth, generosity and freedom of spirit, shown out as brightly as a summer day. She has left us a legacy of history, of learning and of curiosity about the world each child should cherish. I always wondered why such bad things happen to such good people through no fault of their own. Maybe it's because of circumstance or neglect. Or it could be like Millie. Her life was ended by a family member who is very disturbed. In any case, we never know when we will draw our last breath and it's up to us to live each moment in love and comfort to all we meet. We should show Christ in each of us and see Christ in each person we encounter.

Lord, come, live in your people and strengthen them by your grace. Help them to remain close to you in prayer and give them a true love for one another. Grant this through Christ our Lord. Amen."

The Mass of Christian Burial continued with the Communion service, then onto the cemetery for burial.

As they were leaving the church, Father Miller recited the Antiphon,

"May the angels lead you into Paradise; may the martyrs come to welcome you and take you to the holy city, the new and eternal Jerusalem."

After they arrived at the burial site, Father Miller sprinkled the casket with holy water and incensed it. After more prayers and responses from those attending, Father Miller made the commendation:

"We commend our sister, Millicent to you, Lord. Now that she has passed from this life, may she live in your presence. In your mercy and love, forgive whatever sins she may have committed through human weakness. We ask this through Christ our Lord. Amen."

And the ending prayer:

"Lord Jesus, our Redeemer, you willingly gave yourself up to death so that all people might be saved and pass from death into a new life. Listen to our prayers; look with love on your people who mourn and pray for their dead sister, Millicent. Lord Jesus, you alone are holy and compassionate; forgive our sister her sins. In dying you opened the gates of life for those who believe in you: do not let your sister be parted from you, but by your glorious power, give her light, joy and peace in heaven where you live for ever and ever. Amen."

Each person took a flower from the vase next to the casket and placed one on top. They said their final farewells and Shauna took a white rose with her. She wanted it preserved in remembrance of her new friend, so she could look at it and think of what might have been.

Roan thanked Father Miller and gave him a generous check for the Discretionary Fund. He invited everyone to Charles' restaurant for a light luncheon, to share memories of Millie. The sun finally broke through the clouds and shined brightly on the grave as the casket was lowered into the ground. Millie was reunited with her sisters and with Christ.

Maggie stood silently at the grave, sobbing softly as she cried, "I'm so sorry Millie. He had no right, no right to do this. We could have had so much more time—all of us."

She walked slowly toward another grave a few plots down. It was her husband Paul's grave. The flowers were coming up around the neatly attended perimeter and smelled sweet in the fresh air of Spring.

Maggie bent down and whispered, "Take care of Millie. She's a gem. I know you and I will never be parted from one another, Paul, but just know, Tim has come to the rescue like he always has. I know you will be happy for us. He knows he can never take your place in my heart, but he will always continue to be your friend and you know how well he treats his friends, because you were his best one. I love you, Paul."

Maggie dabbed at her eyes with a tissue and walked toward her friends. You could tell the emotion was overwhelming her. Shauna came up and gave her a hug, as did Roan. Roan took Maggie's hand and as they walked to the car, she looked back over her shoulder.

"It's not fair, I know," sobbed Maggie. "None of it is. I never got to say goodbye to either of them—or Lulabelle either. I hope Ronnie spends the rest of his life in solitary confinement without a book or a person to visit. He needs to think about what he's done. I trust they'll give him asbestos underwear when he finally meets his maker."

Katie made a comment that, "Even murderers are capable of redemption, Maggie. But with Ronnie, I just wonder what his life must be like without God in it."

Roan invited the publishers to brunch, because he wanted to know more about Millie's writing and about her personally. These are the men she dealt with for decades and they had stories to share. Everyone could comment about their experiences with Millie and it would lighten the sadness of the day.

As they entered the restaurant, Stephen spotted the tables in the banquet room. He sat down and was silent for a few moments. Of all the friends, Stephen probably knew Millie best. You could see him remembering some of the good times and it made him smile. Her death was probably the most difficult for Stephen to endure, but he tried his best to be happy for her and her new life in Heaven.

After everyone was seated, everyone raised their glass of juice or water in a toast to Millie.

Roan spoke eloquently as he said, "To Millie. A first-class lady and an exceptional human being. You will be missed."

'Here here,' repeated the crowd.

By afternoon, they disbursed and went their separate ways. Shauna and Katie went back to the Gallery, along with Jim, while Roan, Stephen and Alex took the boys back home. The rain didn't last long, which meant the contractors were moving rapidly and it was just possible to get the house livable within the week. Of course, the work would go on around them, but in a house that size, it didn't really matter.

Conor showed Jimmy what his Dad had planned for the bonus room above the garage.

Jimmy said excitedly, "Overly Sweet."

Two words—the boy is definitely coming along!

Shauna called the auto detailing shop to see if they could put logos on the sides of their trucks. She would have the "Whistling Winds" logo on hers and Roan would have his "Ristorante Tuscano" logo, which matched the plane. With that taken care of, Shauna went about painting the walls in the expansion.

Katie had chosen a sand colour for the walls, with accents of taupe, sage and turquoise. The trim work would be a natural maple, tying it all together. This way they could go Continental, Native American, Country Classic— any type of décor. The Bluestone flooring gave the shop a rich blend and accented all the colours perfectly. The restrooms were painted the same, with floral arrangements in the 'ladies' and English footmen statues in the 'gents.'

Shauna decided to put some stone accents on the front of the store—just on the corners to give the façade some dimension. She found a stone with mica and quartz in it, which sparkled in the sunlight. It took no time for the stone mason to put it on and it looked marvelous. Shauna also had an idea to make a feature fireplace in the store and put the same stone on it as well.

Soon the store had a first-class look to it. All they needed was a few more embellishments and the furniture.

It had been a long day for everyone and at 6:00 PM, Katie and Shauna called it quits. Tomorrow would be the tour of the campus for Katie and a quiet day for Shauna, as she put on the final touches for the Gallery.

Alex had been busy investigating Ronald, Jr.'s background in Ireland. She'd found he indeed had been with Interpol, Dublin Branch for ten years as a forensic scientist, but was forced out for 'medical' reasons. She decided to go into the hospital and talk with Parker about this. Alex put the information in a file and drove into town.

Alex hadn't changed clothes from the funeral and looked stunning in her navy suit-dress. She'd borrowed one of Millie's jewelled pins from Maggie and placed it on her left lapel. Her black watch and a pair of tiny gold hoops were her other jewellery. Her shoulder-length brown hair gleamed in the Spring sunshine and a soft scent Shauna had loaned her made her feel feminine.

Parker was sitting up in the hospital bed, reading a report when Alex walked in.

He glanced up to see Alex walking confidently in and said, "You are absolutely beautiful, Alex. Why, I don't think I have ever seen you look this pretty, except the night we got engaged."

Alex began to blush and replied, "Oh come on, Parker. I just clean up well, that's all. Here is the information I was able to find on Ronnie from Interpol in Dublin. It's not that much to go on, I'm afraid, so it's possible I might have to fly over and talk with them in person."

Alex handed Parker the folder and as she did, he got an idea.

"Listen, if you can wait a week or so," explained Parker, "I could probably go with you, since it is my home town. And we could actually have a couple of days off while I show you around, that is, if you want to."

"Ah, I don't see why not," replied Alex. "But I would have to clear it with Roan before I said yes. With Rutherford in jail, the situation seems to be under control and a few days over there wouldn't hurt. We could combine business with a little sightseeing—maybe go down and take some photographs of Roan's cottage in Ardmore for them."

"Great," smiled Parker. "I'll look this information over and have Keller also look at it to see what he comes up with. We're all a good team and we will find the reason for Ronnie's dismissal."

Before Alex left, she leaned into the bed, kissed Parker gently on the lips and said, "See you later, Handsome. Have a gentle night."

It was as if someone had taken a sledge hammer to Alex's stomach and smacked it five times. Those old feelings were running around inside her like a herd of turtles on a race to the sea! Alex drove directly to the cottage to ask Roan if she should go to Ireland and interview some of the doctors who treated Ronnie. As she walked in, she saw Roan and Shauna looking at the contents of his safety deposit box.

"Oh, sorry, I don't mean to interrupt," explained Alex. "I can talk with you all after supper."

"No no, that's fine," replied Roan. "What's up Alex?"

"I've just spoken with Agent Fitzgerald about the information I discovered on Ronnie's background," said Alex. "And I feel we should go over to Ireland for a few days to speak with authorities there, then talk with physicians who treated him. It may shed some light on why he's acted this way."

"Oh, no doubt, sure that's fine with me," said Roan. "You may want something I have in this box, though."

Roan shuffled through the papers and pulled out a set of keys. They were the keys to the Ardmore cottage and Millie's automobile, stored at the local garage.

"I just brought this stuff home today and the keys are here," explained Roan. "If you are over there, you should take a drive down and check it out for us. Take some pictures of the cottage and the area so we can see what it looks like. You can accomplish two goals at the same time."

"Great," replied Alex. "As soon as Parker is feeling better, we can go over. It will take a couple of days to get everything in place anyway. Shauna, I'll help you get supper."

Shauna said to Alex, "Don't worry about food tonight. Charles sent a bunch of it home with us after the brunch, so we're set for food. I think tonight we can just help ourselves. I'm exhausted from the funeral and painting the store. But get it now before Conor hears me!"

Roan continued to pour over the contents of the box. There was a letter sealed in an envelope with a gold seal on the back. It had his name on it, so he carefully opened it, so the seal wasn't destroyed. Inside was a handwritten letter from Millie and several photographs of people in the 1940's. Roan began reading, then sat, staring at the photos.

"What is it?" Shauna asked. "Who are those people? They look a little like the Forsythes."

"Well, they are," replied Roan. "The letter says my father had a half-sister, Millicent, who married a Sir James Sutton, a British Lord and RAF fighter pilot, in 1939. He died in 1940 during the war in the Battle of Britain. It states they never had time to have children. She took her maiden name, Forsythe, back when she returned to the States. This means Millie really was my Aunt, so was Lulabelle and also Emmie."

Roan looked up at Shauna with tears in his eyes and explained, "She owned a piece of property inherited from her husband, somewhere on the Lancashire/Yorkshire border in the north of England. It has some land, a working farm with animals, and a 'large house' on it, plus a river running through the property."

"Oh my," sighed Shauna. "Does that mean you are landed gentry now?"

"No Shauna," replied Roan sternly. "It means I'm Ronnie's first cousin."

SNAP. You could have heard a pin drop.

Roan put the box down on the coffee table and walked into the kitchen for a cup of coffee. He put a shot of whiskey in it to steady his nerves.

As he sat back down, he looked at Shauna and said, "Maybe this would be a strong enough motive for murder, I don't know, but I have NO knowledge of this whatsoever. I think I need to contact Stephen immediately."

Roan picked up the phone and called his attorney, who had additional information waiting to be delivered.

"A package arrived for you this afternoon from England," explained Stephen. "I think it's the deeds to the property, which is why, I suppose, you are calling me now. I'll come out and give them to you. Believe me, Roan, I had no idea either."

"You do know, Stephen," said Roan. "This means Ronnie and I are first cousins. Think that's a motive for murder?"

"I'll be right there," continued Stephen. "Put the kettle on Dorothy."

Alex had been making some calls to Interpol in Dublin. Roan explained the contents of the box and a piece of the puzzle was now in place. Alex continued making notes from the information Roan had in the box. She'd check it out when she was in Dublin.

Within twenty minutes Stephen was there with the documents and photographs of the estate. He headed for the dining room table to spread the information out. He set each item on the table and explained them all.

"Here are the Deeds, land ownership documents, accounts for the property and information on the people who live on the land and farm your estate," explained Stephen. "Now, here are the photos of the little 'house'— Bolton Hall. It's close to the village of Bolton-by-Bowland in the Ribble Valley near the A-59 motorway. Be prepared, this is a manor house, Roan, not a little shack in the country. It was built in the early 1400's and has been in the Sutton family for over two hundred years."

Roan had to sit down. As the family gathered around, they gazed at the photographs scattered on the table. Conor's eyes got huge, while Shauna simply gasped.

"Hey Dad, look at the horses," cried Conor. "I can have my own horse."

The doorbell rang and it was Jim and Katie to pick up Jimmy.

Shauna opened the door and it must have been a shocking site, because Katie yelled, "Is everyone okay in here? What's happening?"

Shauna explained, "I think you and Jim need to come into the dining room and have a look at the contents of Roan's safety deposit box Millie left him. It says Millie was actually Roan's aunt, making him Ronnie's first cousin. And, Roan has just inherited not only a cottage in Ireland, but a manor house and estate in England. Other than that, nothing much!"

Katie looked at Shauna for a moment and stammered, "English antiques. Shopping trip for English antiques."

That broke everyone up, then Jim and Katie settled in to look at the photos. Jimmy and Conor chatted about the horses and Alex sat with Stephen discussing the motives for Ronnie's rampage.

Tomorrow would be Katie's appointment with the University, while Shauna ran the store. Jim asked if he could help, while Roan said Monday, he would take Alex to Minneapolis to meet everyone and show her his property there and get her opinion of the security. Alex wanted to shop a little, too, for her trip to Ireland. If she was going to get her man back, she needed more ammunition than in her bullet clip.

Chapter Twelve

Agent Keller made arrangements for the flight to Dublin, while Parker spoke with his family's housekeeper to open up the guesthouse. Although he had been disinherited years ago, his parents had forgiven him before they passed away, making Parker also very wealthy in his own right. He never spoke of it nor did he spend money like he had it. Parker was simply a regular guy with a high-profile job. And even Alex had no knowledge of his financial status. He'd keep it that way, too—for the time being anyway.

In the meantime, Alex and Roan went over the records for the restaurant, plus the schematics for the security systems in the Lake Minnetonka house. Roan contacted Franco to pick them up at the private airfield, as they would be bringing the company jet down from Bemidji. Roan wanted to treat Alex to a little luxury.

Monday morning, Roan drove his truck out to the airport hangar and parked inside. He and Alex boarded their plane, as Captain Marks greeted them.

"Good Morning, Sir," said the captain. "And who is our guest?"

Roan explained, "Captain Bob Marks, please meet Alexandra Baker, my new personal assistant."

"A pleasure, Miss," responded Captain Marks. "Good flying weather ahead, no storms, light winds and we should be there within the hour."

Alex picked out a window seat inside the executive jet and exclaimed,

"I can see why movie stars like this type of travel. Do you do this often, Roan?"

Roan had to reply, "Not always, but this jet does come in handy when I need a ride fast and the commuter line is filled up. It's just a little jet, anyway!"

They took off and in a very short time, Franco was waiting for them at the airfield.

He ran up to the plane in his usual fashion and gushed, "Oh boss. I am so excited to see you in one piece. Oh oh, who ees dees pretty lady?"

"Franco, this is Alexandra," replied Roan. "She is working with us now as my assistant."

"Allo, Miss Alexandra," he responded. "Eest me, Franco. I am de manager of Ristorante Tuscano. You weel like it here, right Boss?"

"Nice to meet you, Franco," said Alex. "You can call me Alex if you want. Let's go see the restaurant."

The staff was just setting the tables for lunch when they arrived. Marcel had a few things lined up, though. He'd put out some pastries, fresh cappachino and a bowl of fruit. Alex was impressed with the outside of the building and was even more impressed by the inside and the staff.

"Marcel," beamed Roan. "This is Alexandra, my personal assistant. Alex, this is Marcel, my Major Domo and one of my closest friends."

"Marcel, delighted to meet you," replied Alex. "You all have done an amazing job with this restaurant."

Franco ran into the kitchen to bring out his parents and Gramma Giovanna to meet Alex.

But you know Gramma, she burst out with, "Cutie, but too skinny. You could blow this one away with one puff. Going back to the kitchen now. Franco, bring me sausage."

Alex was a bit stunned, but shook hands with Franco's parents and other staff members.

Franco was upbeat and commented, "Gramma likes you. She's going to try to fatten you up. She doesn't DO skinny, I'm sorry. She adores Miss Maggie!"

Alex wasn't sure how to take that, but settled in with Roan and Marcel at a table to enjoy the breakfast he had prepared.

"Marcel, I need you to dig into your past in France for a moment," asked Roan. "Do you remember hearing anything about a Michael DuMonde, who would be in his 60's now? He would be part of the political terrorist movement back in the 1960's."

"DuMonde, DuMonde," mused Marcel. "Maybe, I'm not sure. Wait, would he be tall with a pony tail and haunting eyes?"

"Yes, that's the one," replied Roan. "Is he familiar?"

"Oui, he was a student revolutionary leader in the 60's in Paris," explained Marcel. "He was in the papers for several years, but that's all I remember, except for those eyes. Very scary."

Alex continued, "If you think about any details like associates, friends, habits, anything like that, would you let Roan or me know?"

"Of course," replied Marcel. "Now I must get back to the kitchen. Luncheon will be soon. Enjoy."

After they had eaten, Roan took Alex to the house on Lake Minnetonka. She was pleased the security system was so well designed and it included the little cottage by the lake. Soon there was a knock at the door. Roan peered through the security peephole and saw it was Sandra.

"Hey come in here stranger," smiled Roan. "I want you to meet Alexandra, my new assistant."

"Hi Roan, glad to see you home again," chimed Sandra as she gave Alex the once-over. "I'm the decorator around here. Nice to meet you, Alexandra. I brought all the receipts for cleaning and getting that grunge off the walls. Man, that was nasty. But I figured you would like to see what they did. Franco paid them and they did an excellent job, as I'm sure you've seen."

"Hey Sandra, I have a favor to ask this morning," asked Roan. "Could you take Alex out to Mall of America and show her around some of the shops? She's looking for some new clothes for a business trip, plus a little pleasure trip on the side and she needs something pretty and feminine. I thought you would be just the right person to show her around."

"Great, I have a couple of hours free before my next appointment and I'd be glad to," replied Sandra. "Come on, Honey, let's blow this pop stand and get shopping."

Shauna had already briefed Sandra on what Alex needed, so she had the stores lined up for when they arrived. The ladies went to several petit shops for dresses, skirts, blouses and tops, jeans and hats. Then they went to a lingerie shop for frilly undies and lovely night wear. After that, it was on to several shoe stores and a perfume shop Sandra loved to shop. She had her personal fragrance made there and Alex could, too. Roan had made arrangements to have the purchases put on the company's accounts and would sort out the accountant later. This was, after all, a business trip and Alex was—ah—'under cover!' Within two hours, Sandra called Franco to 'come and get 'em' at the Mall.

With everything packed up in the company SUV, Franco dropped Sandra off at her car in the parking lot, drove back to the house to pick up Roan and get them back to the airport for the return flight.

But before they left, Franco took Roan aside and asked, "Boss, you theenk you cuud do sometheeng about that Sandra woman? She ees driving me nuts. She is so hungry for a man, she ees all over me like chip suit. Eet gives me creepings, Boss. Pleeze help me."

Roan tried to keep straight-faced and replied, "Don't worry, Franco. I will make sure she has lots of work to keep her busy and away from the restaurant. Then she won't be in your hair."

"In my hair, on my face, touching all over. Eeek, I hate dees," cried Franco.

"See you in a couple of weeks, Franco," said Roan. "In the meantime, decide with Marcel about the menu changes for summer. Let's put in some salads, fruit compotes and ask your Dad if he has some ideas. Okay?"

"Bye Boss. Bye Misses Alex," sighed Franco. "I go now."

The flight back was smooth and once they disembarked, Roan loaded all the packages in the truck, then asked, "You and Sandra must have found the bargains of a lifetime down there, didn't you, Alex? Mmm. And you smell delightful. Must have been that perfumer Sandra loves so much. That's an excellent scent. What is it?"

"Vanilla, hazlenut, bergamot and tiny hints of rose and sandalwood," replied Alex. "I think it's excellent and it's my own blend. No one else has it to my knowledge."

"Well, let's get these things home and see how the house is progressing," said Roan. "I'm sure there will be new developments on the home front by now."

They unloaded the packages at the cottage and walked up to the house to see what had been done. The new walls were up and the studio expansion was almost complete. The new bullet-proof glass had been installed and the security system put in. The radiant floor heating system was also installed, with the terra cotta stone tiles lined up for placement. Roan's pottery studio was almost ready to go, as the kilns had been delivered, along with his pottery wheel. Just the lighting had to be sorted out, tile floor completed and finishing fire-retardant shingles for the roof. The sunroom and bonus rooms were both almost completed. The inside would be next and the contractor met Roan as they walked over to look at the sunroom.

"You can probably move back up here tonight, Roan, if you don't mind the mess," explained the contractor.

Alex wandered around the compound to check on the security details and was satisfied it would be safe.

"Looks good to me," she said. "It will be nice to be in here, although I do like the smaller house, if I was there on my own."

Roan walked in the front door and was pleased the cleaner had done such a good job. The kitchen had been fully expanded, with new granite counters, more cabinet space and a double wall oven. There was a bright, extended window over the new sink looking into the sunroom and a pass-through for ease of serving. There were French doors leading out into the sunroom and a larger space for the kitchen table, with the phone lines re-routed to be closer to the table. And finally, there was a large new island in the centre of the kitchen, complete with power outlets for the mixer, coffee maker and bread maker. There was a small sink on the end and lots of cabinets underneath for pots and pans. The built-in glassware hutch had been rebuilt and expanded, with stained glass diamonds set in sections of the doors. The floor tile had also been taken up and replaced with the terra cotta tiles, as many old ones had been broken during the explosion. The pantry was now doubled in size to accommodate all the things they needed for entertaining. Shauna was in for a huge surprise when she saw the new kitchen.

Soon the pool table would be in for Conor's bonus room, along with a big screen tv and stereo system. Roan wanted to go all out for his son.

As Roan walked back to the bedroom, he realised his bedroom furniture was destroyed. Although the windows and deck had been fixed, this room had not been, so Roan looked up the furniture store in town and ordered an identical set, along with the same bedding. Their order was on file from the wedding and also in stock. Roan called the florist and ordered flowers for the bedroom, kitchen and Alex's room.

Soon they were ready to walk back down to the cottage and get things moved back into the house. Shauna was just driving up when Roan spotted her.

"Not a word about what I have done, Alex," said Roan. "This is to be a surprise for Shauna and Conor."

"You got it, Roan," replied Alex.

"Hi Honey. Did Katie have a good meeting with the University today?" asked Roan. "And how did the painting go for you?"

"It was an excellent day for us, Roan," she replied. "Katie did some wonderful sketches for the offices and dorm rooms, plus we had great sales, even with all the mess. Sally came by and ordered a bunch of stuff."

"With what she made on the vehicles, I'm not surprised!" grinned Roan. "By the way, we can move back tonight, so pack up and we can haul things up there."

"Oh thank goodness," said Shauna. "The house looks so beautiful, I can't wait to see inside and get things back where they belong."

"Since we have these trucks, we have the room and Alex can drive the car up," explained Roan. "It won't take long to get our belongings back home, along with the food we bought. So what do you all say?"

"Oh yeah, I'm ready and Conor will be when he gets home," shouted Shauna. "I am so happy, Roan."

Shauna wrapped her arms around her husband and gave him a huge hug. When Conor got home from school, he and Jimmy, who always seemed to be with him now, packed up his things and helped with the food, trying not to eat it all before it could be moved!

Flash, Tyler and Mickey were still a little confused, but happy to be on the way home. Wherever Mom and Dad led, they followed.

The merry band of gypsies was on the move again and up to the house. Roan deactivated the alarm system and they began to bring things into the house. Shauna took one look at the new kitchen and her mouth dropped open.

"Oh Roan, this is magnificent," she exclaimed. "How on earth could they do this so fast? Look at the counters, the island and the double oven. Oh and the new stove. It looks just like Charles and Marie's. And I can walk out to the sunroom? And look at the pantry. It's doubled in size. My china cabinet has stained glass diamonds in it. Oh Roan, you've thought of everything!"

Conor opened the front door to let his little friends in the house.

He looked directly at Mickey and said, "Don't you dare fart in here—not today."

But the dog got that 'look' on his face, so Conor picked up his dog and took him back out onto the porch before he could do any damage to the air quality of the home. Tyler and Flash were almost ready to run upstairs and hide! Mickey trotted back in with a satisfied look on his face.

"Isn't there a doggie etiquette camp they can send him to?" asked Alex. "That dog's odor makes my eyes water."

Once the food had been put away, Roan had to explain to Shauna their bedroom set had been damaged in the blast.

"Well, there is always the studio bedroom, Roan," said Shauna. "We can sleep in there until we can get another set of furniture."

Shauna also said, "Maybe you might like to show Alex around, since she hasn't been inside the house much and there is a lot to see."

So Conor took Alex on the grand tour of the house, the studio, the bedrooms and downstairs into the guest quarters, with the sauna, kitchen, wine cellar and storage room.

"I see why you said it was a rather large house, Roan," remarked Alex. "This is one of those houses in a magazine. You'll have to tell me all about it one day, but for now, I want to unpack and go over some notes for the trip to Dublin."

"I'll get going on supper," giggled Shauna. "Who wants pizza?"

Shauna dialed Mr. Young and ordered the usual but doubled it because Jimmy was staying for supper. After they'd eaten, Katie and Jim came out to pick up their son and Katie wanted to explain a call she had received at the store.

As they walked in the house, Katie took one look at the kitchen and became totally awestruck.

"Would you look at this kitchen, Jim," she sighed. "Have you ever seen anything so beautiful? Oh and look, there is the same range they put in Marie's kitchen. Oh Shauna, that's da bomb—oops, sorry, kid's slang. I didn't mean it."

Shauna broke up and forgave her friend's slip of the tongue. She showed Katie the sunroom and pantry as well. Then they sat down for a chat about the call, which had been from the university. The review board was scheduled for the following Wednesday to decide the bid, but Katie felt it would probably be theirs, since the other firm bidding was from out of town and much higher priced.

Alex found her bedroom and made a personal call to Parker, who had news.

"I get out of the hospital tomorrow, Alex, but I will probably need a little help getting around. We are scheduled to leave on Wednesday, fly into the Twin Cities and fly from there to Chicago and a direct flight to Dublin. I have a friend picking us up. Do you have all the information we need and contacts we need to see?"

"Yes Parker," replied Alex. "We're all set. I will be ready when you are. I can fill Roan in on our schedule and location."

"Great, I will pick you up at 5:30 AM on Wednesday," Parker answered.

"5:30 AM?" asked Alex. "Isn't that a bit early, Parker? I'm fine with it, but wow, that's early. Oh and by the way, we are back at the main house."

"See you then," said Parker. "But before we go, I am going down to interview Ronald Rutherford and let him see what he did to me. See ya, sweetie."

Alex walked slowly into the hallway and down the staircase.

When she got to the bottom she said, "We will be leaving at 5:30 AM Wednesday morning to fly over to Dublin. I'll need keys and directions for the cottage, Roan. We should be there for a week. I have set up interviews with several physicians who treated Ronald and people he worked with at the forensics unit. That should shed some light on his mental stability."

Roan went to his briefcase and rummaged around for the keys and said, "Okay, here are the cottage keys, the car keys and Mille's directions. Speak with Seamus O'Flaherty at the garage and get the car. I'll phone ahead to let him know what day you are coming. He in turn will contact the grocer and the housekeeping service to get the place ready. This information says there is Internet service in the cottage, a fax machine, copier, etc., all the things you will need. There are two bedrooms, a kitchen, hallway, study, lounge and small dining area. The garage is separate next to the house. And it looks like there are tons of roses everywhere. It even has a thatched roof!"

Roan also handed Alex a photo of Roselyn Cottage, to be sure she got the right one when she arrived in town. With that decided, Alex excused herself to get some rest and have the next day to herself, studying her notes and finishing up some details.

Katie and Jim hauled Jimmy away by 9:00 PM and Conor went to bed. That left Roan and Shauna to admire the work on their home. They went into the Quiet Room annex to look around. The statue of Mary had been incorporated into the design of the room and added as a water feature. The walls were done with smooth boulders, resembling a grotto. At the far end were the enormous windows, which allowed for a panoramic view of the lake. On the wall closest to the cottage, a fireplace had been designed from the same stones as the wall, making a quiet statement. The stereo speakers looked just like the rocks, so Shauna wouldn't notice them. The entry way to the outside adjoined the front deck and the old walkway had been covered over by the room. Flash's house was right at the door and attached securely to his own little covered porch. A mini-roof with little shingles helped protect his domain. He could come in and go out at will. No more storms would batter his home.

Shauna was simply amazed at how beautiful the room was and how elegant. There was a space for a family altar under the windows on the lake side, with a stained glass window on order to be placed over the altar. They could leave the lights on in the reflecting pool at night or turn them off during the day. And the statue would also be protected from storms.

They also went into Roan's pottery studio to look at its design. There was a potter's wheel, two kilns of different size, racks with glaze, clay and paints, plus plastic tubs for storage. There were drying racks for the greenware and buckets for Roan's craft tools. The doorway opened into what was the back wall of the studio and there was an exit to the lane by the side of the house, but Roan would use that only in an emergency or when hauling products into his studio. Two sky lights added more direct sunlight and there were plenty of windows as well. A deck ran from the pottery studio all the way to the master bedroom, which enabled Roan to walk over during good weather and not disturb the household. He had a stereo system and a big screen television on one wall, with a couch and two leather chairs, plus a small fridge, a utility sink, a drafting board, chair and a telephone, with an intercom system connected to the alarm system. Everything was ready for production.

Shauna was still a bit overwhelmed, but felt it best to go upstairs and get a good night's sleep. Roan followed with a bottle of wine and two glasses.

The following morning, Conor was up as usual and off to school. Alex was downstairs making breakfast, as Shauna strolled in wearing the ratty bathrobe her mother hated, her fuzzy slippers and her hair out in five directions.

"Glad I'm not the only one who looks like that in the morning," laughed Alex. "You look a fright, Shauna!"

Within moments, Shauna heard hammers, saws and men talking loudly. Her eyes widened as she stared at Alex, then ran to her bedroom to clean up and get dressed. Alex continued to laugh.

Roan came in and thanked Alex for going over to investigate Ronald's life in Ireland. He was happy to have her around and he got to thinking, maybe he really could steal her away from JB's company when the assignment was over. He tucked that idea away for another day and ate a hearty breakfast. Alex was an excellent cook.

Alex went into town to check with Chief Reynolds, get some traveler's cheques and try to get her cash converted into Euros. The local bank didn't have that facility, so Alex would have to get that done in Dublin with the cheques. She had the company credit card, her passport and money, but she needed to stop in at OfficeMax again for folders, batteries and extra tapes for her recorder. She picked up a journal as well, to keep on this trip. It would prove helpful when doing her notes.

Chief Reynolds had no news. Ronnie had been relatively silent but became agitated when he saw Alex.

They walked into the cell area and Ronnie said, "Oh, look at Roan's bitch. Ain't she pretty. Why don't you come on over here and gimme some huh?"

Alex paid no attention him, simply stared. It only made Ronnie madder. He began pacing the floor, glancing over at her, then to Reynolds and back again.

He ran up to the bars and began rattling them ranting, "You'll never convict me, never. I have a plan. You can't touch me."

Alex decided to bait Ronnie and said, "We know all about your little 'plan' Ronnie. You've been a very bad boy and let it slip to the wrong person. That person talked. It's all right here in this nice neat folder. You gave yourself just enough rope to, well, you know…"

Alex shook the folder at Ronald, smiled ever so slightly and walked out of the cells, leaving Ronnie with a shaken look on his face. He ran back to his bed, began tearing at his hair, staring wild-eyed into the security camera in the corner of the ceiling.

After Alex and the Chief got out to his office, he looked at her and remarked, "I'm not sure what you did, but I think it had the desired effect."

"I put it into his head that someone else knows his plans and has talked. It might just bring up some of his real plans and you can get that on tape. I have to be away on investigation for a week, so I won't be in touch, but contact agent Keller if you need anything. He is in the loop at all times."

"Got it," replied Chief Reynolds. "I hope you find what you are looking for."

Alex returned to the house and started packing. She took her service revolver from the safe in Roan's office and placed her identification in her fanny pack to get at it quickly if necessary. She took only her watch and wore her hoop earrings. That's all the jewellery she had anyway. She might pick up something fun in Ireland and certainly something for Shauna and Sandra, maybe even for Katie. In no time, Alex was packed and ready for the early morning flight. She also added some snack bars, baggies of dried fruit and cookies in her carry-on, just in case she got hungry on the flight.

After supper, Alex excused herself to go up to bed and get a decent night's sleep before she had to get up at 2:00 AM to get ready. She charged her phone and made certain it was switched over to International calling. Her converters were packed as well. Now all she needed was rest.

The alarm went off at 2:00 AM and Alex was ready to face the shower. She lathered up with her new fragrance bath gel, then spritzed on the body spray. *Maybe I should call this, 'Remembrance'*, Alex mused. She was pleased with the gentle scent. She wiped the bottles dry and packed them in her carry-on. Alex dressed casually in jeans, t-shirt and blazer. She wore her black sneakers without socks. Parker wasn't the only one who did that!

Alex put her suitcase, carry-on and briefcase in the elevator and went downstairs to wait for Parker. She turned on the coffee maker and before another moment passed, Roan came out to wish her well.

"Let's hope you get some answers in Ireland, Alex," whispered Roan. "I think this will be a good trip for you and Parker. Somehow I am detecting more than a professional relationship between the two of you. Am I correct?"

"Yes, Roan, you are," explained Alex. "Parker and I were engaged in college. Somehow we lost each other and we want to see where our reconnection takes us. The love is still there, but we don't know what time has done to us. Our business is tough on relationships, especially on agents in love with one another and now we're getting too old to let any more time slip by us. Guess we'll see if it can be salvaged."

"I think I hear Parker driving up, so I'll help you to the door with these," said Roan. "Keep in touch and let us know what you are finding out."

"Thanks Roan," smiled Alex. "I'll call daily to let you know. With what I have uncovered so far, this trip should really help nail down Ronnie's history of psychosis."

Parker rang the doorbell and smiled as much as his cuts would allow. He had to use a cane to walk, but he was in excellent spirits, probably glad to be out of the hospital. Roan helped Alex carry her bags to the taxi and waved goodbye as they drove away.

Alex looked over at Parker and said, "I feel like I am running away against my parent's wishes! That's too silly, isn't it?"

Parker took Alex's hand in his and whispered, "I won't tell anyone if you won't!"

Once they were in flight, Alex looked out over Lake Bemidji and saw the lake house. Roan, Shauna and Conor were outside waving in the darkness, with the floodlights shining on them. It was almost like looking at a movie set. The pilot wiggled his wings, because he knew who was waving at them!

When they got into Chicago for the flight into Dublin, Parker had a surprise. He had been able to upgrade the tickets to First Class due to his injuries. They were right behind the cockpit with a sky marshal seated across from them.

The sky marshal was terse but said, "Heard about the blow-up, Parker. Sorry, but you look terrible. Glad you will be okay. No broken bones or anything like that?"

"Thanks Al," replied Parker. "Thank goodness for that. By the way, this is Alex Simpson. She's a private anti-terrorism specialist on loan to the CTB for this assignment, as we are working a case in Dublin this week. Alex, this is Al Foster."

"Pleased to meet you, Al," said Alex. "It will be good to get away from drugs and street gangs for a while!"

The seven hour flight was an easy one. Alex slept most of the time, while Al and Parker talked about old cases they worked on together. Al was a retired CTB agent, who became a sky marshal.

The pilot had taken the polar route and came into Dublin from the north. He landed suddenly and the passengers lunged forward, but there were no injuries. There had been straight line winds forecast across the tarmac and the pilot had avoided all but the tail of one. Thankfully, it was an easy flight.

Al helped Parker to the jetway, as Alex followed. They walked through customs with security clearance and to the immigration station. Because Parker had dual status, Alex took the most time with her American passport. But when they had cleared, Parker gave Al his business card with his local phone number in case Al needed anything during his stay in Dublin. Soon a large black automobile drove up and honked. The car looked like something out of a black and white movie. It was an old 1950's vintage Rolls Royce Corniche. And behind the wheel was a chauffeur complete with cap and buttoned-down uniform.

"Who on earth is that?" asked Alex.

"That's my friend I told you about," replied Parker. "He sort-of lives at the house and takes care of the place while I am in the States. Hello Stanley. This is Alex."

"Hello Miss, pleased to meet you," Stanley said as he doffed his cap. "Welcome home Mr. Parker."

"Oooookay," exclaimed Alex. "And just how large IS this house, Parker?"

"Oh, it's just a town house, Alex. I live in the little cottage out back. It's a guest house, really," explained Parker.

They drove through the center of Dublin, past Phoenix Park, onto a more country estate area, then turned into a gated community. Stanley drove for another few minutes and turned into a beautiful dark red brick Georgian townhouse with a burgundy door. Stanley drove over the gravel driveway to the front entry and the housekeeper opened the front door.

"Good afternoon, Mr. Parker. Welcome home," she said.

"Hello Violet," he replied. "This is Alex and she will be spending a few days with me at the cottage."

"Oh yes, I'd know you anywhere, Miss. Welcome to Dublin," sighed Violet with her hands clasped in front of her.

Stanley unloaded the luggage while Alex helped Parker up the steps to the foyer. They entered under a magnificent white archway into the main hall, with a curving mahogany staircase and a red oriental stair runner going up three floors.

"Tea will be served in about fifteen minutes Mr. Parker, if you want to show Miss Alex around," explained Violet. "Stanley will take the luggage out to the cottage."

Alex was stunned. She stood in the hallway, staring at the portraits of the Fitzgeralds painted over the centuries. She walked into the front lounge and found a huge wood-burning fireplace with hand-carved mantle. The bay windows had heavy claret velvet draperies tied back with gold tassels. There were thousands of books lining the shelves and striped vintage furniture placed strategically around the room. It looked like a museum. A grand piano was placed near the rear windows and on it were photographs in gold or silver frames. There were several of Alex and Parker in college. And there were pictures of Parker's family members, cousins and events. Alex could see a vast lawn stretched out behind the house, with a stable, six-car garage and large glass conservatory. And in the corner was the cottage.

Now this wasn't just any 'cottage'—oh no. This was a fully functional house with three bedrooms, lounge, dining room, large kitchen, two full bathrooms, study and office. But in comparison, I suppose one could call this a cottage! And it had central heating, which the house did not (except for Violet and Stanley's rooms, that is).

As Alex continued to wander through the main house, she went across the hallway to the next set of rooms. One was a large parlor, with chairs, sofas and a television, albeit a 1960's version in a rather ratty cabinet. There was a large liquor cabinet, fully stocked and ready for use.

The next room was the dining room with a massive mahogany table and twenty chairs with matching red and white striped ticking. There were huge scenic paintings of horses and hunt scenes. There was an enormous serving buffet on one wall and a large china hutch on another.

Parker walked in and asked, "So, what do you think of the little shed? I know, it probably isn't what you expected, but hey, it's mine! I sometimes have to share it with my brother, Binky—you remember old Binky, don't you? The banker? He entertains a lot here, so I leave him to it."

"Ah sure, I remember Binky a little, but Parker, this is your parent's home. I thought you were disinherited?" enquired Alex.

"They forgave me about fifteen years ago and since I split my time between my apartment in Virginia and here, I let Binky live here all by his lonesome. Works out perfectly and he is on holiday for three weeks in Ibiza, so this is all ours for the week," explained Parker.

Violet came in and announced tea is served in the Conservatory. Parker escorted Alex to the back of the house, through the enormous kitchen and into the Conservatory. There were birds in large cages at the end of the room, with tropical plants everywhere. The large wrought iron table and chairs at the end closest to the house had the luncheon set out for them. Violet had been busy.

"It isn't often we get to entertain such a special guest of Mr. Parker's," said Violet. "I am pleased to finally meet you after all these years. He always talks so highly of you, Miss."

Alex smiled broadly and her eyes sparkled as they sat down.

Parker explained about Violet and Stanley.

"They have been married for 52 years and have always been in service here since then," said Parker. "My grandparents brought them up from Cork and they have looked after this house and us from that time on. They are as much a fixture as those old portraits. I told them to retire and just enjoy their time, but they still keep up with their duties and keep the place looking tip-top. They do hire a cleaning crew every two weeks and whenever Binky throws a party. And I love them both dearly. They're the ones who really raised us."

Violet had prepared smoked salmon, with a lovely vegetable plate, cold mixed grille, thinly sliced and fresh bread with herbed butter. She served iced tea with mint (something Parker taught her from Virginia) and fresh berry sorbet for dessert. When they had finished, Parker took Alex out into the garden to walk down to the cottage.

"I love this place, Alex," explained Parker. "It isn't just that I grew up here, it's because it's so tranquil in the middle of a big city. We have twenty-five acres here and it's mostly parkland with fields and trees. Binky rents the land out once in a while for car rallies and shows, but mostly it stays as is. I never get tired of walking through the fields, playing with the sheep or riding the horses. I'll show them to you later, but first I want you to see the cottage."

They strolled across the yard to the quaint stone cottage. You could have put it on a post card. The flowers spilled over the planters in a spectacular array of reds, blues, yellows and white.

Alex was so pleased, she said, "After I unpack, may I take a picture of the cottage, the house and the grounds for Roan and Shauna? They would love this."

"Oh sure," replied Parker. "Conor would go wild over the animals, too, I think. He sounds like a great kid."

There was a slight mist hovering over the cottage and even in late May, there was still a chill in the air. Stanley had made up a fire in the lounge to warm them and as they entered, Alex felt amazingly at home.

"Why do I feel so at home here, Parker?" asked Alex. "I feel as if I have lived here forever."

"Maybe it's because I have told you about it over the years," said Parker. "I'm not sure. But this is my favourite place to be on the estate. The house is cold like a canyon. The Conservatory and the cottage are where my heart is. Always have been. Here, let me show you around."

This was a normal sized home. The lounge was arranged with comfortable leather furniture in front of the fireplace. The drapes were velvet, but less massive. There were vertical blinds on the windows, too. The polished wood floors were covered with a white rug and there were books and videos on the shelves. A wide screen television was in one corner. The dining room was attached through an open archway. The round table was small and sat six. That room led into the kitchen. This wasn't massive, but functioned well for a single person or perhaps a couple. The laundry, freezer and pantry were in the 6x9 annex, which led to a patio with barbecue and firepit. There was a study, a small office and shower room close to the stairs, which led to the bedrooms and family bathroom.

Parker excused himself from walking up the stairs for obvious reasons, but told Alex to wander around up there and pick out a bedroom for herself. He would sleep in the study because of his injuries. Stairs were simply too painful to climb at the moment.

Alex walked up the wide staircase, similar to the one at the Sandersons. She found a pretty bedroom at the front of the cottage, with pink, lavender and yellow Laura Ashley-style drapes and bedspread on the double bed. Fresh flowers, including star-gazer lilies, were on the nightstand next to her bed and on the table in the sitting room facing the Conservatory. There was also a hand wash basin in the corner. A small television/dvd player, radio and stereo were also there for her pleasure. This room would suit her perfectly. Alex also walked around upstairs to find the bathroom and look at the other bedrooms.

The second guest bedroom was rather plain, almost as if Parker had redecorated her room only for the visit. This room, however, had two twin beds, a television and stereo, plus a small sitting area and hand wash basin. It looked out over the meadow.

Parker's room was the most spacious, with a walk-in closet and sitting room. His was definitely a man's retreat with wide-screen tv, massive stereo system and racks of dvds. There were books on the shelves, trophies from school and university. There were photos everywhere and one special one, the night Alex and Parker got engaged. That was on his nightstand. There was a Bible on the table in the front window, a rosary and a small standing crucifix, along with a picture of the Sacred Heart of Jesus and the Immaculate Heart of Mary. Alex had forgotten Parker was Catholic. She smiled and went downstairs.

"Did you find everything to your liking up there, Alex?" asked Parker. "I hope the flowers weren't overkill. But I know they were your favourite."

"Still are, Parker. Thank you," Alex replied. "The room is lovely and I will be very happy to stay there. This cottage is simply amazing."

"I put a roast in for later this evening. I hope you still like yours well done," exclaimed Parker. "We can eat on that for a couple of days, but I think Violet will have my hide if I do that to you. We'll be eating out a lot anyway."

"Listen, Parker," said Alex. "I'll get unpacked and we can check messages and reconfirm our appointments for tomorrow. I want this part of the trip out of the way fast, so we can enjoy the rest of it."

"Agreed," sighed Parker. "You go unpack and I'll check in the office to see if there is anything on the fax machine or Internet."

As Parker checked through his messages, he found one from Chief Reynolds. It seems Alex had gotten Ronald so worked up, he was pacing and yelling at himself for the past ten hours. He wouldn't shut up and looked as if he was about to burst.

Parker called up to Alex and asked, "Hey Alex, what did you do to Ronnie yesterday? You must have gotten him really panicked because I think he's about to dump in his pants."

Alex came downstairs and explained what she'd done to get Ronnie to talk. And it seemed to be working. Chief Reynolds had it all on audio AND video. It would be there for them to review when they got back to Bemidji.

"Blood and sand, woman," yelled Parker. "You know more tricks in the book than I do!"

Alex laughed and continued to unpack. She came back down to find Parker reading another e-mail. This one was from Cresswell in Rome.

"Apparently DuMonde was seen in Paris, then Istanbul," Parker explained. "Several high ranking government officials, accused of being on the graft, were gunned down in restaurants in each city. It's DuMonde's MO and people saw a man fitting his description running away from across the street after the kills. Could be a copy cat to throw us off the scent or it could be DuMonde on his normal rounds."

Alex thought for a moment and said, "DuMonde is high profile. He likes the acknowledgment of the kill. He adores the headlines. If this were a copy cat hit, he'd get angry and take out the person who stole his thunder. He's too egocentric to let someone else take credit for his work. No, I think they are dealing with DuMonde. Question is, where will he show up next? I'll e-mail Roan and let him know we arrived safely."

"We have an appointment at the Custom House down on the Quay in the morning with Interpol agents Finnegan and Morris," explained Parker. "They have Ronnie's files, plus physician's statements why his employment should be terminated. We also have two appointments with the psychiatrists who wrote those reports and two of co-workers Ronnie worked with right before he left the service. This should prove quite interesting."

Alex finished e-mailing the Chief and Roan, then asked, "Can we go out to the stables now? I'd love to see the animals, Parker. It will be dark soon and we might not get time again."

"Oh sure, let's go out then," replied Parker. "I'm sure my friends will be glad to see me. It's been a couple of months since I was home. You know, I have a groom who comes by daily to exercise the horses, feed and clean them, but it just isn't the same, is it?"

"No, it isn't," remarked Alex. "You really need to be around them all the time. Oh, here's a beauty. Who is this horse?"

Parker walked slowly up to the stall and scratched the nose of "Twinkle," a dapple grey mare with blue eyes. She immediately whinnied in recognition and bobbed her head up and down. You could almost see her smile.

"This is Twinkle, Janna's horse. My sister was killed in the same accident as our parents seven years ago. I couldn't bear to part with this horse and she knows it. I still think she will see her owner come around the paddock with her riding crop in her hand. I guess I will have to be a substitute, unless you want to ride her?"

"Maybe next time, Parker," replied Alex. "The last time I rode was ages ago and I was sore for two weeks. We have business to conduct and I don't want to walk into the meetings all hunched over."

Alex petted Twinkle and spoke to her gently. As Alex walked to the next stall, Twinkle winked at her.

Parker was laughing with the next horse, "Sparticus"—who was Binky's and explained, "Oh, Binky never rides. It would muss him up something shocking, so I always ride this horse. When Binky comes around, Sparticus defecates on Binky's shoes and he runs away. It's hysterical and Sparticus always laughs with me. He has an excellent memory!"

"I think Sparticus needs to meet Roan's dog, Mickey. They would get along famously," Alex laughed. "They'd be great pals!"

As they continued down the line, Parker came to his own horse, "Patton." Patton was delighted to see Parker and stuck his head out to greet his owner.

"Hey boy, I know, I miss you too," exclaimed Parker. "Look who I have here, it's Alex."

Alex walked up to say hello and the horse stared adoringly at her. He actually made a bow with one leg extended, then came back to the open doorway for a pet and a scratch. He nuzzled against Parker's shoulder, then wiggled his head.

"Oh, he knows who you are. I tell him often enough," said Parker. "I'll have to find a way to ride him before we leave."

Alex gently blew into Patton's nose and kissed him on the bridge. You could see the love in the horse's eyes for his master and for the woman his master loved.

They walked hand in hand through the field to a small sheep pen. There were marvelous wooly jumpers waiting to be sheared and they seemed like gentle creatures.

Alex reached her hand out to pet one and Parker said, "Stop Alex. They will take your hand off! They always seem to think you have food!"

Alex laughed hysterically and they strode back to the cottage. A small cat scurried by chasing a mouse. She stopped in her tracks and sat down. Parker tried to bend over to pet her, but Alex picked her up for a cuddle.

"This is "Sarah" our barn cat," laughed Parker. "She had the best kittens, but last year we had her fixed, so she's now all we have here. We let her in the house, too. She still does quite well with the mouse population. No complaints from Violet!"

"Can we bring her in with us tonight, Parker?" asked Alex. "I love to have a cat cuddling by the fire in the evening. It reminds me of when I was young and the cat was my only friend at the house. She's very pretty."

"Sure, she can come in, can't you girl," replied Parker. "I'll miss this if I decide to sell the property. I won't sell the cottage or the stables, but I'm thinking about doing something with the house. Binky is in Ibiza most of the time at his villa anyway, so he could care less. This will be my last assignment with the CTB and I am retiring after the trial. Just looking at my options is all."

"Well, you could turn the main house into a conference center or a guest house. It would pay for itself and you could have weddings in the conservatory," explained Alex. "I've seen that done in other places and it could work here. There is plenty of space for parking out back and getting zoning permission wouldn't be difficult. It's something to think about."

They walked in the house and Alex smelled the roast. She'd take it out and let it rest for a while, then they could have a nice, light supper.

Alex and Parker sat in the leather chairs by the fire, with Sarah curled up on her rug, her toys in a little basket. Romantic music was playing softly on the stereo and Parker looked lovingly at Alex as she sipped a sherry.

"You know, time has been very kind to you, Alex," said Parker. "You have become a lovely woman, accomplished, well-read, someone with her own identity. I'm glad we found each other again. Do you want to follow your heart with me and take a chance on love a second time?"

"Oh, I've never stopped loving you, Parker," smiled Alex. "Your parents were very cruel to both of us and we could have been married for over twenty-five years with children of our own now. I don't want to lose you again. I do want to see where this leads us. I guess I'm not surprised you want to retire, because I have had the same thoughts. We're almost fifty and have a lot of years left to explore all the world has to offer. Family is everything to me and I need that in my life now. This business has taken too much as it is."

"Then spend the rest of your life with me, Alex," said Parker. "This belongs to you anyway and it's about time you put it back on your finger."

Parker produced Alex's engagement ring from its tiny blue box. It was a magnificent Asscher cut diamond set in platinum with smaller diamonds in a Victorian mounting. It had been Parker's grandmother's engagement ring. Alex couldn't believe it.

"You've kept this ring all these years," cried Alex. "I never thought I'd see it again. Yes, Parker, I will marry you, whenever and wherever you say."

Parker slipped the ring on Alex's finger and said, "I'd get down on one knee, but they're all bandaged up. Now, this looks right—on the hand I first put it on twenty-seven years ago."

Alex and Parker shared a passionate kiss and embrace. Suddenly from the kitchen up popped Violet and Stanley with champagne.

"Congratulations Miss Alex and Mr. Parker," yelled Stanley. "We couldn't let this long-awaited day pass without a celebration. Here's a glass of bubbly for each of us…and a toast. To Alex and Parker. May they finally live happily ever after."

Their exuberance was interrupted by the telephone in the office.

Parker went in to answer the call from Agent Finnegan, who was most agitated, "Parker, it looks like Ireland wants to extradite Rutherford on murder charges. It seems his assistant, Miss Emilie Lonergan, disappeared right after he finished working on the DuMonde case. Her body was just found near where Rutherford lived, in a shallow grave by a grove of trees. Some kids found it this morning. Her id tag was on the clothing and DNA tests confirmed it's Emilie. I'll bring the report with me in the morning."

"Why doesn't that surprise me, Padric?" replied Parker. "I'll explain this to Miss Simpson, who is the agent we are working with. She will want to look at the file as well. See you in the morning around 8:00 AM, right? Make sure the coffee is better than the last time."

Parker hung up the phone and explained the circumstances to Alex. Violet and Stanley made their exit and Parker stared at Alex. He wasn't surprised with Ronnie's actions, but this made the case last a lot longer than expected.

"Sorry, love, but this will extend the case a lot longer," explained Parker. "Too bad we can't put both cases in together and get a combined outcome. This means a trial over here, too. At least we won't have to leave home for that one!"

Alex sat on the bar stool in the kitchen and set her wine glass down on the counter. She stared at her engagement ring and thought back to the time they were first engaged.

The university was on Christmas holidays. Most of their friends had gone home, but Parker and Alex stayed behind to work on articles for the newspaper. The snow was amazing—perfect for a ski weekend. They decided to go up into the mountains and took off in Parker's jeep. There was a beautiful lodge within an hour's drive and Alex had wanted to see it for ages.

The monumental pine forests were blanketed with a layer of fresh powder, making the trees shine with a marshmallow cream frosting of fluffy white snow. The deer poked their heads out from behind a grove of trees, while Parker blasted through a snow drift and onto the lodge. It was a magical time of year.

The stone and timber lodge stood on the ridge top, surrounded by small cabins. Those were booked, but there were two rooms left in the main building, so Parker snapped them up. The great lobby boasted a huge fireplace with a roaring fire blazing and skiers toasted their frozen toes as they lounged on leather sofas. A large fir tree stood next to the fireplace. It was decorated with lights and ornaments depicting skiing, fishing and hunting. Santa was dressed as a mountain man! Red and white Poinsettias dotted the mantle.

Parker took the bags up to their rooms, while Alex spoke with some friends who had the same idea of coming up the mountain for the weekend. It would be fun skiing with them, but Parker had other ideas.

He ordered a gourmet dinner for that evening to be served in a private section of the dining room, overlooking the valley below. Parker had arranged a photographer to snap a picture as they were becoming engaged. He had ordered red roses ahead of time, had the ring in his pocket and wore the new royal blue ski sweater Alex hand knit for his Christmas gift. The candles shimmered and the snow was falling softly outside the lodge. It was a perfect evening to propose.

Parker escorted Alex to the table. She looked beautiful in the soft green cashmere sweater set Parker had given her for Christmas. It came all the way from Ireland. She wore her long brown hair tied up in red and green ribbons and her eyes sparkled in the candlelight as she sat down.

"What's all this Parker?" she asked. "Isn't this a little bit extravagant for a ski weekend?"

Parker looked adoringly at Alex and said, "Nothing is too good for the woman I love. I want this night to be the most memorable one of your life."

"Well, it is, Parker," exclaimed Alex. "The snow is fantastic and the view from up here is amazing. I feel like I'm in another country, like Austria or Switzerland. It doesn't get any better than this, does it?"

Now was the time to pop the question. Parker caught the waiter's eye, who brought over two glasses of sparkling wine, along with one long-stemmed red rose. A violinist played softly in the background and Parker got down on bended knee beside Alex. The little blue box was behind the water glass on the table.

He took Alex's hand in his and said, "Alex, you make me the most complete person in the Universe. You support my choices. You feed my creativity and you fill my life with unconditional love. I can't imagine my life without you and that's why I'm asking you to marry me. Alex, will you make me the happiest man in this lodge and say yes?"

Alex sat is amazement as Parker pulled the box out to reveal an astonishingly beautiful engagement ring. As she stared at the ring, then at Parker, tears flowed from her dark brown eyes as she accepted Parker's proposal.

"I'm stunned," gasped Alex. "Of course I'll marry you Parker. You're the man I've always dreamed about being with. You are kind, funny, charming and good looking. What woman could resist those attributes? I accept!"

Parker slipped the antique platinum and diamond engagement ring on her finger and they locked in a passionate embrace in front of most of the lodge guests and staff, who had crowded around silently to watch Parker propose. The ladies were crying and the gents were clapping.

Alex blushed when she looked up to see everyone huddled in the dining room doorway. Within seconds, the ladies came over to see the ring, while the men came over to shake Parker's hand. It was a Christmas they would never forget. The snow continued to fall gently outside the window.

But time swung back to reality and Alex shook the memory from her head, smiling as she went about fixing their supper. After they'd eaten, it was time to get over the jet lag and get to bed. She kissed Parker goodnight and went upstairs. Sarah came along with her to lie on the end of the bed.

6:00 AM was an amazing time on the estate. The animals were making their morning noise and the sun was peeking through the clouds after a thunderstorm. The grass smelled incredibly fresh and everything was alive. Alex got dressed in her navy jacket dress and navy pumps. She dabbed on her signature fragrance and walked into the office, where Parker was on the phone.

Parker handed her a cup of coffee and explained the conversation.

"Post mortem on Emilie showed heart attack," he continued. "But the woman was healthy, just had her company insurance physical and had nothing wrong with her. I suspect the same poison Ronnie used on Lulabelle is the same one he used on Emilie. I told their labs to check for a curare-based poison which leaves no detectable residue in the body and maybe, just maybe, there will be enough uncorrupted tissue sample left with the poison in it."

"Let's get all this information together after we have spoken with the agents this morning and get it sent over to Stephen and Chief Reynolds," explained Alex. "Somehow I don't think they will be surprised."

Parker got his vintage Morgan Roadster out and drove them into the city to the Custom House for their meeting. They walked through the metal detectors and up to the second floor offices. Padric was glad to see Parker in one piece.

"Damn it son," expressed his friend. "You look like a blast door hit you in the face."

"It kinda did, Padric," replied Parker. "This is Alexandra Simpson, our undercover agent in Bemidji. She's with Serpentine Security Systems in Phoenix."

"Oh, I've heard of you, Agent Simpson," said Finnegan. "You have an excellent reputation in the industry and we're really glad to have you on the team. This is agent Sean Morris."

"Gentlemen, I'm delighted to work with you," she said. "Now, to the matter at hand. May we see the employment records and the psychiatric reports please?"

The agents spread out the files for Parker and Alex to read over. It seemed Ronald was a model worker for the first few years with Interpol. However, he began working with natural poisons, fish toxins and chemicals found during investigations in South American cases. Then he became acquainted with Michael DuMonde in Paris. His behavior became increasingly hostile to his co-workers, including Miss Longergan, who had her Master's Degree in toxicology. Ronald would switch personalities, almost as if he could be two separate people. Both were hostile, but one was violent. He was called into the doctor's for a physical and the notes state he was 'nervous, fidgeting constantly, talking to himself and not answering questions, as if he were in a drug-induced state. However, no drugs were found in his system. Mind altering hypnosis was also considered, as if he were being controlled by someone else.'

The recommendation was he was 'too unstable to continue with his present employment and the psychiatrists recommended termination for medical reasons.'

Two of Ronald's co-workers were outside for their interviews. Parker would take one and Alex the other.

As they walked to the interview rooms, the gentleman Alex was to interview said, "I'm glad to be able to talk with someone about Ronnie. He was sick, very sick and we didn't know how to help him."

They sat down in the room as Alex turned on the tape recorder.

"Please just speak naturally, so the microphone picks everything up," explained Alex. "Please state your name, age and department."

"William Devin, forty-five, Forensic Investigations," he said.

Alex continued the questions, "How would you describe your relationship with Ronald Rutherford, who worked in your department for ten years."

"Oh Ronnie was a good lad in the beginning," he replied. But he got really squirrley toward the end. His behaviour was like part of him was in the room and the rest on another planet. He couldn't concentrate. He'd smash things, beakers, like. Then he'd start mumbling things, 'destroy, kill, stupid old woman'—like that. Then he would turn around and continue working as if nothing had happened. He'd look at the floor with all the broken glass and say, 'How'd that happen? Better sweep it up before it comes out of our pay packets.' And that's how he behaved. It got worse and in the end, the doctors sacked him. It were scary that."

"And how long did you know Ronald?" asked Alex. "Were you friends outside of work?"

"We all knew him almost the entire ten years, but no, we never socialised, if that's what you mean, misses," replied Mr. Devin. He kept to himself, even at lunch. Never went anywhere or did anything, just kept scribbling in a journal—a spiral bound one that was at his desk. I brought it with me, because it had recipes in it for my wife. She likes those things, she does."

Mr. Devin handed Alex the journal and in it were notes on how to kill someone using the curare-based poison, learned from a recent case. Words were scribbled all over the pages, such as 'kill, death to the old battleaxe, stupid Ronnie, Lula is dead, Roan stinks, blow up Roan, kill him.'

"Thank you, Mr. Devin," said Alex. "We appreciate your help in this matter. Did you get the recipes from the journal?"

"Yes and the misses loved them," Mr. Devin said. "They were from a magazine, not from Ronnie, so he didn't write them."

They got up and Mr. Devin returned to his duties. Alex went back to the office where Agent Morris was on the phone to Chief Reynolds.

"Our Ronnie is on a hunger strike now, Alex," explained Agent Morris. "He refuses to eat and wants only chewing gum, but the Chief won't give him any. Gave him quick-dissolving mints instead!"

"That's a good thing," said Alex. "He could chew a bunch of gum and tie up his intestines, forcing a blockage and boom—a trip to a non-secure hospital. He knows how to escape and that would do it. Let him get hungry. He will stop eventually and eat again. He's trying the control angle, but Chief Reynolds knows not to give into him. By the way, take a look at the journal Mr. Devin brought in. He thought it might help our investigation."

Agent Morris looked over the journal and said, "Amazing. This is almost a confession. And Mr. Devin had it in his possession all this time?"

"There were recipes in it his wife liked—from magazines," said Alex. "He'd put it away and had forgotten about it until we asked him about Ronnie."

Parker's interview with another co-worker went much the same. He taped the conversation as well and found Ronald to be psychotic and violent at times to the people he worked with, especially his assistant, Miss Longergan.

"Ronald struck Miss Longeran in the face in front of several co-workers," said Parker. "These people will testify when the time comes. I'm just sorry they will have to. None of them disliked Ronald, they were frightened of his rages. They said he was a good worker, but he couldn't concentrate and he was violent."

"Well, time to meet with the psychiatrists then," said Parker. "Thank you gentlemen. I'll take the journal with me tonight and make several copies at home. We can return the original to you in the morning, along with transcriptions of the interviews. Looks like we are building a very solid case. I just hope we don't overlook something."

Alex and Parker left for their meeting. They drove over to Grafton Street to the private practice of the company psychiatrists. Finding a place to park, however, was the worst part of the interview process! They found a small car park a few blocks away and walked to the offices.

Parker and Alex sat with both physicians in their conference room. Their conclusions were the same. The notes they made on their interviews with Ronald were almost identical. His mind was being controlled in some way, either through chemical enhancement of some kind or through hypnosis. CT scans showed no abnormalities, except heightened brain activity. No drugs were found in his system.

"Could someone control his mind to drive him insane?" Alex asked. "Could this terrorist DuMonde have done something to Ronald during his investigation in Paris?"

One of the doctors said, "Anything like that is possible, but for this extended period? I doubt it. The man is definitely psychotic, capable of killing and we couldn't have him near the sensitive materials or people. It simply wasn't safe for anyone and the company had to release him. It's possible he turned his psychosis on the family at home.

Our staff performed neurocognitive dysfunction testing on Ronald and found him to be suffering from a delusional disorder. We concluded he had affective psychosis moods incongruent with delusions. He didn't take any medications for the disorder and unfortunately, the untreated psychosis had a neurotoxic effect on his body and mind.

We will continue to review the facts as we see them and if there is anything new, we will advise you immediately. I'm sorry we haven't anything more positive to say."

"Thank you gentlemen," said Parker. "We appreciate you cooperation and your professional opinions."

Alex and Parker left with nothing more than they came with. However Alex had a theory.

She tapped Parker on the arm and said, "If DuMonde knew about Ronald's personality quirks beforehand, he could manipulate Ronald through hypnosis and use trigger words. When Ronnie would hear one, even if it was in normal conversation, it could switch his personality on or off? A series of trigger words set off over a period of years could drive anyone crazy, while still maintaining some semblance of normalcy in their daily life. Let's go back in the office."

Parker went back in and caught the psychiatrists before they left the conference room.

He explained Alex's theory and asked, "Given the time frame—a period of years, could this be a possibility? Could a series of trigger words used in normal conversation, throw a person into psychosis?"

"Well, yes, it could be possible," replied one doctor. "It would be a rarity, but with a susceptible mind like Ronald's? Word association is highly likely. This could be the answer."

Parker thanked the doctor's again and took Alex back to the Custom House to talk with the agents. When they walked in, the medical examiner was standing in the office with a file in his hand and he had the news they had been waiting to hear.

He explained the results, "Emilie Lonergan did die of a heart attack—brought on by the curare-based poison. There was enough tissue left to test and there was a trace amount of it in the sample. You were right, Agent Fitzgerald. Emilie Lonergan was murdered."

"We found out something at the psychiatrist's office, too," explained Parker. "Trigger words used over a long period of time, could switch a personality on and off at will. And now with the confirmation of Emilie's death? I think one of the words was 'Emilie.' Ronald's mother was Emmie, which sounds like Emilie. He went over the edge when his mother died and progressed steadily into psychosis. There must be more."

"We can work on it from here, Parker," said Agent Finnegan. "You need to transcribe the interview notes while they are fresh and look over the notebook. See you in the morning."

"Okay, guys," replied Parker. "Thanks for the post-mortem file. See you in the morning."

Alex and Parker went to the car park and decided it would be best to have something to eat at the house, where they could discuss this in more detail. They drove home with some pertinent details, which would help convict Ronald, even if it was on an insanity plea. There was no way he could get off.

Sarah met them at the door to the cottage. Parker went into the office to see how many messages they had, while Alex played with the cat. A moment later, Parker came out with a strained look on his face.

"Mr. Devin had a car accident on the way back home. He's dead, Alex," said Parker. "His brakes failed and he slammed into a building. I'm thinking there is a piece missing here. Someone inside is responsible."

"Inside Interpol, Parker—here?" asked Alex. "From the Forensic Lab or one of the agents? That's ludicrous. Or is it? Let's look at the time frame from today. Given Mr. Devin could have damaging information on someone inside, they wanted to get to him before he said anything more. What do you think?"

"Something definitely isn't kosher here," explained Parker. "Let's get things typed up and in order, make the copies we need and get them back to the office in the morning. I know Finnegan well, but he's relatively new there. But Morris? I want to do some additional background on him."

Parker went about making the photocopies of the notebook and files, while Alex transcribed the interview notes. She printed out three copies and put them in individual files. But Parker left out a couple of pages of the notebook when he copied it. He tore the pages out and put them with his copies in the safe. These were the most incriminating ones and if Morris was the mole, he'd show his hand eventually.

Alex came up with an idea to catch Morris, if it really was Morris, in the act. She suggested they send the copies and notebook over by courier, saying Parker had been called back to the States for an emergency. She'd call JB on his secure line and have him do the background check on Agent Morris and one on Agent Finnegan, just in case, then they would wait for two days at the cottage and see if anyone showed up to ransack it.

Parker agreed, but said, "Let me get Violet and Stanley out of here. I'll send them down to Cork to see their family for a week, which should get them away from any danger. I'll be right back."

Alex continued putting things away in the safe and locked it. She placed the false bookcase over the front of the safe and checked to be certain there were no scuff marks or curling of the rug. Then she locked the pet door on the utility room. There was a litter box in the back, so Sarah could stay safely inside the house until this was over.

About twenty minutes later, Parker came back with a basket of bread, wine and cheese, plus fruit and butter. He felt it would spoil if Violet wasn't there to watch over it! They watched as Stanley put a suitcase in the Rolls. He locked the house, turned on the alarm with his remote and drove away with a very delighted Violet in the front seat.

"Listen, we should be safe in here for the moment, but later tonight, we need to close the drapes, set the alarm and not use the fireplace or the lights," explained Parker. I called for the courier pick-up from the house and they should be here momentarily. I told them I had to go out of town immediately and to come to the main house. So, I will take the files and go back up. Be back in a jif."

Alex kissed Parker as he left and went about making certain everything looked normal. She started an early supper and fed Sarah. A few minutes later, JB called back with some startling news. Morris had just deposited a very large amount of money into his bank account in County Galway and records showed large deposits like that over a period of eight years. And he had been in Paris eight years ago, during the DuMonde investigation. But the strange thing was, Finnegan's bank account in Dublin had the same type of transactions. Both accounts had transfers from a Swiss bank in Geneva, but not on the same date. Their financial investigations showed no stocks, bonds or investments whatsoever. There wasn't one piece of a puzzle, but two. Coincidence? I think not.

Parker returned with another basket of goodies. He'd forgotten dessert! He had ice cream, sorbet, lady fingers and cakes. And he had a gallon of laundry detergent. He was out! He'd also called his security company with a secret code which told them he expected someone to break in within the next twenty-four hours and to keep the property under surveillance.

"All set, Alex," said an excited Parker. "I haven't done this type of snare since agent's school I'm getting a little giddy!!"

"Well, you need to read my notes about my phone call from JB just now," replied Alex. "There are two foxes in the hen house."

Parker made certain his car was locked in the attached garage, with the window shades down. It was 4:30 PM, so he set the alarm. The guards were alerted and Alex put the supper on the table. Around 9:30 PM, the rain began to fall.

It was only a gentle rain, but got heavier as the night went on. Most prowlers wouldn't try to burgle at night in this rain, but it didn't take long before someone tried to open the front door. That triggered the silent alarm. Someone else was at the back. The security people knew not to set off the alarm, but Parker was concerned there could be new people on the team, so he looked out a one-way window. To his shock, he saw Finnegan at the back, dressed in BDUs. Morris must be at the front.

In a split second, a crash of glass could be heard in the living room. Someone had smashed in the front door glass and was trying to get in. The flood lights sprang on around the perimeter of the house and Morris was caught red handed with his arm through the front door. The security men took both Finnegan and Morris into custody, as the Garda arrived.

"What happened here, Parker?" asked the Garda Inspector.

"There is an on-going International investigation and these two 'gentlemen' are with Interpol," explained Parker. "And no, they weren't doing their job. They were trying to protect their arses. They will be charged with breaking and entering, plus duplicity in two or more murders, including one today which was supposed to look accidental. Check into the death of one William Devin. I think you will find his brakes were cut. These boys are going away for a very long time. I need you to contact the head office at Interpol in London and have an agent sent over right away. My first call will be to MI-6 about them. I'll be here another day or two, then I will be leaving. Whatever you do, don't let these guys get away from you. If you need me, call."

Alex swept up the glass and Parker nailed a board over the broken door, then reset the alarm. He called the security men on the two way radio in the office and thanked them for making this a swift clean-up, but asked to continue to watch for the next couple of days. The house was locked up again and Alex put a fire in the fireplace. She poured two glasses of sherry and set one on the table next to Parker's chair and one next to hers.

The rain beat gently on the rooftop and onto the windows. Sarah was curled up by the newly-made fire and now was the time to think about the rest of their trip. Parker contacted his counterpart at MI-6 and explained about the moles inside Interpol here in Dublin. They decided on a telephone conference at 10:00 AM in the morning to discuss what their next step would be.

Parker turned off the lights and lit some candles. It was quite romantic. For the first time in many years, Alex finally felt at peace. She sipped her sherry and nibbled on a lady finger.

Parker looked at her adoringly and said, "We have a lot on our plates in the next few months, but after that, we should decide on a wedding. Good heavens, it could be here, the States, England? And where are we going to live?"

"Well, first of all," explained Alex. "Let's keep the house here and make it a business investment, so it pays for itself. We live in the cottage. Done deal. Secondly, I'm leaving my firm at the end of this assignment anyway, because Roan has offered me an exclusive job with his company, designing security systems. But I haven't said yes yet. I live in an apartment in Arizona, which is rented and JB wants the dog. Done deal. So for now, I'd say we live here and sell your apartment in Virginia."

"That was easy," replied Parker. "I like the idea. We make a good team, don't we?"

"Yes, Parker," smiled Alex. "We certainly do."

The morning sun came streaming in through the bedroom windows. Alex woke to rooster crowing in the yard. She looked out to see the groom taking care of the horses. As she stretched her arms, she noticed the sparkler on her finger and smiled, remembering the first time Parker proposed.

Parker had already made coffee and was on the phone to London. Interpol head office was sending over several senior agents to look into the matter of the rogue agents and was set for the conference call later that morning with MI-6. Parker asked the agents to come out to the house when they arrived.

"Looks like another house full, Parker," quipped Alex. "Too bad you sent Violet and Stanley away!"

"Oh no," replied Parker, "They won't stay here. There are rooms set up for them close to the offices. We can use the dining room for a conference room."

Alex acknowledged and completed making breakfast. Parker was happy to simply sit at his own table and have breakfast with Alex.

He looked up and said, "I've missed your breakfasts. You're an amazing cook, you know that Alex? Oh, think about it. We have our future laid out right in front of us—here in the cottage. Finally."

Parker's face was healing fast and he needed a shave. Alex was quick to point that out.

"Hey mister," she laughed. "You need a shave, 'cause you look like a bum. The scruffy look just isn't your style!"

He got up, looked in the mirror and said, "Oh, you're right. I do look terrible. I suppose it's time. I have to check underneath the bandages anyway. I'll be glad to be somewhat healed up. I can go up after the conference call."

Soon the call was in progress. Alex and Parker told Interpol and MI-6 about the agents, Ronald Rutherford and DuMonde. They were all tied together somehow. Parker explained he felt agents Finnegan and Morris were responsible for the death of their employee, Mr. Devin and could have gone after the other person who testified as to Ronald's condition, thinking he linked them to Ronald's demise. Parker said he would give the agents the paperwork he had regarding the notebook, the port mortem on Emilie Lonergan, the psychiatrists' notes and employee file. And they would need to check the Forensics Lab just in case the poison could have been stored there. Ronnie might be crazy, but he was also careless and the poison could be locked away without anyone ever noticing it.

Several hours went by and Parker finally came down from his shower, shaved, clean hair and changed bandages. The skin on his face was still raw from the cuts, but they seemed to be healing well. Alex was pleased to see her man looking so healthy.

"Those cuts won't leave lasting scars, I don't think," said Alex. "You already look a lot better, Parker."

"Thanks, love, but the jury is still out on several of them," sighed Parker.

"Speaking of juries, I wonder what those Interpol agents will find when they scour the lab for the poison—and what other things they'll dig up on Finnegan and Morris?" pondered Alex. "Shouldn't they be here soon?"

Right on schedule, the doorbell rang at the main house, so Alex and Parker walked up and greeted their comrades.

"Welcome to Ireland, gentlemen," said Parker. "I'd like you to meet Agent Alexandra Simpson of Serpentine Security Systems in Phoenix, who is co-agent on this case. Let's go into the house and make ourselves comfortable."

Alex went about finding makings for coffee and there were biscuits in the tin, so she put some on a plate and brought in the coffee, once it was ready. Parker went on to explain the background and findings they had uncovered, then opened the discussion to questions.

Colonel Philip Larkin of MI-6 and Agents Samuel Smithe-Williams and Daniel Griswold of Interpol studied all the files.

Agent Smithe-Williams was curious and asked, "Do you feel there is a correlation between Rutherford, DuMonde, Finnegan and Morris? It seems like a far stretch, but from what I see here, you might be on to something."

Agent Larkin agreed, "Fitzgerald, I'm amazed. Excellent deductions. I'm almost embarrassed to say this could be company-wide, which might be why DuMonde has fomented his escapades for so many years without being caught. You were right to bring MI-6 and London Branch into this."

Agent Griswold was less enthusiastic.

He commented, "Perhaps we are rushing to a conclusion here, gentlemen—and lady. Let's go over all of the information in context, then see where we are. Any report from the Garda on Mr. Devin's 'accident'? "

"Not yet," Parker explained. "But we do know at least three deaths were caused by Rutherford and that he was under some type of mind altering control. That's certain. And the large sums of money wired into Finnegan and Morris' accounts are incriminating (unless they played the horses in Switzerland!!). I'll leave this part of the investigation up to you fellows. I'm needed down south for a few days."

Alex was content to listen to these 'elder statesmen' of the Intel community. She jotted notes in her planner and listened carefully to their insights. She was getting an unsettling feeling about Agent Griswold for some reason, but she would only tell Parker after the men had gone.

After several hours, the agents left for Interpol offices downtown to investigate Finnegan and Morris, talk with the Garda officers and search the lab. Something would turn up and if Alex was right, this would go all the way up the chain of command at Interpol.

As the agents left, Parker said to Alex, "Nice guys. We should get to the heart of the matter now. And I think I want to go riding. Want to come with me?"

"Thanks, but no, Parker," explained Alex. "I want to get changed and packed so we can drive down later this afternoon. And I have something I need to talk to you about—on the case, but it can wait until you are done riding."

"Fine, love," said Parker. "Be back in a little while then."

Alex went back to the cottage to contact JB and have him do a run on Agent Griswold. She explained something wasn't right about him. Then she contacted the garage and the housekeeper in Ardmore to say they would be down around 4:00 PM this afternoon. Little Sarah came along while Alex changed and packed. Her face became sad as she realised her new friend was leaving.

"Don't worry, little one," sighed Alex. "I will be back to give you all the love you want."

In no time, Alex had her luggage downstairs. Parker came in from a great ride. He managed two of the three horses today and was exhausted.

"I'm getting too old for this, Alex," he wheezed. "I need some coffee and lunch. But let me shower and change, then we can drive down and have lunch on the way to Ardmore. Okay with you?"

Parker hurried and came down looking like a new man. He was packed, took his laptop and the rest of the gear, loaded them into the car boot and was ready to leave in thirty minutes. Alex left a few things behind, because she knew she was coming back very soon anyway. This was to be her new home, so why not start now!

Alex's phone rang as they were driving. JB had information about Agent Griswold. It seems he has a colourful background and isn't your typical Interpol agent. He had been an accountant before joining the service and was now working under cover as the banker in Switzerland, depositing money into Finnegan and Morris' accounts. He was the worm on the hook to lure these corrupt agents into revealing themselves as DuMonde's accomplices. But he also had a criminal record for money laundering. Maybe it made him a better agent for this task, but it also made his actions more suspect to Alex.

They drove down the R755, which was the inner route, but much more scenic. Parker wanted to show Alex Glendalough, with the round tower at St. Kevin's and the Vale of Clara, then have lunch at Avoca in the cafe next to their woollen mills. Then they picked up the R741 down through Wexford and down to Waterford. Parker drove along the coast road through Dungarvan, along the N25 until they reached the R673 and drove into Ardmore. The drive was picturesque. There were mountainous areas, rivers and streams, lakes and harbours. When they got to Ardmore, the strand of beach spread out before them and took them by surprise.

"Oh Parker," exclaimed Alex. "Look at that fabulous beach!"

They rounded the main street and saw several pubs on the left, a custom-made furniture store on the right and just beyond, the parish church where they could attend Mass.

Alex got out the directions and exclaimed, "We're on the wrong end of the village, Parker. We need to go back around and toward the south end, near where St. Declan had his hermitage."

Parker turned the car around and went back up the main street to the convenience store.

Alex ran in to check the directions and the woman behind the counter said, "Well, you would be the lass from America, then. Stop over at the garage first, then I'll follow you to the cottage. I'm Stella, by the way, your housekeeper!"

Stella turned the store over to her assistant and walked across the street to the garage to meet Seamus and get the car. Stella would drive that over to the cottage.

"Come on you two, don't dawdle. I haven't got all day," she huffed.

Seamus came bustling out and told Parker, "It's a crime, it is, Miss Millie dyin' like that. I miss her so."

"Hello Seamus. I'm Parker, this is Alexandra. We'll be checking on the cottage for Mr. and Mrs. Sanderson, the new owners. I think you will like them. He's Millie's nephew."

"Nephew?", he asked. "I thought Millie had only one—that nasty Ronald?"

"It turns out Roan is also Millie's nephew and no one except Millie and her family knew it until she died," explained Parker. "It's a long story, but we'd like to see the cottage now and get settled."

"Oh sure, sure," said Seamus. "Here's the other set of keys to the old Range Rover, Stella."

Seamus tossed the keys over to Stella who yelled back, "Follow me and don't get lost. These are narrow roads, windy, so watch carefully. *Tourists!* And Seamus, follow and bring me back to the store."

Stella chugged off to the south road, past the cemetery, with the beautiful round tower. They drove about a mile and a half, past Ram Head road, then Stella turned into a lovely white, thatched cottage with roses in bloom everywhere. Above the lentil it said, "Roselyn Cottage" and it was evident, how much Millie must have loved this place. Her touches were everywhere.

Stella ambled out of the Rover and unlocked the cottage. She quickly made up the peat fire to take the chill off the rooms.

"You've got central heating in here, don't forget, but this adds a nice touch. Millie loved this fireplace," remarked Stella. "There's food in the fridge and pantry for three days and you can get anything else you want at the shop. Phone's workin' and there's a fax machine, computer and all that high tech stuff you'll be needin' so have fun."

Parker was thrilled and said, "Thanks, Stella. We'll call if we need anything."

Alex stood in the hallway and looked at the front room. It was beautiful. It had a large, three pane window in the front with diamond mullions in each. They looked out over the rose garden and some of the flowers came up to glass level. You could see out to the farm across the road and almost to the Irish Sea. The large fireplace was somewhat plain, but held a decent fire. The acrid smell of the peat was something Alex had to get used to, but it wasn't too bad.

There were photographs on the mantle of Millie, Lulabelle, Emmie and her husband, plus ones of Roan and Shauna, with Conor. Several photos of Lillian and Roddy were there, too. There were no pictures of Ronnie. Stella had placed bowls of flowers on the kitchen table and some in Millie's study, where she wrote her books. It was if she were still there, typing away at a story and had just left to make herself some tea. Parker came in and was amazed as well.

"This is incredible," he said. "It's what a typical Irish cottage should look like. It has all the charm it did a hundred years ago, but with modern conveniences. It's the best of both worlds!"

Alex looked around to find two double bedrooms and a bathroom. There was a small dining room and a nice sized kitchen, complete with dishwasher, laundry duo, under-stairs pantry and stairs which went up to a sleeping loft for additional guests. But for now, that was used for storage. There was a grandfather clock in the hallway, which had been maintained and was on time. It chimed 5:00 PM on the dot.

Parker was looking out the back window of the kitchen and remarked, "Alex, look out the back. There are sheep and horses grazing here. It goes on forever! It's almost like Meadowhall."

There were French doors leading out to a patio, with chairs, table and built-in barbecue. There were pots of geraniums and ivies growing on top of posts and planters with roses and other flowers blooming along the sides of the patio. A sundial told the correct time and there was a small water feature, gurgling through to a pond with several kinds of fish in it.

"The Sandersons are going to love this," exclaimed Alex. "I can't wait to call them to let them know."

Parker went out to bring in the luggage, while Alex called Roan and Shauna. Several of the neighbours came out to say hello and ask if they were the new owners. Parker had to explain the situation and they would meet the new folks soon. One lady came with a coffee cake, another with a tray of biscuits and Parker showed them inside.

"Alex, these are some of the neighbours," explained Parker. "Come over and say hello."

Alex concluded her call and said, "I'm Alexandra Simpson and I work for Mr. Sanderson. I'm delighted to meet you ladies. I was just speaking with him a moment ago to let him know what a lovely community you have here."

"Oh thank you, Dear," said Mrs. Shaunessey. "I live to the West of the cottage and Mrs. Mulgrew here lives on the other side. We knew Millie very, very well we did. Terrible shame what happened to her. She'd been our neighbour for nigh over fifty-five years. It just won't be the same now."

"Mr. and Mrs. Sanderson—Roan and Shauna, are lovely people," explained Alex. "They have a son, Conor who is almost thirteen. I think you will find them excellent neighbours as well and although they won't be here all the time, I think this will be their favourite place to be. They will be coming over next month to meet you both."

Mrs. Mulgrew asked, "You sound like Dublin to me, Parker. Are you then?"

"Yes, Mrs. Mulgrew," replied Parker. "Born and raised east of the M-50 at Castlenock. I still live there."

"Oh lovely," said Mrs. Shaunessey. "Glad to have you with us for a visit. Call on either of us if you need anything."

Parker replied, "Thank you ladies. Oh, can you tell me what time Mass is in the morning?"

"Surely, it's at 6:30 AM and again at 10:00 AM," said Mrs. Shaunessey.

Parker smiled and continued taking in luggage.

He smiled at Alex and said, "Nice ladies. And they brought food!"

Alex chuckled and went about unpacking in the main bedroom, facing the front side of the cottage. There were fresh linens and towels, flowers and several of Millie's books on the night stand, in case anyone wanted some light reading!

Parker took the other bedroom and found it to be very pleasant. It looked out over the pasture behind the cottage.

Once they were unpacked, Alex thought it might be nice to take a stroll down toward the Sea. They walked out into the front garden and noticed a double bench on each side of the front door. Not only were there roses, but multitudes of other flowers tucked away in tiny corners of the plot.

Alex could see a beach about a mile away and as they walked, Parker noticed an old castle, which seemed to be derelict. They walked over toward it and were met by a farmer.

"Afternoon folks. You must be the people from America here to check on the house. I live here in Castle McKenna."

"Oh hello," said Parker. "Yes, we are here on behalf of the new owners, Millie's nephew Roan Sanderson and his family. I'm Parker Fitzgerald and this is Miss Simpson, who works for them."

"We live here at the castle and work the farm. I'm Patrick O'Neill," he explained. "Right now we rent, but would like to buy the old place and fix it up. It was quite a grand place in its day around the turn of the 20th Century. Has an interesting history. One of the first places around to have electricity!!"

"Maybe we can come over tomorrow and look at the grounds," said Parker. "This is a lovely place to live and work, I imagine."

"Yes, 'tis," explained Mr. O'Neill. "And Miss Millie. She was a great neighbour. She kept that cottage in top shape. She'd sit outside on a lovely day and talk to her roses, she did. She'd put on some horse manure, water them and just watch 'em grow. This Sanderson fella. He nice as Millie?"

"Yes he is and he and his family will be as thoughtful as Millie was about the place," explained Parker. "They have a son, Conor who is coming up on thirteen, so you will meet him as well this summer, along with Conor's friend Jimmy."

"Thirteen you say?" asked the farmer. "My son Eamon is the same age. They should have lots of fun together. I'll have to tell him tonight."

"We're off for a walk, Mr. O'Neill," said Alex. "See you later."

Alex took some photographs of the cottage and the castle as they walked along the road. There were additional cottages along one side and wheat growing on the other. Soon they were at the beach on Whiting Bay. It was a popular spot for bathers and family entertainment. It was a great stretch of beach like the strand at Ardmore, but more sheltered. The coastal road went around to the hamlet of Moord and onto the main road to Kinsalebeg and Youghal. But there was no one there today, except some fishermen, bringing in their small boat.

Alex's phone went off and she saw there was a message from Agent Smithe-Williams concerning the laboratory in Dublin. She suggested they return to the cottage as soon as possible. Alex decided to wait on calling him back, because as they strolled up to the front gate, a Garda officer was waiting for them.

"Agent Fitzgerald?" he asked. "I'm Guard Dermott Mitchell and I have news on the car accident up in Dublin regarding Mr. Devin."

"Oh sure, come in Guard Mitchell," said Parker. "We'd like to hear what really happened."

"We just got here ourselves, but I can make you some coffee," expressed Alex.

"Oh yes, miss, that would be lovely," he said.

They sat down at the kitchen table and Guard Mitchell explained the findings.

"Mr. Devin's brakes had been cut, literally severed," he explained. "I don't know why he didn't see the brake fluid leaking out under his car. He didn't get very far and the rest you know. We did find out the hoses were cut with a sharp instrument, like a scalpel used for dissecting things, possibly from their lab upstairs at the Interpol offices. They are looking for it now. But it seems your man Agent Morris, had brake fluid under his fingernails, which matches the fluid from the car. He was a bit too careless, I'm afraid. We don't get much in the way of crime down here, so this is exciting for me. You need anything while you are here—you just ask."

Dermott went on to tell a little about Ardmore, its history and the people who lived in the village. He said it was a very close-knit community and many had opened their homes to tourists over the years. It's a quiet get-away for families, but doesn't seem to have much excitement, unless it's the horse races during the summer and fall. Food in the pubs is good, especially the seafood. There is a laundry, two garages, a hotel, some B&B's, a pottery shop and several restaurants which served excellent, but over priced food to the tourists. The closest thing to a big shopping center would be at Youghal, pronounced 'Yawl'—and their traffic was terrible. You can easily get anywhere you need to in a short period of time and you can hunt for sea glass and shells on the strand after high tide. There are small retirement homes near the beach and a nice library and historical center close by. The cemetery is educational to walk through and you can walk out to Ram Head to look at the 'castle' there. For a village, it's pretty interesting.

Guard Mitchell got beeped and had to leave.

Alex showed him to the door and said, "Please come by anytime while we are here. We're glad to have met you."

Parker waved good-bye and Alex closed the front door. She was amazed at how friendly the people were.

"Shauna and Roan are going to love this cottage and Ardmore," said Alex. "I can't wait for them to see it."

They settled in for a delightful evening with a fabulous sunset. The scent of roses, the rush of the sea and a comfortable setting was all Alex needed to fall asleep.

She awoke the next morning when she heard Parker getting ready for church.

"Would you like to go with me to Mass, Alex?" asked Parker. You have time to get ready if you want."

"Yes, I'd like that, Parker," she replied. "I really do want to learn more about your faith. My parents didn't take us to church and I didn't have a religious education growing up, so I would like to find out more about the Catholic Church."

"I won't force anything on you, Alex," said Parker. "You can just absorb what you want and we can talk about it. If you want to join, that's fine. I'd like us to share our faith together as a couple. Maybe you can talk with Father Miller in Bemidji about instruction when you get back."

After fifteen minutes, Alex came out wearing a pretty floral dress, her sandals and her new skimmer hat. She also had a light cotton sweater with her, because the church would be cold in the morning. And she spritzed on a little of her new fragrance.

"I really like your fragrance, Alex," expressed Parker. "It's feminine and a little mysterious all at the same time. It's very—you."

They drove the Range Rover down to the church and parked on the street near the lifeboat station. The church was filling up quickly and Parker made sure they got a seat in the front. There were statues along the walls, a magnificent white altar with the older, high altar behind it. The walls were a mint green and the benches were wooden—a bit uncomfortable. The stained glass windows lined the sides of the church and the choir loft was behind at the back. Parker spotted the neighbours and waved.

The Mass began with an opening hymn, as the old organ groaned a familiar tune, albeit an out of tune—melody. Alex watched in amazement as the people sang without wincing (they must be used to the poor thing by now) and how they concentrated on the service. After Mass, their pastor, Father O'Malley, met the congregation at the front door.

He took one look at Parker and said, "Oh son, you look like a bomb hit you. You must be lookin' after Millie's place out on the coast road. Nice to meet you. I'm Father O'Malley."

"Hello Father," replied Parker. "Yes a bomb DID hit me. I'm Parker Fitzgerald and this is my fiancée, Alexandra Simpson from America. We're just here for a few days to look over the property for Millie's nephew and his family. You'll probably meet them this summer."

"Oh that's lovely," said Father. "I'll look forward to meeting them, too."

"Bye Father," smiled Alex. "We'll see you again."

As they got to their car, Alex had an idea and said, "I think I have a way to get that church organ restored. Roan wants new projects to spend money on and I think this is an excellent one. I'll e-mail him when we get back to the cottage. I'll also mention central heating."

When they got back to the cottage, Alex switched on the television to see the latest world news. Reception at the cottage was excellent because it was so close to the signal from the UK. There had been another killing accredited to DuMonde. He had stepped up his activity. Agent Finnegan was found dead in his jail cell Saturday afternoon. But did DuMonde or someone else kill him?

They stayed at the cottage for two more days, then drove back up to Dublin for one last check-in with the Interpol and MI-6 agents. Alex was really sad to leave Ardmore, but anxious to get back to Bemidji and put these pieces together. She found out Agent Morris had been placed into protective custody at an undisclosed location outside of Dublin until his trial.

Violet and Stanley arrived home just as Parker and Alex were getting ready to return to the States. Parker replaced the groceries he had taken from the kitchen and added a few things, so Stanley didn't have to go to the store. Violet was delighted to see Alex wearing her engagement ring.

Violet smiled and commented, "It's so wonderful to see you wearing Miss Elizabeth's ring. You know, Parker kept it in his bedroom next to his bed the entire time you were separated. He never gave up hope. Have you decided on a wedding date yet?"

"Not yet," replied Alex. "We want to get these cases wrapped up and by the end of summer, we hope to narrow down a date. We will be living here at the cottage for most of our time though. Maybe we could get married in the Conservatory!"

Parker smiled and said, "We'll have to see what happens. Oh Stanley, could you have some glass put in the front door of the cottage. We had a break-in last week."

"Break-in, Sir?" asked Stanley. "I'll see to it, Mr. Parker."

Alex and Parker loaded their luggage in the taxi and said goodbye. Violet was holding Sarah who waved the best she could!

As they rode to the airport, Alex couldn't get Agent Griswold out of her mind.

She looked in her planner and said, "JB found out a few things I don't like about Griswold, Parker. We may have to do a little snooping of our own in England before this is over. I'd say the sooner the better. Maybe Roan and Shauna will want to go over to Bolton-by-Bowland to see their new home and we can go with them. That would be a perfect cover. We've already started this, so we might as well finish it. If there's dirt on the rug at Interpol, I'd rather not sweep it under but vacuum it up."

They boarded the plane and settled in for a long flight. Their stop-over in Chicago was only an hour, so they didn't have time for a lunch, but got a short drink near their gate. Alex got a feeling someone was watching them and glanced around trying to see anyone out of place, but didn't see anyone. She didn't see the tall, thin man standing behind a large post in a black hat, dark glasses and slicker. He peered out from behind the post and stared right at Alex. As she turned around again to look, he disappeared. Could it be…?

Chapter Thirteen

When Alex and Parker got off the plane in Minneapolis, Roan was there to meet them. He and Shauna had driven down for a couple of days to enjoy Spring at the lake house. Shauna opened the mother-in-law cottage down by the lake to take a peek at what Sandra had done with it. It was a perfect place to write or spend some quiet time alone. Roan would take Alex and Parker out to the house after they had some lunch.

Alex stretched her legs out in the back seat of the SUV, while Parker and Roan chatted about the house, the investigations and the renovation of the restaurant. He hadn't seen it yet and was interested in seeing how it compared with other Northern Italian restaurants in Europe.

Franco met them at the door of Ristorante Tuscano.

"Ah, you must be Parker," Franco exclaimed. "I am Franco, the manager of our ristorante. Welcome to Ristorante Tuscano."

"Thank you, Franco," said Parker. "I am excited to see the ristorante."

Alex looked at Roan and said, "He's been working on his English, hasn't he?"

"Yes, he has," remarked Roan. "I've gotten him to say several decent sentences without messing up, so give him praise when you hear them, okay?"

Alex nodded and they went in for lunch. The place was spotless and Parker was impressed. Marcel introduced himself, along with Franco's folks, but not Gramma Giovanna. She was at church. They ate lightly, because Shauna was making supper. Alex was unusually quiet and told Roan she would explain at the house.

On the way to Lake Minnetonka, Alex explained, "Walls have ears. I didn't want to say anything about this case or what we discovered in Ireland in front of anyone who may have been in there eating. There is a lot to convey and I also want Shauna to hear this. We can wait until we can put it all out on the table."

Roan pulled in the garage and Shauna met them at the door.

"Welcome back, you two," she said gleefully. "Parker you look so much better."

Roan brought the bags inside and closed the garage door. Parker was really impressed with the lake house. Shauna took them all out to the cottage by the lake and showed them a miniature version of the main house.

There was a living room with fireplace, small eat-in kitchen, small conservatory, a den and W.C. on the ground level, with two bedrooms and main bathroom upstairs. There was storage in the attic. A deck surrounded the front of the house and huge windows faced the lake. Sandra had decorated it the same as the bigger house—perfect for guests or the family artist.

The ducks followed them up to the main house, waiting for a handout. Parker got a kick out of them.

"All of a sudden, they started following me," laughed Shauna. "So I made the BIG mistake of giving them some food. Now they won't leave!"

"I bet if Garbanzo comes out here, he will get rid of them," commented Roan. "I'll get Franco on it in the morning."

When they got in the house, Parker opened his briefcase and spread out the information on the investigation. Alex showed them the photos of the cottage in Ireland and explained why they needed to go over to England relatively soon.

"We've hit upon some very extensive corruption and it seems to entail Ronnie, DuMonde, two Interpol agents, one of whom is dead now and one is a top executive. I'm hoping we can get to the bottom of this before the trial, but there is so much involved, it looks as if Ronnie is just a linchpin to a greater problem. Oh he'll do a very long time in an institution, but we have to find out how these other people fit into the puzzle."

Shauna needed a breather and went into the kitchen to work on supper. Alex came in to help and as she put her hand on the counter to pound out the cutlets, Shauna spotted the ring on her finger.

"Alex, is that what I think it is," asked Shauna. "Is that an engagement ring?"

"Yes, it is," explained Alex. "Parker originally gave this to me twenty-seven years ago when we were in college. His parents forbade us to marry and we ended up going our separate ways, but we still loved each other. So while we were in Ireland, it gave us the time to realise we had our second chance right in front of us and he proposed again. And this time, we aren't letting anyone stand in our way of getting married. I didn't tell anyone about our relationship until we were certain. This was his grandmother's engagement ring and I have always treasured it. Now I can wear it all the time."

Roan jumped up and asked, "Did I hear engagement? Well, that means champagne. Let's get some bubbly!"

Roan looked at the ring and said, "That's some bauble you're wearing. It's perfect on your hand. Well, it would be if you had it before! Congratulations you two. That's marvelous news."

After the toasts, Alex wanted to ask Shauna about joining the church. She had lots of questions, but wasn't sure who to ask. Shauna felt honoured Alex had chosen to ask her.

"Well, the technical questions, you probably should ask Father Miller, but the other ones, I can probably answer," replied Shauna.

"How do I go about joining and learning about the faith," asked Alex. "Is there a class I can take?"

"Sure," replied Shauna. "But you are too late for this year, as the RCIA class ends with the Easter Vigil. Then it extends its class to Mystagogy for several weeks following, but for you, it might be best to work with Father Miller on an individual basis and talk with us as well. I can teach you prayers and their meaning, we can go to Mass all together as a family and hopefully everything will fall into place. I'm sure Parker will be a big help."

"He has already," explained Alex. "I've never had instruction in any faith, so this will all be new for me. I think I will enjoy the discussions."

"Great," smiled Shauna. "This will be a wonderful experience for you and you know, if you find out you really don't want to join the church, there is no reason I know of that you have to. You simply need to do what's right for you. But I think being around all of us who love our faith, will give you a really well-rounded view of it. I can act as a sponsor for you, unless you want Parker or Roan. And remember, by keeping an open mind and an open heart, that's what you need to begin this journey."

Alex was really pleased with Shauna's explanation. Although it was still early, Alex and Parker admitted they needed some rest and after supper, they went to their rooms. Alex took Shauna's words to heart and slept very well.

Parker still had issues on his mind about Ronnie's involvement with Emilie's death and couldn't sleep. He came up with a few good ideas.

Since the trial wouldn't commence until late August, they had June, July and most of August to research the issues, they had to interview witnesses and get additional background. Conor needed something to do for the summer months, while Roan and Shauna wanted to visit their new homes in Ireland and the UK. So, wouldn't it be prudent to combine all these elements and take the family to Ireland and the UK while everything was coming together? Maggie could live at the lake house, while they were gone and she could oversee the renovations to her own cottage Millie left her. A perfect solution.

In the morning, they drove back up to Bemidji. It gave Parker and Alex a chance to see the great lake districts of Minnesota. What a wonderful way to see the lodge pole pine forests and reservations. The trees were sprouting new growth and the air smelled clean and crisp with the scent of pine. Parker spoke privately to Alex about his ideas. She agreed, but with the provision all involved agencies, parties and attorneys would be kept in the loop during that three-month period. Parker called a meeting with Stephen, Maggie and Chief Reynolds for the following day.

But before their meeting, Alex wanted to try something. She went down to the jail to visit Ronnie and try out the trigger technique to see if the words

"Emmie" and "Emilie" would provoke a reaction in him. She stopped by Chief Reynolds' office to okay this task with him.

"Oh yeah, sure," said the chief. "You go right ahead and try it. If you get a response, maybe there are other words which could be triggers. It won't hurt to test your theory."

Alex walked into the cell with Chief Reynolds to find a subdued Ronald.

He sat motionless on his cot, looked up at Alex and asked, "Can I go home now? I'm tired and it's cold in here. I want my own bed and clothes. No one likes me here and it's unfriendly. Can I go home please?"

Alex poised for the target response.

"We just wanted to see how you are doing, Ronnie," she explained. "We just came back from seeing your old friends in the department. You know Padric Finnegan and Sean Morris. They told us about Emilie, your assistant who died. You remember Emilie, don't you Ronnie?"

Ronnie's eyes seemed to glow and his brow began to knit tightly.

He started wringing his hands and shouted, "You don't know anything about Emilie. She was wicked. She hated me. All she did is pick on me and tell me I was stupid. But now she'd dead. She's not going to bully me any longer."

Alex went in for the kill.

"Do you mean Emilie or your mother, Emmie, Ronnie?" continued Alex. "Emilie was your assistant and she was good to you. Are you confusing Emilie with your mother, Emmie, Ronnie?"

Ronnie was up now and pacing around his cell. He began to tear at his hair and the wild look in his eyes grew stronger.

His breathing became more intense and as he stomped over to the bars of his cell, he reached out his hand and shouted, "They're dead and that's where they belong. I killed them. They deserved to die. Where's Mike. I want my friend Mike. He'll know what to do. Do you know where he is?"

"We're trying to find him for you, Ronnie," lied Alex. "Should we bring him here for you when we find him? Would you like that?"

Ronald settled back onto his cot and remained silent until he sighed, "Yes, please. You're a nice lady."

Psychosis by word association. That's what Alex was going after. Now she had proof of trigger words.

Alex went back to Chief Reynolds' office and said, "This is what I was getting at, Chief Reynolds. The psychiatrists in Ireland said it was possible to train the human mind to respond to these trigger words and their personalities would be switched, like flipping on a light switch. One moment you have the normal, docile Ronnie. The next minute the violent and enraged killer Ronnie had become through this psychotic manipulation. He knows what he's doing, but can't stop himself."

"Well, I'll be dipped," said the Chief. "I never would have thought this could happen in a million years, but you just proved it. Damn. Okay, Alex. I'll be out to the house in an hour for the meeting and I'll bring the video tape of our conversation with me to show everyone. Scares the life out of me to think someone could be this cruel to someone and turn him into a killer."

"This is just the tip of the iceberg, so to speak, Chief," replied Alex. "This goes further up the chain of command at the International level and I think DuMonde is only one of the characters we have to deal with. Poor Ronnie was just so susceptible to mind control, coupled with his anger, that it made him the perfect pawn for DuMonde and his cronies."

Alex shook her head as she left the station. As she walked to her car, she spotted a little shop with petite clothes. She stopped in to take a look and found several dresses to replace those she left in Dublin. It was a quick sale and she was on her way back to the house.

Stephen was waiting for everyone to arrive. Roan and Shauna had Conor staying with Jimmy for a few days, so discussions could continue privately. Soon Maggie and the chief came in. Parker had put all the supporting documents on the table in order and the chief put his video in the player. Now with Ronnie's confession he killed Emilie AND Lulabelle, there were four deaths attributed to Ronnie and one to someone in Ireland, unknown as yet. There was the attempted burglary, the death of a suspect agent and the continued sightings of DuMonde, plus the one senior agent in Interpol who could be involved, this made a tangled and convoluted web of intrigue and deception.

Chief Reynolds showed the group his video of Ronnie and how he had been controlled through trigger words. In his lucidity, he knew who he was, where he was and why he was there. But in his psychotic state, all rationale went out the window and he became a killer, using all his skills with poisons. Except with Millie, it was sheer brute force on a fragile little lady.

Maggie was almost sick as she watched the video. Stephen sat there in disbelief, as Roan and Shauna sat at the table in shock.

Parker began to explain his theory behind the complicated plot and said,

"We have three months to discover more. My suggestion is we go over as a family—Roan, Shauna and Conor, plus Alex and myself as a couple. We can go to Ireland first and you can see the cottage and get used to being there for a few weeks, then we can go over to England to Bolton Hall. We can spend the rest of the time there and if need be, take the ferry back to Ireland. Conor will have his holidays and it will enable us to work on the investigation at the source. Maggie, if you would live at the house during restoration of your cottage, that would be a tremendous help. Any questions?"

Everyone was still in shock over what Alex and Parker had uncovered. But Roan thought for a moment and expressed his views.

"For us, this would be an ideal vacation," explained Roan. "But would it be safe for us as a family, with Conor—and probably Jimmy?"

"Yes, it would be perfect cover," explained Parker. "Since I am from Dublin, I have excellent connections with the local police there—the Gardai, and they would guarantee safety, plus my own personal security service would be employed if necessary. You'd be very safe in Ireland. As to England, with the investigation underway there, I think that would also be quite safe."

Roan looked at Shauna for a moment, then said, "Let's make arrangements. Marcel and Franco can manage the restaurant, as we have seen during my illness. Katie and Jim can run the Gallery and come over when they want. The girls may have to wait for their trip to Italy for a few months, but they can hunt for their antiques in England. It's going to work."

Maggie explained she would be delighted to help out and Stephen was still stunned.

"Well, do I get to come over and play country squire for a while?" asked Stephen. "I think that would be lots of fun."

"Yes, you can come over any time, Stephen," laughed Roan. "I'm sure the folks in Bolton-by-Bowland would find you a reet git!"

Parker almost fell over with that statement, but continued, "So, it's settled then? Shall we say right after Conor and Jimmy are out of school next week? Oh, what about passports? Does Conor have one?"

"No, no he doesn't," replied Shauna. "I don't think Jimmy does either. Can that be rushed through, Parker?"

"I'll call a friend at the Passport Control office and see if that can be done within a week, Parker replied. "Most of the time it takes over eight weeks to get a passport, so I'll need birth certificates and two photos of each boy. The cost will be around $135 each, I think, with them being expedited."

Shauna called Katie to ask her permission to take Jimmy over to Ireland and England for the summer with his pal and she was delighted. She told Jimmy and you could hear Conor and Jimmy yelling in the background.

"I think you have just made their summer, Shauna," laughed Katie. "We'll be fine at the Gallery without you for a little while. Jim will be there all summer and Maggie can be here if we want to come over."

"Thanks Katie. Once again you are a life saver!" expressed Shauna. "This will be a great summer for everyone."

Just then, Alex's phone rang. It was Interpol in London. They needed to arrange a private meeting with Parker right away. There had been some developments.

"Excuse us for a second folks," interrupted Alex. "Parker is needed on the phone. It's your contact at MI-6 and he needs you in London right away. He won't talk over the phone."

Parker spoke for a few moments then explained, "I have to make a short trip to London for a couple of days. I'm assuming this has something to do with the case. Sorry, but I must leave now."

Parker kissed Alex and told her, "I'll keep in touch as soon as I know why I am being summoned. Wonder if the hornets are out of the nest?"

"Okay, I'll just continue my work here, Parker," she sighed. "Call me when you are ready to come back."

Parker drove away, directly to the airport. A government jet was waiting to take him through Washington, D.C. and onto London. Apparently, the hornets indeed, were out of their collective nests!

Alex came back inside the house and explained, "I think this must be some CTB or Homeland Security business. We really shook things up over there and Parker's bosses may want some details. They need to be briefed and you can't blame them. He will call when he can. But let's concentrate on getting the boys' passports in order and decide what we want to take. We can contact Stella at Ardmore, then the caretakers at Bolton Hall."

Alex went upstairs to unpack, while Stephen and Roan continued talking. Maggie and Chief Reynolds went home and Shauna started the supper.

The jet landed at Dulles and a car whisked Parker away to headquarters. He was met by a deputy director who was flabbergasted as Parker gave his report. The Deputy Director for Foreign Affairs, Jack Kassman, handed Parker a communiqué from Interpol and another from MI-6.

As Parker read them, he smiled and said, "Exactly what I thought—but with a twist. I'd say this is interdepartmental cooperation at its finest—finally. Gentlemen, not only are we co-operating, we are doing so covertly and the high ranking official in Interpol is really a spook! He was investigating his men in Dublin by infiltrating as a banker, while MI-6's man was searching for DuMonde, with the guys in Dublin leading him to Ronnie. My partner and I tied them all together in a neat bow. Now we just have to connect the dots and wrap up the case. I'd say, for my last case with the CTB before retirement, I'm getting the best one yet."

Director Kassman said in disbelief, "Retirement? You've got to be kidding, Parker. You wouldn't."

Parker smiled and replied, "Yes, Director, I am indeed, retiring when this case is completed. I am getting married and we are returning to Ireland. I've literally given my life to the CTB and it's time for me to take some of it back. I'd say almost 25 years of dedication to the service is quite enough."

Director Kassman looked at Parker and asked, "You never have time to meet people, Parker. Who are you marrying? Do I know her?"

"I'm marrying Alexandra Simpson, Jack," explained Parker. "You remember, I told you about her when we first started in this business. Well, she's working under cover for the family involved in this case and we solved this together. Circumstances had kept us apart, but now we need to repair all those years away from one another. We will be married after we conclude this case and get everyone where they are supposed to be—in jail."

"Outstanding, Parker," replied Kassman. "This will be a real feather in your cap. I think the president will have something to say when this case is done."

"Well, Jack, you know me well enough to know I don't care about things like that," explained Parker. "I just get the job done and keep the world a better place without some of its criminals."

"Indeed you do," replied Director Kassman. "You'd better get going and fill those Brits in. This DuMonde has been a thorn in the International community's side for a long time now and if you can catch him? Ah, my boy. You will get a knighthood!"

Parker just laughed and met the car waiting for him outside. They went back to the plane and left for London.

Parker phoned Alex from the plane before they landed in London and said, "You wouldn't believe it, Alex. Kassman thinks the Brits will make me a knight if I get DuMonde put away. Can you just see it, Sir Parker and Lady Alexandra. What a load of bushwa!"

"Oh I don't know, Parker," laughed Alex. "I'd like to be a Lady for a day or so. Would it get me a better parking space at Buckingham Palace do you think?"

Parker just roared. The plane was close to touching down, so Parker concluded his call to Alex. When he arrived at MI-6, there were several agents from both firms waiting to speak with him.

Sir Edmund Chancellor, head of MI-6's task force and Agent James Dobkin, Interpol's chief, were anxious to shake Parker's hand.

"Well done lad," said Chancellor. "You've untangled this mess we've been dealing with for several years. Now all we have to do is get DuMonde and put him out of commission. How on earth did you come up with word-induced psychosis?"

"Actually," replied Parker. "I didn't. It was my partner, Agent Alexandra Simpson. She's working under cover for the family involved. She had studied Ronald Rutherford's behaviour patterns and with no evidence of drugs in his system, something else had to be the switch to turn on his alternate personality. Interviews with the late Mr. Devin and another co-worker, along with the discovery of the body of Rutherford's assistant, led to such a strange conclusion, it had to be real. The psychiatrists affirmed it and now we have video tape to prove it. This is in NTSC, so if you have an international video player, I will show you what happens."

An assistant set up the player and Parker proceeded to play the interview tape with Ronnie. The agents were astounded as they watched the almost comatose Rutherford sitting on his bed morphing into a raving psychotic in a matter of seconds when the trigger words, "Emmie" and Emilie" were used. This had been programmed into Ronnie for years by DuMonde (or someone associated with him, like Finnegan or Morris) and the conclusion is to work with your psychiatric physicians to study this more closely.

Parker turned the video off and finished his presentation saying, "DuMonde will probably hang Rutherford out to dry. He won't come to the USA. He will probably stay on the Continent or in Britain. He knows he has been compromised by Finnegan, now dead. Morris is the only link and he has been sequestered. The only way we can get to him now is to smoke him out and that's what I intend to do. He'll be coming after me next."

The agents came up to shake hands with Parker and one said, "Parker, I'm so impressed by what you and Agent Simpson have been able to do. I hope we can work together again."

Parker replied, "Sorry, but this is my swan song. I'm retiring from the CTB after Rutherford's trial and returning to my home in Ireland. Agent Simpson and I are to be married sometime after the trial."

"Jolly good," said Sir Edmund. "I hope we get an invitation."

Parker had to laugh and said, "We don't know where or when it will be, Sir Edmund. But if it's in the UK, then you all will get an invitation. But it will probably be in Ireland at my family home."

Parker gathered his files and the tape, then walked out with several agents. He asked if they would hold the return flight for an hour, so he could run over to a nearby department store to pick up a gift for Alex.

"Sure, we can come along," said one of them. "My wife's birthday is coming up and I'd better get a pressie or she will have my guts for garters. We'll take you back to the airport after you find something."

It had started to rain, so Parker zipped up his briefcase and ran into the store with the other agents in tow. Once they got to the women's department, Parker was totally lost. He had no idea what to buy.

"Get her some tea and chocolates," said a sales clerk. "She does like those, doesn't she?"

"Right," sighed Parker. "Come on lads, back to the food section."

Agent Philips looked at Parker and exclaimed, "Brown Betty! I'll get her a Brown Betty, a tea cosy and some Earl Gray. She'll love that. I'm so glad we came in here."

Parker selected a large box of hand-dipped chocolates, a pound of tea and a tin of shortbread cookies. The clerk wrapped them up and placed the items in a shopping bag, while Agent Phillips' purchases were gift wrapped. The agents left the store just in time to see Michael DuMonde standing across the street looking directly at them.

Philips wanted to draw his weapon, but Parker warned, "No. He's after me. This isn't the time or the place and he knows it. Holster your weapon."

Parker shook his head from side to side, indicating to DuMonde this wasn't going to happen now. DuMonde acknowledged then disappeared into the crowd.

"Damn it man," said Philips. "How can you be so calm? He was right there ready for the picking and you let him get away."

"No I didn't," replied Parker. "He was just baiting me. The moment will come when it comes down to just the two of us. And he's been planning this all along. This elaborate ruse has been staged for everyone's benefit and it's unfortunate people had to die. This is his chess game now and he thinks he's in check."

They hailed a taxi and drove to the airport. Parker got on the company jet and flew back to the States. They refuelled at Dulles, then headed to Bemidji. It was time to tell everyone why DuMonde had been stalking Roan and Shauna and what would be lying ahead before the trial.

Chapter Fourteen

Parker got back to the apartment and filled Agent Keller in on the meetings. He tried to find the right words to tell Alex, Roan and Shauna about his link to DuMonde. It just didn't click in his mind until the meeting in London. The years had pushed those memories back into Parker's subconscious, but now they resurfaced, becoming sharp again.

He phoned Alex and said, "I'll come out in the morning, Alex," explained Parker. "I'm just too tired right now. I have some findings from the meetings and you all need to hear them. So let's say 10:00?"

Alex was curious but let Parker explain the meeting when he was ready.

She replied, "Sure, that's fine. You get some rest and I'll see you out at the house in the morning. I love you, Parker."

"Thanks, Honey. I love you, too," yawned Parker. "See you in the morning."

By the time morning rolled around, Parker was ready to explain his relationship to Michael DuMonde. He drove up to the house to find Shauna in the sunroom, putting out fresh flowers. He waved at her as he walked to the front door.

"Hi Parker," smiled Shauna. "Coffee's on and I have some fresh Danish. Come on in."

"Is Roan here, too, Shauna?" he asked.

"Sure," replied Shauna. "Alex said you wanted to talk with us this morning. I'll go and get them."

When they got to the kitchen table, Parker sat grimly staring at his folder. He opened the flap to reveal several disturbing photographs. He sighed heavily and began to explain.

"When I was just out of the academy, I was assigned as a CTB liaison to the Paris office of Interpol," explained Parker. "It was a time of turmoil with student unrest—violence was rampant. There were American companies targeted for their political and environmental stances. We were there to protect American interests. I met Michael DuMonde and his wife, Camille at a rally at a university, where he had been a professor of sociology. We didn't form a friendship, but I'd say an acquaintance. Over the next few weeks, we had coffee several times and talked about our families, experiences—you know, just general things. I found him quite interesting. But he hated Americans."

Parker took a swig of coffee and continued, "Then one day, back in the mid-80's, he and his wife were attending a protest rally in the street when a bomb went off in front of an American company. Camille was killed outright and DuMonde was seriously injured. As he recovered, his emotional pain turned into vengeance against all huge corporations, especially Americans and the man you are familiar with now, is the product of that hatred. He kills all who, in his sick mind, 'need to be disposed of'."

Everyone sat motionless in their chairs, wrapped around every word Parker was relating. Alex had a question.

"So, why would he target Roan?", she asked. "I guess I'm not connecting this yet."

"Because I was Irish, with an American job, he wanted his revenge—no matter who it was," explained Parker. "He must have thought I was a plant or part of a covert operation to stop his faction (which actually, I was). Over the years, his resentment built up and when Ronald Rutherford came into the picture in Paris, he must have rambled off his insecurities and hatreds to DuMonde. Of course, Roan, Lulabelle, Emmie, Millie—all of the people back home were swirling around in Ronnie's subconscious and could be tapped into by DuMonde's demented mind. It was then DuMonde began programming Ronnie to be his instrument of death."

Roan was aghast.

He stared at the photographs of the rally bombing and said, "So this is what happened to DuMonde's wife. God in Heaven, look at the broken bodies. No wonder it drove DuMonde into insanity."

"Ronald was the perfect stooge," explained Parker. "He was working in Ireland, so DuMonde continued his programming. Agents Morris and Finnegan were his moles in the organization, being paid great sums of money by DuMonde's clients. For one reason or another, DuMonde decided to come after me and my family. As I look back on it, there's a distinct possibility my parents and sister were killed by DuMonde or his people in Ireland. The accident was investigated but no one was ever charged. The connection didn't even occur to me until I was in London yesterday and now it all fits. I knew DuMonde, but the association had been lost over the years. It should end when we get him."

Roan closed the folder and put his hand on Parker's shoulder.

"I don't know what's next Parker," remarked Roan. "But I'll say this. You have it under control. You and Alex were able to uncover an amazing amount of information in a short time and this investigation is now being handled by all agencies directly involved. They will draw DuMonde out and nab him. He will go away for a very long time—in a very secure prison or he'll die in the process. You've done everything possible to end this torment, especially for Ronnie."

Shauna spoke up and said, "We can enjoy our summer without worry, Parker. All that's really left is Ronnie's trial and I don't think that will be a problem either. I'm ready to go to Ireland and England!"

Parker was still concerned for the family's safety in the UK, but kept it to himself. DuMonde would come after him, not the family, unless Parker didn't co-operate.

Shauna handed Parker the birth certificates and photos for the boys, so the passports could be expedited, then they sat down for a light breakfast. Parker gave Alex the gift bag and she took it upstairs without opening it in front of the family. Then everyone went their separate ways.

Katie called up from the Gallery and explained the bid had come through from the University and they had won the contract. Shauna drove into town to go over the bid with Katie and get the schedule settled for summer.

Alex called Father Miller at St. Philip's to make an appointment for reception into the church and any pre-Cana counselling she and Parker needed before marriage. He could fit her into the schedule later that day.

Roan was on his way to Minneapolis to finalise the schedule and menus for the restaurant. He also had Stephen contact the caretakers in England to get the manor house opened up for their visit. He would call Stella in Ardmore, plus obtain an International driving license, so he could drive in Ireland and the UK.

The next few days went as planned. Parker compiled all his information on the case to take to Ireland. He was still concerned about Alex's hunch about Agent Griswold. How did he fit into this scenario other than being the banker? But who is he really?

All the details were in place and the family was ready to go over to Ireland. Shauna had sent clothing and other items sent via a delivery service to England, as they would be there longer than in Ireland. It kept the luggage down to a minimum. True to his word, Parker got the passports, so the boys were ready to leave.

They piled into the company jet, with Jimmy bringing up the rear with his electronic toys. They had to be turned off during the flight, which made Jimmy fidget. The jet would fly to New York, then the family would change planes to a commercial flight. The company jet was too small for long haul flights.

Conor was mesmerized by the scenery below and took some pictures of another jet passing close to them. He wanted to be a photographer when he grew up. Roan was delighted to keep it in the family, so he gave Conor tips on lighting and composition. He bought Conor additional lenses for his 35 mm camera to enable him to learn about the settings and how to use a light meter. Digital photography would come later, once Conor had mastered the basics.

Once they were settled into their transatlantic flight, everyone slept. It was first-class service all the way and the pilot gave Jimmy and Conor sets of pilot's wings. Yes, they still did that for some passengers! They even let the boys look in the cockpit before take-off to give them a close-up of the controls.

Stanley was at the Dublin airport to pick them up and drive them to Parker's home for the evening, then down to Ardmore in the morning.

Stanley was used to Ardmore, as Cork was only a very short distance away and he would meet his brothers and sister at Youghal for lunch on the way back to Dublin.

Violet had been warned about the boys—they were just about thirteen! But she wasn't worried. They would probably be too awestruck to do any damage and she was right. She greeted them at the front door, wearing her apron and carrying Sarah in her arms.

"Welcome to Meadowhall. Hello Miss Alexandra. I have set you all up in separate rooms. Please follow me."

Violet led the family up to the second floor to the bedrooms. Roan and Shauna had an en-suite room, while the boys had to share the family bathroom. Binky's rooms were locked, while Violet and Stanley lived on the third floor and accessed it via the elevator at the back of the house. Although the stairs led to the third floor, it had been roped off.

"I trust everything will be satisfactory for your stay, Mr. Sanderson," remarked Violet. "If you need anything, please tug on the bell-pull. I will be serving supper at 6:30 in the Conservatory. I think that's the nicest place to be. It's Mr. Parker's favourite room in the house."

"Thank you, Violet," replied Shauna. "This is lovely. I'm sure we will be quite comfortable."

The boys were in twin beds down the hall. There were six bedrooms on this floor, with three additional ones on the third floor. Stanley and Violet occupied the other three bedrooms and bath. The attic was so large, it could also be converted to sleeping rooms—or a bowling alley!

The grandfather clock in the main hall chimed in at 6:00 PM. Alex and Parker had taken Sarah with them to the cottage and Parker started a fire, then got on the Internet to check his messages. They would stay in Dublin for a few days to finish with the agents, then drive down to Ardmore. Alex went upstairs to change and by the time 6:30 rolled around, everyone was ready to eat.

The sunlight was glistening through the leaded glass panes of the Conservatory, making little dancing rainbows on the glass table top. The birds chirped in their cages to welcome the guests. Violet had gone all out, fixing a roast, with glazed potatoes, peas and carrots, Yorkshire Pudding and a fresh, green salad. There was a lovely burgundy wine, soda fizzes and/or milk for the boys. By the time they were finished, there was even time for cake and ice cream, coffee and Drambuie for the adults. Then Parker took the family out to see the estate.

The boys loved the animals and were finally up close to horses.

Shauna was the first to ask about Sparticus.

"Is that horse sneering at us, Parker?" she asked. "Or am I imagining things?"

"No, he isn't sneering, Shauna," replied Parker. "He's laughing at me. This is my brother's horse and he never rides because he will get his clothes dirty, so I ride Sparticus. This horse tries his best to urinate on Binky when he sees him and it makes everyone—except Binky—laugh, including the horse. So every time he sees me, he laughs."

Shauna just shook her head and walked around the paddock area. She spotted the sheep and went over to say hello. Parker cautioned her about their curious need to bite people. Shauna stepped away slowly and simply waved!

Soon it was time for bed and an early start to the morning. Stanley would leave at 9:00 AM sharp, while Alex and Parker had appointments in Dublin with the agents investigating the case. They would be driving down in a few days.

Conor had his camera at the ready, while Jimmy was, of course, playing with his game. Stanley stopped along the way to show Conor some excellent locations for his photographs and Conor learned about shooting in morning daylight as opposed to afternoon sun. Conor's school project would be filled with his photographs and stories about Ireland and England.

After lunch at Avoca and a tour through the woollen mill, they arrived at Ardmore and met Stella at the house. Stanley knew precisely where to drive and Stella was impressed.

"You northern boys sure know your directions," laughed Stella.

"We try, Madame," replied Stanley. "Here we are folks. Roselyn Cottage."

Stanley opened the Rolls' door and Shauna stepped out in amazement.

"Look Roan," she gasped. "It looks just like the pictures. It's beautiful. It feels as if Millie is still here."

"I made up the fire for you, clean bedding is in the linen closet, clean sheets on the beds," said Stella. "You have groceries in the pantry and the fridge is stocked. If you need more, the convenience store is down the lane, around the corner from the cemetery and down the next lane to the intersection. Or call and I'll talk you through it. Have fun everyone."

There were road maps on the kitchen table, car keys for the Range Rover and instructions on how to use the electric shower and heating system. There were brochures about the local attractions, the church and Mass times, plus a history of Ardmore and St. Declan. There was also a brochure about the library and the beaches.

Conor came running in to announce, "There are horses out back. You should see, you should see. And there are sheep and other animals. Wow they are fantastic!"

Roan walked out on the patio, looked over the barbecue and spotted the carp in the pond. He took some food from a small cabinet marked 'fish food' and fed them. It had rained earlier in the day and the sweet smell of grasses filled the air. There were flowers everywhere, in containers and planted around the patio.

Shauna was out front admiring the roses and other plantings when Mr. O'Neill came across the road to welcome them.

"Mrs. Sanderson?" he asked. "I'm Patrick O'Neill from across the road at Castle McKenna. I knew Millie very well and I know she would be glad you are here to take over. My son, Eamon is the same age as your boy, so I hope they can become friends. Welcome to Ardmore."

"How nice to met you, Mr. O'Neill," replied Shauna. "You can call me Shauna. I think Conor would like that. He brought his best friend with him, so the three boys can have a grand old time this summer. I see my husband coming around the corner. Roan, this is Mr. O'Neill—Patrick, from across the road."

"Roan, it's nice to finally meet you," explained Mr. O'Neill. "Millie often spoke of you and how proud she was of you."

"The pleasure is all mine, Patrick," said Roan. "By the way, I have an envelope for you from Millie. It was in my safety deposit box from her and it has your name on it. I'll go in and get it."

"My name, something for me?" asked Patrick. "Why on earth would I have something?"

Roan brought the envelope out for Patrick and he opened it to find a letter and a check in the amount of 100,000 Euros. Patrick had to sit down on the retaining wall at the front of the cottage as he read the letter.

It said:

"Patrick, my dear friend. You and your family have been good friends to me over the years and you helped me with anything I needed. Now it's my turn to give back. Enclosed is the check to help you purchase your land and begin making renovations on the castle. I have spoken with a banker in Youghal (the instructions are in this envelope) to set up a mortgage you can handle and your down payment is all taken care of. Also enclosed is a check for 50,000 Euros for Eamon's education fund and another 50,000 for you and Margot to do with as you wish. Buy some furniture, some new clothes, something fun for the two of you. You have struggled hard, my friend. Now you can take it a little easier. You have my gratitude and my everlasting friendship. Love, Millie."

Patrick couldn't speak.

He handed Roan the letter, who read it and replied, "That would be the Forsythe legacy, Patrick. They wanted to share the wealth around to their friends and family. And so they have. Better run over and tell your wife. She may faint!"

Patrick ran as fast as he could across the road, as Shauna and Roan walked back to the front door. The next-door neighbours showed up on cue and brought over baked goods to welcome the Sandersons.

"Hello there, Roan and Shauna," said Mrs. Shaunessey. "I'm Mrs. Shaunessey and this is Mrs. Mulgrew. We want to welcome you to our little piece of Heaven here in Ardmore."

"Oh how lovely," smiled Shauna. "And baked goods—oh the boys are going to go crazy over these. Thank you so much."

"We were neighbours for over fifty-five years with Millie," explained Mrs. Mulgrew. "Bought our houses at the same time. We're going to miss her terribly you know. But glad you are here. Let us know if we can do anything for you to get you settled."

"Thank you ladies. How sweet of you," said Shauna. "Roan and I are really delighted to meet you. I think he has something for each of you."

Roan came out with sealed envelopes for each woman. He handed them out and waited for the reaction. Mrs. Mulgrew opened hers first.

The letter read:

"Dear Mary Margaret. I know how much you have wanted to upgrade your appliances and get central heating in your home, fix the roof, etc., so I have arranged for a contractor to come to your house at your convenience to do that for you. And I know you have always wanted to travel, so here is a check for 55,000 Euros to do just that. All the taxes have been paid so the money is free and clear. This is 1,000 Euros for each year we have been friends. I'll miss our coffees together and our everlasting friendship. Please dear, enjoy yourself and whatever you want in your house, go for it! I love you, Millie."

Mary Margaret had to sit down on the chair in the rose garden.

She looked over at Mrs. Shaunessey and said, "Sit down first, Myrtle, then read your letter. You're not going to believe it."

Myrtle sat next to Mary Margaret and opened her letter to find the same amount of money and this explanation:

"Hello 'Dolly'. I know this has come as a great shock, but I wanted to let you know how much your friendship has meant to me over these past fifty-five years. So, I have set up a trust fund for your grand-children's education wherever they want to go to college or university. The banker over in Youghal can explain more. The check for 55,000 tax-free Euros is the same as Mary Margaret's. It's 1,000 for every year of our friendship and it will make life a little easier for you. Now you can do whatever you want—travel, buy something nice for yourself. And if you need something for the house, just tell Roan and he will do it for you. I'm going to miss you, but know someday we will see each other again. Happy baking. Love, Millie."

"Whew, I'm glad you told me to sit down," said Myrtle. "I really don't know what to say."

"Millie gave me specific instructions," explained Roan. "Anything you ladies ever need and it will be provided for you. And I mean anything. Millie treasured your friendship and this is her way of keeping those memories alive.

She wanted you to have the best. Maybe you two should come in here and have some coffee and your cakes!"

Conor came screaming into the house, (with Jimmy lost in his game) yelling, "Dad, Dad, there are horses out here, thoroughbred horses. You gotta see them now."

"Hey, hold it son, we have company," exclaimed Roan. "Conor, Jimmy, this is Mrs. Mulgrew and Mrs. Shaunessey. They are our next-door neighbours. Say hello to the nice ladies, boys."

Conor came over to shake hands, then smacked Jimmy in the back of the head to get his attention. Jimmy looked up and came over to greet the neighbours.

"Hello, I'm Jimmy," he explained. "I'm Conor's best friend. We kinda like don't go anywhere without each other. Nice meeting you."

"Sorry, tweens you know," sighed Roan.

Half an hour later, Guard Mitchell arrived at the cottage. He wanted to welcome the Sandersons as well. The ladies decided it was best to leave when the Guard got there, so they thanked Roan and Shauna for the lovely tea and their envelopes. Guard Mitchell explained his visit.

"First off, let me introduce myself. I'm Guard Dermott Mitchell. I'm twenty-five, a bachelor and have lived in Ardmore all my life. If there is anything you want to know, please ask. I am also aware of the situation surrounding your visit and will maintain silence around the boys, who I saw outside chasing after a sheep a moment ago. This is a lovely, quiet place to live, with very little crime. The beaches are grand and the food excellent. There is a lot to do nearby and you should have a brilliant holiday."

"Well, Dermott, I am Shauna Sanderson and this is my husband, Roan," Shauna replied. "Would you like to stay and have some of this wonderful cake and tea? There is more than enough for all of us and you can tell us more about yourself and Ardmore."

"Thank you, yes, but only for a little while. My sergeant will be out looking for me and if he spots my bicycle, he can tell if I'm goofing off!"

"Okay then," said Shauna. "A cuppa and a cake, how's that?"

"Grand, Mrs. Thank you," replied Dermott.

Conor came running back in and tried to yell something at his Dad when he saw Guard Mitchell.

He stopped dead in his tracks and blurted out, "Cheese it, it's the Fuzz!"

"Guard Dermott Mitchell, meet my son Conor Sanderson," laughed Roan.

"And hello to you, too, Master Conor," said Guard Mitchell. "I'm really an old softie, you know, so I hope we can be friends while you are here. Just don't get into trouble—okay?"

"Ah right, sir, I mean Dermott, ah Guard Mitchell," gaffed Conor. "Cool. I gotta go and tell Jimmy—that's my friend who is with us."

Just then Dermott's beeper went off. Stella needed him at the convenience store.

"Thanks for the treats, folks. Got to run. You know how Stella is!" replied Dermott. "Best not to keep her waiting!"

The sun was setting and Roan could imagine Millie sitting outside enjoying the peaceful sunsets. It really was the place to write and be inspired by everything around. It was a special place to unwind. He went inside to unpack, while Shauna started supper. It would be fun to explore the beaches and sheltered coves, see the small villages close to Ardmore and go into Waterford to the glass factory. There was a lot to see and do during their first family vacation.

Meanwhile up in Dublin, Parker and Alex had met with Agents Larkin and Smithe-Williams about the dangling details of the investigation. Alex figured nothing ventured—nothing gained, so she asked about Agent Griswold.

"I don't mean to cast aspersions about a fellow agent, but something doesn't set well with me about Agent Griswold. It's as if he's hiding something from us or covering up for something. My intel says he's an excellent agent, but has a past. He knows how to launder money. Could he be working both sides of the fence here, gentlemen?"

Agent Larkin was quick to answer.

He explained, "Griswold has had a rough patch lately. His wife divorced him and took the kiddies and the house—just about everything. Really nasty business that. Seems she found him, more than once, at her best friend's house and not having tea and bickies, if you know what I mean. He's been on warning for drinking too much, but you can't blame the bloke. Still, he's been handling the money on this sting. We've let him run with it, so maybe it's not all accounted for. Best to check."

Agent Smithe-Williams opened the file containing the transaction printout from Switzerland and it showed equal payments to Finnegan and Morris in the amount of £80,000 each over eight payments. However, according to what Alex had pulled from bank records, only £60,000 went into each bank account—six payments of £10,000 each. £40,000 was missing.

"I don't believe this," exclaimed Agent Larkin. "£40,000 missing. How come we didn't spot this earlier?"

"Maybe we were so focused on Rutherford and the rest of the gang, we didn't even think to look at the bank reconciliation," remarked Agent Smithe-Williams. "This doesn't look good for Griswold. That bloke has had way too much happening in his life and if he's on the take? Man, I don't want to be the one to arrest him."

"Best go and get him now," said Larkin. "Parker, will you come with me. I don't want to do this alone."

Parker and Agent Larkin went down to O'Connell Street to a favourite agent's pub and found Griswold three sheets to the wind, eyes bloodshot from binge drinking. There were beer glasses and empty shots on the table. He'd been drinking 'boiler makers' most of the morning and was pished.

The agents sat down and looked directly at Griswold saying, "Dan, it's Phil and Parker. We need to talk. Dan, can you hear me?"

Daniel Griswold looked up and whispered, "Shhh, don't want to make a scene, do we? Whatta ya want fellas?"

"Dan, did you take £40,000 out of the cash fund on this case?" asked Parker. "Where is the rest of the money?"

"You—you want what now?" asked Griswold. "Money? I haven't got money—the wife has all me money."

Dan squinted, tapped his head and slobbered, "Oh THAT money. £40,000 was it? Yeah, I took it. Nobody noticed did they. Ha. I got 'em good I did. Spent it at the track. Lost most all, too. And spent some on this good booze. Tough to be you, isn't it, Philsie?"

"Daniel Griswold, I am placing you under arrest for embezzlement of £40,000 from money in your care," said Parker. " You have the right to remain silent. Anything you say can and will be used against you in a court of law. You have a right to an attorney. If you cannot afford an attorney, one will be appointed for you by the court. Do you understand these rights as I have read them to you?"

"Oh go to hell, Parker," said Griswold. "You got nothing on me."

Parker held up the voice recorder and said, "This doesn't lie. Come on, let's get him to the police station. Better to get him in a cell to sober up first, then we can deal with him when his mind clears. Put the cuffs on him Phil and let's go."

"Looks like Alex called it again," said Agent Larkin. "Boy, she's good. How can the two of you retire after this?"

Parker smiled and said, "We missed out on an entire lifetime of happiness and we aren't about to let it get away again. So now, this will get wrapped up and we can get on with our new life together."

They took Griswold to the jail, then went back to the office. Alex was waiting with more news.

"Guys, a search of the lab turned up Ronnie's stash of poisons. He had them behind a false drawer in a file cabinet. The drawer had become lodged and it wouldn't close, so one of the technicians became suspicious and pried a false wall away from the back of the drawer—and there they were. She called us immediately and now we have everything he was working on. It's all there, the poisons, his notes—everything."

"Well, we just arrested Dan Griswold," explained Parker. "You were right. He stole £40,000 of the graft money and openly admitted it. I've got it on tape, too. I wish we didn't have to do that to him, but he broke the law."

"Guess there is only one thing left to do," said Alex. "Time to go down to Ardmore with the family. Oh, but where are we going to stay?"

"I've been thinking about that and I had Stella do a little checking for me," explained Parker. "She said there is a darling little cottage by the ocean for sale and I had her put in an offer. If it's accepted, we have a place to live when we are on holiday and we can be closer to Roan and Shauna. In any case, it's ours to rent while we wait for the offer to be accepted."

"Leave it to you to come up with this solution, Parker," sighed Alex. "Let's go down and see it now."

"Bags are in the car, we are ready to leave any time," said Parker.

They loaded up their files and took off for Ardmore. The sun shone brightly on the car as they enjoyed the coast road toward Ardmore. Parker stopped to show Alex the crescent beach from the other end. It stretched out forever, with the village on one end. The little cottage was in the distance, nestled in the cliffs with several other cottages. The water sparkled in the sun and Alex was getting as excited as a little kid with her first bike.

"Is that it way over there?" asked Alex. "I can't see very well, so let's get over there!"

Parker drove around the curved road slowly to avoid the farmer with his cows crossing the road. The gentleman tipped his cap and Parker drove into the village, past the church and onto the lower road. He read Stella's notes and drove to a row of three cottages. There was a sign out front that said SOLD in big block letters, with the number 252 over the door.

"That must be it," exclaimed Parker. "I'll give Stella a jingle and she can bring the keys over."

Alex got out, walked down four steps and up to the front door through the rose-covered trellis to peer inside. The cottage had a red clay tile roof and was made from light-coloured stone. The sheltered door was oak with glass insets in the top and hammered iron hardware. There was a brass bell hanging from the wall to announce guests. Alex could see through the house toward the Irish Sea. The house seemed vacant, without furniture. But that didn't phase Alex. She wandered around to the side of the cottage to find a small garden looking out over the sea. There were steps down to a private beach and she could see a deck surrounding the back of the house and also one closer to the sea front. It had patio furniture on it.

She walked around to the other side of the house. There was a beautiful rose and vine-covered gate leading to an herb garden, with benches and bird houses. The pathway wound around to the back of the house and Alex decided to follow it. It led to a marvelous rock garden with succulent plants and a small water feature flowing out toward the cliffs. The cottage looked like something out of a fairytale. Her daughter would love this.

Soon Stella was walking up the road with the keys and said, "I see you found it okay then. What happened to your fiancée?"

"I think she went around to the back of the house to take a peek," explained Parker. "By the way, I forgot if this is furnished or unfurnished."

"Unfurnished, I'm afraid, Parker," said Stella. "The details mention 'unfurnished' except for appliances. So you will have to call into Youghal and get some furnishings for the house. But if you need the bed right away, you can go over to the custom shop and get one there. My brother-in-law owns it and he has some nice things—rustic kind."

Alex came bouncing back and yelled, "I absolutely love this place and I haven't even seen inside yet. Hello Stella. Thanks for finding it for us."

"Sure thing, Alex," remarked Stella. "I have the keys, so let's go in."

The cobblestone walkway led to the front door, which was inset from its frame to protect guests from the wind. Small bench seats flanked each side of the doorway. There were flower boxes on the white-framed windows filled with scarlet geraniums, ivy and white impatiens. The door opened into an open floor plan with a great room ahead, a kitchen off to the left and a study on the right. There were huge plate glass windows looking out over the cliffs to the sea and a deck which wrapped around the great room, complete with chairs and tables. At least there was a place to sit! All the triple-glazed windows in the house were new, as was the security system.

A staircase led to the lower level, complete with basement laundry, finished game room (with fireplace and lots of book shelves) and small kitchen with bar fridge. There was a walk-out to a stone patio and stairs down to the next deck by the sea. Terraced gardens were on both sides. There was even a work-out room, shower room (with w.c.), chest freezer and lots of built-in storage. Another staircase was on the other side of the basement, which led to the top floor with two bedrooms and a full bathroom with shower stall. This was more than a holiday house. It was a home. The central heating/hot water boiler was also in a mechanical room next to the bath.

The double bedrooms were huge. Both had views of the sea and the front of the house. There were full wardrobes on two walls in each bedroom. The bathroom was in the middle, complete with heated towel racks and claw-foot tub, toilet, sink and shower stall. And there was plenty of under eves, walk-in storage with cedar cladding. Someone had taken great care with this property and it was in move-in mint condition. All they needed was furniture.

The kitchen was also an open plan, with lots of beautiful pine cabinets, a wine refrigerator, built-in double-oven and extra counter space. There was a four hob gas range with hood, dishwasher and American-style fridge. And there was space for a kitchen table in the center. The Belfast sink was in good shape and the wide-plank floor squeaked a little, but that added character.

The great room had a fireplace at one end in the corner. You could sit in front of the fire and look at the sea at the same time. It would be wise to order some rugs along with the furniture and Parker asked Stella if she had the room dimensions.

"Yes, they are here in the details, Parker," explained Stella. "We can see what you need, do a little measuring and go over to Youghal if you want this afternoon. I'm free until 6:00 PM. That leaves us four hours to get this accomplished."

Alex took out her pocket notebook and jotted down: queen-sized sleeper sofa, two big chairs, ottomans, tables, coffee table, lamps, curtains, rods, two Oriental rugs. Two beds—one double, one queen. Linens, comforters, tables, lamps, rugs, curtains. Bathroom rugs, towels. She went from room to room like a tornado.

Then she ran down to the basement. Again, Alex wrote in the notebook, kitchen appliances: microwave, coffee pot, hot pot, popcorn popper, dinnerware, utensils, glassware. Towels, bath mats. Large area rug. Two sleeper-sofas, two chairs, a large storage ottoman, one large television, stereo and dvd player. More patio furniture.

The kitchen was next. She looked in the cabinets to find them empty. Parker and Stella watched in amazement as she continued. Dinnerware for ten, glassware, silverware, mugs, wine glasses, liquor, cleaning products, paper towels and toilet paper, table linens, round kitchen table with leaf and six chairs. Spices, pots, pans, utensils, bakeware, microwave, coffee pot, Brown Betty, hot pot and canisters. Several vases and some green plants. Hammer, nails, some pictures and nicknacks.

Within twenty minutes, Alex was finished with her inventory and turned to Parker and said, "Okay. Done. Let's go shopping. You pay for half and I will pay for half. I think that's fair, don't you, Stella?"

"Well, allrighty then, let's rock and roll," laughed Stella. "I'll call ahead and see if they can have a few sales clerks standing by with carts, so you can whirl through. I'll ask if they can bring everything right over when we're done."

Parker was still stunned with Alex's efficiency and queried, "How in the world did you get this efficient Alex? It boggles the mind!"

"Lots and lots of practice," laughed Alex. "We can get this place looking like home in no time flat. Ready when you are."

In twenty minutes, they were in downtown Youghal. Stella had called to alert the staff at the department store and true to form, Alex was ready. She went floor by floor, department by department. Within an hour, she had everything but the green plants and extra food stuffs. They could stop at the grocery on the way out of town, stop at the garden center at the edge of Ardmore and be finished by the time the delivery vans pulled up. By 5:40 PM, the men were placing the furniture and Alex was swinging into high gear.

Stella got a phone call on her cell. It was the estate agent and the offer had been accepted. Good thing, too, because they had just bought all that stuff!

"Good news people," said Stella. "The house is yours and for far less than you offered. Well, I couldn't let you get scalped, since you knew Millie and all. She always told me to take care of her family and you are kind of family, so you qualify. I think you will like it here. By the way, the fridge and freezer are fully stocked and so is the wine fridge."

"Stella, you are a jewel," smiled Parker. "Thank you for all you have done. We'll have you over for supper while we are here."

Stella departed with a huge grin on her face as she watched the delivery men continue placing furniture with Alex directing them to each room. Soon they were finished and Alex went about making things look like home. She stopped long enough to make a sandwich and get Parker to help with the pictures.

"Here, make yourself useful, Dear," Alex said with a smile. "You can decide where to put the pictures. I see some nails in the walls already and you should use those if they are the right height. The vase of flowers would look nice on the mantle, too."

Alex took the smaller pictures up to the bedrooms and put several in each room, along with some in the bathroom. She came back down and went into the kitchen. She looked in the pantry and found it stocked, too. But there was no broom or vacuum cleaner. The mudroom going out to the side garden had a broom closet, but it was empty. That could easily be remedied tomorrow. But Alex had also forgotten about the study. She went in to find it was a beautiful, quiet room with rich off-white carpeting. She called over to the store and asked for a sales clerk who had helped her. Alex asked for a brown leather sofa, two leather chairs with footstools and two tables, two lamps and an oak office desk. She also asked for two pair of long plaid curtains. Then she asked for the electronics department and ordered a computer, printer and scanner, plus a small television/dvd combo, several telephones, an answering machine and a small stereo. All items would be on the truck in the morning.

Parker had finished hanging the paintings and put a fire in the fireplace. Alex grabbed a cup of coffee and sat on the sofa looking out at the sea.

"I could get used to this real fast, Parker," expressed Alex. "There is something about the sea that calms people. Even if there is a storm, there is power here, but also gentleness—and life. We need a crucifix in here, too, Parker. Maybe we can get one at church Sunday at their little stall in the back. And you know what? We can hear the church bells from here."

Parker sat for a while in one of the new chairs, with his coffee in his hands. You could see him making a decision.

He turned to Alex and asked, "If you had your choice, which place would you want to live in—here or the cottage in Dublin? Be honest with me, because this is important."

"Okay, since I'm being honest," explained Alex. "I think it would have to be here. This is a new place, a fresh start for us. It's not busy, but charming and quiet. The people are great and it's the perfect size home for us. I know how much you love your home in Dublin, Parker and I would never tell you to sell it, but that will have to be your choice. I know it's been on your mind."

"I think Violet and Stanley want to go home to retire," explained Parker. "If I sell the house and property, including the cottage, we could relocate the horses and animals down here, bring Sarah here, too. The antiques could be donated to a museum and we could keep what we wanted. I do want the piano. Maybe it's time I let go of the past."

"That will have to be your decision, Parker," said Alex. "We need to look at where we will be spending the most time when we retire and I think of Millie, who loved this place so much. There was a reason she spent so much time in Ardmore. I'd also say to close up the apartment in Virginia, because you don't need to be near the CTB offices any longer. We might take one of Roan's apartments in Bemidji. It seems to make perfect sense to me."

Parker thought for a while longer and said, "I think it's an excellent idea. It's time for us and this is our place—not mine, not yours but ours. It will be less for us to maintain, easier when we need to go out of town and there is plenty to do and see here. Sorted. I'll call an estate agent in the morning, then phone Stanley and tell them. We can talk to Roan about an apartment, then I can call my realtor and put the apartment up for sale. I don't even have personal items there anymore. I can sell it "as is". One thing about this, we will come out way ahead and can bank a lot of that money. Binky already has his and I think we could set up a fund for Stanley and Violet to keep them comfortable for the rest of their lives."

"I like the idea even better," said Alex. "By the way, I had forgotten the study, so I ordered some things for it. They should be here on the morning delivery truck and we can get it put together. And we needed a broom and vacuum. Then we can invite Shauna and Roan, plus the boys down here for supper tomorrow night. What do you think about that? It would be a huge surprise."

Parker's phone rang. It was Agent Larkin. Apparently Sean Morris was singing like a bird, now that Dan Griswold was in jail. Old Sean gave up names, places, dates, cases—all the things connecting the rogue agents, DuMonde, Ronnie and the deaths. He tried to ask for a plea deal, but with Mr. Devin's murder, Sean was going away for a very, very long time.

"Ooo, that's a good thing," laughed Alex. "I think this deserves a nice dinner and a good bottle of wine. Should we go up the street and see what the "Seaside Restaurant" is all about?"

"Excellent idea," replied Parker. "I am famished. A good dinner with my feet under someone else's table tonight sounds just right."

They walked up the road about two blocks and went into a quaint restaurant with hand-made menus. The hostess sat them at a table overlooking the sea and took their drink orders.

Parker saw several items he might like and asked Alex if he could order for both of them, "Do you trust me enough to let me order? I promise, I won't let you down."

"Sure, go ahead," replied Alex. "Surprise me."

The waitress came over to take the order and Parker whispered it to her. He didn't want Alex to hear.

They enjoyed a lovely evening, holding hands and looking at the sea. Soon the waitress brought a beautifully presented platter of seafood, baked, broiled and fried. There was grouper, plaice and cod. There were beans, carrots and cauliflower, with baked potatoes and wild mushrooms. The Shiraz was smooth and they enjoyed this meal tremendously. Parker introduced himself to the owner after they had finished, then they walked home.

Alex was ready to call it a night. She sat in the chair, with her feet up on a footstool and promptly fell asleep. Parker took a knit throw from the package in the closet and draped it over her. The house would be complete in the morning, so Parker went up to bed.

The waves from the rough sea crashed against the rock ledge near the house. It was an unfamiliar sound and it woke Alex. She stretched the kinks from her muscles and walked over to the windows to watch the dawn break over the Irish Sea. The churning water was the colour of steel and the white foam spread over the rocks like frothy egg whites. Gulls soared and dove into the sea to grab a tasty fish for breakfast. And Alex decided it was time to check out the fridge for something to make for breakfast. She looked on the wall for the time and realised she didn't buy any clocks! Her watch would have to do. It was 6:15 AM and it gave her time to make a decent breakfast for Parker.

Stella had put in rashers of bacon, sausage, eggs, tomatoes, etc., for a traditional Irish breakfast (without the black or white pudding), so Alex set the table with her new linens and dinnerware, then made breakfast.

Parker came down with a grin on his face and said, "Good Morning Sunshine. I see you found everything alright. Mmm, coffee and a good Irish fry-up. Thanks, Honey."

Alex ate quickly, then ran upstairs for a fast shower. By now it was close to 7:30 AM and she wanted to call the department store to add a broom and a vacuum cleaner, along with five wall clocks to the truck. An hour later, the delivery van was at the door.

"Morning Miss," smiled the driver. "Fine mornin' for a delivery! Where should we be settin' these things?"

"They go inside the room on the right," explained Alex. "Sofa under the windows, desk along the far wall, computer equipment can be put by the desk. This will be an easy room. Thanks fellas."

Stella came rolling in behind a delivery man.

She had the broom and vacuum cleaner in hand and laughed at Alex saying, "You really going to use these things? Guess I should put them in the closet in the mudroom. Hey, Alex, the place looks great. You really do know your stuff, don't you. Oh, I ran into Guard Mitchell and he will be along directly to say good morning. Nice fellow Dermott. Wish we could find him a good woman."

Alex smiled at her new friend and exclaimed, "I think I should bring my daughter and grandson over here. Might be good to let her see Ireland. She's just the right age for Dermott, too. There's a plan under foot!"

Parker had finished his shower and was dressed casually in jeans, sweater and his boat shoes. His cuts were healing well and he almost looked like his old self. He walked over to greet Stella, when the house phone rang in the kitchen.

"THAT'S what I wanted to tell you," giggled Stella. "I got the phone turned on to the house. Here's the number. You can use the same Internet connection as the one in Dublin, unless you want to change it. Once you get set up, you can log on."

The delivery men finished placing the furnishings in the study, said goodbye and drove away. Parker came over and explained the call.

"That was Dermott. He received a call from Dublin and Dan Griswold committed suicide in his cell last night. He left a note that said he '*couldn't take the shame of what he did or the pain from his divorce. Life wasn't worth living and he had made such a mess of things. This was the only way out. I'm sorry.*'

"What a horrible thing for his family," said Alex. "We should remember them at Mass Sunday. This just makes me sick, Parker."

"Well, I'll get going now and see you folks later then," remarked Stella. "Dermott should be down soon anyway."

"Thanks a lot Stella," said Parker. "Now I can call Roan and Shauna to let them know we are here. See you later Stella."

Parker went about making his phone calls and found that indeed, Stanley and Violet were considering moving back to their home town in Cork when they retired. Parker had another brilliant idea.

He said gleefully, "What if we loaded all their possessions and whatever they want from the house, then ship it all down to Cork and into a house for them? We'll be swimming in cash when the estate is sold and a house for Violet and Stanley will be a drop in the proverbial bucket. I'll call his brother and see if he can check what's available. I just love it when I can make someone happy!"

Parker continued making calls while Alex was tweaking the house.

He dialed Roselyn Cottage and said, "Roan? Parker here. What are you and the family doing for supper tonight?"

"Nothing that we know of," replied Roan. "Whatcha got in mind?"

Parker moved in for the closing and grinned as he said, "Come on over to our house about five for supper. The address is: 252 Seaside Lane, Ardmore. Just come around from your cottage, as if you were going to church but turn right at the bottom of the road. The church is on the left and you drive about a block and a half. The house is in the middle of three cottages. Watch for the "Sold" sign. I think you're gonna love it!"

"Wow, sure, we can be there," exclaimed a very shocked Roan. "I'll tell Shauna."

Just then, the bell rang and Dermott was at the door. Alex walked over and opened it to find a very shined up Guard Mitchell, but out of uniform.

"Dermott, just the man I wanted to talk with. Come on in here," said Alex. "Would you like to come for supper tonight with the Sandersons, about five? Hope you like ham."

You could see the young man blush bright red and it made his freckles pop out.

He shuffled a little and replied, "Oh yes, Miss, that would be wonderful. I'm sick of me own cookin' and would love a good meal. Ham sounds just fine."

"Sorted," said Alex. "Now, I assume you have something to tell us about Daniel Griswold. I'll get Parker and we can talk about it. Would you like some coffee?"

Dermott grabbed a mug and they sat in the living room with their coffee and some biscuits.

Dermott paced around a little and explained, "Griswold could hear the guards talking about him. They were laughing and putting him down for what he did. I guess it just got to him. No one had taken his belt and he rigged it somehow to hang himself. I guess it was pretty awful. Sorry, Miss Alex, I didn't mean to be so graphic."

"It's okay Dermott," replied Alex. "I just feel so bad about this—for his family, I mean. Divorce is never an easy thing, especially for children, but adding the theft and their dad's suicide? It must be terrible for them."

"Let's think about something much happier, shall we," said Parker. "Let me show you around the cottage, Dermott. Alex did this all in one afternoon."

Parker showed Dermott the entire cottage. They walked outside to look at the sea and even went down to the lower deck. Dermott explained the house had belonged to a professional couple who retired to the States to be closer to their children. They had improved the cottage with all the features they wanted, then decided to leave. Whoever bought the place would get the best of everything. Dermott was duly impressed with the furnishings and its homey appeal.

They returned inside and as Dermott was walking past the mantle, he spotted the photograph of a young woman and a child. He thought the woman was beautiful and decided to ask Alex who she is.

He blushed again as he asked, "Who is this lovely lass, Alex? She's just beautiful. The little boy is adorable."

"Well Dermott," replied Alex. "That's my daughter, Brianne and her little boy Morgan. She's twenty-two and Morgan's four going on forty! She got married right after high school and had Morgan right away. Her husband, Brad, was in the military and stationed in Afghanistan when he was killed. His assault vehicle hit one of those road side mines and Brad was killed outright. He never got to see his little boy. Brianne put herself through college in three years, and is a child psychologist with the school system in Phoenix. She's had a hard life because of so much responsibility so young, but she's doing very well. I'm very proud of her."

"Is she Catholic by chance?" asked Dermott. "Just wonderin'."

Alex smiled because her plan was starting to work and gushed, "Yes, Dermott, she is. When her father was alive, he made sure she went to church and became Catholic, just like his family. And it was her faith that got her through all these trials in her life. Morgan is in Catholic pre-school as well."

You could see the wheels turning in Guard Mitchell's head.

He smiled and said, "Well, I'd best be off then. I will see you this evening around five."

Alex showed him out and waved goodbye.

Parker was standing by the fireplace and laughed, "You matchmaker, you. Are you really thinking about hitching these two up? I must say, that's a bold move, but it might just work. Better e-mail Brianne and invite her over!!"

The afternoon went too quickly and soon Parker got the table extension out of its package, while Alex went about preparing for the evening meal. The boys even had their own table in the corner of the living room, so the adults could talk about "things."

There were some CDs and DVDs in Parker's carry-on, so he put on some music, lit a fire in the fireplace and took the movies to the basement. If the boys wanted entertainment, there was something for them to watch. He checked the liquor cabinet and found it was fully stocked, plus there were cold sodas in the fridge. Soon the bell rang upstairs.

Alex went to answer and exclaimed, "Welcome to our home, Shauna, Roan, Conor and Jimmy. I see you found it alright."

Roan and Shauna looked around in amazement and Shauna said, "How on earth did you pull this off so fast?"

Alex replied, "Stella. Naturally."

The boys ran out to the back to look at the sea, running up and down the steps and waving to the adults on the deck. Shauna loved the gardens and as they walked back into the house, the bell rang again. It was Dermott.

"Come on in, Dermott," smiled Alex. "You know everyone here."

Dermott brought a bouquet of flowers for Alex and a bottle of wine.

His green eyes sparked as he said, "Hello everyone. Isn't this a lovely home? Came by way of the church and saw Father O'Malley. I'd be thinkin' of invitin' him to supper one of these days. He loves to visit with new people and he liked you both."

Roan spoke up and reminded everyone, "Tomorrow is Sunday and maybe we can all sit at Mass together like we do in Bemidji. I want a good look at the inside of the church to see if we could get central heating in there and fix the organ. That was a decent idea you had Alex. Dermott, would you like to sit with us?"

"Yes, yes I would, that would be fine, thank you, yes," stammered Dermott. "It would be my pleasure."

After they ate their supper, the adults walked out onto the deck to watch the sea and the boys went downstairs to watch the videos. Conor didn't understand his dvds wouldn't work on Irish televisions, but Parker's did and there were all kinds of movies boys of almost thirteen could watch.

Alex brought up the fact that June would be over in a few weeks and they should be thinking about getting things to the house in Bolton-by-Bowland.

Shauna looked over at Roan and exclaimed, "Next stop, England! I wonder what that will be like? This manor house sounds really huge. I think we need to give this place a lot of thought as to what to do with it. We'll find out when we get there."

"I've been thinking about that," explained Roan. "We could turn it into a conference centre, wedding chapel and reception hall—something to make money for its maintenance. We could schedule our time in it each year and the rest of the year, it could pay for itself. Anyone got ideas?"

Parker and Alex were laughing and Parker explained, "I'm considering selling "Meadowhall" and had the same thought. You saw how huge the place is. It could easily be a business centre, a place to hold weddings in the conservatory or make it a swanky B&B. We'd keep the cottage for ourselves and just let the place run itself, if we could find a manager. Or I would sell it outright and get rid of any financial hassles."

"Excellent plan, Parker," replied Roan. "Let's talk about this more in the coming weeks. I like how you think."

Alex looked over at Parker and said, "Somehow I didn't think you really wanted to let go of the cottage. But that's fine. I have a feeling we are going to need that cottage in the next year and we might have a couple to run the B&B, if that's what you want it to be."

Parker could see the wheels spinning in Alex's head again and asked, "Are you thinking perhaps Brianne would really like to do that IF she and

Dermott got on and got married? Man alive, you think ahead!"

"Well, think about it, Parker," explained Alex. "Brianne has always had a knack for hospitality and decorating (it's genetic). She's a fantastic cook and think about all the advantages Morgan would have there. She's young and energetic and if she and Dermott fell in love and got married, I think he could be persuaded to change professions and move to Dublin. That's what I'm saying."

"Okay, then, feel Dermott out on this but gently and a little at a time," said Parker. "But don't hit the poor boy over the head just yet!"

It was 10:00 PM and time for everyone to leave. They would all meet at Mass around 9:30 so they could sit together, then meet with Father O'Malley about the renovations. Roan decided to contact Stephen about the house in England and Shauna felt she should call Katie about the Gallery. Life was moving ahead for these families. Soon, there would be more challenges—happy ones and a few not so pleasant. Bolton Hall would prove to be more than a house. It would be a death trap.

Chapter Fifteen

Roan met with Father O'Malley after Mass and got the tour of the church. There was a portion of the roof leaking over the Sacristy and the organ was in terrible repair. The salt air wasn't forgiving on the pipes and the building was still cold during the summer—even colder during the winter.

Roan took down some notes and said, "Father O'Malley. It was Millie's wish we do something for the parish and here's what I propose. I'd like to put in central heating, fix the organ—maybe get a new one which is resistant to the sea air, then get the roof fixed. We can even get the inside painted, because I see water stains on the walls. Is there anything at the Rectory which needs attention?"

Father O'Malley stammered a little and fumbled with his words. It must have been a first for the priest, because he never seemed lost for words.

He thought for a moment, counted on his fingers and said, "I could use central heating too, a few repairs to the roof and foundation. The windows are single glazed and there's no insulation in the walls. There hasn't been a lot of funding available to us down here to repair anything for a long time, but we sure could use the help."

"Fine, Father," explained Roan. "You make a list and I will have Stella make the calls to the contractors. Whatever you need, I know Millie would want you to have it."

"Ah one thing, Roan," he replied. "If there is enough, maybe I could get a better car. Mine's shot."

"Tell you what," said Roan. "Tomorrow you and I will go into Dungarvan and pick out a car suitable for your needs. I saw a dealership over there with some excellent vehicles and you can decide what you want. How's that?"

"Oh Bless You, Roan," sighed Father O'Malley. "And Bless Millie. She was such a beautiful soul. I miss her conversations and our cribbage tournaments here at the parish. She was very active, you know."

"Pick you up at 8:30 AM tomorrow, Father," said Roan. "We can stop and have a cup of tea somewhere, too. I also want to discuss wedding plans for Parker and Alex. "

Alex pulled Dermott aside and explained, "I invited Brianne and Morgan to visit for two weeks at the beginning of August. We should be back from England then and she doesn't start back to work until after September first. She can stay here through the month if she wants. Would you look after her and Morgan when we go back to the States for the trial?"

"You think she would stay the entire month?" asked Dermott. "Oh yes, that would be grand. I'd love to show them around Ireland. I can request my holidays then, because I have four weeks coming. Morgan will love it."

Alex smiled and gave Dermott a hug. He wandered back to his bicycle, grinning from ear to ear, his green eyes dancing and his red hair gleaming in the morning sunlight.

Parker grabbed Alex's hand as they strolled back to the cottage.

He looked at her and said, "You're up to something, I can tell."

Alex smiled and continued walking. She wasn't about to tip her hand just yet.

Roan called for Father O'Malley at the rectory in the morning. They drove over to the car dealership in Dungarvan and walked through the lot.

The owner came out of his office and said, "Ah, Father O'Malley. I see you lookin' for another car again. Have you decided to buy this time or are you still lookin'?"

"This is Mr. Sanderson from America, Mr. Willis," explained the priest. "He's part of our parish now and has kindly offered to buy us a new car— not an old one, but a brand spankin' new car."

Mr. Willis was a bit shocked Father O'Malley would finally be making a purchase after all these years, but was most accommodating.

He exclaimed, "I have just the ticket for ya, Father. Take a look at this beauty on the corner of the lot. It's new, has four doors and a big trunk, steady-grip tyres and a neutral colour of charcoal gray. So, what do ya think?"

Father O'Malley walked around the car, kicked the tyres and said,

"Well Roan, what do you think of this one? It's not flashy, has dignity and will last the rest of me life."

Roan smiled and said, "Looks like a winner to me, Father. Let's get going on the paperwork."

"Will that be cash—or cash, Mr. Sanderson from America?"

"Will you take a check, Mr. Willis?" asked Roan. "You'll need to change it into Euros from dollars, I'm afraid. Today's rate is 1.32."

Mr. Willis was most accommodating and within a few minutes, the transaction was complete and Father O'Malley had a new car. Roan followed Father as he drove off to find a little restaurant to have coffee.

They ended up at the edge of Dungarvan, close to the coast road. There was a tiny café where they could sit quietly and discuss the church. Roan also wanted to talk about possibly having Parker and Alex's wedding at the church.

"We could get all the renovations done first," explained Roan. "Then we could have the wedding in the Autumn, say in late October. Alex will have completed her instruction with Father Miller in Bemidji by then and he could come over as well to concelebrate."

"It's a grand idea, Roan. Brilliant," smiled Father O'Malley. "Ask the happy couple and see what they think about it."

They enjoyed their coffee and fresh rolls, but soon it was time to get back to the family in Ardmore.

The next two weeks went by without a hitch. The families loaded up their vehicles and drove up to Dun Laoghaire, took the ferry across to Holyhead in Wales and drove the A-5 to the A-55, then up to the M-56 through Manchester toward the A-59 and onto Bolton-by-Bowland via the Gisburn Road.

The village of Bolton-by-Bowland was recorded as Bodeton in the Doomsday Book, meaning bow in the river. The first part of the village church was built before 1190 and the local landowners, the Pudsay family, supervised the improvements and extensions to the church in the 13th through 16th centuries. In the church is the tomb of Sir Ralph Pudsay, who had three wives and produced twenty-five children among them. In 1464, Sir Ralph hid Lancastrian King Henry VI, who was on the run from his Yorkshire enemies after the defeat at the battle of Hexham. King Henry's Well is located a few yards from Bolton Hall.

Bolton Hall was the ancestral home of the Pudsay family from the thirteenth century until the end of the line in 1771. The house was later purchased by a rich coal mine owner, who lived lavishly and kept a staff of almost 100. He opened the grounds and parts of the house to the public on Saturday afternoons. Later, the Suttons purchased the estate and it remained in their hands until Roan took it over.

At one time, the gardens were magnificent, with extensive glass houses growing nectarines, peaches, grapes, figs and bananas. There was also an underground palm house. The original stables held over seventy horses and two coaches. After the First World War, it got too expensive to maintain, fell in to semi-disrepair and was occupied for a while during World War II, when German prisoners of war built a chapel on the property. A lot of those things are gone now, but Roan would find the house in an advanced state of decay—something Millie failed to mention in her letters. It would take a lot to restore the hall to its former glory.

As the cars drove along the Gisburn Road into Bolton-by-Bowland, Roan noticed how beautiful the village is. It nestles in the picturesque hills and dales of the Ribble Valley. The parish of Bolton-by-Bowland stretches for several miles and encompasses the attractive hamlets of Holden and Forest Becks, as well as picture postcard Anna Lane. There are lots of little shops and Shauna picked up on those immediately. Conor and Jimmy kept pointing out local sites and all the animals as they drove along. Soon they found the driveway into Bolton Hall. They weren't quite expecting the house that lay before them.

The massive stone manor house boasted at least twenty chimneys, with turrets and arched windows on either side of the main doorway. The crushed stone driveway circled around to the front door to reveal a dual staircase. There were huge plantings of overgrown bushes and wild flowers, with misshapen trees, but someone must have planted several rows of flowers along the drive, especially for their arrival. The dirt was still scattered along the gravel.

Several caretakers greeted the families as they got out of their cars. The housekeeper, Mrs. Purdey Preston, was a robust woman in her sixties. She had a bit of a wild look about her and she frightened Jimmy. Her husband, Milton, was in his late sixties, rather pale and frail, seemed to be the head caretaker. They lived in a small cottage on the edge of the estate. They invited the folks in for the grand tour. Milton had put a fire in several fireplaces to warm the hall up. There was no central heating in the place, something Roan would try to remedy—it was mouldy smelling and dankly chilly.

The main rooms had three segmented windows on either side of the main hall, the same above in two of the bedrooms. There were twelve bedrooms in all, several of which were en-suite. The house covered three floors, plus the attic and basement. There was an enormous great room, complete with massive stone fireplace, heavy draperies and huge Oriental rugs. The windows were single glazed and let in a lot of outside air. Some had roller shades and if left up, the windows did allow for a lot of light to penetrate the main rooms.

The furniture was centuries old and smelled like it. You could tell, some of it must have dated to Elizabethan times. There was electricity, but it was ancient—like the house and must be totally replaced. The plumbing seemed no better, with pull chain toilets, no showers and no central heating. The bathtubs were not in good shape either. The information Roan had said there were six family bathrooms—three on each floor with bedrooms, with the en—suites, making nine bathrooms altogether.

Milton came in with additional figures on the structure of the house. A bank in London was overseeing the property and Roan said that would stop immediately. As executor and heir, he had that right. The accounts showed very little income from the farmers. The stables had been torn down, all except for three, which still had horses, whose owners rented the stalls. The roof on the house needed to be replaced, as holes from storms and age had damaged the third floor bedrooms. The attic was home to a family of bats, which often got into the lower sections of the home, making scary times for visitors.

The kitchen plumbing and mechanicals all had to be replaced, as they looked like nothing had been done since the turn of the nineteenth century. There was an excellent space to work with, though and Shauna could take care of that immediately.

Mrs. Preston came in to show the family their rooms on the second floor. She explained the electricity came on and off without warning, so using candles or flashlights would be a good idea in the evening.

They walked up the massive mahogany and walnut staircase. There were statues of knights perched atop the balusters at the landing and the stairs continued up to the second and third floors. The portraits on the walls were of many generations of Pudsays, then Suttons. There were huge porcelain vases on heavily carved mahogany tables along the walls and a faded blue Oriental runner went the entire length of the hallway—at least 120 feet.

Mrs. Preston showed Conor and Jimmy into a room with twin beds, brought in for their visit. Granted, the room was formal, as it had a big fireplace, plenty of antiques and heavy drapes at the windows. But there was a nice view of the village and they could walk outside onto a large veranda, which was on top of the library below.

Next came Roan and Shauna. Theirs was the master suite, with a huge bed on a dais with steps to get in. There were bed curtains surrounding the bed, done in a rich burgundy velvet. Mrs. Preston said they were from the early 1800's. The fireplace was enormous, with an Adams surround—probably designed by the architect himself. Under the double windows were sets of chairs and tables, with fresh flowers and a dish of chocolates. The en-suite bathroom had a double porcelain bathtub on golden claw feet, a toilet, sink and linen closet, but no shower.

Alex and Parker had separate, but interconnecting rooms, which shared a bathroom. These looked out over the gardens to the rear of the property. Alex's room was a large double room. It had a fireplace, three windows and a seating area. The bed was also very high and a four-step ladder had been provided for her to get into the bed! Bed curtains surrounded the bed, done in a red and navy paisley design. They were a bit more contemporary. This had been Millie's room, when she visited. There were pink star gazer lilies in a beautiful French vase on a table in the centre of the windows, along with a dish of Belgian chocolates from the little shop in the village. Alex seemed pleased with the accommodation.

Parker's room was next and he found himself in another grand bedroom. This had faded red oriental rugs on the floor and a huge turned-spindle, four-poster bed, without curtains. Again, there were steps up to the bed, which had a set of tan bed linens and skirting. It seemed manly enough! The fireplace surround was made from walnut and had a great mantle with grainy black and white photographs of the former residents, including one of a very young Millie and her husband. Parker understood rooms like this.

As soon as they were unpacked, everyone came down to look over the rest of the house. Milton continued with Roan's tour, up to the third floor and the attic, where the damage was evident. There were covers on all the furniture for protection and the floors were very dusty. Roan made notes of what had to be renovated, then went back downstairs to the basement with Milton.

Some of the stone foundation needed attention, but it was basically dry. Despite its problems, this house was built to last centuries—which it had. As they walked around the grounds, Roan could see the remains of the 'Orangery' and several of the out buildings. The beauty of the fields beyond the house was exquisite—filled with rhododendron, lilac and forsythia, along with numerous fruit trees. It was clear to Roan why Millie wanted to keep the place, even in its present condition.

Shauna and Alex explored some of the main level rooms, including the dining room with its massive mahogany table which seated thirty—without the extensions! This was like "Meadowhall" only on a larger scale. When they went into the kitchen, Shauna's mouth dropped when she saw what wasn't inside.

"How could people make meals in here?" she asked Alex. "Look at those ovens and that sink? They're ancient! There must be some kind of butler's pantry in here somewhere. Let's look."

They found two pantries. One was indeed a butler's pantry, complete with large table and chairs, rows of glass-enclosed cabinets with hall-marked silver serving pieces (most of which were hundreds of years old), porcelain dinnerware and chests with silverware. This room had the most light of all the rooms so far. The other pantry was for food. There were two new refrigerators and a freezer, so at least they had food in the house. There were cabinets with shelving for canned goods. Off of that room was the laundry, but no washer or dryer. There was a ringer washer, which should have been a planter on someone's front porch! These rooms would be Shauna and Alex's projects, along with the sunroom on the side of the house. That wasn't in bad shape, but needed attention. The sunroom needed double glazed windows and insulation, plus new tile flooring and furniture, heat and new wiring.

Roan got on the phone to Stephen to let him know the condition of the house and grounds. Stephen wasn't too shocked, but wanted to see for himself, so he told Roan to get his room ready. Stephen needed to deal with the solicitors in London anyway. He wasn't about to let those scoundrels waste any more of Millie's money on their fees, so he'd be there on the next flight.

Light was fading and Mrs. Preston was in the kitchen with Shauna and Alex as they made supper. Alex made notes on what they needed from the grocer, while Shauna looked around for pots and pans. The kitchen needed a good coat of paint, as did the pantries. Shauna decided to look under the paint on the pantry doors. She chipped a little away from one door to find a beautiful wood finish underneath. These could be stripped and varnished to bring them back to their original condition.

Soon supper was on the table. Conor and Jimmy got a taste of real Lancashire cooking. There were hot, steamy meat pasties. There was Yorkshire Pudding and gravy, steamed veggies and mounds of whipped potatoes. There was an apple pie for dessert, with ice cream and a dish of chocolates to pass around. No one left the table hungry!

There was no television in the house, so the boys had to make up things to do for entertainment. Roan asked them to make lists of things they wanted to see in the house to make it contemporary. There was a game room with a large snooker table, so they played pool and cards. That satisfied them for that night. Tomorrow, they would go into town and see what they could find.

After everyone had gone to sleep, the house became eerily still. Someone had told Roan there was a ghost in the house. It belonged to one of the former owners, who died in the house on his wedding night. His new bride never set foot in the house again. There were thump thumps on the third floor. No one was up there. As the night went on, there were sounds of moaning upstairs. Jimmy and Conor didn't hear it, but Parker did. He took a candle, left the bedroom and walked over to the stairs leading to the third floor. When he said, "hello", the moaning stopped. Parker stayed in place for a few minutes, heard nothing and went back to bed. He told Alex about it in the morning.

Alex, Shauna and the boys decided to go into Burnley, a larger town about twenty miles away from BBB. They took their lists and went to the grocery, to the chemists for some of their personal care needs and to department store for towels, linens and kitchen items. The boys found an electronics store with games, a large screen television, a VCR/DVD player and dvds. Those things could be delivered, so they went on to several other stores and bought what they needed. On the way back, Shauna wanted to stop at some of the stores in the village and find a local church. The only church in Bolton-by-Bowland was St. Peter & St. Paul's, which is Church of England. The Catholic Church in Clitheroe would be the closest to attend until the chapel restoration was completed.

Meanwhile, Roan and Parker were calling local contractors, electricians, roofers, plumbers, etc., to get bids for improving the property. Because this is a historic home, the work needed to be authentic to the home, but brought up to current standards. The game room would have the television and modern entertainments, but Roan wanted to leave the other rooms as is, except for the kitchen. That was not his project.

Shauna stopped at Farmhouse Antiques on the way back to the manor to see what they carry. She and Alex were amazed at the beautiful linens, antique jewellery, tableware and quilts. They had wonderful cups and saucers, small pictures and woven throws. This was the place to buy soft furnishing accent pieces.

Next Alex spotted Garden Makers, a landscape gardener. She found unusual statuary, African art, home made chutneys, jams and other food stuffs. Shauna made arrangements with them to do a survey of the house and grounds to see what was necessary to bring the plantings back to health.

Soon it was time to have a late lunch and decide what they wanted to do with the kitchen. Alex thought a commercial-sized dishwasher would do for banquets, along with two six burner stoves like Charles had in the new house, two sets of built-in double ovens and a crystal dishwasher. The refrigerators were new, as was the freezer and would be satisfactory. They needed two large microwaves, two jumbo, 72 cup coffee makers, along with a huge pot for hot tea water. Shauna contacted a restaurant supply company in Manchester to come out tomorrow and give them a bid. Alex also felt a smaller microwave, a hot pot and a coffee maker would be good for the butler's pantry, along with a television set and a stereo. All those cleaning tasks would go a little easier with something to watch or listen to.

Next came the decorating of the kitchen and pantries. Alex called the local paint distributor in Barnsley and told them they needed to come out tomorrow and bring some paint samples to the manor. Shauna was considering a pale sage green and tan combination against the dark wood of the cabinetry once it was stripped. Some gold antiquing would also be appropriate. Katie was taking a Venetian Plaster seminar at home, so that technique would come in handy for the Gallery and possibly at the manor. Shauna decided to replace the island counter top with a black metallic granite and add it over the rest of the old wooden countertops. Keeping it simple was the best design for the kitchen.

Roan came into the kitchen to ask the ladies their ideas for the property. Shauna explained her choices.

"We need to make it pay for itself, give employment to as many people in the village as want it and bring the manor back to its former glory," Shauna said. "Alex and I are considering a banquet facility, weddings in the chapel with receptions in the ballroom, honeymoon holidays, reunions, seminars, retreats, etc. We can schedule our family use around the business and hold classes here on English cooking, competitions, wine tasting, etc., like they have done in the past in the village. We'll let Conor take photographs for a brochure once the place looks right, then find someone to run it."

"Well, that's done then," exclaimed Roan. "You seem to have things well in hand. I see the landscapers will be here tomorrow, along with the kitchen people, so I will just putz around the house and sign checks!"

Just then, Stephen roared up in a little red sports car, spewing dust and gravel everywhere. You had to laugh at this ruffian.

Roan ran to the front door, blurting out, "Dadgum it man, you really know how to make an entrance!"

"Beulah, put the kettle on," yelled Stephen. "The man of the house is home to his castle. Hey, this is a big place Roan. Is this house on steroids or something?"

Parker came around the corner to greet Stephen and help carry the luggage in. Stephen was laughing his head off as he told everyone about his little escapade in London this morning.

He slapped his side and bellowed, "I told those stuffed shirts their services were no longer required and they couldn't collect those exorbitant fees any longer. I told them, ever so politely now—for me, you understand, they could kiss my lily-white anti-patrician arse if they had any objections and I walked out the door. Thought I'd save you a few pounds, I did, I did!! Their final bill is in the post as we speak!"

Roan stared blankly at Stephen, then realised who he was listening to and slapped him on the back.

"Wish I'd been there to see it, Steve, old buddy," exclaimed Roan. "I'm surprised you didn't moon them while you were at it!"

Mrs. Preston called the family to tea, and as she rounded the corner, she came face to face with Stephen.

His eyes popped and once she was out of the room he gasped, "Did she get the number of the truck that hit her? That woman is scary, Roan. She frightens the life out of me."

"You ain't seen nothin' yet, Pally," exclaimed Roan. "We really DO have a ghost in the house. Heard it last night. I'll take you upstairs to your room after we eat. And by the way, Mrs. Preston is very nice and an excellent cook."

Roan and Stephen spent most of the late afternoon chatting, while Alex and Parker decided to walk through the village. The sun filtered through the bushes and trees in full spread. The flower beds in the gardens of the neat stone houses were dazzling displays of roses, primrose and geraniums. The whitewashed cottages and homes along the main street were freshly painted and gleamed as the sun bounced off the facades. They decided to pop into the Coach and Horses Inn, a local watering hole in the village.

This is a typical English pub—not a sports bar like you see in the States, trying to BE a pub. This had the original old oak beams running along a crooked ceiling. The floors were a bit uneven, while the bar wrapped around the center of the room. It had gallons of charm, great food and some of the nicest people they had met yet. Parker ordered two pints of locally brewed bitter and took them over by the fireplace.

Alex was delighted and said, "You realise they have a wonderful hotel here as well? And you can see the beautiful dining room through that archway. This would be a place to bring family and guests. And there are several other places near here just like this, but I think this is the oldest. We'll have to check out the rest of them while we're here."

"This village has the charm, ambience and friendliness I would expect in England," explained Parker. "I guess we are so used to the chaos of the cities, that we forget what extraordinary beauty is here in the countryside."

They finished their pints and walked back to the manor house. Roan and Stephen were still talking, while Shauna was sketching in the sunroom. Mrs. Preston came into the room and asked Roan to come into the kitchen.

"Mr. Sanderson," she said in a very concerned tone. "Things have been disappearing here. First it was batteries and a torch. I thought my husband had taken them, but he hadn't. Then it was some canned food, a basket, a loaf of bread and butter—food items and the like. And then there was the flour. A bag of flour is gone. This happened right before you got here, so it concerns me."

Roan thought about the situation and replied, "I'll check into it, Mrs. Preston. Let's keep an eye out for any empty containers out of place or people who don't belong to the crews here. You've been in the village all your life and you know everyone, you could spot anyone out of place."

"Well, that isn't all, sir," explained Mrs. Preston. "Some in the village say they have seen a light in the manor at night. It goes from room to room, but is mostly in the attic. No one has been up there I know of. People think it must be the ghost we've heard of all these years. I'm not ashamed to say I'm concerned."

"Tell you what, Mrs. Preston," said Roan. "Stephen and I will go up right now and see if we can find anything in the attic. Would that make you feel better?"

"Oh yes, sir, it would," sighed Mrs. Preston. "Thank you kindly."

Roan walked back into the library armed with two flash lights and called over to Stephen, "We have a mission. Mrs. Preston needs us to investigate something on the third floor and attic, so let's go."

"Let's go?" asked Stephen. "Oh, you don't mean the 'ghost'? I'm not sure I want to go up there."

"You're such a chicken, Steve," exclaimed Roan. "I'll ask Parker to join us if you feel you need back-up!"

"No, no, let's go up," sighed Stephen. "I'm not a coward. I just don't like the thought of ghosts."

Roan grinned and the two men walked up the staircase to the second floor. They stopped for a moment to listen for anything above them. Stephen thought he heard faint music, but that could have been from anywhere. So they proceeded silently up to the third floor.

The hallway and rooms were cold, even in July. The furniture was covered with blue tarpaulins in each bedroom. The damage wasn't as apparent at night, but the floors squeaked from the water saturation. The floors seemed dusty, especially in front of one of the bedrooms. Roan opened the door. The room looked normal, except for faint footprints in the dust. A puff of wind flew past the men as if directed at them. Stephen stepped backward and dropped onto a chair.

He could see a window open and explained, "There's the problem, Roan. The window is open over there. It's blowing the dust all around the room."

Roan walked over to shut the window and noticed some empty food tins in a waste basket near the bathroom door.

"Someone has been up here alright," remarked Roan. "Here are some of the missing tins. And it looks as if someone has been sleeping in this bed, but covered it back over. I'll check out the bathroom and see if there is anything in there."

Sure enough, Roan came back out of the bathroom with an empty flour sack and said, "That explains the extra "dust" everywhere. I think we need to search further."

Roan called Parker on his cell phone to get he and Alex upstairs to join in the canvassing. Soon the four began a room to room search, but found no one. Then they went up into the attic. The massive rooms were like parade grounds, filled with corners a person could hide in. There were built-in cupboards, some still filled with antique clothing. There were footprints all over the floor—none of them theirs. Alex began to get that "feeling" they were being watched.

She walked slowly over to Parker and whispered in his ear, "Someone is in here watching us. Let's get the men back downstairs and you and I wait for someone to show."

Parker called over to Roan and said, "I don't think there is anything up here except dust and old clothes. We can search again in daylight. Let's go back downstairs."

Stephen was the first to bolt out of the attic, while Roan simply walked out. Alex and Parker remained at the entryway to the attic in the dark. It wasn't long before someone stepped out of the shadows and crept toward them.

Alex positioned her flashlight to shine directly on the person, as Parker counted silently, "One, two three, NOW."

They turned on the flashlights directly at the face they never thought would be at Bolton Hall. It was Michael DuMonde.

He stood there with his egomaniacal glare and screamed, "So Fitzgerald, we finally come face-to-face. Where's your gun? You always seem to have that with you these days. Or is your little lady friend your weapon of choice, hmm? Your time is coming. And believe me, I am going to kill you—both of you, but I'll pick the time and the place. And it's not going to be now. I want you to sweat a little first. Maybe this will add to your pain."

DuMonde took a swing at both Alex and Parker with a wooden cricket bat he'd found in the attic. It knocked Alex down and Parker managed to rip off a piece of DuMonde's jacket as he ran past. Parker tried to follow but lost DuMonde when he jumped out a second-story window and onto the balcony below. Parker watched as DuMonde ran into the forest behind the manor.

He slammed his fists on the window sill and yelled, "You're a dead man, DuMonde. A dead man."

Alex struggled to get on her feet. The bat had hit her squarely in the shoulder and on the side of her head, which had a large gash on it, bleeding profusely. Parker reached her just in time to catch her as she fainted. He carried her downstairs to her bedroom and called Roan on his phone.

"Roan, call the local doctor," he screamed. "Alex has been hurt. We found DuMonde in the attic. Call the police, too. We need to set up a security perimeter around the manor now. He will come back, it's just a matter of time."

Stephen heard this and poured himself a stiff brandy, making one each for Roan, Parker and Alex. He hated dark, spooky places and this only confirmed his fears. DuMonde of all people. It goes to show, there is no place in the world safe from that man.

The ambulance could be heard on Gisburn Road, along with the siren from a squad car. Soon the police and doctor were at the house. Mrs. Preston let them in and directed them upstairs to Alex's room. Parker met them at the doorway.

"Gentlemen, I'm Parker Fitzgerald of the CTB," he explained. "I know you were apprised of the situation here before we arrived, but DuMonde was living up in the attic. I came face to face with him and my fiancée, Alexandra, has been injured. Doctor, she has a deep bruise on her shoulder and the cut on her temple. DuMonde hit her with a cricket bat."

PC Trevor Adams took Parker aside, while the doctor examined Alex.

PC Adams asked, "You know for certain this was Michael DuMonde? Would you show me where he was and how he got away?"

"Certainly, come up with me and you can see where he had been hiding and the window he got away from," explained Parker. "I have been chasing this man around the world and we were within a foot of one another. I could smell his sour breath on my face and was almost sick. That bastard has caused an inordinate amount of trouble in this world, with death and destruction wherever he goes. It's time to stop him now."

The attic had lights, so Parker turned them on and as the men searched, they found a false cabinet. They opened it to find a pillow, blanket and the basket of food items. There was a rifle, a pistol and a few home-made petrol bombs sealed in plastic bags to keep the smell from alerting anyone. There were newspaper articles about the trial, about Roan inheriting Bolton Hall and photographs of Roan, Shauna, the kids, Alex, Parker and Ronald Rutherford. And there was a charred photo of DuMonde's wife, Camille. He'd been living up there for weeks it seemed. But no longer. Time was running out on Michael DuMonde.

Doctor Griffin said he would need to have Alex's shoulder x-rayed and her head stitched up at the local hospital in Clitheroe. They transported her there in the ambulance, while Parker and PC Adams continued to look at the evidence DuMonde left behind. They went to the second floor to look at the broken escape window, when Parker realised he had the piece of DuMonde's denim jacket in his pocket.

Pulling the piece from his pocket, Parked explained, "I tore this from the back of DuMonde's jacket as he pushed past us," The scent might help the dogs track him, but knowing DuMonde, he has already found new clothes and taken a bath! And look, look at the window. The broken glass has blood on it. So he's been injured enough to leave a blood trail. That's DNA evidence."

PC Adams bagged the piece of jacket and said, "I'll keep going from here, Parker. You need to be with your fiancée. One of my officers will take you over and bring you back. I'll get my forensics team up here and gather the blood evidence and take the rest from the attic. I've heard about you through channels. If the Queen doesn't give you a Gong for this, no one will!"

Parker thanked PC Adams and left with a female officer. Shauna came out from the sunroom to all the activity and questioned Roan.

"What's all this?, asked Shauna "What's going on and what did I miss?"

"DuMonde has been living in the attic and possibly on the third floor," explained Roan. "Stephen, Parker and Alex helped me search both floors, then Parker and Alex stayed back at the entrance to the attic because Alex had one of her feelings of being watched. She was right. DuMonde confronted them, hit Alex with a cricket bat and dove out a window on the second floor. He ran into the woods and now we have the police crawling around the house. THAT'S what you missed."

"What about the boys, Roan?" fretted Shauna. "Are they okay?"

Roan reassured Shauna, but said, "I'll check on them now. They are probably asleep and didn't hear a thing."

Roan walked up to their room and there were the boys, fast asleep in their beds, wearing headphones. Would they ever be disappointed when they woke up in the morning to find they had missed it all. Roan went back downstairs and told Shauna they were fine.

Stephen was in the library talking with an officer, when the house phone rang. He answered it and said it was the hospital. It seems a man came in with glass wounds to his right hand, arm, shoulder and right leg. He had a laceration on his scalp and a cut on the bridge of his nose. The man said he had been installing a window in his house and it had fallen on him, shattering the glass.

The officer took the phone and asked for a description of the man involved and it came back, 'long white hair in a ponytail, dishevelled and unkempt, with extremely bad breath and a vacant look in his eyes. He paid in cash and left.'

Stephen looked at the officer and said, "That's Michael DuMonde. Better get over to the hospital and get the person who tended to him to give you a more in-depth description, maybe take a sketch artist or have them look at a photograph for a clear identification. I'll give you one, because I have a copy in my briefcase."

Stephen called Parker on his cell phone to wait for the officer who was on his way over. He must have just missed DuMonde at the hospital emergency room. Parker went back in the treatment room, where the doctor had just finished examining Alex, given her a sedative and stitching her head wound.

"You are a very lucky lady tonight," explained the doctor. "If the cut had been any deeper, you wouldn't be here. And your shoulder is badly dislocated. It's going to take a while to heal. I've numbed the area so I suggest you go home and be very quiet. You are taped to your side, so you can't use your arm at all. Here is some additional pain medication because when this anaesthetic wears off, you'll be miserable. I'll see you back here in a couple of days. Okay?"

Alex was pretty groggy from the medication and tried to say, 'fine.'

But Parker picked up the sentence and said, "I'll have her here doctor, thank you. I'll let her rest for a few moments longer, because it seems DuMonde was also just treated here and I want to talk with the nurse or doctor who saw him. Be right back.

Parker found the doctor who treated DuMonde and asked about the severity of the injuries.

"He had some deep gashes from the glass and wood fragments from the window. I had to stitch a lot of the wounds," explained the physician. "He will be in a lot of pain for a week or so and won't be able to get around well. The gashes on his leg are the worst, because he went through the window foot first. He's a large man and the window was relatively small in comparison. He will be very easy to spot until he heals. And the gash on his nose will leave a scar. I can talk with the officer about him, if you'd like."

"Thank you, doctor," said Parker. "You have been most helpful."

The other officer helped Parker get Alex into the squad car. She was really groggy now, plus she was wrapped in elastic bandages from her shoulder to her waist. DuMonde had hit hard and with Alex being so petite, her shoulder was no match for the stiff cricket bat. Soon she was propped up on pillows in her own bed, out cold. Parker finished up with PC Adams.

"I spoke with the doctor who treated DuMonde," explained Parker. The lacerations and gashes are severe in some cases and DuMonde will be feeling the pain for a while. He won't be fast on his feet—possibly easier to capture. But he disappeared into the night and no one knows where. I can almost guarantee you this. He isn't far away. His ego won't let him leave. He wants to kill me and soon. This has been coming for years and it's almost to a head. Concentrate on a ten mile radius, but I'd wager it would be more like three."

PC Adams said goodnight and indicated he would be around in the morning with the rest of his team. The search for evidence outside would go faster in the daylight. A patrol was spaced out along the grounds until private security could get their team in place.

Activity came early as the groups of contractors and teams of workers began demolition, renovation and delivery of materials. Everyone came at once! Each employee was checked against a roster by the security people. Each worker also wore a photo identification badge, which could be scanned by the security people. Delivery people were watched. Even the chimney sweeps were watched.

DuMonde was still around. He had studied the history of the area and knew of a place under Pudsay's Leap, where William Pudsay took a header on his horse into the Ribble River. It seems there is a small cave tucked away under the cliff. Some of the older locals would know about it (stores of silver coins were hidden in it centuries earlier), but it didn't come to the attention of anyone else. DuMonde huddled inside, making a home for himself. No one would think to look there for him. At least, no one right now.

The demolition of the kitchen was taking precedence on one side of the house, with the roof the essential focus of restoration up on top. The chimney sweeps gave a report that several of the chimneys were in disrepair and needed to be re-pointed and many of the bricks replaced. Then they could clean inside the chimneys and replace the liners. The landscapers said there is an excellent area for a swimming pool, which could be added easily to replace a section of yard on the side of the house by the sunroom. That was fine with Roan and it would give an extra feature for the guests to enjoy.

Shauna had to do without Alex's help for a while, so she spread the orange gel stripper on the cabinets in the pantry and let them bubble away the ions of paint on the doors. She could peel it off in a few hours and get down to the bare wood. The doors were in excellent condition and bringing them back to their natural shine would make a beautiful pantry. Soon the new kitchen equipment would be delivered, but Shauna asked the contractors to arrange for a painting sub-contractor to help on the kitchen. Within a few days, the kitchen would be finished.

Conor and Jimmy were outside scouring the area for photographs, along with two security guards. Roan wasn't taking any chances with the boys' safety. Conor snapped away happily and no one saw someone else in his pictures—DuMonde—until later that evening. When Conor showed the photographs to the family, DuMonde could be seen lurking in the bushes near where the boys were taking photos. Roan immediately stepped up security. Dogs were brought in and used the piece of cloth Parker had torn off for the scent. The noose was closing around DuMonde.

As work progressed, Alex was feeling a little better. She decided to go downstairs to look around. An elevator had been installed to all three floors and she felt safer using that than trying to navigate the stairs. Soon she was in the middle of a traffic jam of artisans, painters and installers, working on the house. She walked into the kitchen to see the new paint, equipment and countertops, plus the newly varnished pantry. Alex got a cup of coffee and sat at the pantry table, flicking on the television.

The news was all about the hunt for DuMonde and a plea from police to contact them if there had been any sightings. A small blurb came on about the renovations at Bolton Hall—a big deal for Lancashire. It wasn't that often someone was going to such lengths to bring a historic house back to mint condition.

Shauna heard the telly and came in to see who was watching.

She was pleased to see Alex looking better and exclaimed, "Oh my you are looking more chipper today, Alex. How is the shoulder?"

"Better, I think, but it's terribly sore," replied Alex. "By the way, what day is it? I've really lost track."

"You've been up in that room for ten days now, Alex," responded Shauna. "Parker has taken great care of you. Do you remember going to see the doctor at the hospital?"

"No, I don't," replied Alex. "Everything is kind of foggy. Must be the head injury. I know this one will leave a scar."

"Not necessarily," explained Shauna. "The doctor who sewed it up is a plastic surgeon and he put in stitches under the scalp, then some on top to close the wound. If you have a scar, it will be barely visible."

Alex sipped her coffee and looked at the calendar on the wall.

Her eyes widened as she exclaimed, "It's almost August. Oh no, Brianne and Morgan will be over here in a week. I need to get back to Ireland!"

"Not to worry," said Shauna. "Parker has that covered. You'll both drive to the ferry and take the slow route home. The work will take a lot longer here, but we will join you for a week before we all have to return for the trial."

"Thanks," replied Alex. "I have never been laid up like this before and my schedule is all messed up. Say, could you help me take a shower and get dressed? I really want to feel like a human being again."

Shauna smiled as she helped Alex back upstairs. The showers had been installed in the bathrooms and although it was difficult to get into the tub and take a shower, the girls managed it...after a fashion. Keeping Alex's shoulder immobilised was the task. Soon Alex was looking refreshed, ready to tackle her day and some breakfast.

Parker brought up some fresh flowers to Alex and was surprised to see her looking so happy. He filled her in on the progress of the house and the hunt for DuMonde. One, obviously, was going better than the other. Parker asked if she was up to a drive around the countryside and Alex was delighted to get out of the house for a while.

"Sure, let's go," she said happily. "It will be good to get out and see some of the area. It's so lovely here and I want to see more."

Jim and Katie were due in to take Jimmy home for the rest of the summer. Shauna had found a fabulous company that did architectural reclamation and sold all kinds of building materials from homes and buildings which had been demolished. Things such as pilasters, columns, brass bed frames, stained glass panels, railings, mantles, carved statuary, doors and much more, could be shipped back to the States for the Gallery. Katie was excited to go on this journey!

Roan had gone down to Manchester to pick them up. Neither of them had been on such a long flight before and although they were tired, Jim and Katie took in every sight along the way home. Shauna was ready for their visit and had put them in a bedroom on the newly renovated third floor overlooking the front garden.

Shauna heard the car drive up. Jimmy ran out to greet his parents and Katie's eyes widened when she saw the house and Jimmy, who had grown at least two inches during the summer.

"Hey everyone," yelled Jim. "Come out here and say hello!"

"Hi Dad, hi Mom," giggled Jimmy. "Boy do I have a ton of stuff to show you."

"He said more than two word sentences, Katie," exclaimed Jim. "Did you hear that? I AM impressed!"

Shauna came over to Katie and gave her a hug. She explained the work was still going on and would be for a few months, but most of the major work had been done. Roan and Jim took the bags inside and to the elevator.

"Where are Alex and Parker?" asked Jim. "I thought they might be around."

"This is the first day Alex has been able to go out and about, so they are driving in the countryside," explained Shauna. "Stephen will be going home with you when you leave and should be roaming around here somewhere."

Katie was duly impressed with the scope of the house. The idea to turn it into a guest house was excellent.

She looked at the antiques, the rugs and the woodwork, then asked Shauna, "Is this the kind of item we will be able to sell at the store? Something like one of these mantles or a huge vase? We could use some of those."

"Yes," explained Shauna. "I have made an appointment for us tomorrow, so you can see this shop and the type of merchandise they sell. They will ship it via air freight directly to us in Bemidji."

Conor and his security guard came in from riding. Conor was getting very good at riding the horses and Parker had been giving him tips on handling older horses. A world of experiences had been opening for Conor over here in England.

The sunlight streamed into the sunroom. Shauna showed Katie the sketches she had been doing for her Minneapolis clients, plus some for paintings she wanted to do for the shop. The village provided lovely backdrops for landscapes, including the two village greens, with their war memorial and ancient stocks. The plantings at each home were dazzling displays of flowers and trees. Patios shined with lovely wrought iron tables and chairs, set among beds of primrose, geraniums, roses and greens. Even the countryside was resplendent with flowering trees, sheep and horses grazing on the slopes and verdant fields. Katie liked what Shauna had done with those themes.

The swimming pool had been completed and Stephen just had to be the first one in to 'test it out.' The pool had an electronic sensor-controlled cover which went over when the sensor detected rain. It saved a lot on cleaning the pool, keeping it fresh for the guests. Stephen waved at Katie from the shallow end.

"Whooo whee," shouted Stephen. "I can get used to this life very easily. Katie, always good to see you. Is Roan in the house? I need to speak to him."

"Jim and Roan just took the bags upstairs, Steve," explained Shauna. "They should be back down in a few minutes."

Stephen had been contemplating a change in careers. Roan needed a site manager and Stephen Brennan felt it would be the right change for him. He'd ask Roan in a little while.

Shauna showed Katie more of the grounds, then into the chapel. This project was taking more time than the rest of the house. The stucco on the walls had to be removed, along with some of the support beams. Water had seeped in over the years and weakened the walls. The steps to the altar had to be replaced, along with adding insulation, new wiring and plumbing in the Sacristy. The stained glass windows had to be sealed and covered on the outside to protect them from the elements, along with tuck pointing the exterior. Some of the pews were warped and needed restoration. A Bride's Room was added near the Sacristy and an office had been made from a storage closet. Each bit of space would be used effectively.

"See Katie," explained Shauna. "We are almost finished with the refurbishment here in the chapel. We've added central heating, carpeting, some new pews, replaced sections of the floor, redid the windows, sanded and varnished the altar and added a moveable altar for Catholic services. The craftspeople here are unbelievably talented. I suppose it comes from years of tradition, learning from and working with the top people in their fields and just the pride each person takes in their work. We couldn't ask for anything more."

Katie looked up at the rose window above the altar and asked, "Shauna, is that window original or did you add it?"

"Actually," replied Shauna. "One of the stained-glass craftsmen had it salvaged from another church and it fits right into this wall. It's The Holy Trinity and it's about two hundred years old."

"This is stunning, Shauna," exclaimed Katie. "I can see lots of weddings and services in here."

"We met a retired priest who lives a few miles from here," said Shauna. "He's excited about saying Mass for us before we go back to the States and he said he would hold the dedication service for the chapel as well. The bishop has approved the chapel for inter-denominational use once it's blessed. It fills a need beautifully. We can advertise the chapel in our brochure."

"This is so beautiful, Shauna," remarked Katie. "It's like I envisioned an English chapel to be. This entire estate is coming together the way it should."

Everyone congregated in the great hall for cocktails and snacks. Stephen and Roan had an announcement for the group.

"Stephen and I have been chatting about who will run the guest house when we leave and after much consideration, Stephen has accepted my offer for the job," explained Roan. "He will finish the Rutherford trial in Bemidji, then move over here to manage the house. It seems like the logical move to all of us!"

"Bravo, Steve," exclaimed Jim. "Excellent choice for a second career."

The all raised glasses in toast to the new Lord of the Manor! But before too much merriment could happen, one of the security guards came in with some news.

"Sorry to intrude on the party folks, but DuMonde has been sighted all over the parish," said the guard. "He's been in the village, over at Holden and Gisburn. Someone saw him walking over the fields toward the Ribble. He's been sighted in the Mews and down by the village greens. He's very close by, we just haven't been able to capture him. It's like he's taunting us or something."

Stephen looked at the security agent and remarked, "Have you looked near Pudsay's Leap? Remember, there are caves scattered about along the banks of the river where the coins were hidden. Since I'm a gambling man, I'm going to wager DuMonde is hidden in one of those caves."

"We haven't looked there, Mr. Brennan, but I'll get on it right now," said the guard. "If he's been there, we'll know it."

"Steve, how in the world did you come up with that tidbit?" asked Roan.

"Easy," replied Brennan. "There is a quantity of historical information about this region, including the village web site, which is packed full of statistics, history, genealogy—you name it, there is a place to find it. So, I deduced DuMonde could be hiding deep inside one of those caves without being detected from the outside. Let's see what they come up with."

Alex and Parker came in to greet everyone. The day had been a long one for Alex, but she felt better and could move her shoulder a fraction, but that was all. She was hungry for once and grabbed some of the snacks. Soon they would gather for the evening meal Mrs. Preston had prepared in her new, super techno-sophisticated kitchen. She was busy testing all the equipment, with the radio cranked up full blast, dancing around the room with delight. Conor and Jimmy peered around the corner and the look of horror came over their teenage faces.

"Would ya take a look at that," sighed Jimmy. "An old person like that listening to Van Halen and dancing? That's disgusting, Conor."

Conor covered his eyes, then left to rejoin the party. Within moments, the boys heard a dog barking. They walked to the wide open front entry door, to see a Border Collie puppy sitting on the door mat, waging its tail.

"Wow, cool," shouted Conor. "Wonder who it belongs to?"

Jimmy bent down to play with the dog, who knocked him over and started licking Jimmy's face. The boys were laughing so loudly, they created interest from the adults in the great hall. Roan came out to see what was causing the boys to make so much noise.

"Hey, who is this little fellow?" asked Roan. "Gosh he's cute. Oh Mrs. Preston, can you come out here please?"

"She'll never hear you, Dad," replied Conor. "I'd better go in and get her."

Soon Mrs. Preston came to the door, looked at the dog and said sternly,

"Not on MY clean floors you don't. Hmm, I don't see a collar or a tag. He's only a wee thing anyway. Maybe Milton will know. I'll ask him later."

"Dad, can we keep him, please?" asked Conor. "He's just great, can we please?"

"Shauna, please come out here for a second," asked Roan. "We have something for you to look at. Okay Son, here she comes, do the pouty-lip thingy."

"Would you look at this adorable puppy!" exclaimed Shauna. "Oh Roan, can we keep him? I guess it's a him?"

"Ah sure, dear," sighed Roan. "I thought it would take a little more convincing. And yes, it's a little boy puppy."

Stephen came to the door and the dog went right to him.

Brennan looked at Conor and said, "Happy Birthday, Conor. You are officially thirteen tomorrow and I saw this little fellow at a farm close-by, so I thought he'd make a good present for you. He doesn't have a name yet, either and he's really smart. It's your decision."

"Wow, thanks Uncle Stephen!" cried Conor. "Ah, maybe Buster, or Rascal. No, how about Bolton and call him "Bolt?"

That got a clap from everyone huddled in the doorway. Within seconds, the dinner gong sounded and everyone moved into the dining room, including Bolt, who sat quietly in front of the fireplace until the family was through.

A wind picked up and rustled the trees. Some of the branches slapped against the house and made an eerie sound. Up in those trees was someone who shouldn't have been there. DuMonde was perched in a middle branch, wearing night vision goggles and his rifle was pointed directly into the library.

It was primed to shoot at whatever target was in range. But he just sat—watching.

Finally he picked someone and lit the target with a red beam of light. Parker realised what was going on and told everyone to 'hit the dirt.' He ran over to turn off the lights, as everyone scurried into the hallway and out of the heat zone. Roan called the security guards to bring their dogs and double check the grounds.

"Damn," shouted Roan. "How did he get up there without anyone noticing?"

"Remember, he's an assassin," explained Parker. "He is silent—he's stealthy. He can be standing right next to you and you'd never know."

A knock on the front door broke the tension in the hallway. It was PC Adams coming up to give his report. And it was exactly what Stephen had suspected.

"Mr. Sanderson?" called out PC Adams. "It's PC Adams with a report."

Roan went to the front door to let him in. You could see additional guards patrolling the grounds as the door opened.

He stepped into the foyer and explained, "Folks, Mr. Brennan was correct. We found a cave which DuMonde had been hiding in. It was well-hidden, but the dogs found it. He's all set up in there, too. He had a camp stove, food, sleeping bag, ammunition and enough weapons to start his own small army. He could have stayed in there forever."

"Well, he was just up in the tree outside the library and almost got a shot off," said Roan. "Had it not been for Parker's fast reaction, someone in the room might not be standing here in the hallway! Tell your people to look up!"

Alex was getting tired and asked Parker to take her upstairs. She said goodnight and took the elevator up to her room. She had an idea to draw DuMonde out into the open and get this finished once and for all. But it would be dangerous. As she sat in the chair by a window in her room, Alex formulated a plan.

Parker listened intently, then said, "Are you sure you can handle a firearm? You can barely walk without help and it's your shooting arm that's dislocated. I'm not sure this is wise."

"I think we are out of options, Parker," explained Alex. "The family is in danger and every minute DuMonde is out there is a potential incident.

Tomorrow is Conor's birthday party, so let's wait until Sunday night to implement the plan. If it works, we should be rid of DuMonde for good."

Alex spent the night thinking about the plan and got very little sleep, but was ready to go in the morning. Shauna wanted to take Katie to their appointment, then to the Little Red Party Box in the village to pick up her party decorations. Parker said he would go with them. Alex spent the morning directing the workers setting up the party. Roan, Steve and Jim helped the workmen set up the tents and the stage for the band.

There were two large, white tents set up near the swimming pool. One of the tents contained tables and chairs, along with the buffet. The local caterer, 'Mood Food', would be setting up Conor's favourite foods—freshly-grilled hamburgers, hot dogs, lots of pizza, of course, potato salad, chips and salsa, French fries and a pop corn machine sat on the end of the table. The chocolate birthday cake was made in the shape of Bolton Hall.

The other tent had a dance floor, a small stage and a light show. There was a magician slated to perform, plus a band called, "Stinky Badgers", who were from Manchester. The kids could dance and be entertained in the same place.

Conor wanted the teens of the village and neighbouring area to come, just to have a summer party, not really to celebrate a birthday. The vicar even mentioned it during Sunday services! It was explained it would be a "swimming party" at Bolton Hall to celebrate the new swimming pool, so Conor didn't expect gifts, except from his parents.

Katie, Parker and Shauna arrived early at the reclamation center to look over their stock. There were several mantles and Adam-styled surrounds of great interest, which Shauna ordered. There were some columns, a few concrete pieces and old flooring. Parker admitted he was lost when it came to decorating, but the ladies seemed to know exactly what they wanted. Arrangements were made for similar items, the descriptions of which could be sent by fax or e-mail before purchase. The owner of the store introduced the women and Parker to another vendor who dealt in antique reproduction furniture. The Gallery wouldn't have to worry about supply, because they literally had tons of it in this place!

On the way home, they stopped to pick up the party plates and napkins, more balloons and plastic ware. Although Bolton-by-Bowland is a small village, there are stores of great diversity, lots of fun things to browse and buy and perfect items to bring home from holiday. Katie wanted to dash down to the Farmhouse Antique shop to buy some hand-made table linens for the store, along with some for her personal use. They were so beautifully displayed, hanging from a pole in the ceiling and along the wall on etageres. Katie also saw a lovely broach for Shauna and snapped it up. She exchanged business cards with the owner, because this is also an excellent source for the Gallery.

They were home by 10:00 AM and the party was due to begin at 2:00 PM. Shauna put the party goods in the food tent, while Katie went upstairs to pack her treasures. By noon, they were ready for the party. Parents had been invited as well, so there were 'adult' refreshments in the house for the older guests and soft ones for the kids. There was even a registered life guard for the pool area for plenty of safety. The security guards were dressed like party guests to blend in. No sense in scaring the children.

Conor and Jimmy came down from their room, freshly scrubbed and Jimmy smelled like Sandalwood soap.

He grinned and explained, "Well, I figured there would be some young ladies at the party and maybe I might meet one. It's always best to smell nice for them!"

Roan stared at the boys, turned to Jim and said, "I think our boys are leaving their childhood behind, Jim. They are becoming young men. Thirteen. I don't really remember thirteen. Sixteen, yes. Oh dear, that's only three years away. I suppose I'm going to have to give him a car then."

Jim replied, "Yeah, well, I remember us at that age, Roan. Your parents gave you that '65 Mustang, you know, the one in the cottage garage? Maybe you could fix that one up for Conor when the time comes. That's one classy car."

"Oh no," responded Roan. "That's going to be restored for ME, not a kid who just got his license. I'll get him an old Escort or something economical like that."

The men laughed as Conor came into the room.

Conor was puzzled at the two men bursting their sides and commented, "You guys have something up your sleeves, don't you? Well, I won't ask. But I wanted to let you know the place looks fantastic, Dad. I think everyone will have a great time. Thanks."

The family ate first, to allow the guests to eat at their leisure. Soon it was 2:00 PM and the first guests came up the driveway. Most of the children were around Conor's age. Some were a little older and a few younger. The vicar and his wife brought their four children, while the village photographer, Roger Wood, brought his camera to record the event for the village archives. Conor spent lots of time with this gentleman during July, learning about photography. Conor may have found his profession—he was that good at it. His dad even added a darkroom off the main hallway so Conor could develop the photos he took around the manor.

But there was one young lady who caught Conor's eye. She was Meghanne Adams, daughter of PC Adams and his wife Dora. Meghanne was also almost thirteen, a student at the Anglican school in the village and absolutely beautiful. She was tall and had the most amazing translucent ice blue eyes. Her hair was pale blonde, shoulder length and pulled off her face by a blue headband. She wore a white shorts outfit, sneakers and some rubber bracelets, with a little lip gloss on her mouth—that was it. Conor was smitten from the moment she said hello.

"Hi Conor, I'm Meghanne," she exclaimed. "Happy Birthday. Mine's next month, so I guess we are the same age."

"Ah, hi, Meghanne," stumbled Conor. "It's nice to meet you. Come on through and I'll introduce you to the folks and our friends."

Shauna looked at her son with pride. He was transforming right before her eyes. She wished Sam could see him now, but she knew he was watching. Jimmy saw Meghanne coming from across the room and walked right into a post. He turned around, humiliated and ran off. Conor explained Jimmy does that a lot.

Meghanne and Conor walked over to his parents and she immediately introduced herself, "Hello Mr. and Mrs. Sanderson. I'm Meghanne Adams. My father is PC Adams who is helping you with the security here. My mother teaches at the school I attend in the village. It's a pleasure to meet you both."

"It's very nice to meet you as well, Meghanne," said Shauna. "I have met your parents and they are lovely people. I hope you have a good time today."

Conor showed Meghanne around and suggested they have a swim. By now, Jimmy had found some new friends, too, including a very pretty girl with long brown hair, named Olivia. They were in the food tent, naturally, eating and talking.

About fifty children and twenty adults were in attendance, swimming, playing tennis or putting on the mini-put green. About 5:30, the band began to play rock music and by 8:00, everyone was exhausted. Some parents took their kids home, then came back to sit around the pool and chat. By 10:30, the evening was over. Conor and Jimmy had each made a very special friend. Love (or what a thirteen year-old fella calls love) was in the air!

The next morning was Sunday and it was time to dedicate the chapel. Father Aidan Mulroney, the retired priest from Gisburn, came over to bless the chapel and say Mass for the family at 10:30 AM. Conor and Jimmy were the altar servers (having been well trained by Father Miller at St. Philip's) and they helped with the incense, serving at the Mass and cleaning up. Father Aidan was delighted to give the old chapel a rebirth for new generations of the faithful, plus those who would be married there. It also gave him the opportunity to say Mass for the handful of Catholics around the parish of Bolton-by-Bowland who couldn't get into Clitheroe on Sundays. The chapel was also handicapped accessible for those who were in chairs or used walkers.

Mrs. Preston had prepared a beautiful luncheon, which Father blessed. Everyone had a great time, but Katie realised they would have to leave the following morning for the States. Maggie was running the store while they were away and it was time to get back. Stephen needed to prepare for the trial, while Roan and Shauna would stay behind to supervise at Bolton Hall. Parker and Alex had family coming the first two weeks in August over in Ireland, so everyone's schedules were set. Unfortunately for two of the people, their lives would change in a heartbeat.

A cold front was coming in creating a thick fog. It hung low along the ground and blanketed the shrubbery around the perimeter of the estate. Parker said this would be a good time for DuMonde to make his move—

under cover of the fog. It was a perfect way to sneak around without being detected.

Father Aidan bid the family farewell, while Katie and Jim began to pack. Jimmy was doing the same, but also calling Olivia to say goodbye. They promised to write and would get together at Christmas, as he invited Olivia and her family to come to Bemidji for the Holidays. Conor was playing with Bolt, while Alex and Parker were finalising their plans for the evening.

The workers had removed the tents that morning and left over food was given to them for their families. And they took some of the balloons and party favors for their kids. It was nice everyone could share in the festivities.

By evening, the fog choked anyone walking outside. Alex took some pain medication for her shoulder, dressed in black and checked her Lady Smith and Wesson. She could shoot with her left hand just as well, but hoped they could take DuMonde without a shot. That was wishful thinking.

"Parker," whispered Alex. "Can you help me with this Kevlar vest? It's so heavy, I'm having trouble getting the thing fastened."

"I'm hoping these vests will help stop a bullet if DuMonde shoots at us," sighed Parker. "I'm not so sure they will if he shoots from a foot away!"

"Well, at least we have some protection," explained Alex. "The ceramic plates inside are heavy enough. Guess we'll see what they WILL stop."

Parker had also dressed in black and wore his body armour. He inspected his firearm and made certain the batteries in his radio were fresh. He contacted PC Adams to confirm their plans. The local officers would be close to Parker and Alex, as they settled in to bait the trap for DuMonde.

At 11:00 PM, after a final radio check, Parker and Alex left the house and crept into the fog. They settled in at a pre-arranged spot and waited. Around 1:00 AM, Parker heard a rustling in the thicket in front of them. There were human steps, because Parker measured the sound as the steps crunched the leaves and twigs under foot. Soon they heard a hollow metallic "click, click" coming from the clearing ahead of them. A weapon was being readied to fire.

Silently, Parker motioned to Alex to stay still. Within a few moments, a voice spoke through the darkness.

"I know you are here, Fitzgerald," growled DuMonde. "And she's with you. Oh very good. Now I can take you both out at once. I'm gonna enjoy this."

Parker and Alex stayed motionless, as the fog deepened, making the area pitch black. You couldn't see your hand in front of your face and their night vision goggles were useless in that kind of fog.

"I can hear you breathing," laughed DuMonde. "I'm close, very close. And it's time to die."

Parker focused in on the sound of DuMonde's voice, but the fog made sound radiate to the sides. He had to guess where the sound was coming from. In a matter of seconds, four shots rang out in the direction of DuMonde's voice. You couldn't tell who they hit—or missed. However, two of the shots made a 'clink' sound, as if they hit the ceramic plates in a Kevlar vest. But whose vest(s) did the shots hit? Police were all around the grove and you couldn't tell who had fired their weapon.

All of a sudden, two thuds could be heard from bodies falling to the ground and a barely audible voice whispered, "Shots fired. Officers down."

Printed in the United Kingdom
by Lightning Source UK Ltd.
123371UK00002B/50/A